Fatal Measure

BRENT LADD

FATAL MEASURE

A CODI SANDERS THRILLER

NEW YORK
LONDON • NASHVILLE • MELBOURNE • VANCOUVER

Fatal Measure

A Codi Sanders Thriller

Published in New York, New York, by Morgan James Publishing. Morgan James is a trademark of Morgan James, LLC. www.MorganJamesPublishing.com

Proudly distributed by Ingram Publisher Services.

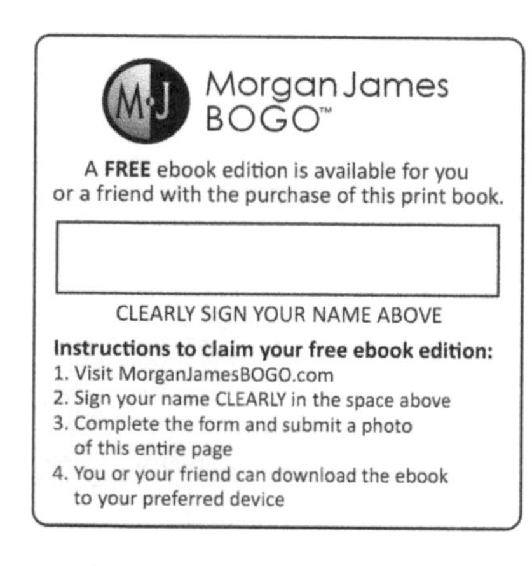

ISBN 9781636980607 paperback
ISBN 9781636980614 ebook
Library of Congress Control Number: 2022945980

Cover & Interior Design by:
Christopher Kirk
www.GFSstudio.com

Dedicated to my son-in-law Justin–a dedicated family man and a first responder who gives and serves without hesitation. We thank him for his service. He is smart, determined, and always eager to bust my chops. Again, we thank him for his service.

Chapter One

(BASED ON ACTUAL EVENTS)

1958 – FIRST AIR COMBAT COMMAND – KAECH'ON, NORTH KOREA – 6:20 A.M.

Head down, Mah followed the heels of the polished black boots in front of him. He was afraid to make eye contact with any of his superiors for fear his expression would give him away. The five pairs of boots clicked in unison against the spotless concrete floor. The large hangar was open with no support beams. It had offices and dressing rooms on one side and held seven of the newest Russian fighter jets in the Korean People's Army Air and Anti-Air Force. They were experimental Mikoyan-Gurevich 17 Frescos, more commonly known as MiG 17s. They were a more sophisticated evolution from the earlier MiG 15s that, during the Korean War, had significant air supremacy over the allied forces, especially over MiG Alley, an area in northwestern North Korea where the Yalu River empties into the Yellow Sea. Numerous dogfights took place there with suspected Russian and Chinese pilots against the American F-86 Sabre.

The interior hangar space was painted white like a clean room, including the metal superstructure. Equipment and personnel moved in a practiced cadence as final checks and last-minute inspections were completed, each step reliant on the next.

On his shoulders, Mah wore the three silver stars set upon a thin blue strip stitched under a brass star of a first lieutenant. His muted brown-green uniform with leather helmet and goggles was starting to show its age. He stood at attention along with his comrades in a shoulder-to-shoulder line-up. The officer of the deck, Major Jang Sok, was a short, rotund man with matching glasses. The kind of man who looked in your direction, but never at you—disconnected from the human experience. He moved like a snail as he scrutinized each of the pilots, more concerned with what was in it for him than with his charges. His face carried the expression of a man who had just tasted a lemon for the first time. Mah could feel himself sweating as he fought to remain still and composed. Twenty minutes ago, he had killed a man.

***

The 1st Air Combat Command base in Kaech'on was a mix of late 1950s state-of-the-art and Korean War rundown. Mah stepped off the bus and entered the base at 05:00, an hour before his shift, the sun only a glimmer of hope for the coming day. He entered the officer's mess hall for a cup of tea and was surprised to see it was not completely empty. The gray concrete walls echoed with even the slightest conversation.

He sipped on his *nokcha* from a table in the corner, his mind lost on the approaching day. His ears tuned out the various conversations.

The locker room was empty as Mah sat on the worn wooden bench and pulled his assigned locker open. The room was lit by metal China-hat lights spaced every ten feet. The floor was concrete, and the beige-colored lockers were set against white block walls. Inside his locker were his flight suit and helmet. Mah pulled out a picture of his mother sitting outside his childhood home and gave it a customary kiss. It was well-worn and faded, like his memory of her. He grabbed his flight suit and draped it across the bench, mentally reviewing his plan one more time.

"You can't do this."

Mah spun around at the words and looked up. "What are you doing here?" he asked.

A thin wiry soldier in a corporal's uniform stood over him. Park Lee was wearing a concerned look with desperate eyes. "I came to stop you."

"You'll have to kill me. My mind's made up," Mah said.

"Seriously, you would put that on me? I came here to set your mind straight, not to go down some guilt trip with you." He paused and sat down on the bench. "I know things are tough right now, but we can get through it, together. You don't have to throw your life away. Think about all the good work you've done."

"There is no one left here for me," Mah said, not making eye contact with his friend.

The words hurt, and Park turned away. "Fine, but I'm doing this for your own good. You might have to spend a few years thinking about your choices, but you will thank me in the end." He stood and turned to leave.

"Park, wait . . . maybe you're right. I've just been struggling lately. My mind has had some destructive thoughts." He stood and placed a hand on the lockers. "We can do this—together."

Park stopped and walked back over to Mah, placing his hand on his friend's shoulder. They stared at each other for a moment. Mah nodded his understanding and then reached out and put his arm around Park. Mah pulled him close, fixing Park in a headlock as he squeezed.

"I'm so sorry, Park."

Park, realizing the danger he was in, fought and struggled for all he was worth, fists and legs flying, body jerking back and forth. Mah caught a fist square on the nose and blood sprayed out, but his grip around Park's neck never wavered. It was like riding a water buffalo cart with square wheels down a steep hill.

Park's resistance slowly faded, and Mah hung on long past the required time for death. He sobbed inconsolably as he held his best friend in his arms. There was no going back now.

The reality of the situation finally pulled him from the moment, and he quickly emptied the rest of his gear out of his locker. It took a lot of effort, but

Mah managed to stuff most of Corporal Park Lee inside. He was kicking at a dangling foot that would not cooperate when another pilot entered the room.

"You're here early today, Mah," said Third Lieutenant Shin Ji as he spun the combination lock on his locker.

Mah shoved the last body part into his locker and slammed it shut with a heave. He quickly wiped the tears from his face and the blood from his nose. "Couldn't sleep. Thought I'd get a jump on the day," Mah lied.

"Nothing like killing time in the military, I say," Shin said.

"Yeah, nothin'," Mah replied in a monotone. He kept his back to his comrade as he put on his flight suit and placed the picture of his mother in his breast pocket.

***

Major Jang Sok paused in front of Lieutenant Mah Choon Hee, one of the five pilots standing at attention. Sok had an undeserved dislike for the young officer, which he had never been able to hide. The lieutenant had been on the fast track with the powers above. Someone up there had a real hard-on for this young man, and Major Sok could not, for the life of him, figure out why. He pushed and harassed just enough to make the young pilot's life a nightmare without it blowing back on him. He looked Mah over from the top of his leather helmet-covered head to the tip of his black boots, letting the man squirm a bit. The humidity was unusually high today, and the room had an oppressive blanket of moist heat, like a locker room on fire. Something caught his attention, and he refocused on Mah's left boot.

"Is that blood on your shoe?" he demanded.

A flash of fear coursed through Mah's spine, and he quickly wiped the spot of blood away on the back of his pant leg.

"What is the meaning of this?" Major Sok demanded.

Lieutenant Mah Choon Hee quickly looked left and then right at his comrades. Finally, he looked back up at the major and lied. "Just a minor nosebleed I had this morning, sir."

The sour expression on Major Sok's face twisted for a beat before he spoke. "Next time, clean up before presenting yourself to the People's Army Air and Anti-Air Force for inspection."

"Yes, sir," he replied.

Major Jang Sok dismissed his pilots and watched as they saluted and scattered for their planes, each happy to be rid of their commanding officer.

Mah, feeling slightly more hopeful in his plan, jogged for the third jet in the line-up.

Today's flight would take them close to the 38th parallel in a routine border patrol and show of force. It was a path this crew had taken many times. The preflight check had gone well, and Mah was finally shedding the last of his anxiety as he climbed the metal rungs that led to the cockpit. The MiG 17 was a marvel of modern fighter aircraft technology. It had proven itself superior to what the Americans flew. With speeds approaching Mach1, the sweptwing transonic frontline fighter was their first jet with afterburners, a technology that injected extra fuel into the jet pipe downstream, significantly increasing thrust. The small gray cockpit was a tight fit, even for the five-foot-seven frame of its pilot. Mah shimmied into position and strapped himself into the ejector seat.

The roar of the Rolls-Royce-copy turbine engine, thrusting air through a vent just below his feet and butt, was intense. It always amazed Mah how humankind had harnessed such power. He pressed the stick between his legs and the fighter moved out of the hangar. He guided it across the tarmac and onto the runway. With the press of a finger, he engaged the afterburners and shot up into the sky, his body slamming back against his seat. A quick bank to the right, and then into a holding pattern waiting for the other jets to be airborne. Once in the air, the five fighters moved into a V-wing formation, much like a flock of flying geese.

Mah slid his fighter into his assigned position for today's exercise, left back, commonly referred to as the Purple Heart position in the formation. The term was first coined during the allied bombing raids over Germany in World War II, as that position always took the most damage. Following the jet in front of him,

Mah followed as the squadron headed south for the demarcation line. Because part of the mission was a show of force, the fighters had to fly low enough to be seen and heard. There was nothing like a formation of five high-tech jets screeching overhead to make a citizen feel pride in his country, and the same applied in reverse for the enemy to the south.

They crossed scores of rice paddies and small villages, which eventually gave way to a belt of green. Mah looked over his gauges and habitually tapped on his altimeter, making sure it was working properly. He had almost crashed several years before because of a sticky gauge. He pressed the transmit button.

"People's Team leader, this is Bravo Three. I have an intake warning light. My turbine is heating up. I think I sucked a bird. I need to slow and return to base. Over," Mah said.

"Copy, Bravo Three. We've got this handled. See you back at the base. People's team leader out."

Mah reduced his speed and pulled the center stick to the right, banking the jet in a tight ninety-degree turn. Once he reached one hundred eighty degrees, he continued for another ninety, pointing the nose of his aircraft straight south. He engaged the afterburners and pushed his fighter to near Mach1. A quick glance over his right shoulder revealed his squadron as nothing more than dots against the blue sky. They were still moving away, unaware.

The 38th parallel or demilitarized zone (DMZ) is an enhanced border that separates North Korea from South Korea. It consists of two parallel high fences topped with razor wire. The earth below is cleared and heavily mined in a four-kilometer-wide buffer zone that divides the country in half. Initially established after World War II, the citizens of Korea could choose to live in the North or South, depending on their politics. Eight years earlier, in June 1950, a full-frontal invasion across the DMZ from the north started the Korean War. After the war, the re-establishment of the 38th parallel included fences and land mines to further separate the two countries.

From the air, Mah watched below as his fighter crossed the border and entered South Korean airspace. Farmland flashed past as the MiG 17 continued south, leaving behind his homeland and everyone he knew. As part of his training, he had memorized every South Korean and American airbase, and a quick lean on the stick had him heading to the nearest one.

First Lieutenant Mah Choon Hee started his career for the People as a military engineer. He had an eidetic memory and solid drafting skills that quickly put him at the top of his group. His superiors had pushed him into the Air Force because of a lack of qualified soldiers. During training, he proved himself competent enough to qualify as a fighter pilot, a very respected position. His small eyes and narrow face, however, had made him less of a hit with the ladies, and he soon found passion in his work rather than wasting it on social frivolity.

Flying low across the open fields in South Korea, Mah could see a military airbase come into view. This would require some luck and timing to finish his mission.

Mah remembered the leaflet that had literally fallen from the sky one day. The US had sent several helium balloons into the sky to float across the border and into North Korea. Each was rigged with five hundred leaflets that automatically released and fell after an hour in flight. The message was clear and specific. Any North-Korean pilot who delivered a MiG 17 to the Americans would be hosted in a country of their choosing and receive one hundred thousand American dollars for their troubles. Mah had picked up the flyer and devised an inspired plan.

He made no deviation and aimed his jet for the tarmac ahead, flaring his flaps and reducing the power as needed. Halfway down the runway, he realized his mistake when an F-86 Sabre suddenly veered left and hit the afterburners to avoid a collision. He had entered the runway from the wrong direction. Mah held his nerve and pushed his fighter into the nearest hangar and cut the engines. The base was caught completely unaware, and soldiers gathered in curiosity rather than assault.

Mah slid the canopy back and clambered down the side of the jet without the usual ladder supplied by the ground crew. More gawkers arrived, trying to register what was happening. A North-Korean communist just flew his new MiG 17 into an American-run South Korean airbase. It started slow, but soon everyone around the jet was clapping and congratulating Mah. He had done something truly remarkable.

Mah let the moment play out. It was a rush to have so many soldiers praise him. His lips curled up, revealing his crooked, tea-stained smile. This was a day he would never forget.

Now, for part two of his plan. The West would never see it coming.

***

The MiG 17 dropped and arced to the right as an F-100 Super Sabre tracked its movement. Mah pulled up hard on the stick and watched as the F-100 failed to replicate his maneuver. He would barrel-roll out of the move and drop in just below and behind his target. A quick flick on the gun control and he called in the kill. It was a game of cat and mouse that had been played many times over the last three weeks, each one trying to out-maneuverer and target the other's fighter jet. A confirmation over the radio had both jets turning and heading back to base.

Mah had spent the last three months working with a team to take the MiG 17 apart and study every piece. During that time, he changed his name to fit into his new world. Lieutenant Mah Choon Hee was now Mark Kroon. He worked hard to improve his rudimentary English and learn the American way of doing things. It was all so different for him.

Once the MiG was photographed and documented, the pieces were reassembled. The completed fighter jet was flown to a Naval air weapons station near China Lake, a dry lakebed in California that stretches for miles across the open desert. Mah . . . Mark had watched as several test pilots took their time familiarizing themselves with the MiG. Even a promising up-and-coming major named Charles "Chuck" Yeager flew the Russian's latest frontline fighter.

After the initial test flights, the MiG was recommissioned as a training jet for new pilots heading to the Vietnam War, now in its third year. Mark was instrumental in testing and running aerial dogfights over the dry landscape, giving US pilots a taste of what they might be up against with the Viet Cong and their Russian training. His ability to look at something once and retain the information made him a quick study, and the US took advantage of his knowledge and skills.

Most nights, Mark would return to his modest dwelling just outside the base and work on his other passion, a series of pamphlets on aeronautical engineering treatises. They covered the basics and a few of the more advanced developments of the emerging technology. Each one contained diagrams and hand-drawn pictures as examples. It was meant to explain to the masses the popular world of aviation and how it all worked. There was never anything top secret or classified, and he made sure the Air Force approved each pamphlet before releasing it. A small educational publisher picked up the series and soon *Aviation Basics—The world of science and technology in the skies*, had a small niche following. It allowed Mark to immerse and pursue both engineering and aviation.

It was an unusually warm night in the high desert, known for extreme temperature drops after the sun went down. As he focused on a diagram on his drafting table, Mark's one-and-only fan was pointed in his direction. It was a dissection of a jet engine. The small cabin-like building had wood-paneled walls and carpeted floors. The furniture was clean and simple. Some might say it was one step up from a trailer park, but to Mark, it was beyond anything he had ever had in North Korea. He was waiting for his favorite TV show to start, *Peter Gunn,* on the first real purchase he had made since becoming an American, an RCA Victor CTC-9 console color TV. A knock on the door interrupted his concentration. Mark stepped to the door and paused before reaching for the knob.

"Yes?" he said.

"Mark, it's me, Harry. I need to talk to you right away."

Mark took a breath and unlocked the door. Harry Wells was one of the government's many liaison officers that were part of the team working out of China Lake. Mark couldn't remember what he was responsible for, as the man seemed to just stand in the background and take notes, never actively engaging in the exercises. But Harry had been kind to Mark. Many other team members harbored racism against anyone "Oriental." First the Japanese, then the North Koreans, and now the North Vietnamese. They had mostly talked behind his back, but a couple of guys on the team were quite harsh. Harry, however, was undeterred by Mark's heritage and treated him as an equal.

The thirty-eight-year-old, blond, blue-eyed man stepped into Mark's living room with a creased brow and nervousness that spilled through every pore. He wore green canvas pants and a madras collared shirt. He moved about the room, too worked up to sit.

"Tea, coffee?" Mark asked.

"No, thanks. I don't know how to tell you this, so I'm gonna come right out and say it. I think there is something fishy going on with your publisher."

"What?"

"Your book publisher. I hate to admit it; I'm a fan of your books. I guess you could call me a secret airplane buff, and as the man responsible for all the BLM land you are using in your training flights, this has been a real dream job for me. And what you did . . . coming over here with the MiG. That took guts. You're like an American hero, though Korean."

"So, what about my publisher?" Mark asked.

"Oh, yeah. I was reading your book on ailerons and their effect on the trailing edge of each wing. 'The aileron,'" Harry quoted from memory, "French for 'little wing,' it is a hinged flight control surface operated in pairs to control the movement of the plane."

This guy really is a fan, Mark thought.

"Anywho, I accidentally spilled my coffee with a little bit of Baileys, if you know what I mean, on my book. I like to end the day with just a splash, along with some creamer."

Mark interrupted Harry's babblings. "I'd be happy to give you a replacement pamphlet." He was still not sure where this conversation was going, but the guy was taking forever to get to the point.

"No. That's not why I'm here. Once wet, the pages got all see-through, and the two diagrams, Figures 3 and 4, when overlapped, produced this." He held out his soggy book and moved over to a lamp next to the small plaid couch. The two pages had stuck together and were translucent when held up against the light. Several words seemed much darker than the rest, the overlay creating a zig-zag message.

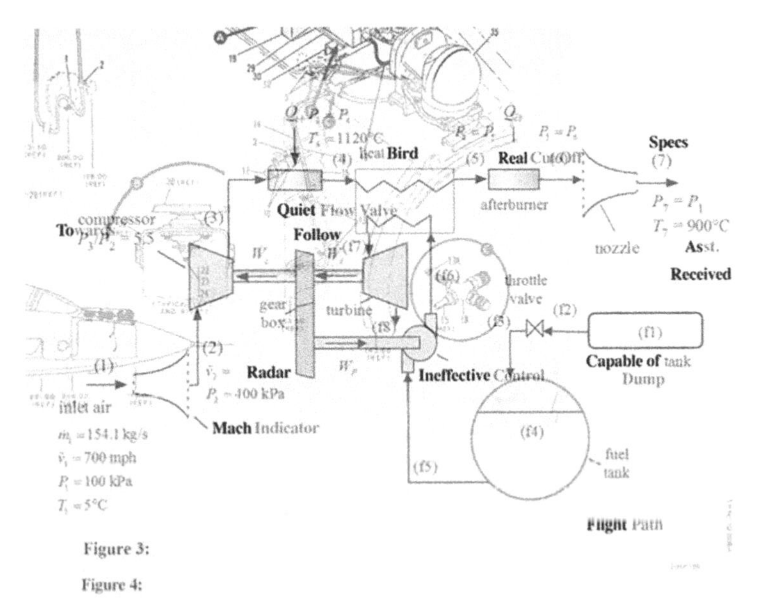

Quiet Bird Real. Specs to Follow as Received. Radar Ineffective. Capable of Mach Flight

Mark pretended surprise. “What on earth?”

“I know, right? This can’t be a coincidence. There is something going on,” Harry added.

Mark’s mind turned at afterburner speed. “Grab a glass of water from my kitchen. I’m going to get more books and a stronger light. Let’s see if this is a one-off or something more.”

Harry headed for the kitchen. It took him three tries to find the right cupboard before turning on the faucet and filling the glass.

Mark grabbed several of his pamphlets and a metal flashlight. He returned and opened the same pamphlet Harry had brought over. Harry spilled some water on the two selected pages and Mark shined his flashlight from below.

“You’re right. It’s on both books,” Mark said.

“Let’s try another book.”

“Good idea.” Mark grabbed the pamphlet on *Take-offs and Landings*. Opening it to a diagram, he handed it to Harry to hold. “Line up the next diagram with this page,” he said.

Harry set down his glass and eagerly placed the two pages next to each other. Mark flicked on the flashlight, but instead of placing it under the pages, he swung it as hard as he could on the back of Harry's head. The flashlight bent and the glass lens shattered as Harry's body dropped to the floor unconscious. Mark just stared at the man on the floor, planning his next move.

He cleaned up the room, throwing away the flashlight and the two wet pamphlets. He then squatted next to Harry and went through his pockets. The license in his wallet told Mark where the man lived. The car keys were to a Chevy 3100 pickup.

He loaded Harry into the passenger side of Harry's pickup and drove. Once at Harry's home, he dragged the man into his living room and took a look around. There was a small spill on the carpet and an empty coffee cup on the side table. A bottle of Bailey's Irish Cream sat next to it. A moan escaped Harry's lips as he started to move. Mark gripped him around the chest and dragged him into the bathroom. He turned the water on in the tub and placed the rubber stopper in the drain, and then he started to undress him. Once naked, Mark pulled his victim up and over into the tub. Harry began to protest as his faculties returned. He struggled and flopped against his foe. With a quick back flick, Harry's head smashed into Mark's nose, sending blood spurting out. They wrestled and squirmed in an ugly, twisting brawl. Eye jabs, elbows, knees, and water went everywhere. Finally, Mark managed to slam Harry's head against the tub spout and send him back into oblivion. Harry's head was now bleeding into the water and mixing with Mark's blood. Mark grabbed a washcloth and used it to stem his own flow of blood.

The bathroom was a mess—blood, water, and a broken towel rack. He tidied up and reassembled the towel rack. From the linen closet, he replaced the dirtied towels he had used to clean up. He left the water running and plugged a radio he found in the living room into the bathroom outlet. Then, without emotion, he tossed it into the water of the tub, careful to keep back from the edge. Harry's body immediately went rigid and vibrated to an unseen current. Sparks from both the radio and the plug filled the room with smoke. Mark closed the door behind him satisfied that the staged accident was complete.

He locked the front door and killed the lights, leaving through the back door, which he locked behind him. He dashed back around to the front yard and exited the neighborhood. It would be light in a few hours, and the walk back home, staying off the main streets, would take time. The only consolation—his secret was still safe.

Chapter Two

PRESENT DAY – FOUNTAIN PARK – SAINT LOUIS – 8:43 P.M.

The metamorphosis was transcending. Cameron Clark, also referred to as "The Scientist" by his employer, lowered the magnifying glass that had helped him witness every detail of the change. First, the dark coffee-brown chrysalis wiggled and squirmed until a crack grew across its body. From out of that crack burst a new being, soon capable of one of life's rare skills—flight. Cameron held out his hand and let the creature crawl onto his finger as it pumped blood into its shriveled wings until they filled with life and purpose. Once ready to take flight, Cameron placed the giant silk moth, known as *Lonomia obliqua,* into a specialized moth aviary that allowed the creature to fly, eat, and mate in the never-ending cycle of life.

Cameron appreciated the yellow-brown moth, roughly the diameter of a teacup saucer, but what he most loved was the two-inch larval form of the creature. A leaf-eating machine with the most unique defense system on the planet—urticating bristles that could inject a specialized venom unlike anything else. The caterpillar itself looked brown and ordinary, but the bushy pale green bristles that covered it looked like a forest of baby twig cactuses with little spikes on the end. Each could deliver its toxic formula to anyone unlucky enough to brush against it, or a creature stupid enough to try to eat it. Cameron picked up a small sample dish with one such caterpillar inside. It moved along in an undulating walk that made the bushy green covering wobble. He held it up to his dark brown eye, an eye devoid of emotion. As much as he admired his deadly babies, Cameron held no love for them or anyone. He had a detached psyche that landed solidly on the autism scale. Curiosity and perfection of actions, however, were always on display.

Cameron Clark was of average height and looks with buzzed sandy-brown hair and slightly sloped shoulders. He had unusually long ears and an elongated face to match. In a word, he was forgettable, and that was fine by him. Being one of the cleverer assassins in the trade, The Scientist could walk through a room, and no one would remember him. It was not just his looks that made him so successful, however. He also had an IQ off the charts. He was a true stealth-style assassin, and right now, his weapon of choice was aptly named—the assassin caterpillar.

Four years back, Cameron had taken a trip to the southern part of Brazil in search of a very rare specimen. He hired a naturalist to guide him on a two-day excursion into the jungles hoping to photograph some of the jungle's least common lifeforms. One of his goals was to find an assassin caterpillar. The caterpillar had become something of a legend in his mind, ever since he first read about it. The fuzzy little larva could kill in a most diabolical way and was responsible for hundreds of deaths. Medical technicians in Brazil were still working on an antidote with no success yet.

The first day was a hot, muggy affair with a lot of weaving, ducking, and crawling as his naturalist guide was against using a machete when at all possible. The humid, rotting air was overwhelming for the Seattle-born assassin. Eventually, they found a clearing for the night and set up two hammocks and a small campfire under a large cashew tree. Cameron was covered in mud and bug bites, despite having continually reapplied his 100 percent Deet insect repellant. His guide thought he would likely die from the diethyltoluamide in the repellant rather than the bugs.

They had come across some amazing finds that first day. Cameron reviewed his camera's memory card, stopping and zooming in on a brightly colored poison dart frog. At one point, his guide pointed out a golden lion tamarin monkey, and he got a great close-up of an eyelash viper. The night was miserable, even with the mosquito netting, and Cameron questioned his decision to venture so far from civilization. This was not to his liking, with every minute seeming like an hour. Eventually, exhaustion won out, and he drifted off to sleep.

The morning glow signaled the end of what was officially the longest night of his life. A quick breakfast and the two broke camp and started back.

Two hours into their return trip, Cameron hit pay dirt. On the back of a large grey tree were dozens of assassin caterpillars. Cameron took many pictures and asked several questions. When he felt like he had learned all he could from his guide, Cameron pulled a knife and ended the man's life without a second thought, sliding the blade between his ribs. He hauled the body into a marshy area and pushed it down with a stick until there was no sign of the naturalist.

Next, he carefully collected all the caterpillars and placed them in a leaf-filled Tupperware container. With a machete in hand, he followed his GPS device and hacked his way out, vowing never to come to the jungle again.

His home-built, screened-in aviary was now a gilded cage to one of the deadliest insects on the planet, causing a death that was effectively untraceable in the US. The Scientist returned the assassin caterpillar to its cage and moved up the stairs out of his basement workshop to his kitchen. It was all white, including the dishes. In fact, his entire home was furnished in various shades of white, from the bleached wood floors to the white leather furniture, and even the artwork. He pulled a Topo Chico from the refrigerator and sat on the couch, nursing the naturally carbonated spring water. His thoughts drifted back to his humble beginnings.

Growing up as a loner had its advantages. As long as you stayed away from the crowds and out of the spotlight, you were invisible. That was particularly important during one's formative years, and it set the pattern and style for everything else that followed. As a young boy obsessed with knowledge and an unnatural love for all things that moved, crawled, or grew, Cameron found his life's passion in the natural sciences at a young age. Humans were the problem. They hunted, smashed, and ate their way through everything Cameron loved. A virus to nature. High school had brought his most troubled years. As a social outcast, Cameron was left alone to pursue his passions, but trouble always had a way of sniffing him out and pulling him from obscurity. Unlike the typical young psychopath, his total apathy toward living things did not extend to small animals. A psychopath in mind but not in deed.

Besides the general ridicule of being a freshman, Cameron's elongated face and ears won him the moniker "Rosie Palm" with the other boys.

"Hey, Rosie! With a face like that, the only action you'll ever get is with yourself!"

"How are the blisters, Rosie?"

"Heard you went on a double date. You used both hands!"

It was a painful and humiliating running joke that came out anytime Cameron was spotted. It was as if he had a target painted on his back just above a sign that read "Bully Me."

Cameron could not shake the stigma throughout his high school years, but he had several moments of satisfactory revenge. It started with the girl he thought was the most beautiful person he had ever seen. Sherri Velsor. She had light brown wavy hair and a slim body and the most perfect smile. She had even flashed it in his direction a few times. But people change, and as she became more popular, her attitude toward him shifted dramatically, to where she joined in with the chorus of insults and barbs. They were only words, and words can't hurt you, could they? Emotional scars consumed Cameron, leaving him with two choices, a complete disconnection or to fight back. And there was nothing wrong with a little payback, right?

Cameron went to the local Asian market and bought the biggest fish they had. He cut off its head and placed it in a bucket of water for two days, to let it ripen. It was Friday evening when Cameron carried his experiment onto school grounds and over to locker number A345. It took him several tries to successfully pick the lock and open the swinging door. He placed the rotting head on the back center hook; its dead eyes gawking forward. Monday was a holiday, so it would be three days before its owner found her surprise.

When her locker door swung open, Sherri saw the hideous fish face. The smell enveloped her so completely that she turned and puked. Word spread like wildfire that someone hated Sherri Velsor. Even after her locker was pressure washed, the smell lingered. Cameron had not expected such an outcry. The amount of talk and energy spent was intoxicating. Only he knew the true culprit and for some very strange reason, no one suspected him. The suspicions and chatter lasted nearly a month before dwindling. That emboldened Cameron to move things to the next level. He would go after Bruce, the jock who had initially given him his moniker.

As the leading wide receiver in the county, Bruce was assured a college scholarship. One Saturday, he had several scouts coming to see him and a few other teammates. Cameron had taken the time to do his homework, along with some eavesdropping and a bit of snooping on Bruce's Myspace profiles. It didn't take long to work out a plan. It wasn't perfect, but the odds of success were high. That week, he watched as Bruce moved through his weekly routine around campus. Timing and plotting his movements, Cameron decided on Friday he would make his move. Last summer, he had read *The Art of War*, by Sun Tzu, and tried to apply one of its teachings: "The supreme art of war is to subdue the enemy without fighting." He would do just that. Keep it simple and strike without warning.

Clare Dawn High School was a two-level tilt up style building with gray walls and black trim around rectangular windows. The flight of concrete stairs leading from the English department down to Social Sciences was the longest on campus. With thirty-two steps of hardened concrete, it was perfect for Cameron's needs. He sneaked onto campus Thursday night and spent ten minutes installing two tiny screws into the wall on either side of the top step. He touched them up with matching gray paint so they blended in with their surroundings. One-hundred-pound clear test fishing line was plenty of strength for his needs and was still almost invisible. He tied it to one screw, carefully pulled it down, and then pressed it into one of the parallel grooves of the rubber non-skid strip at the top of the first stair step. He then routed it back up and looped it once around the second screw on the other side. He rolled up the remaining line and wrapped it around the small accent light that illuminated the step. Satisfied that his contraption would go unnoticed, he exited the campus and hurried home. For the first time in many nights, Cameron slept a full eight hours. Something about his calculated actions gave him a peace he rarely felt.

At 10:30 a.m. on Friday, Cameron perched himself in the alcove next to the flight of stairs. He leaned over and grabbed the excess fishing line from around the accent light. He wrapped it around his hand and waited. Bruce left his English class and hung outside the door chatting up some of his friends. He was bragging about how he was going to crush his try-out the next day and leave this crap bag of a town behind. Eventually, he said his goodbyes and headed Cameron's way. As he neared the top of the steps, Cameron quickly pulled up on the line. The force popped the fishing line up out of the non-skid and brought immediate tension to it just four inches above the floor. Cameron watched from the side of his vision as Bruce went from a self-assured, cocky jerk to a scared little boy, his torso going horizontal as he tried and failed to grab the railing. He tumbled awkwardly down the hardened steps, not stopping until he was a motionless blob at the bottom. Cameron quickly removed his fishing line and headed in the opposite direction. He desperately wanted to see the aftermath, but that would be too dangerous. He needed to put distance between himself and the incident. He forced himself to take the long way around, walking nice and easy until he eventually made it back to the scene. Two adult teachers were kneeling over Bruce with worried looks on their faces. They were telling the growing mob of students to get back and make room for the paramedics. Cameron stood on his tippy toes to get a look. Bruce was lying on the ground crying, his left leg at an awkward angle. The smile that grew on Cameron's face was straight out of *The Grinch. It was an outstanding day!* he thought to himself as his heart leaped with joy before turning and heading to his next class.

***

Light burned her retina and fovea centralis as her lids fluttered open, and then quickly closed with a shot of pain. Her eyes were caked with dried blood, and her vision was blurry as she tried to adjust to the brightness. An urge to sit up outweighed the dizziness. Stabilizing her hands on the greasy pavement helped her stay sitting. A slow look around provided no knowledge of her surroundings. She recognized the objects, just not the location. The smell was familiar and not pleasant. She saw a narrow alleyway, a worn and dented overfilled dumpster, and several bags of trash upon which she sat. Using her hands for balance, she stood and gathered herself. Inspecting her person, she found fitted navy-blue slacks and a light-blue blouse, both stained and grimy. They did little to place who she was or how she had gotten here. Her shoes were saddle leather with wedge heels. They were scraped up but new and fashionable. She probed a dried but bloody gouge on her head with gentle fingers. It explained the pounding in her brain and the dizziness. She tried to think back, but there was nothing, just snippets of childhood and some fragments of college life.

She walked on unsteady feet out of the alley, using the brick wall for support. The day was young, and few people were out and about. A random selection turned her right, down a well-trodden sidewalk. She moved past a closed cellphone store with a heavy gate locked across the front. Through the bars, she could just make out a reflection of a face in the storefront glass. It was familiar but unknown. *Who am I? How did I get here, and where am I?* were just a few of the hundreds of questions that bounced through her muddled mind.

Mid-block, a second right pushed her through the doors of a Starbucks. They were preparing for the day's onslaught. There were two people in line and three partners behind the counter, taking orders and filling them. The smell nearly knocked her off her feet. It was familiar and desirable, calling to her. She forced herself past the glares and judgments toward her immediate destination.

A voice she didn't recognize but understood called to her, "Restrooms are for customers only! Hey!"

She ignored the voice and moved to the door with a symbol of a half man, half woman on it. Once inside, she closed and locked the door, leaning back against it for support, working up enough courage to finally face the mirror. A hollow face stared back. Her mind began to build a story of what was in the reflection. *I am a woman, brunette with brown eyes, maybe five-eight. My clothes look nice but are battered and filthy. I am dirty and hurt, with a wound on my head. I have been injured, and I can't remember who I am.*

The woman stared a bit longer, trying to recall and fill in the missing pieces. She checked her pockets and came away with nothing. *Am I recently homeless or did someone provide me with these clothes? No, they feel right to me. These are my clothes. I think I must have been in an accident. Some kind of trauma or altercation. My shoes are too practical to be in the fashion or corporate world. I must work a lot on my feet. Maybe I am a waitress or sell cars. That makes no sense. I am standing here trying to deduce my past based on a simple reflection in the mirror. I'm a cop or an insurance investigator. Maybe a spy. This is ridiculous. I'm a mess, and I stink. That is who I am.*

She turned on the water and washed away the blood and grime. Her matted hair, her filthy skin, even the muck under her fingernails. Damp paper towels helped remove the large chunks that still clung to her clothes and after a bit of effort, she was feeling better about herself and her looks. One more long look in the mirror and she came to a conclusion. *I don't know who I am.* She left the restroom and headed out of the shop.

"Come in here again like that, and I'll call the police."

She flipped him the bird as she closed the door behind her. The sidewalk was still relatively empty. A siren closed in her direction from the left. It made her skittish. *Am I on the lam? Lam? Who uses that word?* She would take no chances and ducked out of sight as a police car with flashing lights flew past. Quickly jogging across the street and moving in the opposite direction of the police car, she cut across the next block and saw a city park. An empty bench in a more obscure area called to her. She sat to collect her thoughts. *I need a plan.* Wandering lost around a town was not a plan.

The park was coming to life as joggers, dog walkers, and strollers began their daily rituals. The sun was already announcing a hot day as the humidity index started to climb. She watched the passersby move in all directions, a daily pattern that was the lifeblood of the city. A glance at her hands revealed a thin white line on her ring finger. Had she recently lost or taken off a wedding ring? *Am I married? Divorced?* A rift in the morning's symphony caught her eye. Two men dressed in gangster chic got out of a brown van and started to patrol the neighborhood. They were looking for something or someone.

***

The Scientist adjusted his black-framed non-prescription glasses and stepped up the stairs to the lobby, his days as the bullied Cameron Clark long behind him.

The glasses had specialized lenses that, when viewed from an angle, made it difficult for others to see his eyes. That included cameras as well. It forced him to move his neck more as he scanned left and right, but later identification would prove most difficult. A cool blast of air-conditioned air greeted him as he pushed his way through the revolving door, pulling his carry-on along with him. He wore a pilot's uniform with only one bar on the shoulder, making him a junior officer. The bushy, dark, curly wig was making his head sweat, and that, in turn, made it itch. The chair he had scouted previously was empty. He claimed it, knowing the security camera was blocked by a Grecian column.

His path to this moment had been carefully planned down to the last detail. Starting with his first overt act with a rotted fish's head back in high school to the first man he had killed with antifreeze. It had been a journey with purpose and intention. His life had been a series of molding events that had dropped him into the business of eliminating the worst of the worst—man. College had allowed him to learn and embrace his love of the earth. Life had taught him the horror that was humankind. Why the word "kind" was attached, he would never understand.

He had met The Handler; or actually, she had met him at an entrepreneur's convention in the California mountains. She had been intrigued by his ideas and passions. In time, she had shown him a world where he could thrive. It allowed him to use his superior intellect and control his urges by giving him an outlet for them. Killing other humans was the fuel that drove him forward, fulfilling his existence. She had encouraged his passions and even financed his training in areas he had never thought important. But her most important contribution was marketing, something Cameron never understood. It was she who had named him The Scientist, saying it would give him anonymity and a certain *je ne sais quoi,* making him more intriguing and ultimately more valuable than a guy named Cameron Clark.

Now, he had a steady flow of jobs, an outlet for his obsessions, and all the money he needed.

The Scientist placed over-the-ear headphones on his head and connected them to his phone, a sure way to avoid engagement with anyone in a crowd. Instead of music, the headphones were specially built to amplify and cancel sounds in the room. They allowed the wearer to tune in to conversations by adjusting the four built-in omnidirectional microphones by turning them on or off, thus engaging the chosen directional noise and canceling the rest. The system ran on a simple phone app with a graphic circle and a highlighted pointer that could be moved around the circle like a dial. The Scientist powered up the headphones and listened to the cacophony of sounds that filled the space, all overlapping and blending together. He used his finger on his smartphone's screen to engage the system. All ambient sounds fell away, and a very specific sound replaced it, the simple ding of an elevator car. He moved the pointer around the circle slowly, listening to various people and groups. He closed his eyes as he concentrated on each one, slowly circumnavigating the lobby of the grand hotel without looking.

Well, I don't mind if you do . . . Someone will surely be interested in such an ideal property . . . Would you like some company tonight? You look lonely to me . . . Tommy, get over here and stop touching everything . . . Can I help you, sir? I'm here to check-in. The name's Stanisloff. I'm going to go up and check your room, Congressman. Justin will watch your back here until I give the all-clear.

The Scientist sat up. He checked his app and could see he was tuned into a conversation behind him and to the left, at his eight o'clock. Casually, as if he had all the time in the world he lowered the headphones around his neck, stood, and walked to the elevator area with his phone in hand. He leaned against the wall as if sending a text but was actually opening his next program. Ever so carefully, he risked a glimpse of the mark. Just a second but long enough for The Scientist to fix the position of his target. He slipped on a flesh-colored glove that, once in place, mimicked his human hand. Removing a small glass vial from his pocket, he used his gloved hand to carefully pick up the caterpillar inside, holding it between his thumb and forefinger with the spines outward.

The lobby was a grand affair, with large columns and a domed roof. There was a generous amount of marble and complementary beige paint. The Scientist moved, head down, as if he was captivated by something on his phone, pulling his carry-on behind him like a lonely caboose across the patterned stone floor. He kept the phone in his left hand, with his thumb and index fingers holding the caterpillar just above it. His eyes were down on the screen as he walked. The image on the screen was a live video of what was in front of him, beamed via Bluetooth from a hidden camera on the headphones still around his neck. It allowed The Scientist to walk along any designated path while seemingly lost in his phone, never needing to look up. The image on the screen showed two men in suits standing off to the side of the lobby. The older one seemed impatient, and the younger man had his eyes continuously scanning the occupants of the room. Bodyguard. There was an obvious bulge under his coat.

***

The woman suddenly felt vulnerable. She watched the wanna-be gangsters searching the surrounding area for someone. *What if they are looking for me?* she thought. A quick slouch on the park bench lowered her as she looked for a place to hide. The air was ripe with the scent of freshly cut grass. The sounds of the city coming to life were carried on the gentle breeze as her eyes darted back and forth with indecision, the knock on her head pounding in time with her racing heart.

She watched the two men as they moved in a pattern designed to eliminate possibilities. Up one street and back down another. Each time they moved in her direction, she could feel a surge of adrenaline coursing through her body. After clearing the streets, they made their way into the park. It was a half-block affair with open areas and a path that wound through several gardens and a few mature trees. Off to one side was a fountain that had a marble Pegasus spouting water from its mouth.

She stood and walked toward the fountain, keeping her head down as she went. About fifty feet from the flying horse, she noticed a change in the hunter's posture. They were looking in her direction, and one was pointing.

Like a spooked deer, she turned and ran, panic fueling her flight. The men gave chase, each determined to get there first. As she left the park, a brown panel van screeched to a stop in front of her. The driver jumped from the vehicle and reached for something metallic under his shirt—a gun.

A surge shot through her body as instinct took over. Using her right foot, she jumped at the man reaching for his gun. She landed full weight on his chest with her left foot, knocking him back before he could bring the gun to bear. Her momentum carried the man into the side of his van, his head leaving a nice dent in the sheet metal. She used his body as a ramp to vault herself onto the roof. Once on top, she continued over, dropping in a roll safely back down on the other side. Before her assailants could react, she dashed across the street and down an alley. The three men reorganized and gave chase. But their target was nowhere in sight.

***

Bobby Carlyle of the US House of Representatives was an up-and-comer who had been making a lot of news lately. He was a moderate pushing hard for the abolishment of special interest in government. It was a message that played well in the media and public eye, but Washington was too attached to the teat of this unholy cow to let him have his way. Power and money were perfect bedfellows in the cycle of political life, and power almost always got its way.

Carlyle butted heads and intimidated colleagues wherever he could to forward his agenda. He wielded the press as his own personal messiah and connected to millions through social media. It gave him leverage but not security. Making enemies in politics was a given—accepted, really. It was how you controlled the public in concert with your allies that was real power. But if you ever crossed them, they would all turn on you.

The handsome fifty-six-year-old native Philadelphian was a full six feet tall with broad shoulders and a strong chin. He was built for politics. His wife Cassandra and two kids had been slow to adapt to the DC lifestyle. She was the yin to his yang and worked hard to stay out of the public eye. Every other month, Carlyle traveled to his home city for a couple of days to work on his other passion: a non-profit benefiting foster families. It was a good cause and had won him many votes every year. Growing up in a broken and dated system himself, Carlyle had gone on to champion reforms and protections for both the parents and children in the system. He worked tirelessly to make what he believed was a better America, waving off his critics.

Now, he was feeling the tension that always dogged him when he ran behind schedule. It was one of his pet peeves, preferring to be on time or early for every meeting. He waited in the lobby of his favorite Philadelphia hotel, The Rittenhouse, anxiously awaiting the all-clear. He headed for the elevator unconcerned with the procedure the bodyguards required.

The Scientist continued, head down, buried in his phone as he moved through the lobby on a perpendicular path that would pass by the congressman with a yard to spare. Nothing suspicious here. The Scientist could see the bodyguard eyeballing him from a few steps behind the senator, but the man quickly dismissed him as a threat. Just another working-class pilot on his way to or from the airport. When he was less than three feet away, The Scientist slightly skewed his approach. The bodyguard instantly reacted and moved to intercept, but before he could, The Scientist bumped into his target. He watched as his fingers wiped the back of the caterpillar across the congressman's hand and then quickly pulled back, just as the bodyguard pushed him to the side.

The Senator reacted as if shocked by a doorknob on a dry day, quickly pulling his hand away. "Hey!" He backed up.

"So sorry, please forgive me, wasn't paying attention," The Scientist said, as he stepped back and looked up with a repentant face.

"Watch where you're going," the bodyguard called out, unsure if he needed to pull his gun.

"My bad," The Scientist replied, with his phone hand raised in supplication, hiding the bug behind it. He hurried off with the eyes of the bodyguard boring into the back of his head.

Congressman Carlyle rubbed the back of his hand and looked down. *What was that?* There was no scratch or cut. His skin looked normal.

"You okay, sir?" the bodyguard asked.

"Yes. I'm fine, just got a static shock I guess, no big deal. Another citizen not paying attention to where they're going. That's why I'm here, to help them find the right path."

"One hundred percent, sir," the bodyguard replied.

Congressman Carlyle gave his "yes man" bodyguard a sour expression. "Let's head up to the room; I have a lot on my plate today. I'm done waiting for the all-clear."

What the congressman did not know was that three days from now, he would experience flu-like symptoms, and shortly thereafter, he would be dead.

***

Why am I being hunted? Who wants me dead? Am I important or just yesterday's trash needing to be taken out? And how in the world did I just take out that guy with a gun? The thoughts circled in her head as she fought to catch her breath behind a late-model SUV in the parking structure she had dashed into. Images from her past popped by like a broken projector on repeat, but her memories were still lost to her. *Who am I?* A slim view of the street through concrete and sheet metal was her only security. Footsteps approached and then passed as an older woman with a large purse and coffee mug walked by. She let a breath go that she had been holding and tried to calm herself.

The sound of an engine slowly moving in the parking structure reverberated off the hard surfaces. It was coming her way. Carefully standing on the balls of her feet she prepared herself to run or hide. Between the parked cars, she could finally make out the vehicle. It was the brown van, and it was slowly moving throughout the complex. They would be coming her way any second. She crouched behind the SUV trying to make herself invisible, closing her eyes for a moment in hope, as the engine noise drew closer.

A door abruptly opened and closed. Followed by the roar of a V-8 starting up. Before she knew what was happening, the large SUV she was hiding behind started backing out. A call from the driver startled her and didn't go unnoticed by the men in the van. "Hey! What are you doing hiding in front of my car?"

Two gangsters jumped from the van and ran in her direction. She hurdled the cable wires separating her from the level below and rolled with the jarring impact onto the concrete. Once back on her feet, her ankle protested, forcing her to limp-run out of the structure. She could hear the van driver yelling at the woman in the SUV to get out of the way, and a small smile crossed her face as the woman gave it right back to the van driver. Her real problem was the two men in hot pursuit who had jumped over the cable-wire railing just behind her.

With her ankle protesting, they were quickly gaining. Her flight instinct took over, and she ran blindly into the street, just trying to get away. The sudden screech of tires turned her attention as a delivery truck hit her from the side, launching her like a kid on a trampoline. There was sudden silence as the world turned and spun in slow motion, followed by the hard reality of an asphalt impact. Then nothing at all.

Chapter Three

LAGUNA BEACH, CALIFORNIA – 11:09 A.M.

Atlantis was a driven woman with the ability to gain people's empathy when none was warranted. She had little regard for others and held to a strong belief system that governed her actions. As an atheist and confirmed bachelorette, life was all about getting everything you could for yourself. She put 'I' first and all else she disregarded. After several years of a myopic focus on her career, she used that income to build a life filled with comfort. A simple lifestyle that appealed to her desires built around her expensive tastes.

Her business meant everything to her, and she followed a simple adage taken from the only religious verse she had ever agreed with—Isaiah 22:13: "Let us eat and drink for tomorrow we die." It was literally the basis for her entire life. That she was a death dealer was seen as only a means to an end. It gave her the same satisfaction as buying a new handbag. Death was a growing business niche in which she had excelled. For the right price, anyone was a viable target and with the talent she had carefully developed, the outcome was assured.

Atlantis had prospered from the demise of presidents, CEOs, spouses, and even child heirs, but she had always held the line at pets. No animal, no matter how much money was left to it in a trust, deserved that fate. When it came to people, however, no name was out of bounds and once an agreement was reached, you could set your watch to the agreed time of their demise.

At forty-two, she was young enough to not have to fight to maintain her figure but old enough to know that was coming to an end. She was one of the younger handlers in the business, with a ruthless streak that had quickly earned her an exemplary reputation.

Her mix of Asian and European ethnicity gave her an exotic appearance that fit into almost any international crowd. At five-foot-four and only 108 pounds, she was slight, with jet-black hair held back in a simple ponytail most times and dark liquid-oil eyes to match. The tail of a dragon tattoo could be seen on her neck as it peeked out of the heather-gray collar of her fitness top. It had open sides and a mesh back to match the fitted joggers capped with white and canvas sneakers.

Her blanched-almond skin was smooth and flawless, but her real beauty was her intelligence. She was an ingenious planner and strategist, developing a unique and secure business model that had gone unnoticed by authorities.

Atlantis ran only two assassins, but they were prolific. Both very different in their approach and methodologies. She had given each a unique handle that matched their specialty.

The Encyclical was named after the papal letters sent to bishops in the ancient Roman Catholic Church and was used for sending a message. When you wanted someone dead in a public or obvious way, he was the perfect choice. Always messy and always deadly.

The Scientist was the clear choice when there was a need to leave no sign of foul play. Clever and ever so subtle in his methods, not one hit had been determined as anything other than accidental or unexplained or was a clear blame to the intended, like a wife or partner.

Atlantis worked off a website named *Lilies4everyoccasion.com.* It was a simple and colorful site that allowed you to choose your color and arrangement, all sold by the dozen. For those who knew how the site worked, it was easy to order a hit, and for those who did not, they received their flowers a few days later, as ordered.

Each dozen lilies represented a hit. There were two different arrangements available: loose flowers or in a vase. Loose flowers were for sending a message and in a vase was for subtlety. The colors related to pricing, starting at red for twenty dollars, up to one hundred dollars for white. Buyers placed their orders and followed up with an electronic deposit in her Isle of Mann bank account, adding four zeros to the amount. Each purchase required delivery instructions, including name, photo, and address. There were no posted instructions, and knowledge of how to order came from a very closed word-of-mouth network.

Any additional negotiations took place in the comments section of the site, where you were then redirected to a live chat page. Ten seconds after you typed your message it auto-deleted, making it very secure. For those who found or used the site as a flower source, the amount paid told Atlantis exactly what to do. She had a small floral service that fulfilled the benign orders, giving her an additional modest income that covered her business costs. It was simple and highly profitable, with low overhead, high margins, and minimal visibility.

Atlantis set her half-finished caramel macchiato on a rustic table and sat on a neighboring over-stuffed chair. She pulled the Tootsie Pop from her mouth and set it on the small wax paper square in which it was originally wrapped. The room was modern with a bold use of color. Like a flower garden, every color had its presence. Teal chairs with yellow pillows, sky blue walls, and a dusty rose couch. There was a moss green rug set upon a gray slate floor. It would be too much for some, but it made Atlantis happy to be in the room.

Laguna Beach, California, was the right mix of money and anonymity. Atlantis spent a good portion of her time in a beach house built on the tip of a peninsula with a 220-degree view of the water. The house was three stories high, with a single gated entrance. A sheer cliff to rocks and water below surrounded the rest of the property. She had picked it up for a killer price back in the real estate slump, and it had soared in value since.

Placing her laptop, phone, and wallet in the basket of her pink electric beach cruiser, Atlantis opened the gate at her driveway and coasted into town. The sun was up and warming the blacktop as the cool salty ocean breeze countered its effect.

Morning Session was a petite café on Pacific Coast Highway that catered to tourists. It had an ever-evolving collection of patrons and employees. The owners had decorated the place in beach casual, embracing retail's trendy over-decorated look.

Atlantis selected a small table in the back and set up her laptop. She connected to her site through an encrypted VPN that cloaked her IP and address. The prearranged time was in five minutes, just enough time to get her order in.

The purchase request had come in yesterday, and after a bit of due diligence, she had marked the order as pending. She recalled the issue at hand. The order had been for a dozen loose orange lilies, but after some research, she had found the price of $300,000 too low for the complexity of getting to the target. It was a man of means.

She opened her site's chat room and typed a question mark.

A moment later, a question mark returned. This simple protocol ensured both parties understood the topic of the chat. Within a few seconds, both marks disappeared from the page.

Atlantis replied with: *Yellow would be more appropriate for your occasion. There are many hurdles to the perfect venue.*

There was a pause. She leaned back and watched her text disappear. And then nothing. She let out a sigh and started to close her laptop but stopped when letters popped up.

Yes, yellow would be a better choice, thank you.

Her lips turned upward. The client had accepted her counter of $500,000. She typed an account number for the deposit and finished by closing her computer just as a waitress brought her order. She would now have both her assets on jobs. The Encyclical was in Texas, and she would send The Scientist to Miami. She unwrapped a purple Tootsie Pop she took from her purse and popped it into her mouth. It was shaping up to be a great day.

***

Soft beeping called her back to the light as her eyelids fluttered open. Bright white shocked her whole system as she waited for her squinting eyes to adjust to their surroundings. White ceiling, matching walls, and medical equipment. It was a hospital room. The aroma of chemicals, familiar and haunting. She had been in one before. She tried to sit up and immediate pain shot through her body. Her arm was in a sling and there were many bandages everywhere. She felt groggy and could still only remember her recent past and snippets of her history. A nurse entered her room and appraised her. "You're up. That is good news."

"Where are we? What happened to me?"

"You're in DC, dear. You've heard the term, *hit by a truck*? That was you."

She searched her fragile memory. "Oh, yeah."

"My name is Polly, and you are in Howard University Hospital." The nurse waited for a reply. When none was forthcoming, she pressed a bit harder. "And you are?"

A twinkle of fear shot across her eyes as she tried to remember, but there was nothing. "I can't remember."

The nurse nodded kindly. "It's not uncommon to have some level of amnesia after the kind of head trauma you've experienced. Try to get some rest, and we'll try again later." She tucked the sheet back around her patient.

A second after the nurse left, a man in street clothes opened the door to her room and stepped inside, appraising the situation. He tried a smile, but it was clear he was not well versed in the practice. His suit screamed Men's Warehouse, and his shoes were well worn. The eyes said lack of proper sleep, and his voice said chain smoker.

"I'm Detective Gasser, and I'd like to ask you a few questions. The nurse tells me you either don't remember your name or you are not willing to share that information. So I'll skip to a few preliminary questions and come back tomorrow to see if your memory is any better. Plus, I'll have your fingerprint report back by then, so we won't have to play any games. Something I'm not a big fan of."

He pulled the only chair in the room over next to the bed and sat on the peach upholstery. "The driver of the delivery truck said you ran right in front of him like he wasn't there. I have to ask . . ." He paused to find the right words but just blurted out the question. "Were you trying to end your troubles on the bumper of some innocent?"

The question took her by surprise, and a flash of anger built. "Just because I can't remember my name or my past doesn't make me suicidal or crazy."

"And just because you say that doesn't make it true," he countered.

The signs of an overworked and underpaid professional cop hung on him like a sandwich board. He had neither the time nor the desire to be in the room. After all, people were dying all around the city. Why did he get an attempted suicide?

"Okay. So why did you jump in front of the truck?" He looked her over with a judging eye.

"I didn't jump," she replied.

The detective held his palms up. "Hey, I have to ask. Why did you run in front of the truck?"

"I was being chased by three low-level criminals."

This response brought his eyes up off his notebook to look for signs of deception by the possible suspect. "What makes you say that?" he asked.

"They drove a beat-up brown van and wore gangster chic clothes that were meant to advertise, not hide, their gang affiliation. They were young, in their early twenties. Two were Hispanic and the driver of the van was white. Had a lightning bolt tattoo on the side of his face." She gestured toward the right side of her face.

"That is fairly descriptive. Why were they chasing you?"

She tilted her head at the question. She had no idea and shook her head absently. "I'm feeling extremely exhausted. Can we pick this up later? Everything hurts." It wasn't a lie but a convenient coincidence.

The detective nodded slowly and stood. The woman looked seriously beat up. He slid the chair back against the wall and turned to leave. "I'll be back tomorrow, and I'll expect you to be more helpful," he tossed out as the door closed behind him.

***

The view was astonishing. Four hundred-seventy feet up a glass elevator ride to the geo deck observation level. The iconic Reunion Tower, locally known as *The Ball,* is a 561-foot-high observation tower with restaurants and tourist activities that gave visitors 360-degree views of downtown Dallas.

The Encyclical picked at his half-eaten garlic chicken sandwich, not because the Cloud Nine Café didn't make a great garlic chicken sandwich, but because his mind was far from his meal. He checked his watch and paid the bill, leaving a modest tip. The café was not too crowded today. Instinctively, he scanned each diner, adding the face to his memory bank. Should they show up in his path again, he would do something about it.

The Encyclical was an olive-skinned man in his late twenties with a scruffy beard over a chiseled handsome face. He kept his wavy hair just off his shoulders. His ubiquitous sunglasses and shoulder bag suggested a celebrity look-alike. He excelled at the I'm-better-than-you attitude and had no time for humanity in general. Even his clothes said I can afford what most of you can't. He was an island unto himself with a strong sense of self-worth and a grab-what-you-can-when-you-can mentality. A perfect fit for Atlantis's team.

Wandering to the observation deck a few feet away, he stopped at a collection of free high-powered telescopes lining the glass-domed panels that opened out to the city. He selected a predetermined one and adjusted the focus and view to his liking. He watched as a man that ran on a very specific schedule pulled his car out of the A parking structure. It was a British-racing-green Bentley Mulliner GT Number 9, a limited edition two-door coupe loaded with technology and craftsmanship. A faint number nine was etched into the front grill, giving a nod to the manufacturer's racing heritage.

The Encyclical watched as the vehicle merged into traffic and cruised up to a destination less than a mile away. He lowered the telescope, satisfied the mark was truly a hostage to his schedule. This would make eliminating him all the easier. He went to the elevator and hit the button that would take him to the ground floor and mentally walked through his plan.

Texas was a state known for relaxed gun laws, and with that came additional freedoms that you would never have in California or New York. He would use these laws to his advantage. He let his thoughts turn to the freedoms that were slowly being eroded across this great country, freedoms easily given up for a false sense of security. Safety and security were a mirage. No government could truly protect you as an individual. It could make laws and try to enforce them, but if the masses turned against its leaders or even a segment of the population, they would hold no sway. Personal safety and security were your responsibility.

A young couple entered the elevator. They stood hand-in-hand each wearing the glow two people in love seemed to radiate. He pondered the emotion, knowing it was attributed to a mere chemical imbalance in the brain. Real love, devotion, and commitment were just words used by advertisers and movie producers to elicit a response. The thought almost made him laugh out loud, and he had to turn away to hide the mockery on his face.

***

She woke with a start. The room was dark, and the only illumination came from the machines to her left. A moment's confusion faded as she assessed her situation. Her memory had come flooding back. Her past—growing up in San Diego County along the Pacific Ocean. Her parents, friends, adulthood. The struggles and successes of her life, everything. Her career with the FBI, and even her name—Codi Sanders. She sat up.

The first thing that struck her was the hospital room. She hated them. Time to check out. She pulled her feet to the floor and sat on the edge of the bed. That's when she noticed the handcuff. It attached her right wrist to the bed frame. She was a person of interest in some kind of crime. That would never fly. She pulled the IV out of her arm and used the metal tip to pick the lock on the cuffs. In the closet were her street clothes, still filthy and blood-stained. It was the one thing she still had no memory of. *What had happened to me? What did I do?* With one arm in a sling and every muscle protesting, she awkwardly dressed herself. Carefully using the wall for support, she left the room, every step a painful reminder of the three thugs who had put her there.

As she exited the hospital, an older man, dressed like a college professor from the sixties, was waiting on the empty sidewalk. He was illuminated by an orange streetlight that highlighted a first-rate comb-over.

"Hi," she said to him. "I just got released and realize I don't have my cellphone. Would it be okay if I borrowed yours for a quick call to my brother so he can come and get me?"

"Sure, little lady." He handed her his phone with a kind smile.

She turned and dialed, listening to the rings, followed by a sleepy voice.

"Strickman."

The sound of Codi's partner, Special Agent Joel Strickman, allowed her shoulders to finally relax. She had been so lost and confused, but her confidence came flooding back.

"Hello?"

"Joel!"

"Codi? How's your three-day weekend going?"

The words focused Codi on her recent past, but the memory of leaving work on Friday evening faded into nothingness. "I might be in trouble, and I definitely need your help."

"What do you need me to do?"

Codi gave Joel her location, and then returned the phone to the helpful citizen and stepped back into the shadows to wait for him to arrive. The thin white line on her ring finger now completed her memories. She was engaged to Dr. Matt Campbell, a brilliant scientist working for DARPA, the Defense Advanced Research Projects Agency, and somehow, she had lost her engagement ring. Apparently, this was a weekend she would never fully remember.

***

The home he had rented through Vrbo under a false name was an older 1960s home with a garage in the back. The paint was new, and the home was nicely furnished, the owner knowing full well the power of reviews. It had taken him all of thirty seconds to pick the lock on the garage used to store the owner's crap, and set up a small workshop inside, hoping to hide his actions from all. There were wooden shelves holding long-forgotten items along one wall and a few rusted tools for the gardener on another.

Grenades in Texas, as in all states, were illegal, but non-lethal smoke grenades were not. The Encyclical had picked up two at the Texas Machine Gun and Firearms store in Fort Worth. He had worn a specialized hat for the occasion, one that had several hidden IR LEDs installed in the brim. The small but powerful

IR LEDs produced an infrared (IR) light invisible to the naked eye, but that blinded security cameras. Using false identification and his special hat, he would be nothing but a vague memory if anyone came asking. The shop mostly catered to government agencies but did strong business with preppers and patriots. Next, he stopped by a hardware store for a few additional items. The entire trip had taken him through lunch, and he was starving by the time he returned.

He laid the smoke grenades out on a table in the garage, along with a sandwich and a Coke. He carefully dissected both. The smoke grenades looked like pewter soda cans with a pull ring and lever mounted on the top. He unscrewed the top pin and fuse assembly while chewing a mouthful of sandwich. Using an awl, he dug out the starter and the filler mixture packed inside the canister. When the canister was empty, The Encyclical refilled it with cordite taken from fifty high-velocity thirty-ought-six rifle cartridges. Once the cordite was packed into the canister, he replaced the ignition assembly. After a quick gulp of the cold soda, he focused on the next step—installing two hundred 3/32-inch steel ball bearings. He glued a hundred to the outside of each canister with JB weld. Finally, he wrapped the whole thing in FiberFix tape. The result was a lumpy black cylinder about the size of a can of green beans.

Once both homemade grenades were finished, along with his lunch, The Encyclical removed his gloves and stepped back. They were beautiful and as lethal as any real hand grenades, all made from easily obtainable items. His next task would be a test.

He pulled the gloves from his hands, placed the grenades in a shopping bag, and closed the garage door, locking it behind him. He estimated the dangerous part of the blast radius would be around fifteen feet. After that, death could not be guaranteed. He would need to get close.

The Encyclical stepped back into the house and opened his file on the target. He would need to find the perfect time and place to make his new toy a success. The buyer on this job wanted to make a statement. He could accomplish just that. He would take out the man and his status symbol.

***

Danzo Perez rubbed both hands across his face as he tried to clear his head. Hiring and navigating HR was the toughest part of running a burgeoning criminal organization. The thirty-six-year-old crime boss adjusted his black tie set against a white shirt, his trademark look.

He had built his operation in and around DC, dividing it into three divisions. A small gang of purse snatchers and pickpockets delivered their ill-gotten goods to a predesignated location. Said location would change every few months. He would then use the personal information and keys they collected to have a break-in crew hit the homes and offices of those people they had stolen from. And finally, he sold the personal and banking information to a group that specialized in identity theft and credit card cloning. His set-up was small but profitable, and he had been extra careful to stay under the radar of the authorities. He knew full well that if you got too big and profitable, you were asking for a takeover or a takedown, so he stayed small and mobile.

Danzo was currently working from the first floor of a condemned building. He had set up a mobile hot spot for Wi-Fi and a few tables fashioned from giant wire spools with mismatched chairs. There was an ice chest cooler for a fridge and a bathroom that still had running water. The whole operation could be packed up and moved in minutes. He had bigger plans for the future, but they would have to wait until he was big enough to pay for his safety. And once you had a few key policemen in your pocket, you could afford to be more public.

He was a Cuban-born "wet foot" immigrant with dark wavy hair and an unpredictable attitude. At five-foot-eleven, he was taller than most in his organization. He used his ever-present dour expression to help maintain control over the others.

His parents had made the crossing when he was just five, and he still remembered the ordeal. Days in the hot sun with no water or food. The jury-rigged flotilla was overcrowded and sat low in the water. Any swell that came by would wash over the deck, sending bodies into the sea. It was a large, unexpected wave that had taken his mother. One moment she had her arms wrapped around young Danzo and was whispering a prayer, and the next moment, she was gone. That had turned him away from two things in life—water and religion. He would never own a boat or step foot in a church.

He and his father struggled to make a life in Miami before lymphoma took his father as well. At age eight, Danzo had gone to work for one of the many drug lords that loved to use minors to move their product. Now, he was the boss of his own organization, honed and educated by the hardest and darkest minds.

His immediate problem now, however, was that three of his best guys who worked the street had robbed an FBI agent, and he wasn't quite sure how to put that genie back in the bottle.

Two nights ago, Diaz, Garcia, and Rodo, "The Three Amigos," were robbing a man who had stepped out the back door of an upscale bar into the alley to make a call. Diaz and Garcia quickly surrounded and relieved him of all his possessions while Rodo stayed behind to keep an eye out. A woman followed shortly after the man. This was too easy. They were lining up to be robbed. But she was different. Instead of cowering before them, she stepped in their direction, calling out. "Hey, we don't want any trouble. Just take what you want and go on your way."

Before Diaz and Garcia could engage her, Rodo hit her on the head from behind with a small bat he liked to carry in the front of his jeans for multiple reasons. The woman dropped and hit the pavement headfirst without so much as a twitch.

"Whoa, bro, you killed her!"

"That was gangsta."

The man being robbed used the distraction to run for his life, leaving his possessions behind. The boys circled the body of the woman. Diaz kicked her to see if she was dead. Nothing. They hurriedly removed all of her valuables as panic took over. Thinking the woman was deceased, they tossed the body behind a dumpster and ran for their van.

The real problem came when they got back to the boss. An FBI badge was found in her purse. The boss lost his mind and fired them on the spot. He gave the woman's belongings back to them and gave them twenty-four hours to get out of town. Killing an FBI agent would bring his whole world crashing down.

The Three Amigos took it upon themselves to go back and get the body, and then dispose of it. That would surely get them back in with the boss. The problem was, by the time they got there, the body was gone. An angry assaulted FBI agent was worse than a dead one. This fed could ID them.

They had done a sweep of the area, and with a bit of luck, found her in the park. They gave chase, which resulted in a second failure. Now, The Three Amigos were thinking about giving up and leaving town when lady luck smiled down on them. The FBI agent had run right in front of a truck and been smashed, dead. Now, there wasn't any evidence linking their involvement. They were free and clear. It was what Danzo would have called *making your own luck.*

"You sure she was dead?" Danzo asked as he rounded the wire cable spool he used for a desk. The abandoned building had once been a printing press but now was an assemblage of peeling paint and rusted pipes.

"Oh, for sure, boss. That truck pancaked her on the street, and it had nuthin' to do with us."

"Did either of you stick around to make sure she was dead?"

"No. But there was no way she was ever getting up again."

Danzo scratched his chin. "Okay. Dead fed, no connection. You got lucky. What did you do with her belongings?"

"Ah . . ."

"They're in the van," Rodo said.

"Get rid of them. This never happened. *Understand?*"

All three nodded vigorously.

"Now, get out of my sight before I change my mind."

Chapter Four

HOWARD UNIVERSITY HOSPITAL – WASHINGTON, DC – 8:12 P.M.

The Prius pulled to a stop at the patient pickup outside Howard University Hospital. From out of the darkness, Codi tottered to the passenger side door and got in. Without delay, Joel pulled away from the curb, mesmerized by his partner's appearance.

"What happened? When you called, I was sure I would be bailing you out, not rescuing you from a hospital."

"It's a little of both, actually. I got in some kind of accident, and my memory is all messed up."

"Accident? You don't own a car." They pulled to a stop, and the glare of a streetlight illuminated the Prius. Joel finally got a good look at Codi's face. Her nose was swollen and both her eyes were as black as night rain. There were two butterfly bandages on her head, and besides the sling, who knew what else was hidden under her dirty clothes. He had seen his partner in pretty bad shape before. Tortured, even dead once, before she was resuscitated, but now she looked truly ragged. "Whoa, your face is a mess. Are you sure you're okay?"

"Thanks, and I'm not sure. I woke up in an alley with no memory and there were three thug-lites trying to either kill me or catch me."

"Shoot, that's really freaky. Thank goodness you're alright. Let's get you home. Have you called Matt?"

"No, he's off in Oregon on some DARPA project. I'll be fine. I just need to get some rest."

Joel didn't know what to say. Calling Matt seemed imperative to him, but this was Codi.

She used her fingers to smooth out her matted bedhead hair. "Don't be surprised if I call in sick tomorrow. Wait a minute. If the guys who did this to me still have my purse . . ."

"Then they have your address and your keys," Joel finished.

Codi nodded, a concerned look on her face.

Joel spun the car around. "I'm taking you to Matt's."

Dr. Matt Campbell had literally been thrust into Codi's life on an earlier case where the two of them had been kidnapped together and had to self-rescue each other. They now found that slow and easy rhythm that two people who were made for each other experience. His broad shoulders, wavy hair, and penetrating green eyes would be his physical calling card, but Codi loved all of his bits and pieces—most of all his mind. He had a kindness and a simple way about him that contrasted with his incredible intelligence, surely a member of MENSA or maybe even the Triple Nine Society. Recently, the two had become engaged. Codi was still trying to get her head around how extremely happy she was, or how scared. Her family life had fallen into the gutter after the unexpected death of her father, leaving her to fend for herself. The responsibility of caring for someone else ushered in anxiety for her. Maybe with a little practice, she could figure it out.

Eight months ago, Matt quit his job in Boston and started working at Bright Source, a think tank for DARPA, the advanced research and projects agency for the Department of Defense. Bright Source came under DARPA's Tactical Technology Office, TTO. It was used to test and innovate defense systems used for the prevention of strategic and tactical surprise by land, sea, sky, and space. It was his dream job, working on advanced concepts and gadgets, and he was already making an impact.

The move had him living just outside of the city in the small town of Beverly Beach next to the Rhode River, as it drained into the Chesapeake Bay. It changed their long-distance relationship into a next-door romance, and knowing Codi's relational reluctance, Matt worked hard not to add any additional pressure with his new proximity. It took some doing, but Matt finally got the words out—*Codi, will you do me the honor of being my wife?* At least, he felt like he had said the words. It was very possible that Codi had somehow tricked him into saying them. After all, he was hopeless when it came to women and a certified klutz when it came to Codi. She, on the other hand, seemed to have a handle on everything about them.

Joel pulled into the narrow driveway that led around to the garage in back.

Matt had purchased a small beach cottage with a view of the water. It was robin's egg blue with white trim, an accentuated peaked roof, and an extended white front porch that wrapped around two sides of the home.

Codi opened Joel's glove box and pulled out his backup pistol.

"I'm borrowing this, and I'll see you as soon as I can," she said, holding up her left arm that was in a sling.

"I'll get someone to watch the place."

"Thanks, Joel."

He nodded as she walked up the steps to the front door. Life in a small town differed from the city. Codi reached under a small pot by the front door and pulled out a door key. She quickly let herself in and hit the lights. Joel waited and watched, making sure his partner was safe inside before driving off.

Matt was away for the week testing a drone stealth boat or something like that in the Pacific Northwest. Codi didn't even pull the covers back before crashing on his bed and drifting off into an uncomfortable dreamless sleep.

***

Research was just one thing Atlantis excelled in. Her current order called for the mark to be dispatched without any blowback. She spent two days diving deep into the man's background and routines. She pulled information from social media and was partial to Zillow for in and around-the-home photos. Her internet connection was protected with a high-end firewall and custom VPN, affording her the freedom to search without being tracked. Social movements could be charted and habits exposed for even the most careful of persons. Atlantis was especially good at sourcing hard-to-get blueprints and personal itineraries.

She was working on her back patio from a comfy lounge chair. The sun was out, and the shade was a must. The sound of waves crashing below harmonized with the reggae playing in the background. An iced tea dripped condensation next to her computer as she finished adding the last few details. An almost finished Tootsie Pop moved around in her mouth, unconsciously satisfying an oral fixation she'd had and never lost from a very young age.

Once a case file was built that contained all the particulars, it was time to reach out to The Scientist. This was his kind of job. A packet that contained no incriminating evidence, just concise information was FedExed to his home. Now all she had to do was sit back and wait for her next customer. Her margin on this job would be close to 250k. *Not bad for a few days' work*, she thought as she sipped her cold tea.

Atlantis recalled her humble beginnings. Her father immigrated before she was born, but she had heard the stories of his heroism. He had single-handedly duped the North Korea government. There was even a bounty on his head from the premier himself, Kim Il-sung. In America, he was protected and praised. He had taken a wife of European heritage and lived the American dream.

As a mixed-race couple, it was not so easy to fit into the American dynamics of the era, so Mark buried himself in his work. Her mother found a way to manage between the races and spent her time shopping and socializing, much to her father's displeasure. Though he never raised a hand to her, the fights were legendary.

As a young Korean-American, Atlantis was bullied in school and given a strict upbringing by her tradition-driven father, who had wanted a boy. She had always felt like an outcast but hardened her emotions and push through. She was exceptional in school and used her intellect to push herself forward. Her determination and stick-to-itiveness eventually won her father over, and he began to train her.

At first, it was just physical self-defense classes. He rounded out her education with piano lessons and spy craft, pushing her to excel, often to the breaking point. He instilled the importance of being true to oneself and their heritage. Her brain was constantly pushed to find solutions and workarounds to a variety of posed problems.

Her mom died during her sophomore year at UCLA. Her secret drinking that fooled nobody had done its damage. She was followed later that year by Atlantis's dad, but not before he had taken her hand and told her the truth about himself. She had left him that day not realizing she would never see him again. He had placed a folded strip of paper in her hand. "Open this when you are ready."

"Ready for what?"

"You will know."

It was all just another mind game, and she had no time for frivolity. Atlantis left that day with her head filled with anger at the knowledge that her father was a double agent for the North Koreans. He had betrayed his host country. It spun her world upside down, but she found strength in the one thing she could always trust and believe in—herself.

After finishing college, she dedicated herself to a path of success that consumed her. She would do whatever she felt was necessary to be successful. Morals and laws were made for the weak to follow. With money came power, and power was something you could use to change things to your will.

Atlantis first conceived of her business model when a local news story carried the events of a CEO's death and all the shuffling that took place in the company afterward. She envisioned it all like a giant chessboard, where the pieces could be moved and changed. The ultimate move for an impatient underling or jealous competitor seemed to be murder, a growth industry she could perfect and flourish in.

The idea marinated until she decided to pull the trigger.

She would never forget the Saturday morning she had pulled out the folded strip of paper her father had given her to find a handwritten name and phone number.

Chung-Woo was in his late fifties with an impossibly thin neck supporting a spherical, balding head and a paper-thin mustache. He was shorter than Atlantis by several inches, but he carried dead eyes that held an easy menace at all times.

He had paved a way for her by providing contacts and resources. His connection to her father's homeland was clear, but he seemed genuinely excited about her new path.

Atlantis embraced the business of death and opened doors for potential customers. First up was an older business owner with apparently no plan to retire. He was permanently retired to make way for his impatient son.

The transaction had been less than perfect. The assassin she hired was reckless and messy. Chung-Woo made it clear what had to be done to clean up her mess. It was a lesson all must learn. Atlantis personally eliminated the son and the assassin, leaving no trace back to her. This had seemed to excite Chung-Woo, and he continued to help mold her business. He showed her how to operate effectively in the underworld. Atlantis learned quickly and refined her company. She eliminated the need for personal contact and worked with Chung-Woo to hand select and train her employees to fit the company's requirements, at the same time reducing her risks and increasing profits. It wasn't long before her next job came along. There was always someone in need of killing. This time, thanks to the assassin, she called the Encyclical. Things went flawlessly.

Atlantis met her next assassin, the long-faced Cameron Clark, now known as The Scientist, at a business retreat in the California mountains. He had been there attempting to raise money for some forgettable idea. What caught her attention happened at an after-party when a bunch of men sat around joking about one of them killing off his wife. She would never forget Clark's response. He laid out the perfect plan on how to do it and not get caught. She made sure to get his business card that night, and subsequent follow-ups slowly led them to a working relationship that flourished. His unique skill set and quirky personality made him truly one-of-a-kind.

Chung-Woo encouraged Atlantis to keep just two assassins. That would keep her busy, plenty profitable, and most importantly, under the radar. Atlantis added a very talented hacker known as JC to the team and business grew exponentially. Murder-for-hire done right was very profitable.

***

Codi set her new phone down as she bucked up and down. Her face was no longer swollen, but her two black eyes were not a pretty sight. Her driver pulled to the side of the road and got out to survey the damage. He popped his head back in the driver's side window. "The tire is flat. Let me request another car for you."

"Not a problem. I'm only a few blocks away. I'll just walk." She stepped out of the Uber and headed down the sidewalk. Her lean athletic figure was accented by just the right amount of curves and a hidden strength that had left many surprised to be on their backs in handcuffs. Intense brown eyes with flecks of gold surveyed her environment as she walked. Determination and intelligence were her most valued assets, but she found time to laugh even at herself from time to time.

Ten minutes later she regretted her decision. Washington, DC, was having a heat wave and the morning humidity in the city was already suffocating. By the time she reached the FBI Field Office, she was a sweaty mess. After passing through the security gauntlet to curious stares, she found the nearest bathroom and used a damp paper towel to cool down and remove the sweat. She was not going to win a beauty competition, but a quick look in the mirror said good enough. She took the elevator up to the third floor and headed to her office.

The Special Projects division of the FBI, on the third floor of the DC Field Office, was a growing division that took on cold cases and investigated unusual crimes. Criminalities that didn't fall into the purview of the other divisions within the FBI, but still required a federal presence. They were also often asked to help with other mainstream cases for divisions that found themselves shorthanded.

The main room for the Special Projects division was small by FBI standards. It was a square bullpen holding nine desks, each set within tall cubicle walls that formed around a center rectangle. There was a carpeted hallway down the middle, and Codi's office was straight across the hall from her partner Joel's. Daylight glowed from windows on the back wall where a small glass conference room was housed. Function ruled over form.

Down the hall and across from Supervisory Special Agent Brian Fescue's office was a room known as the fishbowl. It was a workspace used when additional staff or specialized investigations were required. It had gotten its name from the two glass walls that allowed anyone in the vicinity to see inside. This was not a purpose-built facility, but rather a division that made their environment work. And work it had, as the team was responsible for clearing some very high-profile cases and stopping several imminent international and domestic disasters.

Codi sat in her desk chair with a thud, still trying to let the air-conditioning seep into her overheated core. She scratched at her arm, which was still in a sling. *Hopefully, the itch was due to healing,* she thought absently.

A slight tap on the side of her cubicle was followed with, "Welcome back. I brought you some exquisite coffee. How's the arm?" It was her partner, Joel.

"No can do unless it's iced coffee. My Uber crapped out, and I decided to walk the last bit this morning."

"Oh, it's a beast out there," he replied.

"Tell me about it. I'm hoping to get this thing off tomorrow," she said, holding her damaged arm up. "What's on the docket today? I'm wishing for an art smuggler with a panache for fine food and good wine holed up in a luxurious walk-in cooler."

"Count me in. Boss has a round table planned for ten."

Codi looked at her watch. It gave her an hour and a half to check her emails and complete her last report.

Her partner seemed to understand. Joel was a tall wiry blond with black-framed glasses and a big heart. His expertise fell more to the technological side of their partnership, but he had proven himself a solid performer. His charming, nerdy good looks and superior intelligence more than made up for his lack of social skills.

"So three days off rehabbing at Matt's. Anything to report?"

"He's still out of town. I can't remember much from my weekend, but otherwise, I'm doing better, and the DMV still sucks at getting a replacement license."

"The DMV sucks at everything," Joel countered.

"Except for queue lines. They got that down to a science."

***

The Encyclical drove a Harley Davidson Livewire out to the woods beyond the city. It was a cash purchase he had made under an assumed identity on the first day he got to Dallas. The orange, black, and silver bike was a testament to the company's pursuit of perfection.

As he passed 50 mph, the subtle whine of the gears was replaced with nothing but wind. The all-electric motor pushed him past 90 mph without effort, having a range of just under 150 miles and a top speed of 95 mph. Its Revelation power train was built for torque, making it one of the quickest motorbikes ever produced. Plus, it was very quiet, leaving only the tires on pavement and wind in your hair for company. It was a marvel of technology packed into a single motorcycle.

He turned off the main road and headed down a wooded trail into a section of secluded land. Once he felt confident no one was around, he unloaded his oversize cargo—four good-sized watermelons. The weight had made the bike squirrelly at highway speeds. The Encyclical placed them in a tight circle in a small meadow. He returned to his bike and pulled the last of his cargo from the box mounted on the back rack. It was one of his homemade grenades. He tossed the box to the side.

Taking the grenade in his left hand, he rode away from the watermelons. The meadow was bumpy, and the bike shook and shimmied across the rough ground. He spun around and headed back at a brisk pace. Just before he got there, he grabbed the grenade and used his right thumb to hook the pull ring. As he stopped next to the watermelons, he yanked the pin from the grenade. With his left hand, he tossed it into the pile and then floored the electric bike, leaving a swath of dust as the rear tire spun for purchase in the loose soil. There was a five-second fuse that ignited the cordite. He looked back just in time to see the homemade explosive detonate. A single concussive blast destroyed the canister, sending the steel ball bearings in every direction. The watermelons were eviscerated. The Encyclical stopped and dismounted. He strolled over to survey the carnage. The test was a smashing success.

With phase one complete, he would need to set a few more items in place before he would be ready. He parked his E-cycle behind the house and headed into town in an older work truck he had bought for cash just yesterday. He had selected a perfect spot to cover his egress from the attack in case things went south. There was a large parking structure with seven levels next to a defunct Woolworths and the Giant Eyeball sculpture on Elm Street. Each level had a large dumpster located just beyond the corkscrew lanes that allowed automobile access to the entire building.

The Encyclical drove the utility truck, with a bogus company logo he had printed and attached to the side, into the parking structure. He pulled in next to a dumpster, turned on his flashers, and set out a few traffic cones. Once the illusion of an actual job was set up, he began his next project. A plasma cutter made quick work on the steel side of the dumpster that was out of view from the exit ramp. Within a few minutes, he cut out two rectangles that made up most of the side of the dumpster. He then reattached them with spring-loaded hinges that held them in place as if nothing had happened to the dumpster at all. A simple push against them from the outside and they hinged inward, allowing access. Once released, they closed with a thump back to their original position.

The Encyclical stepped back and looked at his handiwork. A bit of touch-up paint and the seams were virtually invisible. He then placed a padlock on the dumpster, rendering it unusable. The final piece was a printed note with the Dallas Sanitation Services logo: "Temporarily out of service. Please use dumpsters on level four or six."

***

The sea of the great Northwest was angry today, and clouds bunched together, threatening a storm. From a distance, Dr. Matt Campbell's moppish light-brown hair and solid physique seemed in contrast to your typical nerd scientists, but as you got closer, his piercing green eyes and intelligence showed like a beacon through a foggy night. Dr. Matt Campbell steadied himself as the first of the large rollers swept past the bow of the eighty-five-foot follow vessel. He looked out at the *Sea Hunter,* a one-of-a-kind gray Navy ship with a host of advanced electronics and autonomous navigation. The ASW, or anti-submarine warfare continuous trail unmanned vessel, was one of DARPA's newest developments. The large, unmanned surface vehicle could stay at sea for months at a time. It had undergone several phases throughout its development and was going through one last week of sea trials before being sent to San Diego to interface with the Navy and run test missions.

Matt, along with several other colleagues from Bright Side, had been invited to participate and give any advice or tweaks. He had taken a flight out of DC on Friday and was digesting everything he could about the new ship and its technical specifications. The hotel was small but clean and only a few blocks from the Willamette River, which merged with the Columbia five miles downriver. A call from Codi still weighed heavily on his mind, as she was staying at his place, thinking her place was currently unsafe. The story she shared had him wanting to take the next flight back, but she convinced him to stay, as "she had it all under control."

Dr. Matt Campbell closed his emerald-green eyes and ran his fingers through his tangled hair. The sea always brought out the curliness in it, and the constant breeze didn't help matters.

Matt hung onto the railing to keep himself stable as the follow ship rolled in the sea. The blue and white boat with the high steel bow plowed through the water with ease. Most of the staff was inside the large bridge, viewing the operation from there, but Matt preferred to watch from outside with the wind in his hair. The radio on his hip kept him informed of every command and result the *Sea Hunter* in front of them went through.

Three months ago, he asked Codi to marry him, and they had yet to set a date. It was the kind of uncertainty a person who liked to have everything in life planned and organized to a fine detail would hate. A man like Matt.

He tried not to let it bother him, knowing Codi was a lot more by-the-seat-of-your-pants. She was a free spirit, unbound by dates and plans. How she navigated through the FBI like that was a mystery to him. He was guessing her partner, Joel, took up the slack. He was very buttoned-up, dotting his *I*s and crossing his *T*s.

Matt grabbed his phone and sent her one of his now famous emoji hearts with a *Miss U* text. He knew texts and emojis were hollow at best, but the signature text let Codi know he was thinking of her. In his mind, nothing beat face-to-face for proper communication, or, more to his liking, skin on skin. For now, however, knowing Codi and her situation, this would have to do. He put the phone back in his pocket, not expecting a reply soon.

***

Codi stepped into the alleyway to take it all in. The only thing familiar was the dumpster. She used her toe to move some trash around, but nothing obvious popped up. A buzz on her phone had her checking the screen. A quick smile erupted—Matt.

"It's been a week," Joel said to her. "I'm sure this is at least the second or third round of trash back here."

Codi looked back at the situation, pocketing her phone. "None of it seems familiar except this dumpster. I woke up right here," she said, pointing to the back of the dumpster.

"There was a reported mugging here on the night of your memory loss." He looked at his phone. "An Edgar Rice, male Caucasian, age thirty-eight," Joel read from the case e-file. "You sure you want to do this?"

Codi walked further into the alley, ignoring the question. On the other side of the alley was a metal door with a swag light mounted over it. "Too bad there isn't a camera here."

"What do you suppose is on the other side?"

"Let's find out."

They walked around the block to the other side of the alley. The street was lined with small businesses, each with its own personality. The shop that caught their attention was a black brick façade with a small neon sign: DIVE. She seemed drawn to it by memories just out of reach.

Joel pulled the door open, and the two agents entered. A dark room with many tables surrounded by chairs led to a four-sided bar in the middle of the room.

"We're not open yet," a voice from behind the bar called out. A fortyish man with a cleaning rag and a shaved head watched with a perplexed scowl as Codi and Joel approached.

They showed the man their badges.

"We were wondering if you recognize me. I was here a week ago Friday night."

The man looked her up and down. He liked what he saw. "No. I would have remembered you." He turned his head to the rear and called out. "Hey, Roger, got a second?"

A younger man in all black stepped from the back room. He had crazy large sideburns and a square-shaped body.

"Hey, welcome back," he said, looking at Codi. "I see you got out alright."

"You remember me?" Codi asked.

"Sure. Last Friday, 'back door girl.'"

Codi looked confused. "I'm sorry. I don't remember."

"Whoa, that must have been some night." He chuckled.

"You have no idea," Codi replied.

"You were here partying, came up to me, and asked if there was a back way out of here. I figured some creeper was making the moves, you know. We get a couple of those a week in here."

Codi understood the words, but there was no memory to go with them. "Do you remember who I was with or anything else about me?"

He thought back for a moment. "Let's see . . . you came in with a brunette with a party vibe. That's something you recognize in a person when you've been doing this as long as I have."

"Katlyn," Codi said to Joel.

"She left first, and you went out the back, and that's that." He pointed with a jerk of his thumb at the back door.

Joel asked a few more follow-up questions, and they thanked Roger and left the building.

"You know we're not supposed to be working this case, right?" Joel said to her. "They have some agent named Greta from the field office assigned to it."

"Joel, it's my memory, and until I get it back, I'm no good to you or anyone else."

Joel looked into her eyes, trying to make a decision. "Our boss is gonna . . . it's going to be bad."

Codi just stared at him without concern.

"All right," he said. "We might as well get this over with. Let's go check out this mugging vic, Edgar Rice. I have his address in case . . . well, you know."

They drove six blocks to the Law Offices of Rice and Burrows. It was a small office with three paralegals and an office manager named Dawn. Attorney

Edgar Rice was surprised to see FBI agents interested in his mugging case. He led them into his office, and they all sat down in unison. There were plaques on the wall boasting of his higher education and an original Jean-Michel Basquiat framed prominently.

"Now, what can I do for you two agents? Wow, looks like you got hit by a truck," Edgar said, noticing Codi's black eyes as he sat behind his glass desk.

"You should see the other guy," Codi threw back lamely.

Joel started the questioning. "Ah, we, we were wondering if you . . ."

"Hey, I know you!" Edgar said, interrupting. "You saved my life. Didn't recognize you at first. What's with all the bruising?"

Codi looked stunned. "I'm sorry. I can't remember. How did I save your life?"

"Wow. You came at the guys who were mugging me and about to kill me. You're a guardian angel."

"Can you tell us everything?" Joel prodded.

"Like I told the police, I had been celebrating a big win for Rice and Burrows. I went out back to have a smoke and clear my head when these two guys came out of nowhere and held a gun to me. I don't mind saying I was scared. They took everything, including my Patek Philippe. Then, two days later, my home was robbed. It's been a crappy week, but I'm alive, all thanks to you."

"What about during the robbery?"

"Yeah, they took everything, like I said, and then you popped out the back door and started giving them hell. They forgot about me, and I ran off," he said, with a sense of pride.

Joel adjusted his glasses and suddenly looked perplexed. "Wait, you ran off, leaving her to do your fighting?"

The blood drained from Edgar's face, as did his pleased look. "I called 911!"

"She nearly got killed trying to save you, and you ran off!" Joel stood in anger.

Codi grabbed his shirt and pulled him back. She hastily stood and made a hurried exit from the room along with apologies and thanks, pulling Joel with her.

Once outside, Joel exploded. "That jerk left you to die!" he screamed.

"That jerk solved the missing moments of my life. You can't expect citizens to come to your aid by putting their own lives at risk."

"Well, you should."

"Yes, Joel, you should."

***

Smart vehicles were making the world a different place. With the ability to drive and park themselves, drivers were slowly becoming more dependent on them every year. Modern cars worked by having the key fob transmit a low-frequency signal, which the car's computer verified. As long as the signal was paired to that specific vehicle and within a few feet of the vehicle, it provided access to the doors, trunk, and ignition. But for a technologically savvy person, there were ways to clone a fob. The latest generation of smart cars addressed this weakness by taking security to a new level, forcing The Encyclical to enlist one of the most egregious hackers unknown to authorities, but well-known to him.

He placed a message on a public e-board on the dark web and waited two days before getting a reply. Con Air was a troll of a man who still lived in the nineties, from his haircut to the clothes he wore. The only exception was the work he did. It was cutting-edge. He had done several jobs for The Encyclical in the past.

The Encyclical stabbed a piece of grilled chicken and stuffed it into his mouth. The street-side café was in the middle of downtown Dallas. As the workday finished, people moved to new destinations. He was never a fan of in-person meetings, but if you were going to pay in cash, it was the only way to do it.

Con Air had yet to learn the meaning of punctuality or personal hygiene. The Encyclical could smell him before he saw him. A short, bald man in a purple tracksuit sat down across from him with a plop. He had a hunched posture and a large bulbous nose that preceded him almost as much as his odor. The Encyclical poked at the last of his dinner with his fork without looking up. "You're late."

"Thanks for noticing."

"Can I get you anything?" The Encyclical asked.

"Do you think they have Monster or NOS here?" Con Air asked.

"Doubt it."

"I'm good."

The Encyclical tried to casually breathe through his mouth as the proximity to the foul-smelling man was all-encompassing.

"I have this for you," The Encyclical said as he slid an envelope over to the hacker.

The man pocketed it and leaned back in his chair. "What's the turn-around time?"

"Yesterday. But I only need the passenger window. Don't need to start it or unlock it. Just a simple up and down."

"Here." Con Air tossed him a simple key, and The Encyclical caught it. "Any time after four tomorrow. Two blocks down." He gestured the direction with his head. He then stood and hurried off as if the sunlight might burn through his skin.

The Encyclical watched the little man scurry away like a rat being chased by a broom. He placed two twenties on the table and left the café behind. He was curious what Con Air had meant by two blocks down, but once he got there, it all made sense. Mailboxes & More. It was a key to a mailbox.

Chapter Five

PACIFIC OCEAN – PACIFIC NORTHWEST – 11:16 A.M.

The project manager for the ACTUV, Giles Preston, was making the rounds. He had a nervous energy about him as he tried his best to spin the entire week to his narrative. It was understandable. The fifty-five-year-old from New Hampshire had spent years of his life developing a technological marvel like the *Sea Hunter*. Now, he was being forced to lift her skirt and show a bunch of fellow scientists her glory. It was disconcerting at the very least. He rubbed his hands together as he spoke in low tones.

"We have rough seas today. The tri-hull configuration makes her fast and stable on the water, but in this chop, she'll need to throttle back a bit. It will be a great test of her reliability."

"Only time and missions will really show her reliability," Matt said, with a noncommittal air. "But you're right, we shall see."

"Yes, of course," Giles replied.

"I'm sure she will pass with flying colors. Sometimes things that work great in the lab don't work so well at sea, but it is all part of the process. I have gone through her capabilities and am quite impressed with the level of redundancy you have given her."

"If one circuit is good, two are better. A failure now would be bad, but during a battle, catastrophic." He paused his mini-lecture and looked Matt over for a brief second. "Thank you, Dr. Campbell," Giles said as he moved back to the safety of the bridge to ply the other scientists.

Matt gave the man a sideways glance. He remembered feeling the same way testing his own invention. Matt had been the recipient of his grandfather's work, which he had started some sixty years earlier and bestowed upon Matt through a colleague. Matt had gladly taken over the reins and had both completed and enhanced the project. It was a machine that broke down compounds to a cellular level before transmitting them through the air. Similar to how helium can pass through a balloon, the smaller molecules pass right through larger molecules. Matt's dream was to fly over a remote village and vaccinate every person in a single pass.

Almost four years ago, a man named Nial Brennan entered the picture. He stole the technology, renamed it SkyStorm, and planned to use it as a weapon, something Matt had never considered. The thieves had kidnapped him along with a young GSA agent named Codi Sanders in order to force his hand. The whole debacle ended in a race to stop a madman bent on death and destruction.

Nial loaded SkyStorm with a deadly agent and aimed it at London, planning to infect millions of innocents. This act changed everything for Matt. He realized there would always be vile people in the world willing to do anything to promote their diabolical agendas. It had exhausted his passion for his project and made him more vigilant.

Matt and Codi pushed themselves to their breaking points to stop the weapon. Luckily, Codi and her team prevented the attack and retrieved Matt's invention.

After getting it back, the military took charge. They gave the device the odd acronym, "FCBT" for focused cellular beam technology, and appropriated it, citing national security. The government buried the whole thing in secrecy and layered it with a giant heaping of painful bureaucracy.

The time spent together during that intense fiasco had forged an incredibly strong friendship that had blossomed into something very special. But maintaining a high-octave relationship was always doomed to fail. It was the quiet time they spent together after the case on a beach in Ireland that cemented their genuine feelings for each other.

Since that time, Matt had run several trials with the FCBT and was getting exceptional results, but after everything he had been through, he eventually left it all behind and started anew.

Now, things were going well, and their engagement seemed to have cemented their love for each other. He thought of Codi. She was an extraordinary woman. He had never met anyone so determined and driven, yet still willing to give. She made time for life and tried to get as much out of it as she could. The woman would shoot you in the head if it was warranted and kill herself to save you. He let his mind wander to the more primal parts of his brain as he imagined them together. Her thin waist and seductive butt that accentuated her athletic form. Her amazing breasts that seemed to defy gravity. And her smile that cut right through him every time.

A gigantic wave crashed into the ship, sending icy ocean spray over the bow. Matt's unexpected cold shower sobered his thoughts and brought him back to the here and now.

The *Sea Hunter* was a dual, catamaran-style, tri-hull ship with ACTUV software instead of sailors. ACTUV was designed to allow the ship to operate and navigate safely at sea, including interfacing with other ships in its path. Its specialty would be tracking the very quiet diesel-electric submarines that many countries used and dispatching them without remorse.

Since leaving the dock site in Portland, Oregon, just over an hour ago, Matt watched, mesmerized, as the ship in front of him manipulated its way down the Columbia River through ship traffic and out to sea, all without a single command correction from the follow ship's technicians. As they came around the protective finger of Fort Stevens State Park, everything changed. Giant swells and strong winds put a damper on the whole exercise. Welcome to the Pacific Northwest.

***

Working for the FBI's Special Projects division out of DC came with some unexpected moments, but it was all part of the job description. Codi transferred there after a bout with the GSA (General Services Administration), where she and Joel cut their teeth on a high-profile case that launched them to federal agent celebrity status. The FBI recruited them, and it wasn't long before they made a name for themselves there as well.

Supervisory Special Agent (SSA) Brian Fescue moved down the hallway toward the conference room, carrying his laptop. Codi's boss had a casual way about him that hid the seriousness of his position and the cases he often oversaw. He was proud of his Jamaican heritage but kept his accent well-hidden unless upset. Brian was about three inches shorter than Joel, but he was built like a tank. And his cappuccino-colored eyes seemed to get to the truth no matter how hard you tried to hide it. He was good to his agents and worked just as hard as they did.

After a particularly intense case where Brian first worked alongside Codi, he stepped away from the field and into an office job. Brian's wife had given birth to their second child, Abigale, and he felt strongly that the field was no place for a good father.

He was a committed husband and father. When the administration offered him his current position, he was happy to take it. It offered him a chance to blend the job he loved with the home life that was so important to him. Now, he was the driving force behind the FBI's Special Projects division based in the DC Field Office. He had personally recruited Codi and her partner, Joel. Together, they had solved several high-profile cold cases to become two of the division's shining stars. Codi, and even her partner Joel, flourished under his tutelage. And their results had gone a long way with the brass to confirm that Brian was the right man for the job.

It was not often that he met with all of his agents at once. Most days, they were off following leads or hip-deep in the enormous load of paperwork the government agency seemed to thrive on. Today's meeting, however, had been on the books for quite some time, and he was excited to reconnect.

Brian was all business as he traipsed the gray carpet toward his seat at the head of the table. The small conference room was filled with agents and support staff. He laid a replacement badge in front of Codi as he passed. "Try to hang onto it this time."

His words were followed by some good-natured ribbing and a couple of laughs from the other agents.

He was wearing a fitted black suit with a light blue collared shirt and a red checkered tie and pocket square. Brian unbuttoned his coat as he sat at the head of the rosewood oval table. Behind him was a tandem whiteboard and a pull-down screen.

"Morning all. Thanks for being here. I wanted to start by saying you have been doing some solid detective work, and it has not gone unnoticed. He pointed to the group with a sweeping finger. "So good job." He cleared his throat and continued. "As you know, we are asked from time to time to help out with other departments' caseloads. So check your emails after the meeting.

Brian powered up his laptop and plugged it into an HDMI cable leading to a projector. The screen lit up, showing his homepage, a happy family picture partially covered in icons. Brian clicked over to the page he wanted and read the list of cases to be distributed. "Also, as you know, we get a lot of unsolved cases to work on. Well, today is no different. Our fellow agents from the cold case division have sent us some overflow."

A consensus of moans filled the room.

"I know, I know. But what they are asking is for us to take a cursory look at several unsolved that haven't been looked at in years. A couple of them have been haunting the FBI for decades, and a few are just dust bunnies. We all know there are new technologies that most of these cases didn't have access to. So go through them, and if any opportunity or a new way of looking at the evidence comes up, follow it. I'm sure you're all aware of the Carroll Bonnet case that was solved thirty years after the fact, thanks to DNA evidence. Well, we are hoping to do the same here."

He passed out a single page to each set of agents with a list of cases. Brian always had agents in mind as he assigned cases, but he was willing to listen to their feedback.

"Most of these are available electronically, and some are stored at either the vault or the National Archives." He paused until every agent turned in his direction. "Remember, every case matters."

"Did you get that from a cereal box?" someone mumbled.

"Who here still eats cereal?" Codi asked no one in particular.

The meeting disbanded, and Codi was one of the first out the door.

Codi could hold her own with most men. She was an avid swimmer and took physical fitness seriously. She had even competed in college swimming in both relays and as an individual.

After graduating college with top honors, Codi received several promising opportunities, but she left them all behind and joined the Marines as an enlisted soldier. She had something to prove to herself and to her dead father. Three arduous years later, she was one of the few females ever admitted to BUD/S training. Becoming a SEAL was something she had set as a do-or-die goal. Nothing would stop her from achieving it. Nothing except a misogynist "boys' club" that conspired against her. She was forced to tap out or, DOR, drop on request, after a tragic injury left her ankle shattered, along with her dream. She would never forget the pain as she rang the brass ship's bell three times, signaling her exit.

Afterward, Codi spiraled down into a dark place that put her out of the military and practically on the street. Eventually, she phoenixed from the ashes of despair and destructive behavior. It changed her in many ways. She found that there were some things more important than success. A softer side blossomed, and she united it with her driven side. It allowed her to appreciate and trust others in a way she had never before.

She accepted a job as a GSA Agent where she was responsible for tax and fraud cases, essentially a paper cop. Though feeling like she had let herself down, Codi put her best foot forward. She embraced the job with fervor and quickly got the attention of her superior, Director Ruth Anne Gables, a strong politically connected leader who took Codi under her wing. She pushed Codi when needed and supported her when there was trouble.

Codi was assigned to work with Joel Strickman, a computer-savvy agent with a heart of gold. His wiry figure and unkempt blond hair framed his naturally positive curiosity about life. They found success in bringing to justice several individuals who had defrauded the US government. But it took a cold case from the forties to really test them. It started benign enough but quickly escalated to international implications and ultimately global terror. The case pushed Codi to her breaking point, unleashing her full potential. She fought through the impossible to stop a madman bent on global destruction.

It seemed the harder someone pushed her, the harder Codi Sanders pushed back. It wasn't stubbornness but determination born of a confidence her father had instilled in her at a young age. In the end, she was credited with saving hundreds of thousands of lives.

The case got her noticed at the FBI, and she now found herself Special Agent Sanders, assigned to the Special Projects division. For Codi, her career was back on track. Even her personal life was finding its groove. It was a good time to be her.

She glanced at her phone, hoping for a text from Matt. Dr. Matt Campbell was often in her thoughts. He had won her heart, and that was something she thought impossible. Now, as they moved their relationship into something more permanent, Codi's thoughts wandered to a possible date for the wedding—spring or fall?

***

Rodo inserted the key and tried to turn it. Nothing. He wiggled and jiggled it to no avail. "Feds changed the lock!" Garcia stammered.

"You sure this is the right door?" Diaz asked.

"Three C just like on her license," Garcia answered.

"Here, let me try," Rodo said, as he kicked in the door in one violent motion. He stood there perfectly still, looking into the room. There was a nice living room that opened to a modern kitchen and dining area.

"What are you doing?" Diaz asked.

"Making sure there isn't an alarm," Rodo replied.

"By standing still? Move over. If there was an alarm, it would have blasted off as soon as you kicked the door, numb nuts," Diaz said as he pushed past his partner and into the apartment.

"Take anything of value," Garcia said rhetorically.

"And smash what we don't take!" Rodo called out as he followed them into the room, opening his knife and closing the door behind him.

Twenty minutes ago, The Three Amigos were drinking at Whiteys Bar, a small dark pub owned by a very black Nigerian with the most unusual white hair. They had managed to save their job with Danzo, thanks to a random truck accident. The boss would be slow to return his trust in them, but it would come. After a few drinks, they were feeling much more confident about their situation.

"What did you do with the fed's stuff?" Diaz asked.

"Tossed it, like the boss said," Rodo mumbled.

"Too bad. I was thinking we could start our own little side hustle and help ourselves to her stuff."

"Yeah, too bad," Garcia said. "Where did you dump it?"

Rodo hesitated before answering. He downed the rest of his drink and finally confessed. "Glove box of the van."

Three smiles spread around the table.

***

Joel pulled to the curb and hopped out of his Prius. He had promised Codi he would pick up a few of her things from her apartment since he had an appointment in the neighborhood. The weather had cooled in DC, and now, you didn't start dripping until after ten minutes outside instead of two. He hustled into the red brick building and visibly relaxed as the cool air inside embraced him. A quick jog up three levels and he turned left. Apartment 3C was one of four others on the floor. He grabbed for his keys, selecting the new one Codi had given him. As partners, they traded home keys for emergency purposes.

Joel reached for the lock and suddenly stopped. He could see the doorjamb had been breached. Automatically, he pulled his Glock and racked the slide. He pressed his ear to the door and listened. Voices. Dithering between bursting in and sneaking in, Joel followed his partner's training and kicked the door in. With his gun raised and pointed, he spied three men ransacking Codi's apartment. "FBI. Hands in the air," he called.

Instead of stopping in their tracks, the three men took the call as an invitation to war. They dove, simultaneously firing their pistols at the intruder. Joel hesitated, initially not wanting to shoot them, but bullets coming his way changed everything.

The door frame splintered, driving Joel back as he emptied his mag in their direction. The wall was no sanctuary as the bullets punched right through it. He dropped to the floor and reloaded. He grabbed his phone and hit 911, then dropped it on the floor next to him.

"Cops are on the way. You've got ten seconds to drop your guns and come out with your hands up, or we're going to make that room a kill box. I got three other agents with me. You hear me, ten seconds. Come out now!" Joel didn't feel as confident as his words sounded. Yes, the cops would come maybe in ten minutes, and, truth be told, these guys had him three to one. They had plenty of cover inside, and he had no chance of getting through the door unscathed.

"Five seconds!" he called as he waited on the floor, his gun shaking slightly in his hands.

"Hold your fire. We're coming out," a voice from inside called.

"Yeah, don't shoot!" another yelled.

Joel stood on shaky legs and moved back down the hallway. One by one the three men exited Codi's apartment with their hands in the air. As soon as they saw there was only one cop, they moved apart.

"On the ground now, or I'll drill you where you stand."

They froze, then two of them got to their knees, hands still in the air.

The skinny one with crazy eyes lowered his hands and made a move to approach Joel. "You lying mother fu—"

Joel shut him up with a shot from his gun that whizzed barely past his head. The gangster dropped to the floor and joined his cronies.

Fifteen minutes later the police arrived and took over.

Joel sat on the steps leading into the building, trying to calm his breathing. The fear he had barely subdued was pouring in as his adrenaline wore off. It had been more than he was willing to admit—a real brown-stained-pants moment.

An Uber pulled into the circus that was now forming in the street, and Codi ran from the car, past the yellow caution tape, and up to her partner. She slowed the last few steps and joined him on the stairs.

They sat wordlessly for a moment.

"I hear you shot up my apartment," she said.

"Yeah, a little," Joel replied.

"That's the last time I ask you to do me a favor."

Joel looked up, still trying to calm himself.

"It's alright. I was thinking about remodeling anyway," Codi added. She smiled at her partner, who looked up with a nervous grin.

"You would have been proud. I went at them Codi-style," he said.

"What, shoot first so you don't have to ask them any questions?" she said.

Joel nodded.

"Well, three-to-one, not the best odds. I see you dodged a few bullets."

"What?"

Codi pointed to a bullet hole in Joel's crotch.

He looked down and panicked. A quick unzip and a finger check that returned with no blood was too much for Joel, and he suddenly felt lightheaded.

Codi caught her partner as he turned as white as a ghost and fell over. She laid him on his back and just shook her head at the best partner she could ever ask for.

***

Matt watched as the *Sea Hunter* slapped back down against the white water. The sea was a boiling cauldron of froth and waves and the water had taken on a dark blue-brown color. There was a small craft advisory in place, and it was no picnic on the follow boat. The initial assignment was for the autonomous boat to reach a designated point in the water ten miles northwest and then change course and patrol southward for one hour. Finally, it was to return to the mouth of the river and navigate back to the dock in Portland. A fairly simple routine for the technology, but the weather changed everything. The computer was constantly adjusting course for the strong wind and current. It had reduced speed to six knots, which made the follow boat feel like a wine cork in a bubbling jacuzzi.

Soon everyone was turning green, and they were less than a third of the way through the test. Matt used his legs to act as shock absorbers as the boat plunged up and down with the undulations. Five minutes later, they had to abort. Both boats corrected course for home. Matt closed his eyes to avoid looking at the constant flow of projected stomach contents over the side of the boat from his colleagues. He moved upwind to avoid the smell, hanging onto the railing on the bow. With his eyes averted and his nose free from the odor, he only had to deal with the sounds of multiple repeated upchucks until there was nothing but bile.

His mind flashed back to Taco Bell. He was spending the weekend with his sister Cindy and her two young children while her husband was out of town. TJ was four and Lexi was three. They had made a run to the popular fast-food taco chain for an early dinner. Lexi was not feeling herself since lunch that day, and it had been an afternoon of whining that nearly sent Matt to the edge. TJ did his normal routine and ate two tacos before Matt could finish half of his. Lexi ate part of a taco and then complained that she was done. Matt decided, as an uncle, he needed to step up and help his sister out.

"Lexi, if you finish your taco, I'll take us all for ice cream," Matt said.

TJ immediately chimed in, forcing Lexi to eat more. Matt took small pieces of taco and pushed them into the resistant child's mouth. Eventually, the pressure of not getting ice cream won out, and Lexi finished her taco. That's when she stood up in the booth and moved toward her mother. Eye to eye and without warning, she projectile-vomited all over Cindy's face and mouth. Matt turned white as a ghost and yelled at TJ to help while he ran for the door and the safety of the car outside.

It had not been one of Matt's finest moments. As a scientist, he was supposed to be unaffected by variables. It was his job to calmly eliminate them and find an answer, but when it came to his sister covered in her child's vomit, the scientist departed, leaving a useless hulk with severe emetophobia. He shook the memory from his head. His sister might someday forgive him, but how would he ever be able to raise a child? Perhaps he'd bitten off too much by getting engaged.

The ship calmed as the mouth of the river came into view. Matt had fought hard not to succumb to the effects of the sea, but just before they cleared the point back to the safety of the river, it hit. Between the barf flashback and the unstable deck, he barely had time to get his head over the railing to launch his half-digested breakfast to the ocean creatures following the human chum-bucket.

It was another hour of seasick agony before docking. Twelve scientists and technicians all scrambled off the boat for the sanctity of land, each praising its stability.

Chapter Six

DALLAS, TEXAS – 9:29 A.M.

The Encyclical set the package he retrieved from the local mailbox store on his temporary workstation in the garage. Inside was a smartphone. Attached to the back of it was a black box equal in size. A piece of paper was taped to the box with a note.

"Turn on and once you are within twenty feet press the green button."

He powered up the phone, and after a few seconds, the screen lit up with a single large red button. "Okay. Looks simple enough. When does it turn green?" he wondered. There would be no way to test it, only a full-dress rehearsal that would take place tomorrow. He mounted the device to a holder on the handlebars of his motorcycle and powered it back down. The ten thousand dollars he had just splurged for the modified cell phone had better be worth it.

The Encyclical thought back to the last time he and Con Air had done a job together. The hacker built a keyboard that would explode when the Enter key was pressed. The job was not too difficult; the real trick was replacing the target's regular keyboard with the exploding one. The man's office was a fortress, and security was always on high alert. In the end, a five-thousand-dollar bribe to the cleaning woman made the exchange simple. The next morning, before most of the staff arrived, a small but deadly explosion took the hands and face of the corporation's leader.

The Encyclical hadn't always been an assassin. His childhood was incredibly average. Growing up as Stuart Nichols in the suburbs of Gary, just south of Chicago, Stuart was the middle child of a happy family of five. He made decent grades and had none of the special needs most young boys have. They lived in a stacked-stone two-story a couple of blocks from Lake Michigan. The family made time for vacations and church. His dad ran a local hardware store, and Mom worked part-time as a realtor.

The closest he had ever come to getting in trouble was with his ten-year-old friends Parker and Jaxson. The three pals, along with two other friends and a girl named Kylie, had taken two M-80s and a few BB guns onto school grounds one night. Kylie had black mascara smeared under her eyes like a football player. Parker wore an old leather helmet. Jaxson had a fully automatic BB gun, but it held only thirty BBs, and reloading was a drag. The plan was to stage an epic war against another group of friends.

Stuart and his gang wore blood-red t-shirts with a hand-painted dragon on the front. They had just finished making them and the paint was almost dry. The other boys wore gray with a black cobra painted on the front.

"Hey, dudes, nice uniforms," Conner, the leader of the other group said, with no small amount of sarcasm, as the two groups met up. They were under a streetlight across from the school.

"What about you guys—did you get those shirts at ThugLife.com?" Stuart chided.

"Funny guy." Conner stepped forward and addressed the group. "Okay, here are the rules. No shooting in the face or the balls."

"What about the ears?" asked a nerdy kid from his group.

"Ears are the face! Everything else is fair game." He looked around to make sure everyone got it. "Red Dragons, you have the north half of the school, and we'll take the south." Conner pulled out a video game cartridge and held it up for all to see. It was the latest *Call of Duty.* "Here is your prize. You want it, come and get it," he said.

"Black worms, here is your prize," Stuart said, as he lifted a *Tony Hawks Underground* game cartridge as well.

"It's Black Cobras, douchebag," Conner said.

"Oh, thought it was a worm."

"Just make sure the prize is in plain sight!"

"Yeah, yeah. Come on guys," Stuart called as he and his team turned and ran into the shadows of the school.

The two groups split, and each established its territory on opposite sides of the school. The war began. Stuart organized his team by building an offense, leaving only one man back to protect the prize.

The battle started off fairly normal, with both sides pinned down, each shooting at the other. Multiple hits were scored with a yelp or a scream, but none so bad that anyone gave up or surrendered. At one point, Parker was getting overrun, and Stuart had to double back to help. He lit both M-80s and chucked them at the enemy. The explosions scared the attackers back, but they also alerted a police cruiser in the area.

Conner took a BB right to the temple and screamed out in anger, "Hey watch the head shots, butt wipe!"

"It was a ricochet!"

"Here's your ricochet!"

Bullets followed bullets, the rules forgotten, and guns were aimed at any body part. A powerful flashlight beam suddenly swept across the fray.

"Gary Police. Everyone stop shooting and put your weapons on the ground. *Now!*"

Half the boys froze in fear and complied. The other half jack-rabbited away like cockroaches fleeing the light.

The police had been watching the war just long enough to realize it was a bunch of kids. Now came the part where they would scare the holy crap out of them. The first officer moved to corral the kids that complied with their demands. The second officer lifted his radio to his mouth but didn't press the button. He called out in a loud voice. "All units, be advised; we have runners with loaded weapons coming your way. Consider them armed and dangerous."

That had most of the other kids stop in their tracks and drop their BB guns with their hands in the air.

The officer smiled at his partner, who just shook his head at the devious ploy. Soon, all but one boy were herded up and captured. Their guns were piled up, and the two officers laid down the law in the harshest terms. Parents had to come to the school and pick up each warrior. The officers hoped that what waited at home was more of the same.

Stuart had been too scared to stop, even when he heard the bit about other police officers waiting to shoot him. The fear was so engulfing, he involuntarily peed his pants as he ran for his life. His heart was practically bursting from his chest, and he couldn't catch his breath. Finally, after five minutes, which seemed like an eternity, he hid behind a neighbor's trashcan. He lay there, too scared to move, whimpering at the terror that filled his soul. It wasn't until early morning that he was finally able to stand and walk home. His parents had been worried sick and had just finished calling the police before Stuart walked in the door. The whole thing had been a disaster for all parties.

The experience had focused Stuart on a new path. One where he would build and find control over himself and his environment, never to experience that feeling of fear again. He enrolled in a dojo the next week and soon found himself there four days a week. He excelled and added more disciplines to his training until he was proficient in Jeet Kune Do, Taekwondo, and Jiujitsu.

Stuart kept mostly to himself from there on out, never feeling the need to prove his skills against anyone. Soon, the word on the street was *don't mess with the weirdo*. It wasn't the best reputation for high school, but it got him through. And once out, he was never going back.

***

"Hey, Sanders!"

Codi leaned back and rolled her chair out into the hallway. The office was unusually busy today as all the agents were just getting started on their new assignments. Codi was finally feeling like herself and was glad to have the sling off her arm. Supervisory Special Agent Gordon Reyas was standing a good twenty feet away, looking her way.

"There's someone here to see you. In the fishbowl," he added.

Codi raised a hand in acknowledgment and slowly stood, rolling her chair back into her cubicle. She massaged her arm as she padded down the hallway.

She pushed her way into the fishbowl and was greeted by a familiar face.

"Detective Gasser . . . Good to see you again," Codi said, without an ounce of truth.

The fortyish blond detective looked like he had swallowed mouthwash as he fumbled for his voice. "I wanted to come by and apologize for the way I treated you in the hospital. I get a lot of—"

Codi interrupted his attempt at softening his apology. "Let's just stop right there and move on. Apology accepted. And by the way . . . Hi, I'm Codi."

"Chris. When your prints came back FBI, you can imagine my surprise."

Codi stared without emotion at the man.

He adjusted his tie like it might suddenly be too tight. "The thing is, I think you stumbled onto a new gang we've been trying to identify. Any chance you would care to give me a description of the men you ran into?"

"Sure. I mean, we're all on the same team, right?" Codi deadpanned.

The detective pulled up his notes on the case. "So, in the hospital, you told me you were being chased by three low-level criminals in a beat-up brown van. They were young, in their early twenties; two were Hispanic, and the driver of the van was white with a lightning bolt tattoo on the side of his face. Why do you think they were chasing you?"

"I'm not one-hundred percent sure. My memory of the weekend has not returned." Codi went on to tell him what she remembered and the things she and Joel had learned.

"They definitely came back looking for me. I'm not sure why. I mean they got what they wanted. They could have killed me then and there if they'd wanted to," Codi finished.

"Well, if it's the gang I think it is, they make a habit of robbing the more well-to-do. And then, they use the information they glean from their ill-gotten goods, selling personal identification and credit cards. Finally, they burglarize the victims' homes and offices using their own keys."

Codi said nothing in reply.

"I'd like to send you some mug shots. Maybe it will jog your memory."

Codi reached into her pocket and pulled out a slightly bent card with her information on it. She passed it to the detective. "You can email additional questions. But I can do you one better. The three suspects who attacked me are cooling their heels in a federal holding cell."

Detective Gasser's mouth moved, but no words came out, like a fish recently pulled from the water. He paused for another beat, trying to organize his thoughts. He looked straight at Codi. "That's good. I'd like to talk with them. Maybe they will shed some light on the operation and tell us who's in charge."

"Good luck with that. As soon as the AIC is done with them, I'd like to turn them over to you."

"Good, good. . . . You say you were a victim of theirs, but why they came back for you is a mystery to me. Murder is not on their resume." Detective Gasser scratched the stubble on his head. "Was your badge in your purse?"

Codi nodded.

The detective snapped his fingers. "I'm betting they found the badge and got spooked. Maybe they came back to finish the job. The last thing they'd want is a hot fed . . . pardon me." The detective's face flushed at the *faux pas.* "A fed who can recognize them hot on their trail."

"Okay, I can see that," Codi said. "So what now?"

"Now they got a lot more than a fed on their trail. These pukes poked the friggin' beehive."

***

The Scientist set down the file folder Atlantis had shipped to him, analog-style via FedEx. It had a wealth of information without containing anything incriminating, in case it fell into unwanted hands. As far as anyone from the outside could tell, he was a reporter doing a story. He spread the contents out on the aged zinc tabletop in the center of the room, the white pages contrasting nicely with the pewter gray surface. The subleased apartment was small but functional, with good overhead lighting and bamboo flooring. Two large computer screens were mounted side-by-side on a standing-height desk on one wall, and a large shelving unit sat on the opposite. It was filled with collectibles from someone's travels.

The Scientist took his time and went through everything carefully, applying no prejudice to the information. It would tell its own story. There were several photos, mostly taken from social media, a bank statement, and a copy of a business contract. He pulled up a chair and read through the pages. Atlantis had been thorough. She supplied enough information for him to get a good picture of the Hemmings' daily life.

He flipped through the contract. It was between two partners in a business called GutBuster. The ownership division was spelled out clearly. Should one of them die, Mrs. Hemmings would get her husband's ownership. They had no children, family, or other heirs it would pass to after that. If both Mr. and Mrs. Hemmings died, the ownership would revert to the surviving partner, a man named Dicky Castro. The Scientist sat back in his chair. He could see the picture clearly. Even though he had no idea who had hired them, it was most likely the wife or the business partner who ordered the hit. He flipped over the last page of the pile. An equation was handwritten in the middle of the page, which cleared everything up.

HW-H=W†

HW meant there was a husband and wife living in the home. The *minus H* meant he was to remove the husband, and the *equals wife down-pointing symbol* stood for discredit or frame the wife if possible.

He now knew who was behind the contract—Dicky Castro.

The Scientist moved to the living room and started the electric fireplace. He took the time to make sure every scrap of paper and all photographs were thoroughly burned. With his assignment well-defined, it was time to move to the next stage.

The walk from his parked car to Atlantic Way was a short ten minutes. The Scientist wore tourist chic and flaunted every bit of it. Ocean waves could be heard over the traffic noise. There was a funky humid smell in the air, as rotted vegetation and sea air mixed.

The Hemmings' estate was near the end of Atlantic Way, along the ocean-side strip of desirable North Beach in Miami. The Scientist walked a forty-pound speckled mutt with floppy ears and a curious expression. They headed down the narrow street dividing beachfront from beach access. He had adopted the pooch from a local shelter and chosen a name to match this operation—Castor.

Mr. Hemmings had succeeded immensely as one of the first to market with a line of nutraceuticals designed to eliminate gut problems. The digestion market had grown exponentially as American diets fell to the greasier and less-healthy side of the food pyramid. He and his partner, Dick Castro, whom everyone called Dicky, had taken the two best-selling probiotic products on the market to a local lab to reverse-engineer and combine them. They rebranded the product GutBuster and made some extreme claims. They also discounted the first order by half of what their competitors charged. Eventually, the competitors filed complaints about the GutBuster claims to the FDA, which forced GutBuster to drop a few of them, but not before they had captured a huge part of the market.

The two partners had grown the company into a three-hundred-million-dollar business, expected to double in the next five years. The problem was the partnership had soured. Dicky tried to buy out the Hemmings several times but was met with a hard no. Mr. Hemmings had become increasingly irritable and blocked Dicky's attempts to grow the company in the direction he believed it needed to go. It finally got to where the two no longer spoke to each other.

Dicky was at an impasse.

The Hemmings' home was second-to-the-last on the street. The Scientist let his trained eyes take it all in. It was a modern, white stucco affair set back from the street with a gated entrance. There was plenty of "Look at me. I have money" in the design, and more space than any two people could ever use.

The Scientist casually placed two micro-cameras on a neighbor's fence, pointing back at the property. He used a specialized program on his smartphone to execute a brute force attack on the Hemmings' network. The relatively easy password was cracked in seconds, giving him access to their Wi-Fi and connected cameras.

He then uploaded a hidden remote access application that would give him access to the network from anywhere. As he continued, he noted the home's security cameras and their placement. The last home on the street was undergoing a complete teardown and remodel. It had a large green fence surrounding the property with the construction company's sign attached to it.

Atlantic Way empties at 79th Street, which becomes a walking path to the sand. A trail took him to the backside of the home, where he could see the grass courtyard and pool that filled the Hemmings' backyard. The other side of the trail revealed a white sandy beach and the ocean beyond.

Once back in his eighth-floor apartment on the other side of the peninsula overlooking Biscayne Bay, he connected to the Hemmings' network using a VPN and bounced his IP from London to Tahiti. Once connected, he piggybacked the camera feeds to his laptop and turned on the recorder. Now, all he had to do was wait. He poured some food into a bowl for Castor and scratched behind his ears. Within a few days, he would have a good idea of the comings and goings of the residents.

The Scientist changed his clothes to something less in-your-face, cargo shorts and a green t-shirt, and then added a floppy hat to the mix, before grabbing a preloaded backpack and saying goodbye to his four-legged partner.

The Kampong is a botanical garden once part of the estate of Dr. David Fairchild, a famed botanical explorer. It is in Coconut Grove next to the bay. At 3:00 p.m. mid-week, the foot traffic was light. The Scientist had done his research and followed a pre-set journey along several winding paths until he came to a large plant with deeply lobed leaves, each roughly a foot in diameter. He sat on the low stone wall meant as a decorative divider for the planter. There were several reddish, spiky seed pods hanging from the bush, including a few that had fallen to the ground and spilled their contents.

The Scientist waited until there was no one in the area before harvesting several pods and collecting the seeds that had fallen to the ground. He placed the contents in his backpack and glanced one last time at the placard in front of the bush. *Ricinus communis* or castor oil plant. The seeds or beans from the plant could be pressed to make oil, long used in medicinal treatments, but the shell of the seed contained one of the deadliest naturally occurring poisons known to man—ricin. A dose of purified ricin the size of a few grains of salt could kill an adult human. Now all he had to do was process the seed shells. He began a languorous return to his car, finally able to enjoy the spectacular array of tropical and exotic plants throughout the lush grounds. The thought of what was to come kept a whistle on his lips and a smile on his face.

***

Director Lyon stood and shook Brian's hand as he entered the office. It was a large room somewhere in the neighborhood of three times the size of Brian's. It had a cream leather sofa and several comfy blue high-back chairs. The window looked out onto DC, and the desk was big enough to land a small plane. Brian's boss was a politically connected power dealer in Washington. He had enemies and allies and knew how to use both to his advantage.

Brian took a seat and looked around, amazed. He had met his boss several times in the past, but this was the first time here on the top floor. FBI Headquarters, known as the J. Edgar Hoover Building, was at 935 Pennsylvania Avenue, its deteriorated façade a blight on the agency's reputation. The powers-that-be had tried and failed several times to rebuild or relocate their headquarters, but politics and budgets had stalled them. It would only be a matter of time before the iconic building would be demolished. Director Lyon sat down across from Brian on the couch to show he was a man of the people.

"It's good to see you again," Director Lyon opened with. "How's the family?"

"They are doing exactly what a father hopes for his family, sir, growing up without a care in the world."

Director Lyon put his head down for a second, unable to fully comprehend Brian's response. His family life was a disaster, and Brian knew better than to ask about them.

"You might recall me mentioning an opportunity the last time we met."

"Yes, sir," Brian said. He indeed remembered. In fact, he remembered the exact words his boss had said. *I have an opening coming up for an assistant director, and a man of your talents who can follow orders would fit the bill nicely.*

"Well, at the time, the case you oversaw got the eyes of the kind of people that matter. I mean, you and your team literally saved the planet. That sort of thing just doesn't go unnoticed."

Brian suddenly felt squeamish with all of his boss's praise. "Thank you, sir."

"I'm now in a position to make good on one of my threats. I'd like for you to consider taking Stu Halaby's job. He's retiring, and we think you'd be perfect for it."

Brian looked confused. He didn't know Stu.

Director Lyon clarified. "Deputy Assistant Director of our ERTU, over at Quantico."

Brian was left speechless. Yes, the director had promised him a promotion if he could tidy up his last high-profile case. A case that had gone totally crazy with a self-ordained billionaire philanthropist trying to save the planet by infecting and killing half its population. Codi and Joel, along with a few others, tied a big fat bow on the whole case at the last possible second. Even Brian was surprised at the outcome.

"So finish up the month and then give yourself a week off. I want you primed and ready by the ninth. And don't give me an answer till the end of the week. Talk it over with your 'not a care in the world' family and let me know. I'm sure you'll make the right decision."

"Yes, I will, and thank you, sir. I won't let you down," Brian replied.

"Of course not, son. I would never allow that to happen."

Brian stood on suddenly uneasy feet and shook Director Lyon's hand. His elation had just been tempered, probably for the best. He needed to get home and sell this to the missus.

***

The double-check was automatic, like riding a bicycle. Codi checked the three-ring system and verified her RLS was attached properly. There was no wear on the loop or cable, both pull handles were connected properly, and the leg and chest straps were good to go. The parachute had an automatic activation device (AAD) computer, capable of releasing the chute at a preset altitude. Codi turned it on and checked the batteries, and then, for some unknown reason, turned it back off. She placed the chute on her back and strapped it to her body. It was a familiar feeling. Skydiving always made her feel alive.

The twenty-six-week SEAL qualification training program was almost over, and Codi had proven herself where others had failed. Being the only female in her group didn't help since the entire program was clearly modeled after a boy's club.

Other females had paved the way, and she was determined to carry on their sacrifice and effort. Once she was chosen for BUD/S training, Codi felt like she could do anything, even if most of the other candidates wouldn't give her the time of day.

This was competition personified and nothing punctuated that more than the bell of shame, a brass bell that hung on a post where morning musters took place. When you couldn't take any more or go on, all you had to do was ring the bell. The instructors reminded the candidates of that fact every day.

She had watched as several other soldiers succumbed to the rigors of the training, each eventually just wanting to make it stop. With the pull of a string attached to the clapper, they were done.

Night after night, in freezing cold conditions, without sleep, there wasn't one applicant who hadn't considered ringing that bell, but the walk of shame leading to it left a permanent stain. For Codi, failure was never an option. No matter what, SEALS don't fail, and nothing could sway her in that direction.

She had something to prove to herself and to her father, who had been taken when she was just thirteen. She used him as a spirit guide in her life and, more than once, had pushed herself beyond her limits to please the figment of his memory.

Growing up north of San Diego, most people would think that Codi had it easy. But after her dad passed, she became a latchkey kid with a mother who would dip into depression and disappear for days at a time. They moved every year or so, her mother in search of a new job and greener pastures.

In time, Codi found that the only person she could really count on was herself. She had used that as a motivator to find her independence and stand on her own. In high school, she found that few people were as fast as she was in the water, and she capitalized on that ability to pay for college.

"Everyone up that tree—now!"

They were words spoken by her instructor that she would never forget.

There was a large tree twenty feet away. The lowest branch was at least fifteen feet up. The group didn't hesitate. This would require serious teamwork.

Codi and her squad set up a human platform that the other trainees used to scale the tree. The squad leader pushed off and got his hands around the branch, but it was wet. Just as he started to pull himself up, he slipped fifteen feet down, bounced off Codi, and hit the ground flat on his back. Everyone stopped, not sure what to do. He struggled to get to his knees and take a breath. The instructor walked around the tree once and said, "Now, you've got four minutes."

The squad leader sucked it up and tried again. This time, he got a full grasp around the branch and hauled himself up. Others followed until it was Codi's turn. She pushed off with everything she had and got a firm grip on the squad leader's reaching hand. She dug her feet into the trunk and held tight to his hand while he pulled her up. She slipped a bit on the wet trunk but recovered and continued to climb. Just as she was within reach of the branch, she felt his grip loosen. She looked up into his eyes and could tell something was off. "No, no, don't you dare!" she screamed at him.

She tried to reach for the branch and caught just a finger on it, but it was too late. The rain and the *male-only* military mindset conspired together, and Codi fell. She tried desperately to tuck and roll when she hit, but the cracking sound and the shooting pain in her ankle told her it was futile. She looked down to see the distorted shape of her ankle. It was broken—and so was everything that mattered to her at that point in her life.

The bell of shame rang loudly, and Codi would not let them see her cry.

After failing her BUD/S training, Codi found herself adrift. She had taken a few odd jobs and made close friends with a bottle and a death wish. Pushing her limits more and more each time was the only way she could feel anything. Her normal senses long ago dulled and were set aside as her life spun out of control.

She had put all her eggs in one basket, and when that basket was smashed, so was she.

Codi strapped on her parachute. The other skydivers on the plane seemed distant, as they suited up and made ready to jump. The Twin Otter aircraft leveled at fifteen thousand feet, and the large side jump door was rolled up. Within seconds, skydivers took to the air, some in groups, one in tandem, and Codi by herself. She pushed herself out the door and let gravity and the plane's momentum take her.

The droning of the two turboprop engines faded as she plummeted in a controlled freefall toward the earth. She quickly reached terminal velocity at 120 mph and let her body relax in the moment. Ducking her head and pointing her body toward the earth with her arms to her sides, she increased her speed to nearly 150 mph. It was an action known as speed skydiving. It was a rush with nothing but the wind in your face and a weightless high that only true sky junkies crave. A brief smile returned to Codi's face for the first time in two weeks. She closed her eyes and just let everything else fade away. No more dead father. No estranged relationship with her mother, and no failure at BUD/S. It was glorious.

Codi wished it would never end. That's when she realized it could. All she had to do was stay just like this, and it would all be over. Go out in a state of euphoria and never have to deal with life again. She thought of the ones left behind. Other than a few college friends, there was no one. Her mind-numbing, soul-crushing life could be fixed with the easiest of tasks—do nothing. She let the dark contemplations float through her mind and embraced them. A sudden beeping interrupted her enraptured thoughts. The altimeter she wore on her wrist was alerting her that she had just passed five thousand feet. It was time to pull her chute. She ignored it and returned to the fleeting bliss. She forced her eyes open and decided she wanted to see it coming. Her alarm changed tones, indicating she was now below two thousand feet. It was the last chance to pull her chute and self-arrest her plummet.

Codi's smile grew full across her face. All her anger and frustration melted away as she ignored the final warning. It was strange how far away the ground looked, and then all at once, it came flying up with no time to react. Codi moved her arms around her torso in a final embrace as terra firma seemed to jump up and grab her. And then, nothing.

Chapter Seven

MIAMI, FLORIDA – 12:43 P.M.

The Scientist placed a mask and goggles on his head. He poured some of the brown variegated castor beans into a small pot of water on the stove. On low heat, he let them heat up and absorb some of the water. After twenty minutes, he pulled the pot from the stove and strained the contents. Wearing gloves, he skinned the beans and tossed the innards into a trash bag. The skins were then mashed and pounded to a pulp and spread on parchment paper. He placed it in the oven on the lowest setting.

Once dry, the pulp was put into a mortar and ground into an off-white powder. That was poured into a glass flask and mixed with acetone. The new formula was then precipitated through a paper filter, leaving a pure white paste behind. Once dried, the paste was powdered and placed in a Ziploc baggie. The Scientist held it up to the light, about two tablespoons worth. The white powder was ready.

His computer gave a brief alert.

Friday night was as good as any in his mind. He watched the image from the surveillance camera as the red Tesla X pulled away from the Hemmings' home on his laptop screen. The Scientist quickly dressed in all black and drove his rental to within three blocks of the residence. He made his way through the shadows up to the back of the house on the small walking trail that separated the homes from the sand. Stepping to the last home, which was under construction, he quickly jumped the fence.

The backyard was dirt with piles of lumber and equipment. The structure was partially rebuilt with tar paper on half the outer walls. He climbed up to the second floor and pulled a rope from his backpack. Once alongside the Hemmings' home on the neighboring lot, he tied it to a beam, and then swung out and over the fence, landing in the side yard next to the kitchen slider.

He knelt and quickly picked the lock. Taking a calming breath, he pulled a rare earth magnet from his pocket and placed it next to the alarm sensor at the top of the door. He slid the slider open about two feet. While still holding the magnet in place, he used a small jumper cable to bridge the contacts on the inside alarm sensor. Once that was done, he released the magnet and entered the home.

Moonlight illuminated the all-white kitchen in a blue cast. The Scientist went to work, placing three micro-cameras in the area, making sure they would not be discovered. A quick final check and he reversed his actions and left the home, relocking the slider. He used the rope to climb the wall between the Hemmings' property and the construction site next door. Once back over the fence and in the darkness of the beach, he removed his outer clothes revealing board shorts and a tank top. Just another tourist walking the beach in the moonlight.

***

Brian opened the front door to chaos. A three-year-old is a very challenging being. Add a seven-year-old to run interference and then top it all off with no nap, and you have the perfect storm. There were toys strewn across the house and small bowls of half-eaten snacks left as if they were forgotten mid-bite, which they were. Seven-year-old Tristian was trying to help, but his brand of justice was unacceptable to his younger sibling. There was crying, raised voices, and desperation. Brian had seen this many times before and knew it would not last. A three-year-old's attention span was ever-changing, and by the time he put his things down, a squeaky voice with tear-strewn eyes and wild hair ran toward him calling out, "Dadda, Dadda."

They were the best words he had heard all day.

"Istin *(unintelligible) (unintelligible)* red choice."

She couldn't quite pronounce Tristian's name, but the fact she was tattling about something he had done was a whole new thing.

He tried not to ignore her concern and consoled her with a hug.

"It's been one of those days," Leila said as Tristian ran past her to tell his father his version of the traumatic event and, of course, get his hug.

"Honey, you have thirty minutes. Babysitter is on the way, and we're going out to dinner."

As if on cue, Tristian asked, "Can we order pizza?"

"You're a godsend," Leila said to Brian as she kissed him and ran for the bedroom.

"Can we, can we?" Tristian pleaded with his mother.

Brian watched as his wife headed down the hallway and answered without looking back. "Yes, of course we can order pizza."

Leila was the best thing that had ever happened to him.

"Pizza!" Tristian screamed from the depths of his soul, and then he and his little sister started doing the pizza dance. Brian turned and joined in.

"Pizza, pizza, pizza. Pizza, pizza, pizza."

The Dabney was located in the trendy area of Blagden Alley. It had a large center wood-burning hearth with bare wood tables and historic-looking, exposed brick walls. The service was refined and relaxed, just what the couple needed to unwind. Leila ordered the black bass and Brian the grilled lamb. He waited through most of the main course, making small talk and mostly doing a lot of listening before bringing up his news about his promotion at work. Leila was overjoyed for her husband and the prospect of his improved paycheck, but within a few minutes the conversation turned to, "What about Joel and Codi and your other agents?"

"I have been giving this a lot of thought . . . and I have to do what's right for us and our family. They would understand and support that. The FBI is not so big. We will cross paths again."

Leila slowly nodded. "Isn't there some way you can take them with you?"

"Sure, but the ERTU would kill Codi. Too many walls lining the box there. She is more of an—"

Leila interrupted, "I know, 'an outside the FBI box' kinda girl."

"Exactly."

***

After graduating from high school, Stuart Nichols enlisted in the Navy. His first year was filled with mediocrity, and he put in just enough effort to go unnoticed. But everything seemed to change when he was stationed in Subic Bay.

In 1979, tensions between the US and Philippine governments slowly increased until the Navy lost Subic Bay as a result of a financial disagreement between the two governments. Thereafter, the US became a guest and not the landlord of the naval base of operations in the Philippines.

By 1991, the US had completely pulled out, leaving the infrastructure to the host nation. The once-largest military presence in the Pacific—gone. Opinion swayed back and forth, and by 2012, the US was allowed to utilize the base again as a staging area, with permission, of course. In 2016, the Pacific saw the largest mobilization of allied naval forces since the war, and the base was active again. Seaman Stuart Nichols was stationed and assigned to base security during the exercise and war games. It was a Wednesday night just after 1:00 a.m. when he was relieved of duty. Nichols hurried to his bunk for a change of clothes and a condom from his sea bag.

His friends had all left much earlier, heading into town for a bit of fun and hopefully a good woman to spend their pay on. Nichols pocketed his pass that allowed him off-base for the night and ran to the gate. A fanciful jeepney was flagged down. He hopped in the back and hung on for the ride down Rizal Highway into the town of Olongapo.

It took him a few tries to find the Voodoo Bar on Bugallon Road where they had planned to meet up. It was an island-themed bar with thatched roofing, bamboo, and rattan accents. They served traditional Filipino food, and the entertainment was geared toward American servicemen. The girls were young and well-trained. Nichols entered the main room, and the first thing he noticed was the amount of smoke. Smoking had been all but eliminated from most indoor establishments in the US. The next thing he noticed was the smell. There was no escaping that bar room smell, a mix of alcohol, cigarettes, and body odor, with just an extra hint wafting in from the overused bathrooms. It elicited a comfortable feeling that immediately took the edge off.

He had some catching up to do and powered down two Red Bull and vodkas before he sat with his friends to watch the entertainment. It took all of ten minutes before he had fully assimilated into the party, bragging and laughing with his pals. Before long, the girls came around, selling their wares. A little negotiation and a price was reached. The floor above the Voodoo Bar was a massage shop that rented rooms by the hour, and soon, most of the lads had made their way upstairs.

By the time Nichols had made it into one of the rooms, he was feeling the effects of the catch-up drinking. The girl told him her name was Amihan, a name he forgot almost as quickly as he heard it. She wore short shorts and a white bikini top holding up nice-sized breasts and revealing a firm belly. Her right hip was decorated with a full-color lotus blossom tattoo.

"You handsome man. I like," she said, with a practiced cadence.

Nichols had trouble getting his clothes off, and it took very little effort for his newfound date to help him out of his pants along with his wallet, watch, and phone. It was just her bad luck that his phone beeped with an alert text just as she was pocketing it in her very short shorts. Nichols sobered up immediately, and the young girl panicked when caught. She ran from the room screaming "rape" at the top of her lungs. Nichols managed to get his pants back on and gave chase. The steep wooden steps leading down from the massage parlor were nearly the death of him as his feet moved too slowly for the sudden gravitational pull on his body. A last-minute self-arrest with his hands on the railing saved him from disaster.

Once in the street, he turned left and followed the girl down an alley at high speed. It took about twenty steps before he realized his mistake. Four men armed with Bolo knives stepped out from the shadows as the girl ran to a fifth man just beyond. Nichols stopped, sucking in air and trying to calm and center himself. The area was mostly lit by a large blue advertisement sign above the rooftops that reflected off the wet pavement. The men now surrounded him.

"Yankee boy. What are you doing coming into my web?" the fifth man said, with gold teeth and about a zillion matching chains around his neck. His beer belly pushed against a stained white collared shirt, buttoned halfway. He stood and allowed his girl to hide behind him. The four goons with knives held their ground, waiting for their boss to give them the go-ahead.

"Is this your play? Robbing your customers?" Nichols said.

"Only the ones too drunk to know. I'm afraid Amihan has made a mistake. She will pay for this. That is a truth." He looked at the frightened girl behind him with fire in his eyes. "But you have made the real mistake by chasing her here." He looked around, surveying the back alley—his kingdom. "And now you have seen my face. That is a problem."

"Your problem, not mine," Nichols replied. "Return my things, and I will go, like this never happened." He wiped his hands together and then held them up empty. "I would hate for you and your men to lose face, money, and time over me."

The boss smiled like he had heard something funny. "You no understand . . . I am ghost. I will mess you up and be gone without a trace like the Flash."

"A superhero you ain't. So what's it gonna be, my money or your blood?"

The boss crossed his arms and looked at his fellow thugs. "Enough talk, Dalhin, *mo siya mga lalki*," he said in a calm voice, before turning and sitting back down to watch.

The thugs closed on the seaman. Their long almost sword-like knives, moving and circling as they did.

Nichols knew he couldn't take all four armed men at once. He needed to isolate them and give himself a chance to reduce the odds. He also needed to be a bit more sober. He took two deep breaths and let the added oxygen perk him up. The length of their weapons required him to fight the gangsters from a longer range. Fighting in close quarters made swinging the blade as dangerous as a gun.

At five-foot-eleven, he was taller than everyone in the alleyway. It took him about one second to identify the leader of the four men. Before he could make a move, Nichols lunged forward and used a center-line kick to the attacker's chest to knock the wind out of him, sending him to the ground hard, his blade skittering away. Before Nichols could fully recover, a second man swung a blade in his direction. He ducked and rolled away, ending up behind one of the other men, who turned and stabbed at Nichols with an overreaching lunge. Nichols took control of the Bolo and let it slip under his arm. He then twisted his body back around, snapping the man's arm and relieving him of his weapon. In less than five seconds, it was two versus one, and everyone was armed. The soundtrack to the fight was moaning coming from the two downed men.

The remaining two were suddenly more cautious. They teamed up and worked together to gain an advantage. There would be no overconfidence this time. Nichols quickly repositioned himself and with exact efficiency, thrust his foot against the side of the head of the broken arm man to finish him off. Then he used the butt of his newfound blade to send the first man who he had kicked into unconsciousness. The fighting soundtrack stopped, and the only noise now was the white noise of the city.

Two blades in unison spun and swiped at Nichols. He parried them away amid sparks that flew off the steel. The action was repeated several times. These guys were skilled with their blades, and Nichols kept his distance, using his own knife to stop their attacks. More sparks flew, and the clanging of steel on steel echoed through the alleyway. It was risky, but he would need to get in closer. Most fighters with longer blades were not adept at fighting in close. It would give him an advantage if he could keep from getting stabbed.

He waited until the two thugs attacked and swung his blade late, letting the range between them close. He dropped low and swept around, letting both blades fly just past his head, keeping the edge of his blade positioned up in a roof block to fend off their steel. As they swung through, he came back up, moving closer to his attackers. He used his kali training to sweep the knife down across the first attacker's fighting arm, continuing the blade's movement down and then up in a crescent-shaped swing that had the business-end slicing the second man's knife arm. The first move cut deeply into the first man's forearm, rendering it all but useless. The upward slice cut through the second man's wrist and tendons. Both blades dropped to the wet pavement as the men grabbed their damaged arms and howled. Nichols dropped once more and did a leg sweep, dropping both men to the ground in a two-for-one. He finished them off with kicks to their heads.

Nichols stepped back, making sure all four men were down for the count and would not be re-engaging him. As he turned to the boss, movement caught his eye. The man had pulled his own Bolo knife and was lunging at his torso. Nichols could hardly react to the unexpected assault in time, and a quick feint saved him from a mortal wound but not from a nice slice across his chest and arm. The boss turned and countered for another attack. Nichols went into autopilot and parried the man's blade before plunging his own into the man's thorax.

He released his blade and watched as the boss slumped to the ground with a gurgling that ended in a slow wheeze.

Amihan was screaming hysterically and yelling in Tagalog. Nichols took her in his arms and held her till she calmed. He then released her and held out his hand. She returned his belongings, and he gave her a simple gesture to get lost. She was gone into the night before he could plan his next move, but one thing was for sure: the military was far too boring for him. He had killed his first man, and he liked it.

Nichols thought back to his experience in the Navy. After the incident in the Philippines, he followed Navy protocol and alerted the OIC (officer in charge) and the local authorities. He was immediately arrested and detained while the two sides had a pissing contest over who was in charge. The Navy assigned an NCIS officer to sort it all out from their side, and the local authorities seemed happy to stonewall the investigation at every turn. The Navy had been torn. Seaman Stuart Nichols had stopped a crime, but he had killed and maimed foreign nationals. It was destined to be a political hot potato, and as soon as the press got wind of it, they spun it out of control. It forced the Navy's hand. Nichols gave them the solution—just discharge me.

Thirty days later Seaman Stuart Nichols was citizen Stuart Nichols.

He followed a path that led him down the dark web in search of work. At first, he was more lucky than skilled, doing an occasional odd job for an outfit that wanted total deniability. Jobs were slow to come by, and Nichols soon found himself living out of his car, just another veteran struggling to fit in and get by.

Sometimes, however, luck can go your way. A chance meeting with a one-time client led to an introduction with a man named Chung-Woo. He saw Stuart's potential right away and introduced him to the beautiful woman named Atlantis. She liked his brashness and determination. That he was quite handsome didn't hurt either. Her plan was to marry his current traits with cunning and skill, making him a truly deadly weapon, one that she controlled and used for both their gains.

She paid for advanced training and tactics classes in some of the worst places on the planet and sat back and watched as he refined himself in the forge of the underworld. If he lived to see the other side, he would be astonishing.

Nichols took on the challenge much as he did his martial arts training. Soon, he was at the top of every test and challenge. After three intense years, The Handler called him home. He was ready, and her first step was to rename him. She chose The Encyclical. He would become a brash assassin who would leave a message with every kill.

***

With a sudden jolt from her pillow, Codi was fully awake. She was drenched in sweat and breathing heavily. The skydiving dream was a recurring one, but she hadn't had it in a couple of years. She sat back against her propped pillow, reminding herself that it was just a dream. In real life, she *did* pull her chute seconds before it was too late, but all those feelings and desires had been a part of her psyche. After calming down, she reminded herself of how far she had come. From her humble beginnings as an agent for the GSA, General Services Administration, to a now lauded FBI special agent.

In truth, she had surpassed her own expectations and done more for her country than most. Her fire and drive were back, and the darkness and hopelessness were now on a back burner, set to a low simmer. She cracked her lips in a near smile at the visual. That's when it all came back to her. In the quiet reflection of the moment, the memory of her one of her worst weekends returned.

Codi's BFF, Katelyn Green, worked in DC for Senator Hightower from the great state of Wyoming. Katelyn was outgoing and had been the genesis of several regrets over the years for Codi. The two women met in a Poly Sci class at the University of California San Diego and had been best friends ever since. Katelyn's curvy figure and carefree attitude drew boys like a magnet to steel, but Codi's sexy, athletic build and genuine charm kept them around. They had set a recurring date at one of their favorite places, The Black Cat on Fourteenth NW. Matt was in Portland doing some consulting, so it was a girl's night out. Katelyn supported her relationship with Matt wholeheartedly, but only as long as she could still have occasional access to Codi. Anything else was a non-starter for her.

The evening had taken a turn when the two girls met up at The Black Cat and read the sign posted in front: "Closed for a private party. Sorry for the inconvenience."

"Probably some political fat cats spending their ill-gotten gains," Katelyn said.

"I'm surprised you weren't invited."

"Who says I wasn't? But tonight is—"

"Girls night!" the two sang in unison.

Katelyn drove them to a dive bar her co-worker had been talking about, appropriately named DIVE. It was a small club covered with used brick and natural oak, with just enough of a stage for a small local band. The place was just starting to pop when the two beauties entered and established their territory at one end of the large square bar dominating the center of the room. They snacked on bar food while Codi tried a few local beers and Katelyn sipped white wine. It was all going great with a bit of dancing and a lot of catching up.

Katelyn had been dating a guy in the Pentagon for almost eight months, which was a record for her. He worked as an operations analyst and was, according to Katelyn, a really good guy. She had moved into a new apartment near DuPont Circle and was getting a raise. Codi, who couldn't talk about work, was mostly required to listen as Katelyn went on and on about the crazy politics in DC and her office. Apparently, there was a real misogynist in her office, making things a challenge. Codi offered to shoot him, and Katelyn considered taking her up on it.

"I was just kidding, Katelyn."

"What? Oh, I know, but the thought is so appealing."

They shared a laugh.

"Hello, beauties. What would it take for you to let me buy you both a round of drinks?" A man in a slick business suit with a gold Rolex stood next to Katelyn, leaning over.

"Well, it's girl's night out for us," said Katelyn, "so you would have to lop off the oppressor in your pants and grow a vagina."

Codi added, "And wear less cologne."

The man who had stepped up so brazenly to the women paused, not sure if they were for real or not. He had a sudden uneasy look that slowly transformed into a smile.

"Good one, ladies. Here's to girl's night out!" He lifted his glass of bourbon and waited for them to follow suit.

"Girls night out," they replied and knocked glasses before following him in a drink.

"Barkeep," he called out. "The next one is on me." He pointed to Codi and Katelyn. He then leaned in a bit more. "Enjoy your girl's night out, ladies. I'm off to the clinic to get a sex change." He then gave a mock salute and moved down the bar to try his luck elsewhere.

Codi and Katelyn burst out laughing.

"Who says *barkeep*?" Katelyn asked.

"That guy."

"He did buy us a round, though."

"Yes, he did."

"Maybe I should dance with him," Katelyn said.

"Don't you dare," Codi ordered, followed by more giggling by the two now slightly drunk friends.

The night went on and the pickup lines got worse. Katelyn and Codi tried hard not to look like the best cut in the meat market as they used the time to reconnect.

Eventually, it was time to leave, and they each ordered an Uber for the trip home. Before Codi stood to leave, she spied the man from earlier eyeballing her from the entrance.

"Oh, my ride's here," Katelyn said as she gave Codi a hug and they said their goodbyes.

As her friend left the bar, the man moved to a standing position between Codi and the door. With Katelyn gone, "girl's night" was officially over. His glazed-over stare locked on her as he undressed her with his eyes.

Codi had no desire to embarrass the drunk, so she turned to the bartender and asked in a hushed voice. "Is there a back way out of here?" She used her eyes to point out the problem.

The bartender, a man with large sideburns, took one look and realized what was happening. "Of course, darlin'. The door opposite the ladies' room leads through the kitchen and out the back."

"Thanks."

He gave her a nod and went back to finishing his pour.

Codi stood and moved to the bathroom. The man started to follow but stopped when she went down the hallway. He would wait until she returned.

She ducked through the kitchen and out the back door. A waft of garbage and urine hit her in the muggy night air. She was standing in a back alley, and she was not alone.

Two thug-types held a man at gunpoint as they relieved him of his possessions.

Codi immediately stepped forward, calling out to them. She cursed herself for not bringing her gun.

"Hey, we don't want any trouble. Just take what you want and go on your way," Codi called out as she approached the robbers.

Before they could answer, a sharp pain filled the back of her head, and she dropped to the ground with just the spinning flash of a man standing over her before everything went dark.

It was a revelation and a nightmare, as her memory flashed—truly a bad weekend. Codi finally remembered the back alley. It was the same thugs who had chased her in the park. The one who hit her from behind and then stood over her drove the brown van. The same guys Joel had arrested now connected to her past, but someone up the food chain was running them and issuing orders. Codi knew exactly what needed to be done. She was going to help Detective Chris Gasser and Special Agent Greta Goodson bring their operation down.

Chapter Eight

MIAMI, FLORIDA – 6:58 A.M.

Sunrise dimmed as the sound of thunder heralded an unusual morning storm passing across the tip of Florida. The Scientist moved from his bed to his laptop and turned it on. Three square images popped up showing the Hemmings' kitchen from different angles. He started a kettle and rummaged through the refrigerator for something to eat, yawning and blinking the sleep away.

Cold pizza and ginger tea were consumed while he watched the screen in anticipation. It didn't take long before the first occupant appeared. Mr. Hemmings was wearing pajama bottoms and a V-neck white tee. Soon Mrs. Hemmings followed in a pink terry robe. He watched with rapt attention as the couple went through their daily routine. About halfway through, he froze the image and zoomed in on it. He scrutinized the picture and then leaned back, crossing his arms. Everything he needed was now in place.

"Castor. Come here, pup," he called.

The adopted speckled mutt, whose coloring looked much like the castor bean, popped up from his bed and ran over for some affection. The Scientist scratched behind the dog's ears, and Castor placed his head on the man's leg.

Ricin was one of the earth's deadliest naturally occurring poisons. It had often been sensationalized beyond its actual effectiveness. It is a Type 2 ribosome-inactivating protein also known as a holotoxin. Due to its high heat tolerance, several countries tried to weaponize the poison by making ricin bombs. At one point, bullets were coated with it. All of the programs eventually failed and were canceled. A recent president and a congressman were sent letters with ricin in them, but they were discovered and thwarted before they could do any harm. The Russians tried to kill two defectors with it but succeeded in killing only one, leaving the unharmed man to bad-mouth them for the next three decades.

The problem wasn't the effectiveness of the poison; it was the delivery. One needed to ingest at least twenty milligrams, about an eighth of a teaspoon, to achieve the desired result. If inhaled or injected, only twenty-two micrograms were needed, about the size of three grains of table salt, but that required a very close-up application. Without the proper delivery component, you would not be successful. As a skilled assassin, The Scientist knew the numbers and planned his delivery well.

The Scientist thought back to the last person he had killed with poison. While poison is typically the weapon of choice for females, it often proved a perfect choice for him as well. The best type in his opinion were poisons that incorporated a fuse or delay before they killed. This would leave enough time for The Scientist to get away, simultaneously confusing the timeline for investigators. With ricin, it took two to four days before symptoms presented, at which point there was nothing the victim could do to reverse the damage other than updating their will.

He replaced his safety gear and moved to the kitchen. Using a magnifier, he scooped ten milligrams of the white powder into a gel capsule. He repeated the process several more times until it was gone. Everything was then placed carefully in a plastic container, which he stuffed in his backpack. Now, all that was left to do was wait.

He called his dog over, and they left the apartment for their late morning walk, Castor wagging his tail in pure joy.

***

Codi and Joel looked over the files they had been given. They contained only top-line details, and each probably corresponded to a mountain of boxes stored somewhere else. The duo commandeered the small conference room to establish a presence there before the other agents beat them to it.

"Love the smell of cold case dust in the morning," Codi said, rubbing her hands together.

Joel glanced over at his partner. The thought of dust made his nose itch.

"Glad your swimmers are okay." Codi gave Joel a sideways glance, trying not to smile.

He stopped typing, remembering the incident with the bullet to his crotch. "Let's not talk about that."

"Too soon? Close call, though. I would hate to have to give you a new nickname."

"New nickname?" Joel asked, not understanding.

"Like One-Ball Paul, Stubby Stu, or maybe Junkless Jim."

"Okay, okay. Not funny. I didn't know you had a nickname for me in the first place," Joel said, with curiosity.

"I guess it's really more of a pet name than a nickname. Something . . . endearing," Codi said, without looking at her partner.

Joel spun in his chair to face her. "You're not going to tell me, are you?"

Silence returned.

"Will you tell me if I guess it?"

"No. I'll tell you when the time is right."

They just stared at each other for a beat until Joel got self-conscious and changed the subject.

"Let's start with a quick machine-gun approach this time."

"What do you mean?" Codi asked.

"I'll run through the names and cases quickly, and we'll prioritize them based on instant gut reactions."

"Why?"

Joel took a breath. "Because next time, I'll do it alphabetically and after that, by date."

"Trying to keep it fresh, I get it. Okay, go!"

It took Joel a second to start back up before rattling off all the cold cases they had been given. He quickly slid the folder off the pile and restacked them as he went, identifying the name, location, and type of crime.

Two cases stood out to Codi as the most interesting to start first.

Joel reread the highlights. "Special Agent Marjorie Madison shot in her home in Colorado, and Judge Jesse Kenworth of Indiana unknown cause, possible poisoning." He looked over to Codi. "Okay, why Marjorie?"

"She's the only woman in the bunch, and historically, women have been given less attention in clearing their cases versus men."

"So . . ." Joel started.

Cody motioned her hands to hurry Joel to come to the conclusion she was hoping for.

". . . that means they might have missed something?"

"Exactly," she said, with a tilt of her head. "I'd hate to waste our precious time returning another cold case to the unsolved pile."

"You realize that is the destination for 99 percent of these cases?"

"I know, but a girl can dream."

Marjorie was a special agent assigned to the Denver Field Office. She had been working there five years when it all came to a sudden stop with a 45-caliber bullet to the back of her head in June 2006. The bullet had come from outside her apartment, most likely the street.

There were a few crime photos and a headshot of her Quantico graduation picture in the electronic file.

"She looks happy," Codi said warmly.

"I know I was when I finished Quantico." Joel tapped in an address to his search bar. "It looks like this case is new enough that the whole thing is backed up electronically." He pulled up the case details, and the two agents divided up the work.

It took both agents the rest of the day to read and double-check all the evidence. At 5:00 p.m., Codi closed her laptop with a slam. Her eyes were bloodshot, and she was nursing a growing headache.

"I hope you found something because I got bupkis," she said with a huff.

"If you are referring to nothing at all, that's what I have as well. Seems it might have just been a random drive-by."

"Do you realize the odds of that?"

Joel felt helpless, as he knew the odds exactly—bupkis.

"What about the boyfriend?" Codi asked.

Joel scrolled up to that section of the file. "He was pretty broken up, according to the investigating agents, and had a solid alibi."

"I wouldn't say solid. We should take a pass at him, and then if we still have nothing, we can move to the next case."

"What's your thought here, Codi?"

"Just got a feeling there is more to his story."

"Okay, I'll see if Brian will approve the travel based on your gut," Joel said.

"I better go with you."

***

The Harley Davidson Livewire cruised along South Field Street, past the Dallas Police Memorial. The Encyclical kept pace with the light traffic, not wanting to draw attention. The sun had popped up, and the day was quickly heating up. It would be another Texas scorcher. He was wearing all-black leathers and a generic black helmet to match, the warm humid air making him sweat in the City of Hate. He took a right on Commerce and pulled to the far left on the one-way street. A quick glance at his watch had him ten seconds ahead of schedule. He slowed slightly, no longer worried about being noticed, as his motorbike made virtually no sound.

The Adolphus Autograph Collection was one of downtown Dallas's premier iconic hotels. Hand-built by European craftsmen in the early 1900s as a passion project for beer magnate Adolphus Bush, it had an old-world-grey stone with a carved relief façade in the style of the Ecole de Beaux-Arts. Its elaborate details, brazen ornamentation, and heavy-handed masonry were countered with a simple curbside valet.

The Encyclical pulled to the curb two blocks away and pretended to chat on his phone, his eyes squarely on the valet parking area ahead. There were currently no cars in sight, but his research had shown him a man possessed by routine and schedule.

Donald Rightmen was a botanist. A botanist who got lucky. After college, Donald had taken the graduation money his mother had given him and left for New Guinea, a South Pacific island just above Australia. He spent four grueling months in the jungles with malaria and a bout of dengue fever collecting and cataloging plants, unique plants that might have the potential to heal. A lucky break came when he collected an unnamed mushroom that grew only in the April Salome Forest region. He discovered it growing behind a small waterfall. The yellowish-pink brain-shaped fungus grew to the size of a human palm. It was in danger of becoming extinct because of the vast logging operations in the area. Donald had determined it was filled with hypocrellin.

The substance had been breaking new ground in anti-tumor and anti-inflammation research. After many failures, he was able to grow a synthesized version in a controlled environment. The early tests yielded astonishing results. Instead of selling his discovery, he licensed his find to a large pharma company, Phlaxco, which specialized in arthritis remedies.

Last week marked the company's move into clinical trials. Donald used this new development to renegotiate his side of the deal, already worth millions. The Phlaxco Board consisted of old-school political players and a former CEO who would not be bullied. The end result is what kept assassins like The Encyclical in business. A simple purchase on a certain flower website and Phlaxco's problems would be solved. They had requested the loose flowers, meaning they wanted to send a message—don't mess with us.

Donald hummed an absent tune as he checked the time on his phone. His reflection in the wall mirror portrayed confidence, with a subtle darkness that few ever saw. He flipped a stray hair back into place and checked his teeth for clinging breakfast bits. The elevator car came to a stop, and the doors parted, revealing the warm tones of polished wood paneling that reached up to a forty-foot ceiling. The scent of sandalwood and fresh linen filled the air as he padded across the muted rust-colored carpet.

The last two years had been a rocket-ship ride to a position of power and wealth. Donald had taken his discoveries and leveraged them into a small but profitable company that allowed him to manage his assets rather than build or design anything new, much like a slumlord. He purchased a nice home in the suburbs and leased the car of his dreams, a British racing green Bentley Mulliner GT. Tuesdays and Saturdays, he had a recurring rendezvous with alternating escorts at his favorite hotel, The Adolphus. Last night had been a spectacle of debauchery and new heights in kinky perversions. The twenty-two-year-old Carmine was truly gifted.

The Encyclical watched as the green Bentley coupe pulled curbside. It was one of only one hundred cars manufactured and built through the Mulliner custom division of Bentley—truly a work of art. Each car had a piece of the original racing seat from Sir Tim Birkin's iconic 1930 No. 9 Le Mans race car displayed in a glass-filled, gauge-like case on the dash.

The Encyclical placed his phone back into his jacket and moved into the flow of traffic. Timing would be critical. He powered up the specialized phone device mounted to his handlebars. A red button appeared on the screen. Every new Bentley comes equipped with *My Bentley Connected Car* running through a 4g embedded sim card. It allowed one of the most sophisticated automobiles on the planet to do many of the driver's tasks automatically. The modified smartphone allowed The Encyclical to hack that system, but it could only operate one feature—the passenger side window.

The target strode to his waiting car with a smug expression and a five-thousand-dollar suit. He ignored the valet holding open his door and sat inside, reaching for the seatbelt. When the motorbike was within twenty feet of the vehicle, the red button turned green—just as advertised. The Encyclical pressed it. The passenger window on the Bentley started rolling down. He repeated the process practiced with the watermelons in the open meadow. He pulled out his modified grenade, used his right thumb to hook the pin, and pulled. The fuse inside the device ignited and began its countdown. He slowed just enough to use his left hand to toss the explosive through the now open window. Without looking back, he silently zoomed away and around the corner, just as a muted explosion concussed the area behind him.

The Encyclical didn't need to look back to see what fifty stainless steel ball bearings set in flight from a sudden and violent exothermic reaction had done to his target. A Jackson Pollock painting came to mind. His only remorse was the damage to the nearly one-of-a-kind automobile.

The sound of a siren was hardly unexpected. When you plan for everything, anything is possible. The fact that a cop was just finishing up writing a ticket a block away and happened to catch the explosion and a subsequent e-bike making a getaway was just bad luck. The Encyclical accelerated his bike around the corner, leaving his obliterated target behind. He floored the bike down the next street where he took a hard right. Using the side view mirrors, he calculated the distance the police car had gained. The Livewire had better acceleration than just about anything on the street, but with a top end of only 95 mph, he was not going to lose the police car on a straightaway. Plus, there was no outrunning a police radio.

The cop followed right behind, matching his maneuvers with ease. The Encyclical slid to the middle of the street, pressing his luck while waiting for an opening in traffic.

Another police cruiser joined in the chase. He took a chance and flew through the intersection at a red light. The drivers of two cars panicked and screeched to a halt as the police cars slowed, and then quickly navigated through the car slalom. That move had given him a half-block lead that was now slowly diminishing as other cops closed in from other streets.

Finally, the gap he was looking for opened up. It was a small space between two oncoming cars. The Encyclical yanked the handlebars and swerved between them, making a quick U-turn. The police all spun to give chase, but the other cars got in the way. The Encyclical turned his bike right again into a parking structure, accelerating up the corkscrew access road that led to the top. He could hear the sirens following behind, and he slowed to give them a chance to close the distance. What he had in mind required the police to make a visual of him just before he hit the fifth floor. The moment he glimpsed the first chase vehicle, The Encyclical twisted the throttle and pulled ahead. His bike hit the fifth floor of the parking structure, and he exited the corkscrew that accessed that floor.

The bike leveled out as it shot forward and then did a quick U-turn back toward the lone dumpster sitting against the wall. The Encyclical headed straight for it, dropping low on the bike, hitting the hidden modified metal side doors just as he hit the brakes. The front tire knocked the two hinged panels back, and the bike disappeared into the metal bin. Once inside, the doors slapped closed, and The Encyclical killed the bike and parked it. He got off and dropped his helmet and coat, and then squatted by the panel, listening as sirens shot past, searching the parking structure. Another siren could be heard continuing up to the sixth floor. He waited inside the dumpster and realized his only mistake. He should have cleaned the dumpster. The heat of the day was cooking the residual contents inside into a most unsavory and foul odor. With his eye pressed to the hairline crack where the two doors met, he watched as police cruisers searched the fifth floor in vain. Eventually, they left and headed to the upper floors.

The Encyclical exited the doors and removed his gloves and the sign posted on the dumpster. He casually walked to a red Prius parked a few slots over and put on a pair of clear glasses. Running his fingers through his long hair, he removed the helmet imprint. The shirt he was wearing was a bright paisley blue and white that said "Look at me, I'm creative." He entered the car and started it up, cranking the AC. As he drove toward the exit ramp, a police cruiser swooped from the upper floor and pulled up next to him.

"Did you see a motorcycle up here?" the cop yelled.

"No, why? What's going on?" The Encyclical asked, lamely.

The cop didn't give an explanation, just drove off searching for something he would never find.

The Encyclical continued down the ramp in no hurry and left downtown Dallas for his Vrbo.

***

His luggage dropped to the floor as he hit the couch with an exhausted expression. He looked up to see Codi round the corner. She was wearing nothing but one of his oversized t-shirts. Her hair was in a ponytail, and her expression bordered on sultry. She strolled over and joined him on the couch, intertwining arms and legs.

"Welcome home," she said, punctuating it with a kiss. They both let the tingling sensation that followed flow through their tired bodies. It had been almost a week since she had seen Matt, and after the drama she'd been through, holding him was magical.

The kiss seemed to revive Matt, and he held Codi in a strong embrace, each letting their auras mix and mingle. It was like releasing a fifty-pound weight they had each been carrying. The two let out a simultaneous sigh as their lips parted.

"We're never getting a boat," Matt said, looking Codi in the eyes.

Her brow crunched. "Okay, got it. No boat."

He then told Codi about the boat trip that cost him his sea legs and breakfast.

"And once you're sick, there is no cure until you get off the dang boat. We are talking stomach completely drained, and it just kept going and going for hours."

"Okay, okay, enough barf talk. I'm losing my appetite, and I have something very special prepared for us tonight," she said.

Matt sat up, trying to not be alarmed. The last time Codi fixed dinner for them, it was a five-star disaster. He forced a smile and braved the question. "What are we having?"

"Reheated Pad Thai I brought with me from the city."

Matt visibly relaxed. They moved to the kitchen and resumed their comfortable connection. The food was good, and each shared stories of their adventures while apart.

Matt showed genuine concern when Codi spoke about her street thug drama. The missing engagement ring didn't go unnoticed or talked about either.

Eventually, they ran out of words and shared the calm quiet only two people truly in love can enjoy.

"I've been giving our wedding some thought." Codi's words felt like they were taken right out of Matt's mouth.

"Me too!" He had been going crazy trying not to overplay his hand, to give Codi all the time she needed.

"Great. So what are you thinking?" Codi asked playfully, not one hundred percent sure she wanted to go first.

"Codi, we have been doing so great together. I don't want to screw that up by adding the pressure of a hard date."

Codi almost choked on her iced tea. She could tell Matt was having second thoughts. It was perfectly natural. She was having the same thing but had pushed beyond it. So much so, that she had picked a date and was eager to share it with Matt. "So you don't want to set a date?"

"Ah . . ." Matt suddenly felt pressured. Had he said the wrong thing? He was sure this was what she would want. "Not unless you want to," he threw back lamely.

Codi's face turned serious. She was hurt and needed to cover that up. "Look, we don't have to set a date. We don't even have to get married. It's not like we have worked so hard to get here or anything." Codi set her napkin down and left the room, slamming the door behind her.

Matt put his hands to his face. Boy, had he played that one wrong.

***

The Hemmings had a fairly active and healthy lifestyle. It was what The Scientist would call the perfect storm. He would have many opportunities to complete this operation.

They left their house on Wednesday night for dinner with friends. The Scientist hopped the fence at the construction site just like he had before. It was important that he leave no evidence, so he wore a beany to cover his head and gloves on his hands. He climbed to the second floor of the house under construction.

It was now completely covered in tar paper and wrapped in steel meshing in preparation for the stucco coat. The Scientist found a seam in the mesh and cautiously removed the staples tying it to the house's frame. Replacing the rope, he swung through the open gap over the wall and toward the Hemmings' side yard.

Repeating his prior actions soon had him inside their kitchen. First up was the removal of the three cameras. Then he moved through the home until he found the master bathroom. He used a specialized tape to lift several fingerprints from a hairbrush and curling iron. Back in the kitchen, he transferred the prints to several of the items he had brought with him.

He placed the flask he used into the back of an upper cupboard along with the mortar and pestle. Leftover castor beans were stuffed in the back of their junk drawer in a blank white envelope. Finally, he placed the ricin gel caps in the prostate nutraceutical bottle sitting in the vitamin basket labeled *His* on the counter.

The Scientist slipped out of the kitchen and moved to the trash cans by the front gate. Staying out of sight of the camera watching the front driveway, he opened the lid and judiciously untied the plastic trash bag inside. The paper filter he used to precipitate the ricin out of the acetone solution was placed inside. A light suddenly flashed across the area and illuminated him. He dropped behind the cans. A red Tesla X pulled to the front door, and the couple exited. They were home early. The Scientist stayed low, listening to the casual conversation as Mr. and Mrs. Hemmings walked to the front doors. He hurriedly finished tying the trash bag the way he found it and silently lowered the lid. Hugging the wall, he dashed back to the slider in the kitchen. It was still open. Lights came on in the home, and his heart pounded. The second he heard the chime of the home alarm deactivating by the front door, he pulled his jumper cables from the alarm sensor and slid the glass slider shut. He didn't take the time to relock it, but instead scaled the wall back to the construction site. Once on the other side, he paused to catch his breath. The prints and items he left behind would be damming evidence that investigators would eat up.

The Scientist replaced the tar paper and mesh, then exited the construction site. As he walked along the beach back to his car, he realized just how fast his heart was beating. He took a few calming breaths to remind himself his work here was done. All that was left was cleaning his apartment and abandoning Castor.

By tomorrow's lunch, he would be out of the state, and if all went well, Mr. Hemmings would not show any signs of distress for another two to three days.

The ricin would be absorbed by his cells and start inactivating his ribosomes. At first, slowly, but ultimately, it would cause irreversible cell death. Symptoms would manifest initially as diarrhea, followed by extreme dehydration, then slow organ failure, and finally circulatory shock. By the time Mr. Hemmings died, they would know the cause, and Mrs. Hemmings would be on the hook for his murder with some robust evidence pointing in her direction.

The thought of it all was most pleasurable. The Scientist suddenly felt an extra pep in his step.

Chapter Nine

FBI SPECIAL PROJECTS – WASHINGTON, DC FIELD OFFICE – 10:23 A.M.

"Good, you're just in time," Brian said as his agents knocked and entered his office. "I have some news. Take a seat."

SSA Brian Fescue seemed amped-up and anxious. Codi and Joel took a seat and waited for their boss to start. The brief silence inevitably made the room feel too small for Joel.

"First off, how are you feeling?" he asked Codi.

"I'm good to go," she replied, moving her shoulder more freely.

"Glad to hear it," Brian said as he organized some paperwork. "You're still staying at Matt's for the moment?"

"Thought I'd give it two weeks before I move back home," Codi said.

"Sounds smart. Don't need you bumping into another pack of angry gangsters right now." He changed his focus. "And you, Joel?"

"Uh . . . " Joel didn't have an immediate answer.

"Good." Brian flipped his laptop open and typed his password. "I checked with Special Agent Greta Goodson. She's the agent at the DC Field Office running your case. She is confident they'll have your attackers rounded up soon. Seems someone anonymously dropped some new evidence her way."

He paused and gave both his agents a scrutinizing look. Joel withered a bit, never liking the spotlight on himself, especially knowing the new evidence had come from them, even though they were not supposed to be working the case.

"Thanks for that, by the way." Brian's knowing look transitioned as he leaned back in his chair and glanced at the ceiling. "So I've been processing how to say this, and in the end, I think we would all feel better if I just blurted it out."

Joel and Codi shared a curious glance.

"I have been offered an AD position at ERTU."

"In Quantico?" Joel asked.

"Correct."

Joel knew an assistant directorship at the Emergency Response Team Unit was a very high-profile bump for his boss. This was a golden handshake from the higher ups. "Wow! That's great news. Congratulations," Joel said, in genuine excitement.

"Yes. It's good for me and the whole family. Regular hours and no more chasing around the world after you two," Brian added.

"I'm so happy for you Brian, but I know you'll miss us," Codi said, hiding her disappointment.

"Already am." Brian smiled. "It'll never be as glamorous as some of the cases we've worked, but it is one of the Bureau's most important crime-solving divisions and an opportunity I can't pass up. And before you ask, the wife's very excited as well."

"Wasn't gonna ask," Codi retorted.

"Hmm . . . sure."

"Who's your replacement?" Joel asked.

"Haven't been told yet, but I'm sure they will be very capable."

"Well, since you're in such a good mood, how 'bout you approve travel for one of the cases we're checking out," Joel said, with his fingers crossed.

"Sure."

"What about a raise?" Codi prompted.

"Not a chance," Brian countered as he met Codi's stare eye-for-eye.

"Had to ask."

"Had to say no."

They each looked at one another for an awkward moment. Then Brian stood and called out, "Come here. Group hug. It's been a pleasure working with you both."

***

Rodo sat at the stainless-steel table picking at something between his teeth with his left pointer fingernail. He had a string of tattoos up his arm that disappeared beyond his dirty wife-beater. His deep-set dark eyes were jittery, and he reeked of fear. The old-school, stained, soundproof walls were placed there back when interrogations had few rules.

The Metropolitan Police Department was on Indiana Avenue. It had seen its share of bad guys over the years and had just managed to weather the storm, with a unique smell and dim pallor to match. Older fluorescent lights struggled to do their job as Detective Chris Glasser stepped into the small room. He sat across from the suspect and placed a file folder on the table next to him, hands splayed across the top. He started a recording device attached to the camera system and spoke clearly stating the occupants and the situation.

"Rodriguez Gutierrez, a.k.a., Rodo. Age twenty-eight, current address unknown. Just so we are clear, I am not here to interrogate you or ask any questions. I'm simply here to explain the charges and what is going to happen next. You are welcome to have an attorney present; just remember anything you say is being recorded and can be used against you."

Rodo looked around the room, uncomfortable with the detective's eyes staring him down. He leaned back, trying to increase the distance between him and the cop, hoping it might change his circumstance.

"Rodo, I'm going to need a verbal answer from you," Gasser said.

"Yeah, man."

"We are charging you with several things corroborated with physical evidence like street cameras and eyewitnesses, as well as the fact that you were caught red-handed on a B&E."

Special Agent Greta Goodson watched from the other side of the one-way glass. She was out of the DC Field Office and had seen her share of collaboration between departments. At thirty-eight, she had been there and done that enough to know when to step in and when to let others carry the load. Her main concern was the attempted murder of a federal agent. The breaking and entering along with several other charges were for the local authorities. Together, the two agencies had let the police handle the case with her on oversight to protect the Bureau's interests, a decision she had personally helped push through.

A soft knock on the door was followed by Special Agent Codi Sanders's entrance.

"Oh, good. You made it," Greta said, looking over her shoulder.

"How's it going?" Codi asked as she closed the door.

"Just getting started. I wanted you to see the perps, and I have a couple of follow-up questions to your interview with Detective Gasser. If it goes like I think, we'll have three less thugs on the street. Right now, we are looking at federal and state charges, which should keep them incarcerated for at least ten, providing one of them cracks."

"Sounds good." Codi took a seat next to Greta and immediately recognized the man Detective Gasser was interviewing.

He continued to read off the list of charges. "Plus, we have a confession from one of your partners naming you in the attempted murder of a federal officer. All that will lead to a conviction and a long visit to one of our state's finest steel resorts."

Codi pointed to the man on the other side of the one-way glass. "That's one of them. He chased me at the park. And I have a brief memory of his face right after he clubbed me on the back of the head."

"Here are the other two they arrested." Greta placed two photos on the table.

"Yep, Thing One and Thing Two. They were the ones robbing Edgar Rice when I stepped out of the club," Codi added while looking at the drama playing out on the other side of the glass.

Detective Gasser slid pictures of Codi's apartment across the table, followed by footage on his laptop of street security cameras showing Rodo and Garcia chasing Codi. The final two were pictures of Diaz and Garcia in similar rooms, gesturing like they were talking. This was a tactic Detective Gasser had used many times when there was more than one suspect—a printed picture of what looked like one of their buddies talking.

They could have been chatting about the weather in up-state New York, but when paired with the implication they had turned on their colleague, it was gasoline to a fire.

"What?" Rodo grabbed the two photos of his buddies. "You said one of them snitched against me? Was it Garcia? I bet it was Garcia; he never liked me. Squealing Chimba, never trust a Columbian." He turned and spit on the floor. "I'll tell you something. It was all his idea to hit the dead agent's apartment. He's the one that hit your agent over the head, not me. He lied to you. Stuffed her behind a dumpster like she was nuthin' but trash. Danzo was hoppin' mad when he found out, just about fired us all. Then she goes and gets blasted by that truck. Some luck, huh?"

"You're right. Garcia told us all about it, but he said it was *you* that did the fed."

The shot of fear that crossed Rodo's eyes told the detective he was on the right track. In truth, he had gotten nothing from the other two suspects, but Rodo was turning out to be a goldmine of information. "You can't pin her death on me. I only hit her on the head. She was fine after that."

Detective Gasser collected up his pictures and placed them back in the file folder. "Danzo must have been pretty upset when he heard the three of you got pinched. I bet anything, he's moving shop and distancing himself far away from you three."

Rodo hung his head in defeat. "He'd be smart to do so."

"Where's he working out of, Rodo?" It was the first question Detective Gasser had asked him.

"Back of Rumi's kitch—. Hey, wait a minute, you said you weren't going to ask questions, just tell me the charges."

Detective Gasser leaned back in his chair and crossed his arms.

Rodo suddenly realized he'd been played. His eyes blazed with hatred as he banged his handcuffed hands down on the table.

"Lawyer!"

"Looks like your case is coming together," Codi said as she stood.

"Yeah, I'm gonna be here a bit longer. Thanks for coming by to ID the suspects."

Codi started to leave when Greta said, "Hey, I have a few more questions I need to ask. You wanna meet for lunch later this week? I can ask you my questions, and maybe we could share some war stories."

Codi looked over at the African American agent in the blue blouse and navy slacks. She had her hair pulled back in a simple ponytail in what Codi liked to call "FBI easy." Intelligent eyes met her stare with equal yoke, along with two of the biggest dimples Codi had ever seen. "Sure. I could eat."

***

Morning came with an intensity Joel wasn't expecting. Burning sunlight assaulted his face long before the alarm. He had forgotten to close his curtains the night before. He rolled away from it and moved through the practiced motions of his morning routine. He placed his to-go coffee order on his phone app and finished with a tap on his aquarium. Sushi and Sashimi stirred awake before he shook a few flakes into the water. They rushed to the surface and slurped up the food as Joel watched with rapt intent. The two large Oscars battled for their share until the flakes were gone. Then they began their ritual search of the rest of the tank for any that had gone astray.

"Okay, guys, have a great day!" Joel said as he left his home and headed for the garage out back. Sushi and Sashimi paused their search and stared after him.

Joel had bought the pair of fish shortly after a case where he had nearly been killed, twice. The first via carbon-monoxide poisoning and the second by drowning in the frigid ocean. Somehow, he had survived both incidents and decided he had always wanted a pet, and fish were about as low-maintenance as he could get away with, considering his schedule. They could easily go a couple of days without food and survive. As he closed the back door behind him and locked it, he made a mental note to close the curtain to his bedroom before retiring that night.

At the office, Joel could tell something was wrong before he stepped off the elevator. No, just different. The office had an unusual vibe. He marched past the boss's office and took a sip of his Kona Peaberry with just a splash of monk-sugar, before sitting at his desk and turning on his computer.

Codi's shadow loomed over him, and he glanced back without stopping his typing.

"Morning."

"Is it?" Joel mumbled.

"Someone got up on the wrong side of the bed."

Joel stopped typing and tried to regroup.

"By the way, the new boss is here, wants to see us," Codi said, breaking the moment.

Joel spun in his chair. "Already? What's he like? Is he mean or nice? Where did he come from?"

"Joel, take it easy. Let's just go ask her."

"Okay, good, yeah, we'll just ask her. Her! Wait, he's a *she?*" Joel said, nervously rubbing his hands together as he processed the situation. "This could be good."

"Come on," Codi threw back at him as she left.

Joel scurried to catch up.

"Special agents, hi, come on in and take a seat." A short woman with light-brown hair and a face with more creases than an unfolded origami dragon stood to greet them. "I'm Bruster Holloway, Acting Supervisory Special Agent in charge here at Special Projects." She shook both of her agents' hands and turned to go back to her desk. The suit she wore screamed professional agent. Her chewed fingernails belied a nervous habit developed over a lot of anxious hours spent in worry. Small beady eyes and a false smile finished her look. "Before we play twenty questions let me tell you a few things about myself since I feel like I already know all about you two hot-shots." She placed her hand on a stack of personnel files.

Codi and Joel shared a brief glance.

"I'm here from the Seattle Field Office where I was the SAC (special agent in charge) for just over three years. While I was there, I trimmed the fat out of their procedures and run an extremely efficient operation. I have been asked to do the same here, and I figure the best way to go about that is to be right up front with my plans."

"Plans? Sir—er, ma'am? We follow the current FBI guidelines," Joel said, with a pained expression on his face, not sure where this conversation was going.

Codi crossed her arms and looked bored.

"Please, call me Holloway. I was never a fan of my first name, given to me by an alcoholic father on a BOGO beer night." She picked at her cuticles as she spoke the unexpected and honest words. "Anyway, I'm implementing a new set of procedures here. I call it 'fiscally responsible intelligent case solving,' or F. R. I. C. S., FRICS for short. That means *no* to quite a list of things and *yes* to several new ways of investigating. I've gone ahead and sent the list to your emails. A couple of examples of my new FRICS policies are no more travel unless absolutely necessary and approved by me. From now on, we are using the FBI's resources to their full extent." She paused to look at her two agents to make sure they were tracking. "Example. Say you have an interview in Galveston. Make a call instead and have an agent out of the field office in Houston handle it. Or if you have a lead that needs following up in Louisville, enlist a local detective to do it for you, or just Zoom with them. This one change alone will save nearly three hundred thousand taxpayer dollars in our department alone every year. Now, imagine those savings spread across the entire FBI." She spread her hands in the air to illustrate her vision. "And that's just *one* of the changes we'll be implementing."

"So, is this some sort of pilot program we're testing?" Joel asked.

"No. This is the new standard . . . as soon as it gets approved through the higher levels." She said the last part as if throwing it away. "Think of it as virtual investigations, 'VI.'"

"Will we have virtual arrests as well? I'm not sure the guilty will take a Zoom call," Codi responded with not too subtle contempt.

"One of the biggest advantages we have since 9/11 is the sharing and homogenous crossover of information from all agencies, and I plan to use that to its fullest." She pounded a fist on the table to accent her message.

"We will work off of evidence. No more following our gut down a dead end. Because hunches don't pay for agent's lunches."

"ASSA Holloway, hunches have been a major part of our success," Codi said. "Sure, they don't always pan out, but we have been more than average in closing our cases."

"I'm sure you think that to be the case, but from now on, we will do things a little differently around here. No more running off on your half-baked assumptions that have everyone in the Bureau watching their backs and taking cover from the fallout. No more disappearing mid-case so I have to enlist extra agents to track you down."

"We were kidnapped against our will," Joel reminded her.

"Exactly. And if you had made a Zoom call instead of a personal visit, it would never have happened."

Codi and Joel stared, dumbstruck.

"From now on, no unnecessary risks, understand?"

"We are federal investigators. We are paid to take risks to protect the public," Codi said, practically pleading.

ASSA Holloway just tilted her head and gazed in contempt. "Fiscally responsible intelligent case solving—FRICS."

Codi stormed down the hallway with Joel barely keeping pace.

"What the FRICS is wrong with her?" Codi mumbled as they headed back to their offices.

"I know. 'Hunches don't pay for lunches?'"

"Or humongous crossover something or other? She's certifiable."

"Homogenous," Joel corrected.

"I think we're in for a bumpy ride with our new boss, Acting Supervising Special Agent Bruster Holloway."

"Bruster? What kind of name is that? I think she might not like me. Did you see the stare-down she gave me?" Joel asked.

"She's just another woman trying to prove herself in a man's world. Nothing new. It shouldn't be necessary, but the world is still out of balance. It takes good, intelligent females and forces them to overdo everything just to be heard. Give it time. We'll get on the other side of this, Joel."

He couldn't empathize, but he could sympathize. He could only imagine how hard and frustrating it must be to not be appreciated for one's full potential.

***

Danzo lowered the phone, slowly processing the call he had just received. He stood and paced back and forth in his make-shift office. The sounds of the heavy construction equipment outside did little to interrupt his thoughts. The abandoned warehouse was next on the list to be demolished, and it was time to move locations, but recent intelligence was changing his plans.

"Chico!" Danzo called.

A young Cuban with a scar across his nose and cheeks entered the room. He was Danzo's number two and mirrored his look with black slacks and a tie against a white shirt. To that he added a black pork-pie hat and two gold front teeth. "Yes, boss?"

"We're moving."

"I'll see to it," Chico said as he turned to start the process.

This was not an uncommon event. About every three to four months, Danzo moved his operation to a new place around the city, never staying in one location too long.

"Any thought where, boss?"

"Out of the city, maybe Atlanta," Danzo replied.

"Wow. We're running away? What's up, *hermano*?"

"The Three Amigos got pinched, undoubtedly spilling their guts as we speak."

"We can't leave the city with our tails between our legs. Nobody will respect us. I might as well get a job at McDonalds."

Danzo knew his number two was right. The smart move was to leave the city, but the right move was to fight back. He had been part of a gang earlier in his career that had successfully done just that. He would take his operation to the next level, screw the cops. It wasn't time to run; it was time to go on the offensive.

"Do you know who's running the case?" Chico asked.

"Same guy that's been chasing his tail after us for the last eight months," Danzo replied.

Chico took off his hat and twirled it in his hands. "You know what this means?"

"We're going to war, Scarface-style."

There was a sudden rumble, and the building shook.

"Hurry up!"

The giant steel ball swung in a pendulum motion. Each time gaining distance and speed. The crane operator expertly adjusted his position so the front swing would make the ball impact with the building's corner. The destruction was severe and permanent, leaving a giant hole where there was once sturdy brick and mortar. As he returned the ball to its oscillation, a policeman wearing a vest suddenly flashed a badge and told him to shut it down.

Special Agent Greta Goodson exited the SUV. She wore her blonde hair in a ponytail and almost no makeup on her face. Detective Gasser circled the vehicle to join her. They were both wearing bulletproof vests with their place of business blazed across the front—FBI, POLICE. They were with a group of ten other officers all dressed accordingly. Each knew their part in the upcoming dance, and like a well-rehearsed troupe they moved out in unison and covered all the exits. The location Rodo had given was a bit vague, encompassing almost an entire block. The center of the block was under construction, as heavy equipment demolished several old buildings to make way for a new high-rise. One of them was just being torn down, and the corner had crumbled under the wrecking ball's weight.

With practiced efficiency, the team unsuccessfully cleared several buildings. As they surrounded the last one, the foreman from the site called out, "That building's not safe!"

"I'll take the responsibility," Detective Gasser called back, as he and Special Agent Goodson stepped across a pile of fallen bricks.

"Sergeant, hold your men here," Gasser said as they disappeared into the maw.

The two officers slowly cleared the decrepit building, working from the ground floor up. Once done, they moved together down to the basement. The room was filled with brick dust, and there was evidence of recent occupation.

"Looks like someone left in a hurry," Gasser said as he put his gun back in his holster.

Special Agent Goodson picked up several purses laying in a pile. "Left something behind." She checked the license in the wallet inside. "Mrs. Fern Hemery."

Gasser pulled out his phone to check the list of reported muggings in the DC area. "Bingo. Rodo was right. They were operating out of here. The question now is, where did they go?"

"If they were smart, another city," SA Goodson replied.

***

Living alone was just one of the many things he loved about being an assassin. It was a lifestyle centered on death, but it was a great way to take all you can while you can. He didn't expect to live forever. All he wanted was a challenging job that only he could do and a paycheck that was in accordance with the risks and effort taken. If you look that up in Google, "assassin" is one of the first categories to pop up.

Murder-for-hire was a growing field, and the world was becoming more and more accepting of what was once deemed abhorrent behavior. He could see a time in the future where he might be on the talk show circuit. Wow, would the audience get a kick out of some of his stories and methods! He finished his tea and rinsed the cup and saucer in the sink. After drying both and placing them in their assigned spots in the cupboard, The Scientist locked his front door and headed for his E-pace Jaguar. His thoughts filled with the imaginings of his own self-worth. His bright red car was a marvel of modern technology. He was a firm believer in the more you shined, the less others noticed you. It had served him well many times. An alert on his phone had him hitting the button. It was a news story he had been tracking.

"Authorities say the death of businessman Alan Hemmings has been upgraded to murder. Mr. Hemmings died from ingesting the deadly toxin ricin. You might recall ricin . . ."

The story went on to give highlights of the deadly poison's history.

"Authorities are now looking at his wife, Mrs. Carol Hemmings, as a suspect. She has been arrested in connection with her husband's murder. Details have been withheld, but an insider has suggested she poisoned his vitamin pill bottle."

It continued, but The Scientist had read the part he was interested in. He started his car and headed for the electronics store. There were a few items he needed for his next project. This one would definitely be a story to share with a TV audience. Maybe he should start writing his memoirs.

Chapter Ten

DENVER, COLORADO – 1:48 P.M.

The flight to Denver was first-class. As a going away gift, Brian had arranged two seats on one of the purpose-built FBI business jet G5s heading for the West Coast. There had been no wait at the airport and nothing but luxury and comfort on the way over.

"I've been saving something for you," Joel said as he sipped his Diet Coke.

"Oh, yeah?"

"Yeah."

"But you're not going to tell me till the time is right?" Codi said.

"No. You know that other case we wanted to investigate after we handled this one about Special Agent Marjorie Madison?"

"The judge?" Codi asked.

"I couldn't sleep last night, so I went through it too," Joel said as he opened his laptop.

"And what did you find?" Codi said, trying to care.

Joel was famous for going the extra mile when it came to research. He loved it and would often spend hours into the night chasing the smallest thread.

"Nothing new, so I hope you're up for a pub crawl through the Mile-High City because that's about all we're going to get on this trip."

"So you're saying we should just rubberstamp these cold cases and be done with them? Okay, pub crawl it is. First drink's on me," Codi said.

"ASSA Holloway ain't gonna like that."

Once on the ground in Denver, the rental car company had oversold their cars, and it took another hour before they were on their way south. By the time they made it to the hotel, the sun was setting for the day. Codi and Joel looked weary as they ate a simple dinner at the attached Coco's restaurant. The conversation was sparse, and time seemed to move slowly. Their booth was near the back of the restaurant, and Codi had a view of the mostly empty eatery.

"This might be our last road trip for a while," Codi said, breaking the silence.

"Well, by all means, let's spend it in a Coco's and a Motel 6."

"Better than the cave in Quebec or the cell in Hong Kong," she replied.

"We have had some crazy cases. Now, we can just do them virtually," Joel added.

"Catch me a murdering terrorist from my desk . . . I do like that!"

"Here's to the new ways!" Joel lifted his iced tea, and Codi joined him in a toast.

"The new ways. May our new shoes never get worn and our guns never fire. Oh, and may the boss get what she deserves."

Joel's eyes narrowed as they clinked glasses. He sipped his tea and leaned back, pushing his mostly eaten plate away. "I've been thinking—we should give ASSA Holloway an acronym to go with all her acronyms."

"How 'bout S. A. P. I. C., SAPIC?" Codi said.

"What does that stand for?"

"Self-absorbed person-in-charge."

"I think self-absorbed is hyphenated so it would be S. P. I. C., SPIC?" Joel said, with a concerned look on his face.

"That doesn't sound right."

"No, it doesn't. Might be considered racist. Okay, SAPIC it is."

The next morning, the ride south was mostly quiet. Codi sipped on a hot chai latte while Joel drove with his customary coffee in hand. The suburbs of Denver were sprawling and ever increasing. They pulled up to a blue and white Tudor-style home with a slightly curved driveway. Joel killed the engine and popped a breath mint as he hopped out of the vehicle. They knocked on the wood and glass double doors and waited as a rattling sound followed by several clicks preceded the opening of the front door.

A gray-haired woman with a forced smile stood slightly hunched over. "Well, come on in . . . that is, if you are the two FBI agents I spoke to over the phone."

"Yes, we are. Mrs. Madison?" Joel asked.

"You're from DC?"

"Uh-huh. I'm Special Agent Strickman, and this is Special Agent Sanders."

She waved them in. "We'll see how special." She led them over to a small but comfortable living room. The furniture was dated and well used, with a lifetime of collectables organized on shelves around the room. A lone man sat in the corner of the room. "Frank," she said to the man, "these are the FBI agents that are looking back into Marjorie's death."

A nearly bald man with impossibly long white eyebrows looked up from his green La-Z-Boy. He had an oxygen tube attached to his nose and was breathing with an audibly labored sound. Lying next to him on a small table was a set of dentures that he picked up and installed before speaking. "About time you took her case seriously," he said. "The numb-nuts doing the original investigation botched the whole thing up."

Mrs. Madison looked back and forth between her husband and the two agents nervously.

"What do you mean?" Joel asked the man as he sat down on a yellowish couch across from him.

"I mean the local investigators did a half-baked job. No follow-through or actionable evidence when it was staring them right in the face the whole time!"

The words were followed by a coughing spell that had Mrs. Madison popping up from her chair to turn up his oxygen.

Joel and Codi waited for the coughing to stop.

"We've carefully gone over the case," Codi said as she leaned forward, "and like you, we feel there are a couple of unanswered questions that maybe you could help us with."

Mr. Madison seemed intrigued by her comments, and his milky eyes shifted in her direction.

"What can you tell us about Granger Stevens?"

"I can tell you he shot our Margie in a fit of rage. Then shot himself over the guilt."

Codi and Joel listened as the lamented couple told a story of jealousy and anger that pointed toward Special Agent Marjorie Madison's fiancé, a man they had never approved of and had no love for.

After two grueling hours, Mr. Madison seemed to fade away between coughing fits. Mrs. Madison said he needed to take his meds and was kind enough to walk them to the door before relocking and chaining it.

Joel and Codi drove in silence to their next destination, a myriad of unsubstantiated facts swirling through their heads.

Joel was the first to speak. "Well, that clears it all up."

"Too bad there's no evidence to support any of their claims," Codi said, with an air of distraction.

"Yeah, too bad. I hate cold cases."

Mrs. Stevens was mid-fifties with a bobbed haircut and too much makeup. Her lips were as chubby as two red sausages and her teeth, impossibly white. The meeting took place in a large estate home devoid of furnishings.

"Thanks for meeting me here. I have to put on this open house today," she said as she finished placing a tray of small sandwiches on the kitchen island. She looked at her phone and took a deep breath. "I've got thirty minutes before I open, so talk."

Joel stepped up as he spoke. "What can you tell us about Marjorie and your son Granger?"

"Well, I can tell you he doted on her. They were a perfect couple."

"That seems contrary to what we've heard," Codi said.

"Been talking to the Madisons, huh? They're just looking for someone to blame. I don't hold it against them. I was like that, too, for a time. But sometimes bad things just happen. Life and all, you know . . . there's no blueprint. No way of predicting what comes next. One second you win the lottery, and the next, you get hit by a truck on the sidewalk. It just happens," Mrs. Stevens said, with a faraway look.

"Yeah, we've seen our share of that," Joel said as he leaned against the island.

"So there was no friction between them during the last few days?" Codi asked.

"No. In fact, just the opposite. Grange and Margie were at my house for dinner the night she died. They were holding hands and laughing. It's pretty special for a parent to watch their child so in love with such a good person. And just for the record, she was a very good person. Granger had found his soulmate. They were drawn together like two beautiful people at an ugly party. He couldn't live without her. That's why he killed himself." Mrs. Stevens wiped a tear from her eye, too broken up to continue. "Now look what you've done. I'm gonna have to redo my makeup." Mrs. Stevens started digging in her purse for her makeup bag.

"We're sorry to put you through this again," Codi said. "Was there any chance of another man or past boyfriend?"

"No. Nothing like that."

The rest of the conversation revealed little to no new information. Joel got a flyer for the house, and the two left after submitting to a tour.

"Thoughts?" Codi asked.

"The master bath is a bit small."

"No, about the case."

"Oh, accidental shooting?" Joel replied.

"Maybe. Let's hold off till we do our next interview."

Special Agent Watson was a tall African American man with wide hunched shoulders and the darkest irises Joel had ever seen. He had a smile that lit up the room with a tangle of crooked teeth. His gaze never seemed to stop investigating his surroundings. "I'm sure you've read all about the case. So what is it that I can help you with?" he said as he led them into a small conference room at the Denver Field Office. "By the way, can I get you some coffee?"

Joel glanced over at the archaic Mr. Coffee machine in the corner, resisting an extemporary cringe. "No, thanks."

The table in the small room had a well-worn surface with a slightly sticky texture. After making initial contact with it, Joel squeamishly lowered his hands to his side. "We were wondering if you could take us through the events following Marjorie's dinner at the Stevens' home the night of the shooting."

Watson looked through his notes and then read through them, paraphrasing.

"Granger and Marjorie left 231 Dove Street at approximately 9:00 p.m. They stopped by the Circle K on Roosevelt, and then drove to her place around 9:40 p.m. He left there about 12:15 a.m. At about 12:30 a.m., 911 got a call from a neighbor about some gunfire, and the police that investigated the call found Special Agent Marjorie Madison thirty minutes later. Three slugs were found in her apartment. One of them was fatal."

"Talk to us about Granger's alibi," Codi said.

"Pretty solid. The security camera at his home recorded him entering at the time of the shooting."

Joel piped up. "Did you discover anything unusual or out of place at her apartment?"

"No, nothing like that," responded SA Watson.

"Was there camera footage from the Circle K?" Codi asked.

"Yes, but nothing out of the ordinary."

"Is there a chance we could see that and the security footage from his home?" Joel asked.

"Sure, but I'll have to send it to you. All that stuff is filed away in our warehouse. It's been a few years, you know. What is it you're looking for, Agents?"

"Just trying to turn over every rock, plus a few more," Joel answered. "This is not a reflection on your case, just fresh eyes. You never know."

"True," SA Watson said.

"Three bullets doesn't sound like a random drive-by," Codi said. "It sounds more planned to me."

"That's what I initially thought as well. But we never made any connection to prove otherwise."

"Were there any other cases she was working at the time that might have caused this kind of reaction?" Joel asked.

"Nothing we could find. And let me tell you, I looked. Special Agent Marjorie Madison was well loved here."

"Thank you for your time, Special Agent Watson," Codi said. "We get these cold cases every so often in Special Projects, and we gotta ask and pry."

"I get it. I had the opportunity to personally work with Marjorie, and she was a good person. I hope you find something we missed." SA Watson stood as he spoke.

"We'll let you know."

"Appreciate it," SA Watson said as he shook Joel's hand.

***

Detective Chris Gasser left the yoga studio feeling refreshed. He had taken it up on his captain's advice, something to keep him healthy and mobile. It also served as an outlet from the crazy that was his job. He almost always wore a grin leaving the studio, not just because it was 70 percent females doing various poses, but it re-set his soul. He hadn't bothered to change into street clothes tonight because his next stop was home. An older apartment in Highland Park with an ice-cold Heineken was waiting for him. He slipped into his '97 black convertible Ford Mustang and started the engine. It was easily one of the model's ugliest designs, but the thing just wouldn't die, the one criterion Detective Gasser required before buying a new car.

He pulled out of the parking lot and down the street, listening to the rattle in the air conditioner as it worked overtime trying to push away the accumulated heat. He let his thoughts wander to his personal life. It was an unsolvable case with no end in sight. His landlord had just given him notice; they were selling the building. He had not yet put much thought into the idea of moving. Perhaps he'd move out of the city. Lately, the only good news was the report back from his colonoscopy.

He had yet to find a woman who would put up with the fluidity of his job. His relationships started off great, but soon, one or the other found a reason why it couldn't go on. After so many years, he had just stopped trying. Now in his early forties, it seemed like he needed to give it one more shot. He figured if it was meant to be, it would just happen—organically, the yoga way. The thought made his grin fade. That would be like fishing without bait. He needed to make an effort if he expected a reward. Maybe he would finally try one of those dating sites.

Detective Gasser didn't notice the late model white sedan that had fallen in pace behind him as his thoughts freely flowed. It stayed two car lengths back and had to make a quick lane change and accelerate to catch a yellow light. Three blocks later, it pulled behind him at a red light. The passenger got out and walked calmly up to his passenger side window. A couple of taps on the glass pulled Gasser from his thoughts, and he looked over. It was Danzo, and he was pointing a pistol at him.

Immediately, Gasser reached for his gun. The sounds of gunshots and broken glass were the last thing he heard as everything dimmed.

The light turned green. Danzo ran back to the car and jumped into the passenger side. Chico pulled out around the Mustang that was slowly creeping into the intersection. They turned right and zoomed off.

A couple of blocks later, Chico pulled to the side. "Boss, get out of here. I'll go dump the car and wipe it all down."

Danzo stepped from the car. "I'll meet you at the club, and we can plan round two."

A curt nod was followed by the car driving away.

***

The return trip to DC was uneventful, just what you want from a major airline. Codi had gotten back to her apartment just before lunch. She was torn on whether to go into the office that late on a Friday, ultimately deciding to take an Uber south to see Matt. They had unfinished business, and the few benign Zoom calls and unreturned texts were not doing it for her. No more investigating for the day. Besides, her apartment was still a mess, and she had yet to decide what to do with it.

She was supposedly engaged to Matt, though that was somewhat in question after their last encounter. He was trying to slow things down just as she was trying to speed them up. The conversation ended with high emotion and a few tears. Since then, she had put the whole thing out of her mind. But with each mile she closed on his house, her thoughts intensified.

Matt lived in a cute beach house. Maybe she should forget about everything, her apartment, their recent drama, and just move in with him. On the other hand, she still liked her independence. Codi fidgeted with her ring finger. The missing engagement ring was just another question mark in their current relationship.

Now that her assailants were under arrest, her apartment was safe to return to. Why push it? Besides, Matt didn't seem anxious about pushing it, either. She sent Matt a text of her ETA and resolved to make a decision once she spoke to him face-to-face. She tabled the seesaw of conflicting emotions, focusing instead on her apartment. Her insurance company had sent her a nice check, and she wanted to take the time to remodel it right.

The Uber pulled into the driveway, and she got out. A dim orange glow came from the front of the house as Codi walked to the porch. It was always cooler down by the water than in the city. As the sun dipped for the day, the weather was finally tolerable.

Codi swatted at a mosquito as she unlocked the front door and entered the house. The lights were out and candles were burning in the dining room.

"Power outage?" Codi called out.

Matt entered the room with an apron on. "Nope, romance is on the menu, and I have ordered myself an extra-large helping of idiot pie. Please, please forgive me and let me make it up to you. He offered her a hand-written menu and escorted her to the dining room table. "Right this way, madame."

The table was set with his best dishes and a bottle of champagne chilling in a silver ice bucket. There were several covered dishes with wisps of escaping steam and even linen napkins. He pulled her chair out for her and guided her to her seat. Once seated, Matt tossed his apron away and took the seat across from her. He sat there with a goofy, expectant look.

Codi opened the menu and inspected the contents. There were pictures of several magnificent wedding venues pasted inside, with dates of availability written below them. Codi shot a look over the menu to her fiancé.

"All you gotta do is pick one," he said.

***

Joel left the office after writing up most of the report for their Denver travels. The case was now better known to them, but there was no new or compelling evidence to progress it. Monday, they would re-shelve it and start on the next one. Just another failed cold case. It was frustrating but expected, something with which they each had come to terms. He clicked through his mental list for the rest of the day. Stops by the dry cleaners and grocery store were next, followed by a hot shower and some grilled chicken and hummus. He pulled his Prius out of the car park and turned north toward Brightwood. A quick stop at Whole Foods provided everything he needed for his planned Saturday dinner with Shannon. They had been officially dating for a little over a year, and just the thought of her gave him a warm feeling.

Shannon Poole of the Royal Canadian Mounted Police was stationed in DC as a liaison officer. She had long auburn hair with steel-blue eyes and a button nose. His mind flashed to the more curvy parts of their relationship as the corner of his lips reached for the sky. She was toned, with a very appealing mole right next to her—

"Hey! Watch where you're going!"

Joel popped out of his trance to realize he was standing in the street. He quickly moved back to the curb with an "I'm sorry" wave.

Shannon had worked with the Special Projects team on a previous case that involved some careful US and Canadian collaboration. She and Joel had found something special between them and a bond soon formed. She loved Joel for all the right reasons: his loyalty, honesty, and kindness. She even put up with his quirky ways, the book smarts over street smarts. Joel had been infatuated since the first time she walked into the office. He could still remember her scent as she strode past him down the hallway with a sexy saunter that nearly dropped him to his knees. It wasn't long before they had taken a weekend trip to meet her parents. Joel rubbed his butt subconsciously, feeling the memory of her extremely active parents and the snowboarding trip that left him bruised and battered trying to keep up with them.

Joel had grown up in the suburbs of Chicago and had excelled as a pianist. Then he'd spent most of his youth on a computer. He earned a full ride to MIT at age seventeen but struggled to find a way to fit into the social side of the college experience. He would often find a corner of the library and hide out on Friday nights, doing homework or gaming. His parents were both professionals who were happy to see their only son leave home and go off on his own. The family had a once-a-year perfunctory Christmas get-together and rarely talked in between.

Joel had a natural likability with his individual, uptight, waggish style. He was never a threat to other males, and women found him cute but geeky. The real issue was his nervousness around strangers. He liked people and people liked him; he just was not good at being normal around people he didn't know. It was the chicken or the egg quandary that he couldn't quite get past. So he ended up spending more time alone than not.

Shannon was a bright shining light in his life who had transformed Joel. He was becoming a new man. He was even trying to find a way for her to meet his parents, but the timing never seemed to work out. He asked them for their schedule but got only a vague answer. In his heart, he knew they weren't interested. They didn't represent the best of him and that, in itself, was like a stuck anchor to his planning.

Would Shannon be turned off if she didn't like them or they didn't like her? Would she think less of him?

Joel pulled into a parking stall and got out of his car, his thoughts still on the woman of his dreams. He collected his dry cleaning and headed back to the vehicle. Hotel Zena across the street was a small boutique that catered to foreign and political visitors. Joel looked over just in time to see a familiar shape. It was Shannon, walking down the steps from the lobby. He raised his hand and started to call out when a man in a business suit stepped out of a G-wagon and into her arms. There was a passionate hug followed by a kiss. Joel froze with his hand still up and his mouth open, unable to breathe as he watched the two turn and head back inside the hotel. It took a good five minutes before Joel could move. A passerby had laid two dollars at his feet for his skills as a human statue. Joel spun, leaving the money where it lay as he dragged himself back to his car. His heart was beating out of his chest with fear and anxiety. His thoughts spun in circles but went nowhere.

He had no memory of driving home or of leaving the food behind in the car. The only image in his mind was Shannon kissing another man. It was locked in slow-motion auto-replay, and he couldn't see anything else.

Chapter Eleven

LAGUNA BEACH, CALIFORNIA – 9:46 A.M.

Atlantis closed the door to her office and moved to the polished wood desk in the center of the room, a room that smelled of lilac and roses. A strong overhead light illuminated the documents she laid down as she sat. Chung-Woo had some influential friends, and Operation Redirect, as far as she could tell, was far-reaching and a bit scary in scope. Though she wasn't one to play politics, the idea of systematically killing off any person of power that opposed you seemed like political suicide. Kim Jong-un seemed to have none of those concerns. His bid to maintain control over his country came with very few rules or regrets, and if he could win world favor by eliminating his nay-sayers, why not?

The list she had been delivered was not only large, but it also contained some very high-ranking officials. She would need to be clear and careful from here on out. She had no concerns over killing these people, just concerns over not leaving a trail to her doorstep. Chung-Woo had promised support and resources. The pay, however, was not on par with her usual fees.

She pushed the documents away and leaned back in her chair. Fingertips circled her temples as she processed her current situation. The North Korean hit-list was just as she had expected. A list of names to be crossed off. Some were unfamiliar to her; others were well known. The president's chief of staff would be hard to get at, but the vice president would be even harder. She had heard both of them speak out publicly against the DPRK and its policies.

This was a tall order, one that would require her to be at her absolute best. She popped a Tootsie Pop into her mouth and moved it from cheek to cheek, dwelling on the matter.

***

Special Agent Gerald Whitestone scratched at the back of his thirty-eight-year-old right hand as he paced the small white waiting room. A potpourri of harsh chemicals and decomp spilled into the space, just enough to give him a small sample of what was to come. It was a familiar smell, one he loathed. He had only been sitting for a few minutes, but the walls seemed to be closing in, so he stood and moved instead.

The FBI Field Office in Philadelphia had been his home for the last five years, and he was considering making it permanent. He had bounced around a few cities throughout his career, but this felt more like home to him than any place so far. That he had always been a big Eagles fan helped. SA Whitestone was a short man of dubious origins. Some might say mulatto, with a Haitian mom and a Hispanic/Greek dad, according to a mail-in DNA test.

His friends were envious of his perma-tanned skin, showcasing a bright and happy smile and brownish-green eyes. But none of that seemed to match his name's origin or how he identified himself in this world. The disconnect had triggered his natural investigative spirit to find out more. Both his parents had died young, and he had no other family to give him clues about his heritage. But he had long ago come to terms with his obfuscated past. What really concerned him now was his future, which was something new for him after years of trying to discover who he was and where he came from.

Following a complex path, he met a like-minded woman, Callie Morales, at a genealogy forum at a local church. She had shown him the ins and outs of tracing one's family tree, and he returned the favor in the bedroom after they'd known each other just three hours. It was not the norm for Gerald or Callie, and it had stirred something in each that had them both forgetting their ancestors and looking in the other direction on their timeline.

Gerald's thoughts turned to that first night as he watched a decorous thirty-year-old Callie with perfect olive skin and stunning milk-coffee eyes acquiesce to his unusually forward actions. He had heard the term soulmates before but was sure he was destined to never know the true meaning. It was as if they were two magnets placed in proximity to each other. Gerald started off slowly, but the moment his lips touched Callie's, there was some sort of transference. Like an electrical current that flowed between them, it ignited something deep within him, and he could tell she felt it too. They had gone from that simple kiss to ravaging their clothes so fast that both completely lost all control. The intensity was like nothing either had experienced before, and once their clothes had been stripped away, revealing the raw nakedness of lust and passion, there was only a single pathway left to follow.

"Special Agent Whitestone?"

The words pulled at Gerald's conscience like a child with a loose thread. He blinked the images from his mind's eye and turned to the source of the voice.

"Yes, I'm he," Gerald said as he showed the man his badge.

"I'm Doctor Goto. Sorry to keep you waiting." He held the door open for Gerald and dispensed with a handshake having learned long ago that most people were hesitant to shake a coroner's hand. The smell hit Gerald like an unseen stone wall, and he pushed through it into the room. It was a direct contrast to the odor, modern with bright LED lighting and white subway tiled walls. There was plenty of stainless steel and a drain in the center of the floor. An examination table in the room had a thin white sheet outlining the form of a human corpse.

Gerald stepped to the center of the room, letting his senses adjust to the environment. He lifted the sheet just enough to confirm identity and then returned it. As he looked at the doctor, he tried to place his heritage—*Japanese, Korean . . . and Irish?* "So what can you tell me, Doc?"

The forty-something coroner with a short haircut and stature had a straggly beard and several smears of blood on his lab coat. He had an unsettling habit of standing perfectly still, even when speaking. Only his lips moved as if he was a robot running on low batteries.

"From what I can tell, this man died suddenly of natural causes."

"That makes no sense," Gerald said while turning to read the doctor's facial expression.

"I would agree, but there is nothing here to show otherwise and, as I'm sure you can appreciate with your own heavy caseload, we do the best we can in the time allowed us."

His body had not moved, not even his hands, as he spoke. He just stood like a statue, staring. Lips hardly parted with each word.

"The file's on the table if you want a look. The basics are disseminated intravascular coagulation along with a consumptive coagulopathy as the cause of death."

Gerald picked up the file and stopped mid-flip of the front cover.

"You doctors love doing that, don't you?"

Dr. Goto made no movement of any kind to answer.

"You use your medical lingo like a barrier to keep us mere mortals in the dark. You talk above your patient's heads and force them to rely on your judgment as the all-knowing expert. I guess it's some kind of God complex. But let me see here . . . disseminated intravascular coagulation—blood clotting throughout the body. Consumptive coagulopathy—that would be blood so thick it won't pump anymore."

"Impressive and close enough," Doctor Goto said, "and might I say you detectives are all the same. Always trying to find a crime even when there is none. You can get a confession out of an innocent person just by leaving them in the room long enough and waiting for them to talk. I guess it's your suspicious nature."

"Touché, Doc, but we are talking about a United States congressman here." Gerald opened the file and thumbed through it. He scanned words like ecchymosis and hematuria. Afraid to ask, he turned the page and saw a close-up photo of the patient's left hand. A small rash in the shape of Long Island was clearly visible on the back of the hand. Gerald moved to the victim and pulled his left hand from under the sheet. There it was.

"What do you make of this?" Gerald said while holding up the vic's hand.

"A rash. Not suspicious by itself and, honestly, I could make no connection to it and the reason his entire system failed. According to the hospital, he came in with severe flu-like symptoms and died three days later in spite of their best efforts."

"What do you think caused it?" Gerald asked.

"There are a few things that lead to mortal disseminated intravascular coagulation, like sepsis or cancer. Both tested negative. Less common causes are frostbite and some snakebites, but there is clearly no evidence of that here."

Mortal disseminated intravascular coagulation. The words were familiar to Gerald. Had he seen them in a previous case, or maybe it was a movie? He shook the thoughts from his head. "You looked for puncture wounds?"

"Hundred percent, and there was no mention of it from the patient before he died. If a snake bit me, I'd know it, and he would too. We also did a careful inspection for an injection site—nothing."

Gerald nodded, taking it all in. "Could it be some kind of poison, possibly transmitted through the skin?" He held up the hand with the rash as Exhibit A.

"No known poisons showed up in the tests." The doctor barely moved his head from side to side. "I did a skin scrape as well."

"What about *un*known?"

Doctor Goto just stared at Gerald.

"Any idea what could suddenly cause a healthy person to die of hemorrhagic syndrome so quickly?"

"Other than some kind of extreme sepsis, none, and, as I said, that wasn't the case."

"Okay, Doc, you made your point. Died suddenly of natural causes. But do me a favor and have the lab run the blood again. Have them check for all known toxins and poisons and send me the e-file when you're done. Thanks." Gerald handed the file back to Doctor Goto and started for the exit door eager to get outside into some fresher downtown Philly air.

"Oh, Special Agent?"

Gerald turned around.

"It's a shame. Representative Bobby Carlyle was doing good things for this town."

Gerald just nodded and left the room.

The short drive back to the eighth floor at 600 Arch Street was filled with a series of "what ifs" running through his thoughts. Gerald never liked to close a case until he was absolutely sure, and in the current mindset of the Bureau, that had no place. If the facts lined up, close it, no matter your feelings or hunches. Luckily, he and his boss were on good terms, and a little out-of-the-box investigating would be tolerated.

The dark brown building with small vertical windows filled his windshield as he turned into the underground structure and parked. A swift security check and an elevator ride with a young lady consumed by her smartphone led to his office. The room was an open, bullpen style, with nine desks in three rows. Additional offices bordered on two sides, and a series of boxy windows on the west wall allowed the waning sun to cut across the beige carpet. The familiar smell of bad coffee and failed dreams filled the room, but no one seemed to take the time to notice. They were all caught up in the machine that demanded constant attention.

Gerald ran his hands across his shaved head and removed his black-rimmed glasses. The ever-present scruff on his face disliked by management was his only hold-out against Bureau best practices and standards. He turned his computer on and, against his better judgment, began his report on Representative Bobby Carlyle's unfortunate death, not murder. He would wait for the final lab tests to return before sending it in.

His thoughts turned back to Callie and what she might be up to. As an up-and-coming actuary at a prestigious accounting firm, her life had been ruled by logic and numbers. *Math can't lie*, she said, *but humans do, and they often let you down.* She had experienced that many times in both the work and dating realms. Gerald had felt sorry for her at the time, but quickly realized he had an opinion just as extreme. *Everyone lies. The truth falls somewhere in between their words.* The two of them were surely meant for each other. Peas of the same pod. He would do everything in his power to not let her down.

***

"What, no coffee?"

"No, didn't have time," Joel answered, with a morose expression.

Codi watched as her partner moved robot-like into his cubicle and plopped down in his chair. His shoulders slumped, and his body language was all wrong. She wheeled across the hall and into his space.

"That's not like you. Rough weekend?" she asked.

"Had better," came the reply without his turning toward her. He just sat, staring at his blank computer screen.

"Okay. Been there. I'm right in my office if you want to talk about it. I'll finish up our report on the Denver trip. It's gonna be like reading a bad short story with no conclusion or results, just a lot of flowery words that lead nowhere. I just have to spin it in the right direction. How do you spell *fiasco*?" Codi said as she watched the back of his head for a response. Still nothing.

"I already sent it in," he said.

"Okay . . ." Codi slowly rolled back into her space and opened her computer. It was going to be a long day.

"Can I have a chat with you two in the conference room?"

Joel and Codi looked up from their desks to see ASSA Holloway standing in the hallway. They followed her to the room across from her office with two walls of floor-to-ceiling glass, known as the fishbowl. Today, it was a conference room, Codi concluded, as she sat at the folding table in a blue molded plastic chair.

"I read your report on the trip you two took last week."

Codi glanced over at her partner, wondering what he had written, as she had not had a chance to open the file and get up to speed.

"I realize my predecessor approved your travel, and I was not yet in a position to stop it, but I just wanted to take a second to reiterate our current policy and go over what I am talking about so you two can clearly understand my goal. It is always best when we work together with the same goals." ASSA Holloway turned on the laptop she had placed on the table and looked at a file. "According to your report, you had three interviews in the Denver area and were not able to progress the case forward. The total cost to our department, including airfare and hotels, is just under . . ." She pulled up something from another program and read from it. ". . . just under three grand. Three grand for nothing. I have three words for you—Skype, Zoom, Teams, Facetime."

"That's four wor—" Joel suddenly went silent, realizing his error.

"The point is, I intend to fix this broken system, and I can't do it alone. I need good people to help me make it happen, people I can count on and trust to do things my way. There are over 35,000 FBI agents in the US, and that doesn't account for the many police officers and sheriffs out there. It is my intention to take advantage of this network and solve cases while saving taxpayer money."

Codi let her thoughts wander while her head did an occasional nod. The boss continued for several more minutes before asking for their commitment to her plan.

"Of course," Joel said with forced determination. Then they were dismissed, leaving the room like school kids late for recess.

Joel kept his head down as they walked back to their offices. "Does she want us to close cases or solve them, and how are we supposed to do that over the phone?"

"I'm not sure," came Codi's intentionally lackluster response, "but it sounds like we are about to find out if we can."

She plopped down into her office chair just as an alert on her phone popped up with a 20 percent-off furniture store coupon.

"Hey, Joel got a second?" Codi rolled over to her partner's desk.

"What is it?"

"Which do you think? Beige or cream?" Codi asked.

Joel looked at her phone displaying two nearly identical couches. "I would call those taupe and linen."

"Joel."

"Sorry, please tell me you are going to add some throw pillows with color to this."

"Absolutely."

"Okay. So not all linens—I mean creams—are created equal. You have to judge the frame; make sure they have sinuous springs and high-density foam inside the cushions."

"Joel, just pick one."

He paused, disappointed, and then pointed to the one on the left. "This one looks more design-neutral, so it won't date as fast."

"Probably get shot up again before that happens," Codi said as she pressed the green order button.

"How is your apartment coming?"

"Almost done patching and painting. They replaced the whole door and frame. It was shot to pieces. That wasn't you, was it?"

"No. I was diving for my life when they blasted your door and wall to pieces. I'm the one who shot up your couch."

"Well, I am planning to move back in on Thursday." Codi picked up a file on a stack next to Joel's laptop and opened it. "Some of these cold cases they gave us are *really* cold."

"You're just now noticing that?"

"Check this one out." Codi set the file on Joel's desk. He eyed it suspiciously. "A federal agent for BLM gets whacked in his home in 1960, and they think we have some hope of solving it, what, fifty years later?"

"B. L. M., Black Lives Matter?" Joel said as he picked up the file.

"Bureau of Land Management. Part of the US Department of the Interior. They're the people who have stewardship over public lands not owned or designated as part of the park system."

"Like for grazing and mining," Joel said as he perused the file. "I read something like they maintain control of the entire US helium reserves."

"Sounds like one of your late-night conspiracy theories. Anyhow, this BLM law enforcement officer . . ." Codi looked at the cover page of the file. "Officer Harry Wells gets killed in his home, not on federal land, but because he is technically a federal employee, it gets dumped on our desk."

"Harry Wells. Sounds like a bad place to go for water."

"What?"

"Harry Wells?"

"Really."

Joel quickly changed the subject. "Doesn't look like any other agents besides the agent in charge of the original case has ever gone back through this."

"That's weird."

"Everyone deserves justice," he added.

"Nice speech. Did you practice that in the mirror this morning?"

The flash of red across Joel's face told Codi she was probably right.

"So . . ." Joel said.

"So what?"

"So let's see if we can close a case the boss's way."

"Hard pass," Codi quickly replied.

"What other choice do we have?"

Codi leaned back in her chair, hating the very thought of it.

Joel looked at her expectantly.

"Okay, just this one case, and then I'm going to break so many of ASSA Bruster Holloway's new rules, she'll wish she was back at Quantico babysitting NATs."

Joel remembered when he was a new agent in training at Quantico and didn't know what to say, so he just kept quiet.

Codi rolled back into her office without another word, holding the folder.

"I'll need a copy of that case file," Joel called out meekly.

***

"Sorry I'm late," Codi called out to be heard. "I think Uber is on strike. Had to find a cab. What's with the tourist location?"

The wharf along the Washington Channel was just under the I-395 freeway. It was a popular tourist stop with multiple seafood markets, cafés, and novelty stores. The air was ripe with damp seafood and seagull crap.

"Jessie's makes the best spiced shrimp in town. Come on." SA Greta Goodson led Codi through the crowd over to a large white metal building with red awnings. She wore her hair in cornrows with blonde streaks woven into each one. She had on black fitted pants and a matching black blouse with red buttons. Codi felt a bit self-conscious, as she had barely gotten her hair into a ponytail, and her clothes had come from a suitcase at Matt's house.

They joined the line of people all waiting to order. Codi looked over the menu board posted for all to see. There was a raw bar, steam bar, fry bar, and grill.

"So according to the case notes I'm working, you lost your wedding ring?"

"Engagement ring," Codi countered.

"Who's the lucky person?"

"His name is Matt, and he works at a think-tank for DARPA," Codi replied.

"Went for the brains, huh? I feel ya. It's good to know where you stand."

Codi gave Greta a curious glance.

"Hey, I'm just askin'."

"I'm just sayin'," Codi replied.

There was a moment of awkwardness as each agent refused to make eye contact.

"Greta, you didn't lure me here to make a pass at me, did you?"

"In a way, yes. But it's not how you're thinking. I'm the kind of person that likes to collect strong people in my friend circle."

"Friend circle?"

"That's what I call it. And I'm especially fond of women. I mean, we gotta stick together, am I right?" Greta said the last part with her eyebrows raised.

"Especially if we are to rule the world," Codi added.

"Exactly. So what are you thinking?"

Codi wasn't sure what was being asked of her.

"To *eat,* girl."

"I'll have what you're having," Codi responded.

"Oh, sister, it is hot. Hope you brought some pepper spray in that purse of yours to cool it down." Greta's dimples were on full display.

"The hotter the better," Codi shot back, with doubt in her words.

"You sure you're not single?"

The two agents laughed at the comment as they stepped up to place their order.

***

Danzo lowered the iPhone he was using to zoom in all the way on the camera app. "Impossible."

"What is it?" Chico asked.

"The other woman. It's the fed the Three Amigos saw get killed."

"Apparently not."

"Remind me to have them killed the day they walk out of prison."

They had discreetly followed the agent working their case from her office. She had stopped by the police station and then led them here.

"So what now?"

"It looks like it's time to feed the birds. You go right, and I'll head left. Here, put this on. Unlike the intersection with the detective, this place is loaded with cameras."

Chico put on the baseball hat and pulled up his hoody. Danzo matched his actions.

"I'll meet you at the lot afterward."

They moved off in different directions.

***

"I see you've done this before," Codi said while watching Greta use her open purse to hold a cold bottle of Perrier. They were standing across from each other in a space that most people considered the eating area. Families, couples, and singles all stood around, holding their fresh seafood and eating it while standing. Some had their drinks in the crook of an elbow and others just put them down. An assortment of birds did their best to fight over anything that hit the ground.

Codi used her fingers to pop a shrimp into her mouth. It took exactly two seconds for her to realize what she had done.

"Oh, wow! You aren't kidding. That is packing some heat!" Codi exclaimed.

"Uh-huh," was the only reply she got.

"Might need some milk after this."

"Uh-huh."

The comments made Codi laugh, and the two agents took turns eating and cooling with their ice-cold drinks.

"There is something you should know," Greta said as she wiped some excess sauce from her lips.

Codi looked up at Greta, waiting for her to continue.

"It might be nothing, but Detective Gasser was shot and killed three days ago. If it had anything to do with this case, it might be wise for both of us to watch our backs." She finished the thought and then went right back to eating as if she had never said it.

Codi paused and let her lips burn, thinking about her destroyed apartment. *Were they gunning for her or just her money and belongings?*

***

Danzo moved through the crowd, stalking his prey. He had spotted the two feds from the overpass walkway but had lost them once he was down on their level. He hoped Chico was having better luck. A child shot into his path, nearly knocking him over, but he paid the kid no mind. Even the mother's attempt at an apology was lost on him. He left the lines of people waiting to order or receive their food. Closer to the water, there was a large gathering, people eating and chatting in groups. He began a search pattern, meandering back and forth, culling the herd as he went.

***

Codi grabbed several French fries that came with the shrimp, hoping they would help dampen the fire in her mouth. As they reached her lips, something caught her eye. A man was moving through the crowd with purpose, and he was headed in their direction. He wasn't carrying food, and his hand was reaching under his sweatshirt. Once he was within a few feet, she stepped closer to Greta and placed her hand around the back of her neck.

Greta immediately stiffened, the look on her face filled with confusion. "What are you doing?"

"I think they're here."

As the gun came out of the man's belt, Codi reacted. She pulled Greta toward her and down, sending her sprawling away from trouble. Then she launched her spicy hot shrimp, sauce and all, at the attacker. The Scoville rating on pepper spray is around two million. The spicy shrimp was just under a million, but it was enough. As the dark red sauce contacted his skin and eyes, the gunman stopped in his tracks. He let out a high-pitched scream and dropped to the floor. Codi stepped over and used a stomp-kick to further disable the man. His gun dropped and skittered off. She placed her knee in his back and quickly handcuffed him as he continued to scream about his eyes. People all around started to back away from the ruckus.

***

A scream to Danzo's left sent his eyes that way. A body flew in his direction, making contact, and he went down in a heap.

The woman pushed up and off of him. It was the fed he was after.

"I'm so sorry," she said while reaching out a hand. "Here, let me help you up."

"You!" Danzo said as he reached for his gun.

It took Greta only a second to recognize the man as the missing suspect/boss from her case. He was reaching for his gun, and she was not going to get to hers in time.

Codi spun back to check on Greta. When she had yanked her away from the first gunman, she had flung her a bit too hard. Poor Greta had taken out a civilian. Codi moved to help make amends for her actions. As she got closer, she saw he was reaching for a gun. She sprinted at her lunchmate, crashing into her back and sending her into the man on the ground. There was a *humph* and a smack, followed by the man's gun scraping across the blacktop as it left his grasp. The man on the ground spun and rolled toward his gun. He collected it up in one fluid movement, then he rose to a knee and fired.

Codi and Greta instinctively dove in different directions. The bullet never reached its intended mark, instead making impact with a man's thigh who was walking past the fray, completely unaware. He dropped to the ground, spilling his blood and his lunch.

Danzo tracked Greta, firing at her as she tried to get away. Several innocent bystanders fell in the onslaught. She pulled her own Sig P226 attempting to return fire, but people were running in all directions screaming. Her site picture was a chaotic mess.

Codi rolled to her stomach next to a trashcan and pulled her weapon. She stayed prone trying to make herself a small target and used the trashcan for concealment. The shooter was about thirty feet away, focused on Greta. She took careful aim and patiently waited for the bodies to clear. Legs of every size and length ran through her sight obscuring her target and making it impossible to make the shot without casualties.

An obese man, blinded by fear, ran crazily through the masses. His only focus was the parking lot in the distance. Birds flew in every direction as the large man plowed into the kneeling Danzo without even slowing down. Danzo's body was like a speed bump to a monster truck. Danzo, however, looked like he'd been hit by a freight train and was thrust airborne, spinning out to the left. For just the briefest second, as he made his trajectory, Greta had a clear shot. She tracked him through the air and pulled the trigger twice. The Sig held true, and both bullets found their mark.

It was over. Danzo collapsed to the ground. His last view was of the two women who had taken him down. His face turned to rage as pain took over and his heart gave out.

Codi stood, shaken but unharmed. She looked down without remorse at the man who had orchestrated so much pain in her life.

Greta moved to the lifeless body and removed Danzo's gun. She checked his pulse and then collapsed next to him.

"You okay?" Codi asked as she stepped over to Greta.

"Yeah, just never had to shoot anyone before."

"It was us or them."

Greta nodded slowly, then reached out for a hand up. Codi could see blood on both knees, but it was superficial. It occurred to her that the man who had been screaming like a child behind her had stopped. Codi pulled her gun and pointed it without looking back.

"I don't think so," she called out.

Chico was trying to get away in the aftermath. He stopped and plopped back down, tears streaming from his bloodshot eyes. The agents cuffed him, helped the wounded, and took control of the crime scene.

Soon, sirens could be heard in the distance, and Codi looked around at the concession stands to see if anyone sold milk. Her lips were still on fire.

Greta looked over at Codi's flushed face. "That was a bit extreme to get out of having to finish your spicy shrimp, don't you think?"

Chapter Twelve

NATIONAL ARCHIVES – WASHINGTON, DC – 9:48 A.M.

The National Archives is one of several repositories where old FBI case files are stored. It is located north of the National Mall at 700 Pennsylvania Avenue. The impressive stone portico entrance gives way to the famous rotunda inside that holds the country's founding documents, including the Declaration of Independence. The Archives are also the storage site for FBI hard files dated from 1907 to 1993. The more recent federal case files are stored along with the corresponding electronic data at the various offices that investigated the cases. The most famous cases of the past have been transferred to electronic data and are used as training scenarios at Quantico. The more well-known unsolved cases periodically make their way around various FBI offices in hopes that new technologies or new evidence will shed new light. Several buildings throughout the US share the burden of storage, depending on the location. Joel had tracked the case files for Officer Harry Wells to the Riverside Federal Records Center in California. Upon request, the files were then shipped out to the National Archives Building in DC.

Joel and Codi had been to enough storage facilities looking through dusty old evidence files to know the drill. But Joel asked beforehand to review the case files along with all evidence, and once they cleared security, the agents found a table with everything waiting for them.

"This is way better than digging through the dust in an old basement," Joel said.

"If you don't mind waiting four days for it to get here."

"It's not like this is a pressing case."

"Granted," Codi said as she opened the box.

"So how are you doing?" Joel asked.

Codi gave him a cryptic look.

"You know, after the shooting?"

"Oh, that. Good . . . fine. Just tired of wearing more bandages than make-up. Glad I didn't kill anyone this time. OPR is a real bite."

Joel nodded knowingly. The Office of Professional Responsibility was the FBI's version of internal affairs. Anytime there was a killing, even in self-defense, they would be called in.

Codi pulled out the first thing in the box and held it up. "Looks like an old miniature film strip," she said holding it to the light, the black and white celluloid stiff in her fingers.

"Whoa, microfiche, that's cool. Never thought I'd use one," Joel said with genuine excitement. "This is how they stored case file photos back in the day."

Slowly, they removed everything from the box. Joel documented it all with his smartphone and tried to organize it. There were two vials of blood.

"Looks like this one dried up," Codi said while holding a vial up to the light. "The other one seems fine." She set them down on the table and reached into the box and pulled out a bag with an old radio in it. Joel reached out and Codi handed it to him.

"One of the early compact AM tube radios. Probably worth some money if it still works," Joel added as he wiped his glasses on his sleeve.

"Says here it was the murder weapon but no other details."

Joel set the radio down like it was radioactive.

"Not much else except this black hair." She held up a small glass container with a single dark hair inside and set it on the table. "Okay, let's see what's on the film strips."

"Microfis—" Joel stopped himself mid-word.

The librarian showed them how to work the microfiche/film reader. They took the time to print out each black and white page. It was a laborious process. By 1:00 p.m., they were both thinking about food.

"I'm starving," Codi said, without looking up. "Chicken parm? I know a place nearby."

"Sounds heavy," Joel replied as he flipped a page of the report.

"Okay. What are you thinking?" Codi stopped what she was reading and looked up.

"Anything is fine with me," Joel said, still lost in his reading.

"Okay, chicken parm."

"Except that."

"You said anything."

"You know what I mean."

"No. Not if you don't tell me, I don't."

Joel seemed unfazed by Codi's dialogue, lost in his report.

"Okay, how 'bout tacos?" she threw out.

"Had that for dinner."

"Seriously? Why is it you know what you don't want to eat, but you don't know what you *do* want to eat?"

"It was Taco Tuesday."

"Okay, so no Italian and no Mexican. How 'bout Mediterranean? I know this Turkish place with the best *fladenbrot* with shaved chicken."

"Meh." Joel made a not-in-the-mood face.

"Joel, you are starting to tick me off."

Joel suddenly looked up from his reading and gave a sheepish smile. "Sorry. Okay, chicken parm."

Codi took a calming breath and then realized something. "No, you're right, it does sound heavy," she said, mostly to herself.

Joel sat there frozen, waiting for what was next, hoping he would say the right thing this time.

"How 'bout a salad? And don't say no."

"Yes?" he gambled.

"Perfect."

***

The lab work finally arrived in his email inbox. SA Gerald Whitestone opened it with a click of his finger. He skimmed through the results and frowned at the conclusion of the tox screen—no known toxins or poisons. He pulled up his report, completed the last few paragraphs, and turned it in. It wasn't his best work on a case, but there was nowhere else to go. Case closed. On to the next. He walked out of the building, thinking about his plans for the night. But something at the back of his mind preoccupied him, and he struggled to bring the thought to the surface. As he pushed the elevator button to take him down to the parking structure, it hit him.

Gerald quickly stepped out of the car as the doors slammed back shut. He hurried back to his desk and reopened his computer. It was from a case a year ago where a federal judge had died under suspicious but inconclusive circumstances. He remembered the frustration he always felt when he marked a case unsolved. It was the same way he was feeling now, and there was a forgotten memory in the back of his thoughts that was screaming the similarities. Something familiar. He opened the old case and scanned the autopsy report. His eyes flicked over the words until he found what he was looking for. "Cause of death, mortal disseminated intravascular coagulation." Gerald tapped on the screen with his right hand before leaning back in his chair.

"Gotcha."

The odds of two people in a year, both elected federal employees, dying from an obscure illness with no preexisting conditions were extremely low. And Gerald always played the odds.

Now, to prove his hunch.

He picked up his phone and dialed, but before he could connect, his cell phone vibrated. He dug into his pocket and peeked at the screen before stabbing the green answer button.

"Are we still on for tonight?" It was a sultry voice with a touch of a smile behind the words.

A chill of excitement went up Gerald's spine. "Yes, but I have a couple of things to follow up on. I'll be thirty minutes late, at the most."

"Good, that will give me time to slip into something more comfortable," Callie said, maintaining the pretend deep voice.

Gerald almost booked out of his office right then and there, but thirty minutes he could do. He hung up. It took a moment before he remembered what he was doing and redialed the first number.

"Medical Examiner's office, may I help you?" a metallic voice said on the line.

"Yes, this is Special Agent Gerald Whitestone. I'm looking for Dr. Goto."

"One moment, please." There was a clicking noise followed by a very upbeat music track for a morgue.

Gerald drummed his fingers on his desk as his thoughts raced with the possibility of a connection.

"Yes?"

"Dr. Goto? It's Special Agent Whitestone."

"What can I do for you, Agent?"

"I need you to send a sample of Representative Bobby Carlyle's blood over to the FBI lab at Quantico."

The call was brief and business-like, and Gerald followed it up with a carbon copy to the morgue in Mount Holly where his federal judge case originated. His last call was over a cell phone as he drove to Callie's house. He had a contact at the FBI lab, and he wanted to give him a heads up as to what he needed them to test for.

Once that was done, his mind finally drifted back to the night ahead of him, and his usually stoic face started to beam.

***

"So what do we know? Besides the obvious," Codi asked as she wrote on the whiteboard in the small conference room. Officer Harry Wells, Law Enforcement Division of the BLM. Single. Electrocuted.

She had started her day doing laps in the pool. It was nice to be getting her old routine back after all the excitement lately. Plus, she always felt invigorated after a good workout.

Codi and Joel had spent the rest of the previous day combing through the documents printed from the microfiche. There were case files, including the autopsy, photographs, and newspaper clippings. For whatever reason, Joel seemed to be just going through the motions. But even then, he was a formidable investigator.

Joel started, "Orphan. He had no family at the time of death. The trauma to his head was antemortem. And there were two different blood types found in the tub water."

Codi wrote the facts down.

"There were two partial prints found that did not match the vic's, a black hair not belonging to Wells was found in the bathroom, and the guy who investigated his murder did a crappy job."

"Joel, I can't write that on the board."

"Did a poor job?"

"No, I can't write it because it is not evidence."

"Right. They found a footprint on the bathroom rug much smaller than the vic's and faint heel scrapes across the living room floor, heading toward the bathroom."

Codi taped the old black-and-white pictures to the board and then stood back to look at the collage. There was a headshot of the blonde-haired Officer Wells next to a shot of him naked and dead in his tub. Codi's list filled most of the middle of the board, and two rows of crime scene photos were hung on the left. "Best guess?"

"Sounds like a smaller person with dark hair dragged Officer Wells's unconscious body across the house and into the tub where the officer came to and put up a fight. There was a brief scuffle causing both men to bleed, and ultimately, Wells gets knocked out and the radio was then dumped into the tub. The killer must have been nervous because he didn't clean up all the evidence before he left. So he was clever but not a professional."

"Seems about right," Codi said. "Pretty clear cut that he was murdered. Could have been knocked unconscious somewhere else, and the killer moved the body and used Wells's house to try and cover it all up. So why did they put 'accidental tub fall and electrocution' as the cause of death?"

Neither had an answer. At least, not yet.

"Hey, Codi!"

The two agents looked toward the voice.

SA Gordon Reyas was leaning in the room. "There's an agent from the field office here to see you in the fishbowl."

"Thanks, Gordon," Codi replied as she headed for the door. "Joel, time for a deeper dive," she called back over her shoulder.

SA Greta Goodson looked up as Codi entered. "I've never been up to Special Projects before. What is it you guys do here?" she asked as she gave Codi a quick hug and took a seat.

Codi followed her. "The weird and boring. Anything that doesn't fit into the Bureau's normal investigative lane. Plus, there are cold cases and overflow. Why? Thinking of making a move?"

"No. Just naturally curious. How are your lips feeling?"

"Fine," she smirked, "but I'm not the one who has to go in front of OPR for shooting someone in self-defense. Good luck with that. It's what I call the FBI's 'torture chamber.'"

"That bad?" Greta asked.

"Think Monday morning quarterbacks with axes to grind and fingers to point, all while holding your future in callous disregard."

"Wow. How many times have you had to go through that?"

"I have a frequent flyer card."

"Okay, noted." She lifted a bag and placed it on the table. "I wanted to give you an update. Your case has been turned over to the DA, and it's in the prosecutor's hands. She feels like it's a slam dunk."

"That's good news. What's in the bag?" Codi asked.

"I pulled a few strings," Greta said as she slid the bag over to Codi.

Codi opened it and was surprised to see her cell phone, wallet, and old badge. She rummaged to the bottom and pulled out her engagement ring. A smile sprang across her lips. "Thank you. This means a lot to me."

"Happy to help," Greta said as she stood to leave.

"If you ever change your mind, there's always room here for good agents," Codi added.

Greta turned back. "I hear the new ASSA is making changes."

"On second thought, you'd hate it here. Got any openings at the field office?"

"Always room for good agents." Greta smiled back. "See you around, Codi."

Codi waited until Greta left the room before placing the ring back on her finger. It was still a perfect fit.

As Greta was leaving, ASSA Holloway stepped into the fishbowl and closed the door behind her.

"I've been looking for you."

Codi stood and let the comment lie. If the woman really had been looking for her, she hadn't been trying very hard.

"SA Sanders, you are one of the most decorated agents in my department. The other agents look up to you for guidance and decorum. You are a real asset to this department."

Codi stayed on her feet, waiting for the other shoe to drop. Anytime a supervisor built you up, they were leading toward a fall, and the bigger the compliments up front, the farther the fall.

"It has been just over three weeks since I took over here, and there has already been a shooting involving one of my agents. You, specifically. Now, I was brought into this department to mitigate this sort of thing. That's why I have implemented FRICS to keep you in the office more and not out shooting your gun. I know you didn't shoot anyone, but there was an agent-involved shooting, and you were there. Trouble seems to follow you, Special Agent Sanders. That has got to stop. I won't tolerate it on my watch. I need you to get back to doing things by the book and setting the new standard for all the other agents." ASSA Holloway paused to gather her thoughts.

"Is there a question in all that, ASSA Holloway?" Codi asked.

The woman was taken aback for a beat before responding, "No, but I am watching you. I need my agents safe, and the last thing I'm interested in is having an international incident."

"I couldn't agree more. I have never liked getting kidnapped and being shot at. Thank you for your concern." Codi left the room before her boss could respond.

Codi was at a loss about what to do within her current situation. She was not going to last much longer. A decision for her was looming.

***

Codi helped Matt clear the dishes. It was "Thursday-night-at-Codi's-place-when-she-was-in-town" night. Now that she was not going to be traveling as much, it could become a routine, especially since her apartment was back to normal. The couch had arrived the day before, finishing off her forced remodel. Her landlord had been unusually helpful and efficient at getting the bullet holes patched and repainted.

The space still smelled like fresh paint, but that was better than cordite.

The routine was something they could both look forward to again—Codi's house on Thursdays and Matt's on the weekends.

"Where does this go?" Matt asked, holding up a grease screen.

"Not sure. Where did you find it?"

"In the sink."

"Okay let's put it back there," Codi replied.

"Okay." Matt placed the grease screen back in the sink, even though he had already washed it. "I like your storage system."

"Right," Codi replied.

"That was sarcasm."

"Mr. Sarcasm, can I fix you a drink?"

"Only if you're having one."

"Okay, two ice waters coming up."

Ever since Codi had fought a brief battle with overindulgence, she made it a practice to limit her alcohol intake. Thursday nights were not one of her self-allowed drinking nights. She sat on the couch, and Matt dried his hands and joined her. He put his arm around her, and they both just sat, enjoying the moment.

"Notice anything?" Codi asked, holding up her left hand.

"You got your ring back!"

"They were kind enough to release it from evidence. The thugs kept all my stuff in their van. All that did was further incriminate them, but it allowed me to get it all back."

"That is awesome, but you should have let me put it back on your finger."

Codi looked askance at Matt.

"You know, one knee and all. Now that we're re-engaged again."

"Meaning we weren't engaged while my ring was missing? Dang, I could have stepped out with that blond from the gym who's been hitting on me."

"Wait, what?"

"You're the one with the conditional love," Codi added.

"I think I'm going down the wrong trail here again."

"Ya think?" Codi replied, trying to hide her smile.

Matt squirmed on the couch. "Subject change. I have news," he said.

"Oh yeah? Is this something you can share or are you just going to announce the fact that you have news?"

"Boy, you sure are feisty tonight."

"I think my new boss has managed to get under my skin. Sorry. First, she says I'm an asset and then, in the same sentence, she slams me for things that are completely out of my control."

"Well, you do . . . or have a really nice asset."

"Funny. So what's your announcement?"

"You know how I invented or finished inventing the Skystorm, which the government took over and now calls FCBT?" Matt asked.

"The Skystorm that got us kidnapped and almost killed?"

"It did bring us together."

"True, nothing bonds like blood and bullets. What about it?" Codi asked.

"Well, as you know, my dream has been to fly over a remote village and vaccinate every person in a single pass. Of course, that was before it was stolen and used as a weapon. Anyway, that technology put me square on the radar for this new project. The higher-ups at DARPA have been working with a group that has developed a new way to vaccinate John Q. Public. In fact, the average person will immunize themselves."

"Sounds dubious."

"No, it's really quite unique. It works like a bandage that you put on the back of your hand and then peel a backing off that sends the inoculation through many small snake-tooth-like needles into your skin. Practically painless. They have assigned me to head up the final phase."

"That's fantastic, Matt. I'm so proud of you."

Matt gave one of his boyish grins, and his face turned a light shade of pink. It was a look Codi couldn't resist. "I think we should celebrate," Codi said with renewed enthusiasm.

"Oh, yeah? What did you have in mind?"

"How fast can you get your shirt and pants off?"

Her phone started buzzing, and she glanced at the screen, intending to ignore it, but it was her partner.

"Shoot, hold that thought." She picked up her phone as Matt put his shirt back on. "Hey."

"I have something," Joel said.

"Just a sec, I'll Facetime you. Okay, let me have it," Codi said.

Joel's image popped up on her phone. He was driving with his phone in its holder aimed at himself.

"Say hi to Matt."

"Hi, Matt!"

"Joel," Matt said, while buttoning up his shirt with the look of a sad puppy.

"What are you doing working late? I thought you were seeing Shannon tonight," Codi said.

"Naw, I canceled. This case is in my head now."

Codi let the comment slide. She knew there was nobody better at prying the evidence out of an old case than Joel, but she also knew he would never cancel time with Shannon for a cold case. Something was wrong.

Joel interrupted her thoughts. "In the late fifties, early sixties, the US Air Force was doing secret tests over China Lake in the California desert. Officer Wells was the BLM officer assigned to that chunk of land."

"What kind of secret tests?" Codi asked.

"Back in the fifties, the Russians came out with a MiG that gave them air superiority. The US government offered a $100,000 reward to anyone that would turn over a working one."

"MiG?"

"Yeah, at the time a state-of-the-art Russian fighter jet. In 1958, Lieutenant Mah Choon Hee flew his MiG across the 38th parallel into South Korea where he landed at a US Air Force base. Our government took the jet and disassembled it. They photographed and measured every single part and then reassembled it for testing and training."

"Over the California desert," Codi stated rhetorically.

"Right. That's what was going on when Officer Wells was murdered. There's more to tell, but I'll give it to you at the office tomorrow."

"Sounds like a cover-up to me."

"I agree," Joel responded, then finished the call with, "Catch you later. Bye, Matt."

"See ya," Matt tossed back as the screen went black. He finished tucking his shirt in.

Codi put down her phone, her mind a million miles away.

Matt watched her like a child waiting for a parent to play with them.

She slowly leaned back against the couch, taking it all in as she placed her hands behind her head. She turned to look at Matt. "What?"

"Ugh, nothing. I was just . . . nothing," Matt said, looking a bit forlorn. His dreams of a few moments ago, crushed.

A smirk crept across Codi's face, and she picked up her phone. "Starting the timer now. *Go!*"

Matt realized what she was timing and shifted gears, ripping at his shirt with heedless abandon.

Chapter Thirteen

FBI SPECIAL PROJECTS – WASHINGTON, DC FIELD OFFICE – 8:01 A.M.

Codi wandered into the conference room the next day with both eyes at half-mast.

Joel looked up from his laptop with concern. "Who died?"

"After Matt and I have our Thursday night get-togethers, Friday's a recovery day," she mumbled.

"Can I get you some caffeine?"

"No, just some good news." She sat and rubbed the back of her neck.

"Well, I have booked our first Zoom interrogation for 10:30," Joel announced.

Codi's forehead scrunched up as she lifted her head to her partner.

"You said you would give it a try. Luckily, this is an ex-FBI guy, so odds are good he'll answer the call."

Codi looked up at the board and saw a few new notes Joel had added since her last time in the office. But something more pressing concerned her, so she just said it. "So what's going on with you and Shannon?"

Joel looked like he had swallowed a large gumball that made it only halfway down. "Nothing, why?"

"Joel, it's me, Codi, your partner. Come on, I know all your moods. Something's going on with you. Now, if you don't want to talk about it, fine. Then it's none of my business. But if you do, I'm always here and happy to help or just listen. Okay?"

Joel nodded but said nothing.

Codi held her stare at her partner. He got anxious and looked back at his screen.

"Fine. Bring me up to date on the case you seem so preoccupied with."

Joel nodded and stood, moving to the whiteboard. He used his pointer finger to reinforce his words. "Okay. We know about Lieutenant Mah Choon Hee and the Russian jet he brought with him when he defected."

"MiG," Codi added.

"Right. He . . ." Joel paused like all his energy suddenly left him. He turned and sat back down with a defeated look.

"So you do want to talk about it. What's up?" Codi asked.

He took a large breath to steady himself, then blurted out in one collective groan, "IsawShannonkissinganothermanlastweek."

The words seemed to bounce off the walls several times before Codi could say anything. "What you see and what is real are not always the same."

"I know that," Joel said.

"Have you talked to her?"

Joel hung his head and gave a subtle shake no.

"It might answer a lot of questions." Codi leaned back, thinking where to take this conversation. "Describe to me what you actually saw."

Joel was practically crying as he tried to steel himself for the heartbreaking trip down memory lane. "She was at the hotel when a man with curly blond hair in a fitted Brooks Brothers suit stepped out of a white G-wagon and walked right up to her. They grabbed each other in an embrace and added a very lustful-looking kiss to the hug. They turned hand-in-hand and entered Hotel Zena." He looked spent by the time he finished.

"Hotel Zena, that's nice. And you were?"

"Just across the street. Had a perfect view of the whole thing. How am I supposed to compete with a G-wagon? Maybe I need to go car shopping."

"Ah, no, that is not what's needed here. We have to get more details. When you say lustful kiss, what do you mean by that?" Codi asked.

"Like when you and Matt go at it."

"Oh, this is not good. How could she? You are such a prize, Joel. She is going to regret the day. It will haunt her for the rest of her life. The nerve. You were right to break things off, get clear of that double-dealing playgirl and move on."

Joel tried to nod his head at her words, but tears welled as emotions came to a boil. "But I love her."

"Oh, Joel. I'm so sorry. I can't imagine how you're feeling. Maybe you should take the day off."

"I have an appointment later with the Mercedes dealership in Arlington," Joel said, blinking the tears from his eyes and taking short staccato breaths.

Codi knew Joel had money from his parents, but he never flashed it around. The man was very conservative. "No, on second thought, you need to stay right here with me and work this case. What's next?"

Joel slowly nodded his head and stood back up at the whiteboard. With little to no energy, he continued his debriefing. "The US made Hee a full citizen, and he Americanized his name to Mark Kroon. So, along with the $100,000 they paid him, he also got a job."

"Testing the MiG against what we had?" Codi asked, trying to encourage her partner.

He nodded. "He flew hundreds of training air-to-air dogfights in the MiG against our best pilots and the F101 Voodoo. They tracked and recorded everything, helping our side build a better fighter and teach young pilots how to beat the enemy. They called it Operation Quiet Bird."

Codi stifled a yawn and forced herself to focus.

"Mark even used his aviation knowledge to write several pamphlets for readers who wanted easy-to-understand technology along with aviation knowledge." Joel looked down and sorted through a few pages on the table called *Aviation Basics—The world of science and technology in the skies.*

"So Mark Kroon was a big part of this Operation Quiet Bird?"

"Yes. He is considered an American hero for bringing us the MiG, and our government treated him accordingly."

"Well, somebody murdered Harry Wells and tried to hide that fact. And someone else or the same person covered it up," Codi said.

"To keep our nation's secrets safe."

"Or to get away with murder."

The silence after her comment hung in the air for a moment.

"Assuming someone on the 'secret team' was involved in the murder," Codi said, "what are the chances we can even get a list of people to eliminate suspects?"

"FOIA to the rescue."

Codi gave Joel a curious look.

"Freedom of Information Act. Most of the sixties are available, unless they are still critical to national security. In fact, I have tracked down a list of everyone involved in Operation Quiet Bird along with their pictures."

"Of course you have."

Joel spun his computer screen around to Codi, doing what he called 'billboarding.' There was a list of names and their positions.

"Wow. Nice work. Let's start with the man in charge." She leaned in and read the name, "Colonel Frank Ricks."

***

SA Gerald Whitestone picked up his phone on the first ring. "Whitestone." He listened for a second and then realized the caller was changing over to Facetime. He reached for his glasses as he hit the button and waited for the image to appear.

Dr. Tang blinked his dark eyes behind wire-framed glasses. He was wearing a lab coat and a youthful, all-knowing stare. He had a round face and jet-black hair.

Gerald inspected the man's face and thought to himself, *Japanese, Taiwanese, and French.*

"Hey, looks like you were right," Dr. Tang said. "No sign of any known poisons, but there is evidence of venom. Both samples are corrupted with the same issue—a type of venom that is not registering on any chart that we have. Might need to find someone who specializes in exotic snakes or pets to source it. All I can tell you is that it's some very nasty stuff."

"High potency?"

"No. It works quite differently. Based on the original autopsies, both vics never reported any kind of bite, nor was there any evidence of it. They developed flu-like symptoms, and by the time they went to the hospital, there was no stopping the damage."

"So it works slowly at first?" Whitestone asked.

"Exactly. A person envenomated by whatever this is doesn't start to show symptoms till a couple of days later. It is unlike any known snake or spider bite, at least known to us here at the lab, and honestly, our database is very comprehensive," Dr. Tang said, with a hint of pride.

"There were no puncture marks on the vics. How would you envenomate a person without biting them?" Whitestone asked.

"If there was an open wound or, say, you have open sores in your throat like from acid reflux and drank venom, that would do it, but neither vic had either of those conditions. And who would ever knowingly drink venom? My best guess is something like a box jellyfish. They leave a nasty rash where they make contact, and they can be deadly."

"Like the rash on the back of our vic's hands?"

"Not quite. It would look more like a burn. The other problem is you experience immediate pain at the contact point, and if you don't take action quickly, you will most likely die. Not like some secret killer sneaking around in your body, killing you over the course of a week, like what we have here."

SA Whitestone leaned back in his chair, trying to make sense of it all. "If I was to numb an area of your body, and then wipe a box jellyfish on the numb spot, that would explain half the problem."

"You would have to do all that without the person knowing and somehow modify the venom to act much slower," Dr. Tang said.

SA Whitestone rubbed his temples to thwart a growing headache. It was an impossible task. He was missing something.

"You got yourself a very clever killer out there," Dr. Tang said. "For all we know, these two are just the tip of the iceberg."

"Thanks for the encouragement, doc."

"Ah, sure?" Dr. Tang replied, unsure if the statement was sarcastic.

They signed off, and SA Whitestone tapped his pointer finger absently on his desk. He had solved the mysterious cause of death. Now, all he had to do was find a clever killer and his or her venomous pet. Piece of cake.

***

The sun was nothing but an orange slice as it dipped below the horizon. Atlantis heard an alert on her computer and sauntered over to inspect the screen. She loved this time of the day, as her house served as a large viewing platform to watch as nature painted the end of another day. Her home was a haven from the prying world, and she relished her time there, alone with her business and her thoughts. She remembered her childhood, living in a lower-middle-class home in the San Fernando Valley. Her father lived modestly and mostly kept to himself.

It wasn't until she was older that Atlantis realized it was racism and a mixed marriage behind the bigotry her family frequently felt. It had strained the relationship to the breaking point. A Korean father and a white mother inspired hatred for many in her neighborhood. Even when she was young, some parents refused to allow her to play with their children. The feeling was tangible in their neighbors' looks and actions. As quickly as the world modernized, it failed to address racism in its forward progress. Life is often a matter of timing. Twenty years later, it would have been a different story. By the time Atlantis had finished high school, she had learned the science of hate well. She used it to fuel her forward journey.

College was better, as time and age had begun to heal a broken country. With the promise of a united, color-free America, opportunities were opening up all around, and once she filled in with womanly curves, her exotic mixed-race heritage made her very popular with the boys. All were willing to try her out for the night, but none were willing to commit beyond that. It was a hard lesson that furthered her education in reality. Racism was not dead; it was just moving underground. Her total disregard for humanity only grew.

The only exception was her sophomore roommate, Mollie. She had taken Atlantis at face value the moment she had moved in. There was never comment or judgment. They became good friends, and Atlantis could see the possibilities America provided more clearly. Spending long hours talking about how to break through the glass ceiling as women, they determined that their destiny was to change the world.

By the spring semester, Mollie had contracted a rare ovarian cancer and never made it to the end of that school year. Three months later, Atlantis lost her mother. It was a rough year. She was emotionally crushed, and all the old feelings of hatred seemed to refuel her. She finished college on her terms and left for home, still not sure of her career.

That same year, her father died, but not before confiding in her about his background as a spy for North Korea. It was a surprise and shock that had left her hurt until she looked back on her upbringing and all the little details of her father came into view. The things he had taught her growing up. It was not a normal childhood. Cyphers, shooting, martial arts, and even piano lessons now seemed to have a dark context.

Atlantis had been furious at first, and then a change of opinion followed. Her father had duped the entire United States government. He was brave, smart, and incredibly clever. It wasn't until her mother died that the wind vanished from her father's sails. He lost his way and drive.

Atlantis remembered him sitting in his La-Z-Boy, staring out the window as if waiting for an assassin from his homeland to put an end to his misery. She tried to engage with him, but each visit home was separated by more and more time.

Finally, that Christmas, a stroke took him from her life.

Atlantis buried her father next to his beloved wife and said her final goodbyes. She sold the family home and used the money to start her own version of the family business. A business that was now booming.

***

The image started pixelated and frozen, but after a second call in and an adjustment to the placement of his phone, the man's image cleared up. Gallagher Allworth was a seventy-nine-year-old retiree. He wore a well-worn Hawaiian shirt and had a clean-shaven face with a few missed spots of grey hair sticking out. His milky cataracts hid green eyes that appeared to focus nowhere. The wisps of hair that remained on his head had a mind of their own, and his yellowed teeth moved loosely behind weathered lips. The background on the screen had more of a trailer feel than an actual home.

"Special Agent Strickman, hello," Gallagher called out.

"This is my partner, Special Agent Sanders," Joel said, introducing Codi.

"They're making women special agents now, huh? Hmm, must have lowered their entrance requirements."

Codi was taken aback at the overt chauvinism. Her first response would have been to verbally slam the bigot to the ground. *Yeah, and they are not letting misogynists join anymore.* But she held her tongue and let Joel take the lead.

After the 'pleasantries' were over, they got down to business.

"We want to talk to you about an old case you had," said Joel.

"You must be desperate. I haven't worked for the Bureau for over thirty years. What case could still be active? The statute of limitations has unquestionably run out on any of my old cases, and then some." He leaned too close as he spoke, making his face look distorted.

"Not the murder of a federal agent," Joel replied.

This got Gallagher's attention. "Okay, I'm listening. Not sure I'll remember much, though."

"BLM Officer Harry Wells. He was electrocuted in his bathtub, but the evidence doesn't add up."

The sudden dilation of his eyes told Codi that he remembered the case and the man.

"That was a long time ago, but I'll never forget it. Of course, the evidence didn't line up; it was a total sham." He rubbed his red bulbous nose and sucked in a wet breath. "A filled-out report was sent to me by my boss's boss with very strict instructions to sign and submit it as written. Said the orders came from high up in the military. Someone working on a secret military operation was a suspect, but I wasn't allowed to investigate."

"They were rubber-stamping it?" Codi said, talking more to herself rather than the caller.

Codi's words made Gallagher's face scrunch like he had just cracked open a rotten egg.

He ignored her and spoke to Joel. "Of course they were rubber stamping it. Some big national secret that didn't need attention, I reckon."

"It's strange the military didn't investigate," Joel threw back.

"The military didn't do jack wad. Besides, Harry Wells was a federal agent under our jurisdiction. They just wanted all the *T*s and *I*s taken care of."

"What did you do?" Joel asked.

"I did what I was told. Something this new generation doesn't understand. I signed the darn thing and submitted it."

"Wait," Joel said, "you submitted the case as solved? Then how did it become an unsolved cold case sitting on our desk?"

"That might be my fault," Gallagher said.

Both Codi and Joel were stunned but tried to hide it.

"The whole thing never really settled well with me. So years later, before I left the FBI, I resubmitted it as an unsolved. Slid it into the bottom of a very large pile. I guess it just finally made its way to the top." He leaned in again for emphasis. "Officer Harry Wells deserves justice and should not have his murder swept under the rug."

Joel and Codi shared a look and let the comment lie. They couldn't disagree. The three agents finished up the conversation and signed off.

"Okay, first Zoom interrogation is on the books," Joel announced.

Codi wasn't listening. "Hmm, oh yeah. So odds are good someone on that list is our suspect."

Joel held up the printed suspect list. "Odds are good just about everyone on this list is already dead."

***

Joel smiled as the seventy-year-old woman strutted down the hallway toting a large shoulder bag. She was tall with dyed red hair that curled like her perma-hunched shoulders that had lost the battle to overly large breasts. She looked lost but unwilling to admit it. Joel popped up and reached out a hand to greet her. "Mrs. Robinson?"

"Yes. Not the famous one, but just as randy," she said as they shook hands.

Joel almost pulled back his hand mid-shake, afraid he might have unintentionally committed to something.

"I'm just messing with you, son. Or am I?" She said the last part with one eyebrow raised.

"I'm . . . I'm Special Agent Strickman. Please follow me." He led her to the small conference room where Codi and he had been working the case.

"I understand you have some experience with HCS?" Joel said.

"HCS?" Mrs. Robinson glanced at him for confirmation.

He nodded.

"Well, that's all I did for thirty years. Is that what you got me out of retirement for, Sonny?"

"Joel," he tried to correct her.

"Hmm?" she said, oblivious to his efforts.

"We are working on a case from the sixties, and we have a couple of partials we tried to compare against a stack of suspects. We loaded everything into AFIS but got back nothing conclusive. We thought maybe going analog for these old prints might work, and as I understand it, you were considered one of the best on the HCS system."

"It's just HCS," Mrs. Robinson corrected him.

"What?"

"HCS literally stands for Henry Classification System, so you don't have to say the word *system* after it."

"Gotcha," Joel mumbled, duly reprimanded.

"I like this one, Joel," Codi spoke up.

Joel and Mrs. Robinson both looked up to see Codi standing in the doorway.

"Hi, I'm Special Agent Sanders," she said as she entered the room and took a seat.

"Pleased to meet you," Mrs. Robinson replied. She sat down and started digging in her purse. She extracted a pair of reading glasses that were so thick, the glass extended way beyond the frame.

Joel tried to refocus the meeting. "We were hoping you could match this . . ." Joel slid over a fingerprint card with two partial prints on it. ". . . to one of these," he said as he slid over a small stack of complete fingerprint cards, each from one of the people working on Operation Quiet Bird at the time of the murder.

"Well, no guarantees, but let me take a look." She pulled a magnifying loupe on a gold chain out of her cleavage and spread out the photos on the table. Joel and Codi watched with fascination as forensic history came to life in front of them. She placed the magnifier on a card and hunched over even further to examine it. She focused on the whorl pattern somewhat visible on one of the partials. The first two suspect cards had ulnar loops and she quickly dismissed them. "This'll go a lot faster without you two watching," Mrs. Robinson said, without looking up.

"Copy that," Joel responded. He and Codi left the room to let her have at it.

Codi sat in Joel's office and gave her partner a sideways glance.

"What?" he said.

"Oh, nothing, Sonny." The corners of her lips reached for the ceiling, showing her parting white teeth.

"Not funny."

"Maybe not to you. So what's next?"

"Next? I think it's time you shared your pet name for me," Joel demanded.

"I told you I would tell you when the time is right."

"Yes, but I'm going a little crazy trying to guess it."

"Joel, you have got to learn to let things go."

"Said the pot to the kettle," he replied.

"Fair, but it's not going to work on me. And I don't think it's my pet name for you that's the problem, is it?"

Joel sighed. He had been a bit of a mess ever since seeing Shannon with someone else. His heart was torn asunder. He had serious bags under his eyes, and his ability to think two steps ahead was compromised. He gave up and shifted back to the case. "We have three pieces of evidence that need lab time. I sent off the two vials of blood to see if we could get anything more, including DNA."

"The dried-out one is gonna be hard," Codi said, trying to keep her partner on task.

"That's exactly what the girl at the lab said. The hair is still viable, and we should get quite a bit of information from it."

"Okay, that's something. How long?" Codi asked.

"Cold case. Last priority. I'm guessing at least a coupl'a weeks."

"Hmm, let's shift to tracking our suspects down and talking to them. After that, we'll have to jump on another case until we get the lab results back."

"I have a list of who's still alive." Joel opened his laptop and pulled up a file. On the screen was a list of six names with their ages and titles. A couple of them had current addresses, and two of those also had phone numbers.

"I'm still trying to track these others down."

Codi and Joel worked the rest of the day trying to put a current address and contact number to the rest of the list. At ten after five, a voice interrupted them.

"Okay, I got what I got."

Joel and Codi followed Mrs. Robinson back to the conference room.

"There is a definite whorl pattern forming here on your suspect's partial print," she said. "That allowed me to eliminate everyone without one. If you look closely here, there is an anomaly. It's probably the start of a scar, a birth defect, or maybe debris taken from the original lift. I'm not surprised AFIS didn't find a match. It's inconclusive at best, and nothing here could win in court."

"With a cold case, we don't have quite the same burden of proof," Codi said hopefully.

"Unless they go to trial," Joel added.

"Well, either way, I have narrowed your forty-six suspects down to five."

Joel and Codi were stunned. The room took on an uncomfortable silence.

"That's great," Joel finally sputtered.

Mrs. Robinson looked pleased with herself and slid the five suspects over to Codi. It was a good day's work.

***

The sudden strike from the African horned viper took SA Whitestone unaware, and he jumped back, almost falling into another deadly snake, his reaction much slower than the viper's. The only thing saving him from a painful death was the glass wall of the aquarium. He regained his wits and continued down the rows of glass habitats, deciding not to look inside again.

The nearly four-hour flight to Huntington, West Virginia, along the Ohio River, was humdrum, but for everything else, he had to fight crowds every step of the way, including an over-sold flight and a massive line at the car rental counter.

SA Whitestone marveled as he drove through the iconic campus made famous through film and tragedy as seventy-five of the school's football players, staff, and boosters lost their lives in a 1970 plane crash that left Marshall University's Thundering Herd and community gutted and grieving.

He pulled up to the hepatology lab and got out of his rental car. The lab was world-renowned for its collection and study of reptiles. The vivariums that held the snakes were placed on raised platforms and extended on both sides for nearly fifty feet. There were species from all over the world, with a specialized section specific to West Virginia. Most of the recent lab work was primarily geared to medical uses for venom, and secondarily for the production of antivenom, so nearly the entire reptile collection was venomous.

SA Whitestone found the door he was looking for and gave a brief knock before entering. Inside, he found a messy office with reports and documents piled nearly to the ceiling. A curly-gray-haired man with olive skin and brown eyes turned. He had a square face and a mild manner.

Lebanese or Syrian with a pinch of Italian, Whitestone guessed. They made introductions, and the head of the department, Professor Hyme, invited him to see the lab.

"We have an extensive collection here and a few less exotic specimens in our annex. You'll have to pardon our specimen room; it's kept warm for our cold-blooded friends."

Gerald noticed the professor walked with a slight limp. *Probably an old snake bite,* he imagined.

"I was surprised to get your call. We're usually contacted by doctors, not law enforcement. So what is it the FBI is looking for, Special Agent Whitestone?"

"Please, call me Gerald." The room gave Gerald the creeps. There were venomous snakes everywhere, with only a thin piece of glass separating them from freedom, and the overpowering smell was off-putting—a combination of feces, wet dog, and bleach. But the most overpowering thing was the heat. It was at least ninety degrees in the room.

"This is a remarkable specimen . . . a blue Krait. I collected him myself. Over here, we have an Eastern green mamba. And that's a puff adder, the fastest striking snake in the world," he said proudly, as he pointed out several of the snakes in their vivariums.

Gerald swallowed the bile rising in the back of his throat. He hated snakes, and sharing the room with so many made him start to sweat.

He placed a few photos on a counter at the end of the row and arranged them side by side. "I'm investigating a case of envenomation, where the victim died, but there were no fang or bite marks. I was hoping you might be able to shed some light on the 'how is this possible' page in the case."

The professor looked carefully at the photos. "What was the official cause of death?"

"Mortal disseminated intravascular coagulation," Gerald replied.

"Ah, a hemotoxin."

Gerald looked up at the professor.

He took the look as an invitation to lecture, and so he continued.

"There are four types of venom. Proteolytic, which dismantles the molecular surroundings of the bite area. Cytotoxic, which has localized action at the site of the bite. Neurotoxic, which acts on the nervous system and brain. And finally, what you have here, hemotoxic. It affects the heart and cardiovascular system. Those are mostly your vipers and rattlesnakes. There are a few sea creatures that can cause similar symptoms, like the box jellyfish or the striped pajama squid, but they are extremely rare in this part of the world, and both leave telltale marks."

"Okay, so we have an envenomation of a hemotoxin without any bite or sting marks?"

"Well, when you put it that way, I'm afraid I have no idea what killed your victims. Even if you were injected with a small needle, there would be discoloration at the injection site."

"What do you make of this rash on his hand?" Gerald showed the pictures of the rash.

The professor looked them over, slowly shaking his head. "Sorry."

SA Whitestone thanked the professor for his time and left the building. A long trip for very little information.

It was the nature of cases. You could go for days with no results, and then suddenly the smallest detail opened new doors.

But not today.

***

Codi played with the ring on her finger. It was just a bit of metal and a few shiny stones. But it was connected to a promise. A promise that was much bigger than the worth of the ring. She was going to marry Matt. The concept was challenging and exciting all at once. She spun it around on her finger with her thumb, letting her thoughts and fantasies run free. This would be a new chapter in her life, and she would do everything in her power to make it work. She would take the best parts of her family life and drop the rest.

When her father died unexpectedly, everything that connected her to her mother died with him. They had grown apart as her mother spiraled out of control, and Codi fought for a sense of normalcy in her life with both parents effectively gone.

After years of no contact, Codi and her mother reconnected, trying to heal the past. Just as things were beginning to make sense, her mom was murdered while waiting in Codi's apartment for a dinner date. Codi had never been able to fully process the emotion and shock she experienced. But the past was something you should learn from, not live in. It mostly carried a bad aura, so she focused on looking forward not backward.

That's what she would do with Matt. One day at a time, pushing and looking forward.

Joel finally stopped typing and looked up. His partner seemed lost in her thoughts. "I cross-referenced the names Mrs. Robinson gave us with this list I have of those still alive," he said to Codi. "There are three that overlap."

Codi's eyes refocused on the matter at hand: the investigation into the case of BLM Officer Harry Wells, who was electrocuted in his bathtub back in the sixties. They spent the rest of the morning trying to Facetime or Skype the names on Joel's list. The technology was problematic when paired with anyone over the age of sixty-five. Eventually, with Joel's technical assistance, they finished the calls.

"That was painful."

"And it took forever!" Joel added. "I used to help an older widow that lived next to me with her computer. Man, was that rough. The same questions over and over. I'd set everything up so it was bulletproof, and the next day, we were back at the beginning. This is a mouse. You move it like this. I hate to say it, but I was glad when she moved to an old folk's home."

"That's a bit harsh, but I get it. So what do we have next?" Codi asked.

"Two from Mrs. Robinson's list are dead. Let's contact next of kin and see if we can learn anything."

"Staff Sargent Kyle Fuller has a son, Kyle Jr., and Mark Kroon has a daughter, A. Kroon. There's a whole file on Fuller, but next to nothing on Kroon."

"That's odd."

"I know, right?"

"What's the *A* stand for?"

"I have no idea."

"Let me call one of my contacts and see if they can shed a little light," Codi said.

Codi left the conference room, and Joel tried contacting Kyle Jr.

"Hey, Cap?" Codi said in a direct voice as soon as the call connected. She sat at her desk and let her chair slowly rotate in circles.

"Codi! Good to hear from you. I take it you're finding a way to stay cool. It's been blazing here."

"I'm always keeping it cool. You know that."

"For sure you are. What can I do you for?" Cap asked.

"I have a name that our data banks draw very little on, and I was wondering . . ."

"If I could run it through the MI database?"

Before Codi could answer, he continued. "Well, lay it on me. I'm on the Military Intelligence server right now."

"Mark Kroon. Originally born Mah Choon Hee in 1933 in North Korea. He's the guy that flew the MiG over the 38th parallel in the fifties. Had something to do with an operation called Quiet Bird, later on in the California desert."

"Whoa, going way back. I remember reading about that."

"There is a lot of information about him initially, but everything goes blank after that. I caught a cold case with a murdered federal officer, and I'm trying to eliminate suspects," Codi explained.

"Gotcha. Well, he's a national hero if you ask me. Let's see . . . Hmm, this is interesting. I got some stuff here, but most of it is redacted, and the file is seriously incomplete. Something's not right."

Codi remained silent.

"Let me send you what I have, and I'll add a contact of mine over at the CIA that might be able to add to this," he said.

"CIA? Isn't this guy domestic?"

"Just read the file, and it will all make sense. I gotta go. Nice to hear your voice."

"Thanks, Cap," Codi added as the line went dead.

Chapter Fourteen

BRIGHT SOURCE – DARPA RESEARCH FACILITY – 3:52 P.M.

Matt rubbed his eyes. He had been staring at the screen for too long. The Microneedle Patch was shaping up nicely. It looked like a bandage on steroids. It had a patch of microneedles that, when applied, could deliver a vaccine painlessly and then simply dissolve away. Its potential was enormous. Imagine receiving your next shot or vaccine in the mail, and all you had to do was stick it on the back of your hand for a short while.

Initially, a team at the Georgia Institute of Technology had come up with the idea. The real genius had been the water-soluble needles that could deliver their payload before breaking down. Favorable results had shown the technology to be just as effective as a classic injection. Next week, they were testing a new batch of subjects, and he hoped they would continue to have the same success.

Being connected to the military through DARPA meant that control and development could be changed at any time. It was something Matt had learned since taking the job. As the lead project manager, Matt had the responsibility of pushing the project forward without skipping any details. He knew full well the devil was in the details.

Matt was right at home in covering every angle and then repeating the work multiple times just to make sure. He thrived on the process and was always careful to move methodically through it. The Microneedle Patch would be a success.

He let his thoughts wander to Codi. He had nearly blown it the other night. What he had thought was reluctance on her part was just excited nerves. He had to embrace the fact that he was just no good at reading or truly understanding women, especially Codi. In the future, he would ask her opinion first and then adjust accordingly. He might not be able to read her thoughts, but as a scientist, he could apply the scientific method to eliminate many of the variables before he blundered again. Observe, measure, study, and develop a hypothesis.

He decided to start a list in an attempt to identify key emotions and moods. Next, he wrote out a second list of facial expressions he felt were connected to her emotions and moods. If he could identify one of these looks, he could counter it and eliminate the negative emotion that was behind it, effectively reading her mind and dodging the inevitable spat stemming from a misunderstanding. He might not be good with complex emotions, but he could use science to uncover them.

A thought hit him. *I should write a book. Three Easy Steps To Scientifically Understand Women.* It would be amazing. The scientific community would laud him, and every introverted brainiac who'd had no luck in the past would praise him. His shoulders and smile both slumped as he realized he had no idea what the three steps were or had any hope of ever truly understanding them.

He wadded the paper up and threw it away.

***

As Cap had said, the file was useful, but not complete. Codi printed it out and handed it to Joel. They laid out the pages on the conference table and took turns adding to the profile they were building on the elusive Mark Kroon. There were details on his work on Operation Quiet Bird and a couple of paragraphs about his technical aviation manuals, but that was it, nothing more. From his personal life, there was a birth certificate for an Atlantis Kroon and a death certificate for a Mrs.

Grace Kroon. Someone had redacted several sections, making it more of a jigsaw puzzle with missing pieces than a report.

"Are you sleeping at all?" Codi asked Joel.

"I'll sleep when this case is closed," Joel said with caffeine-powered words. He had developed a slight jitter that came from multiple days of living on the stuff.

Codi knew his heart was hurting and that he had buried himself in work to keep his mind busy. The lack of sleep, however, was disturbing.

She pulled up the last page and showed it to Joel. It was a name and a phone number.

Joel read out loud, "'Fuzzy Fassbinder.' Sounds like an animated character in a Disney movie."

"He's CIA, and we have an appointment this afternoon."

Joel took his glasses off and cleaned them. "CIA. Cool."

***

The Central Intelligence Agency took security to the next level, and Codi and Joel took mental notes as they were processed through. The famous lobby with the giant floor seal was just like in the movies, and the stars on the wall below the words "In Honor Of Those Members Of The Central Intelligence Agency Who Gave Their Lives In The Service Of Their Country," were sobering.

They were met by a short, rotund man in his late fifties. He wore a white shirt with a black tie to match his curly white and black hair. "Special Agents Sanders and Strickman?"

"Hello," Codi said as she reached out to shake his hand.

"Call me Fuzzy. My original name was Faddey, but once I moved here from Egypt, it got all Americanized."

He led them to his office on the second floor and closed the door as they entered. He took a seat behind a cluttered desk and drummed his fingers on the table. "What can I do for our brothers and sisters at the FBI?"

Codi handed him their incomplete file on Mark Kroon. He picked up a pair of readers and slapped them on his nose.

"We were hoping you could shed some light on this man," she said.

Joel added, "As you can see, there are some serious redactions to his military file."

Fuzzy looked over the documents and then glanced up over his glasses. "May I ask how you got these?"

Codi saw no reason to lie. "I have a friend at Military Intelligence."

Fuzzy nodded briefly and then removed his glasses and sat back in his chair. He looked from Joel to Codi like he was measuring them for a coffin. "I am familiar with this case."

Joel shot Codi a look.

"You are wasting your time. Mark Kroon was a national hero. He significantly helped keep us in the fighter jet race against what was, at the time, a superior Soviet force. He had nothing to do with your federal officer's death. He was cleared and even helped the military catch the person responsible. As you can imagine, Operation Quiet Bird was very hush-hush, and the government wanted to close the case and keep it out of the papers. I will send you the details so you can close out your case."

"That would be fantastic, Fuzzy," Codi replied.

They finished up, and he escorted the two agents out of the building.

"Wow, that was easy," Joel said, plugging his phone into the car charger.

"Yeah, too easy." She pulled the car over to a stop sign.

"What are you talking about? Now, we can close out the case and move on to something else. ASSA Holloway will be thrilled. We proved you can close a case her way."

"You're not helping, Joel. Something doesn't feel right in my gut."

"It could be the Pork Vindaloo you had for lunch. Remember, we are not supposed to be using our instincts anymore."

Codi turned the car onto the interstate to take them home. Something was not right, and that feeling was not going to go away.

***

The case of the two murdered federal employees was turning out to be one of his biggest to date. SA Gerald Whitestone had not been popular with his boss when he asked to reopen two closed cases. Now, the pressure was on him to deliver. He started by running a search to see if there was anything that connected the two men—nothing. Next, he tried to retrace their movements as far back as a year before their death. That took almost three days and left him with no new leads.

A week on the agency's dime, and he had zilch to show for it. His next move was to see who benefited from their deaths. Congressman Bobby Carlyle had been a big proponent of the abolishment of special interest in government. That alone made the suspect list almost infinite. Carlyle had butted heads and used the press to his advantage, but that seemed like politics as usual. He had also worked hard on his non-profit benefiting foster children. His wife was still grieving and had her own money, so she was out as a suspect. Nothing else seemed to rise to the surface, so he moved on.

The federal judge, Dabney Silverman, had been in the middle of a high-profile case. He had ruled that some of the defense's evidence should be disallowed. Three days later, he reported to the hospital, and the case had to be reassigned. The new judge allowed the evidence, and ultimately, the defendant was acquitted. Now that was something he could work with. He set the congressman's file aside and put all his focus on the defendant in the deceased judge's case, Victor Kozlov.

Kozlov was a fifty-eight-year-old with cropped gray hair and a matching trimmed beard. He ran a construction company and looked connected in Gerald's eyes. He had been on trial for the murder of a city employee, and there was an eyewitness who had IDed him. The defense countered with security camera footage that showed him somewhere else during the time of the murder.

SA Whitestone knew that, nowadays, both eyewitnesses and security camera footage were unreliable. Witnesses were often wrong and when it came to video . . . just ask Hollywood. Anything was possible.

His thoughts turned to how he might get good ole Victor to tell him who he hired. It was always an issue—do you show your hand, or do you sneak around in the shadows to find out more first? There was never a set procedure. SA Whitestone let the details play out in his mind. His boss had given him two weeks to come up with something solid, and he had next to nothing so far. The only logical way to proceed was head-on. He headed for the motor pool, planning his next steps.

Kozlov's construction company turned out to be a gravel yard. There were many house-high piles contained by concrete borders. Besides gravel, some had rock and several others contained sand. Large equipment loaders scurried about filling various trucks who then shuttled their load to a construction site. There were two crane-like conveyor belts designed to refill the piles as they were depleted. SA Whitestone exited his vehicle into a cloud of dust. The air was filled with it. He headed to a small prefab building that matched the color of the dust. The mostly covered sign on the door read "VK Sand and Gravel." He pulled the door open on squeaky hinges and stepped inside.

"Can I help you?" a man in brown overalls called from behind a battered desk.

"I was wondering if I can speak to Victor Kozlov?" Gerald showed the man his badge.

"What's this about?"

"That's between Victor and me."

"I see. Just a second." He stood and started moving toward the back-office door. "I can't guarantee he'll see you."

"It's either here or the station," Gerald lied.

A few moments later, the man stuck his head back out. "He'll see you."

SA Whitestone stepped into the back office and closed the door behind him.

The office was average at best. Nothing fancy, just functional decor and poor lighting. The man behind the brown Formica desk was quite the opposite. He had piercing dark eyes that looked at Gerald as if he was part of an old-school line-up back at the office. He was wearing a Chelsea football club jersey and a gold Rolex with more diamonds than taste allowed. He gestured for Gerald to take a seat across from his desk.

As Whitestone sat, he studied the man in front of him. *Russian? No. Belarussian with some latent Turkish or other Ottoman influence.*

"What are you doing here, detective?"

"Special agent. And I have a few questions for you."

"Should I have my lawyer present?"

"That's your choice. We can do this officially down at the office or keep it simple right here."

A smile grew on Victor's face, and then he chuckled. "Okay. I like you, Special Agent. What are your questions?" He looked at his gaudy watch. "You have five minutes."

SA Whitestone was unfazed. He crossed his legs and leaned back in the chair. It creaked in protest. "I have solid information linking you to the killing of federal judge Dabney Silverman. What I want to know is who did you hire? That's it. Nothing more. I could care less about your involvement. If you give me the information I am looking for, I will simply walk out of your office today, and you will never see me again."

There was a moment of silence as the two men sized each other up, each trying to figure the other's angle, like two high-rollers at a poker table.

Victor burst out with a gut laugh. "I knew I liked you—a comedian. I have no idea who this Dabney Silverfish is."

"Silverman was the judge that disallowed your security cam footage at the first trial," SA Whitestone prompted.

Victor looked to the ceiling as if just now remembering. "Yes, the judge with a prejudice against me, of course. He got what he deserved. It was quite lucky for me, yes?" He turned back to SA Whitestone, and his eyes drilled into him with a menacing glare. "You have nothing on me or you would have a team here to arrest me. Take your jokes and go. Oh, and your two minutes are up."

SA Whitestone had played his best hand and lost. He thanked Victor for his time and left.

***

Codi pushed open the door to her apartment. She had a love-hate relationship with the place. It had been the site of two different attacks, the first one leaving her mother dead before they could fully reconnect. That tragedy often overwhelmed her.

But it was also her sanctuary. A place where she could get away and just let herself go. No rules, no responsibilities. Just Codi and her whims.

Coming home to an empty apartment triggered a mix of emotions for her and, depending on her mood, was welcomed or cursed.

She sat on her new linen couch and let her body melt into the soft cushions. The colorful throw pillows played against the neutral colors, giving the place a happy feel. She processed her current situation. Work had finally become just that—work. It had lost its allure. Her new boss was making it harder and harder to care about what she was doing, forcing her to contemplate her options.

Codi knew her bad attitude was a choice, but right now, she was choosing apathy and disdain for the FBI. She leaned forward and pulled her laptop to her thighs and checked her email. There were a few new messages.

Halfway through the second one, she picked up her phone and dialed. "Hey, what are you doing?"

"I'm reading an obscure article translated from Korean," Joel answered.

Codi rolled her eyes, knowing her partner's propensity for conspiracy theories and odd facts from the internet. "So we *are* descendants of aliens?"

"Most likely, but this article came out in a North Korea newspaper right after our guy defected. It says he was a deep-plant American spy sent over from South Korea to infiltrate their fighter jet program."

"Well, that would jive with the CIA wanting to whitewash much of his background."

"Then they should just admit it. I mean, it's been sixty-two years. Who cares?"

Codi sat up a bit and switched her phone to speaker. "We still have a strained relationship with North Korea. Letting that information go public would not make it better."

"That's because the DPRK wants to kill every American they can. Right now, they are working on a new biological weapon they plan to fire at our lakes."

"I worry about you, Joel. Maybe you should ease up on the late-night internet searches and try streaming a show or two. I hear Netflix has some good content."

"What? Do you have stock in Netflix?" His words were met with silence.

"Have you seen the lab report? It just came in through our email," Codi finally said.

"Hang on a sec." Joel clicked on his computer. "Yep, got it." There was a brief pause while he read over the highlights. "Whoa."

"Exactly."

"Okay, so what next?" he asked.

"I say we call bull crap on the CIA."

"That sounds like a bad idea."

***

Special Agent Roddy Chen was an unusually tall man with broad shoulders and a narrow face. He had an inquisitive mind and a love of the outdoors. He had a habit of chewing gum to where his jaws ached by the end of each day. But it helped him focus on the matter at hand.

He knocked on the massive door to the estate on Moss Point overlooking the Pacific Ocean. The drive down from the city of Orange had taken only thirty minutes, which was a minor miracle. After a second press of the doorbell, an older Asian woman opened the door. She was five feet tall with heels and had an expressive nature, which, at the moment, was displaying a scowl.

"May I help you?"

"Yes, Special Agent Chen, FBI. I need to speak with the homeowner, Atlantis Kroon."

"You have warrant?"

"I don't need a warrant to ask a few questions."

"We don't answer your questions without warrant."

"Look, this is about her father. We are just trying to put closure on a few details of his life."

"He hero. You go away and never come back."

"Ling, what's going on?" A voice from inside the house called.

"Some FBI man trying to waste your time."

The voice in the house appeared at the door. She was an exquisite beauty with just a dusting of pink on her lips. "I'll take it from here."

The old woman left muttering a collection of Chinese swear words.

The special agent repeated his request, and this time, was met with a different reply.

"Please come in. You'll have to excuse Ling. She gets paid extra for each person she turns away. You see, I like my privacy."

The entrance was grand, with a fountain and tall spiral tower. She led him to a sitting room that was decorated in pink and green. Through the large windows, Chen could see the waves crashing on the rocks below. The view was magnificent.

"So what is it you want, Special Agent Chen, was it?"

"Yes, I'm here at the request of two special agents out of the DC office. They are looking for closure on a few details about your father. I would like to put them on the phone if that would be okay with you?"

"I see no problem with that, not sure why you are investigating him though."

Chen connected his phone to Joel's cell and pressed the Facetime button. Two agents' faces popped up on the screen. They were sitting in a conference room of some type. SA Chen pointed to the phone so they could all see each other. He made introductions as he sat in a chair across from Atlantis.

"Ms. Kroon," SA Chen said, "we were wondering if you could tell us anything your father might have shared during his time working for the US government."

Atlantis looked at the ceiling, trying to recall the past. "As I'm sure you know, I was not born yet. My father married my mother while he was working on a joint project with JPL."

"The Jet Propulsion Laboratory, north of Los Angeles?" Chen clarified.

Atlantis nodded.

"Did he ever tell you anything about his time up in the California desert on Operation Quiet Bird?"

"Never heard of it. He didn't speak much about his early days in the US. But I am almost certain that working in the desert as a test pilot was one of his first jobs here."

"There is a rumor that he was a spy for the US," Joel threw out.

Codi tried not to react to his off-base comment.

"Actually, he was a spy," Atlantis said boldly. "Just not for the US."

The three special agents were dumbfounded.

"I would have thought you federal types knew this. It's certainly no longer a secret, at least not in my mind. That was a long time ago."

"Can you elaborate?" Chen was the first to recover and ask the question.

"Sure. He was a spy for a Russian-North Korean operation. He was sent bearing a gift, the MiG, which got him a pass to the inner circle. That allowed him to leak information to his superiors. I'd be happy to show you how he did it." She got up and walked over to a set of drawers as she continued. "I know this might seem strange, but I'm very proud of him, and as an American citizen I am allowed to be. The cold war is long over, and my father did what he considered right to win it."

"By duping the country that welcomed him with open arms?" Joel hit back, a bit flummoxed.

"In the end, the right side won out," Atlantis replied cryptically.

Special Agent Chen opened another gum wrapper and added a fresh piece to the wad inside his mouth.

Atlantis sat back down with two pages and a flashlight. "These are pages from an aviation technical guide my father published called *Aviation Basics—The world of science and technology in the skies*."

Joel spoke up. "Yes, we are aware of his interest in the field. He was quite prolific."

Atlantis aligned the two pages and turned on the flashlight. It shined through the pages. "As you can see, when the pages are overlapped a message appears in English. He was most brilliant to design and detail these schematics that were accurate and yet still served a second purpose. He made close to fifty of these pamphlets, all with secret messages for the communists hidden in the schematics." She turned off the flashlight and placed the pages next to her on the couch. "The authorities that welcomed him with grateful open arms never suspected him."

Joel had seen the bold words that made up the message. "Quiet Bird Real. Specs to Follow as Received. Radar Ineffective. Capable of Mach Flight."

"Any idea what Quiet Bird was?" Codi asked.

Atlantis shook her head. "My father was a complex and brilliant man, agents, but he is gone and, and unlike the adage, 'the sins of the father are not the sins of the son.'"

"No, they are not," Codi replied. She thanked Atlantis for her time, and they closed out the phone call.

Special Agent Chen walked back to his car, unaware that Atlantis was taking pictures of him and his vehicle from inside the estate.

Operation Redirect might have to wait until she knew what the FBI was up to.

***

ASSA Bruster Holloway paced in her office.

"So let me get this straight. You two took a sixty-year-old cold case and managed to connect it to a cover-up at the CIA, of all places?"

"Sixty-two," said Joel.

"What?"

"It's a sixty-two-year-old cold case."

ASSA Holloway stared daggers at him.

"The lab work doesn't lie," Codi added. "It ties Mark Kroon directly to the murder. The hair evidence gives us age, gender, and place of origin. The blood evidence gave us DNA, and a partial fingerprint match confirmed it."

"And the CIA claims he had nothing to do with it," Joel said. "But we know he was working as a spy for a joint task force between the Russians and the North Koreans."

"Oh, come on. Seriously?" ASSA Holloway massaged her temples as she listened to her two agents. "This was just the sort of thing I was trying to prevent."

"What, us following the evidence?" Codi asked.

"No. You two causing the Bureau headaches." She stood and then changed her mind and sat back down. "But I suppose this couldn't be helped. Take another run at your contact over at the CIA and hit him with the evidence you now have. Let's see what comes back."

Joel and Codi gave brief nods and stood to leave her office.

"Oh, and, agents, don't forget the all-departments meeting at 4:00 p.m. today."

Codi left as Joel tried to acknowledge their boss.

Once back at their desks, the two worked up an email together and sent it off to Fuzzy at the CIA.

Within ten minutes, Codi got a cryptic text from an anonymous sender.

Queen Vic 9p

She showed it to Joel, and after a beat, the two figured out its meaning.

As 4:00 p.m. rolled around, they finished up for the day and headed to the conference room. The two whiteboards were filled with case clippings, notes, and photos. Everyone was there, including the few secretaries Special Projects employed. ASSA Bruster Holloway entered after Codi took a seat and headed to the front of the room.

"I'd like to thank you all for coming."

Everyone looked around as if saying, *like we had a choice?*

She erased a list on the left whiteboard that Joel had been working from. Then, using a red marker, wrote the letters F R I C S. Underneath, she followed up with Fiscally, Responsible, Intelligent, Case Solving.

Codi rolled her eyes and whispered to Joel. "Oh, FRICS, here we go again."

***

At 8:45 p.m., Codi entered the Queen Vic.

It had a red and black façade with several Liverpool Football Club flags and signs. The English-style pub served excellent fish and chips and bangers and mash. The long bar overlooked a collection of liqueurs and a row of flat screens playing only "the beautiful game." Codi sat on the end and used her vantage point to take in the quaint space. Open ceilings, plenty of wood, and they were pouring proper pints. She ordered a Wells Bombardier, allowing the unique British atmosphere to consume her. Joel was next to enter. He hurried over to sit by his partner, ordered a Guinness, and tried to hide a nervous jitter. "So, who do you think we are meeting?" Joel asked.

"Look for a guy in a trench coat," Codi answered.

"Really?"

"No. More likely a woman packing some serious heat."

Joel looked up at the entrance as a shadow crossed and sat next to him.

He immediately reacted. "We are saving that seat for a fr—" He stopped mid-sentence when he recognized the man sitting there—Fuzzy Fassbinder.

"Pour me a Pimm's, mate," he called out over the heads of the two agents. The three sat sipping their drinks as the crowd cheered a goal for the reds. Once the commotion died down, Fuzzy leaned over and spoke in a quiet voice. "Thanks for meeting me here. There are too many ears at the farm."

The three shared a toast once the drinks arrived.

"What I'm about to tell you is not classified, but it is sensitive," Fuzzy said.

"We understand," Codi responded.

"Not all secrets should be kept. The truth should still mean something." Fuzzy said the last part more to himself than anyone else.

Codi said to him, "We need you to tell us about the spy, Lieutenant Mah Choon Hee, later known as the hero Mark Kroon."

Fuzzy nodded.

"There is strong evidence that points to him being a spy for the Koreans," Joel added.

"We know he killed BLM Officer Harry Wells. We just don't know why," Codi finished.

Fuzzy took another drink as he processed this information. Then he said, "Mark Kroon was a spy, but for the US . . . well, not in the traditional sense."

"What do you mean?" Codi asked.

"He stayed true to his home country," Fuzzy said as he lowered his voice even more. "After his defection, he worked hard to help the US understand and reverse-engineer the MiG he brought us. Following that, he flew and trained new fighters to help them understand North Korean fighting tactics. He was soon trusted and given access to more intelligence than he should have been."

Chen took a sip of his Pimm's Cup before continuing. "You see, it turned out the MiG he brought us was very useful, but it was two generations back from what the Russians had at the time. The tactics he shared with us were North Korean tactics, not what the Russians were teaching. It all amounted to just a blip of an advantage. What he did most for our country was publicity. His defection was big news, news that was leveraged to the max." Fuzzy hesitated before taking another sip of his Pimm's. He continued. "The real coup was that a few higher-ups in the two communist governments sent Kroon here on a mission."

Joel shot Codi a look.

"At the time, we were working on a project called Quiet Bird. The first stealth fighter."

"We know about Quiet Bird," Codi added.

"A stealth fighter back in the sixties?" Joel asked.

"That's right. His mission was to ingratiate himself so he could get access to that information."

"So he was a spy for the communists, and we welcomed him with open arms," Codi summarized.

"It's hard to put a value on the initial damage he did. Officer Wells discovered how he was communicating with his handlers."

"And he got killed for his troubles?" Joel asked.

"Right, but not before Wells sent a sample to us. He was not working for the BLM. He was one of our agents used for over-watch, something we do for many classified projects."

Codi and Joel let the words sink in before speaking.

"So why was he never arrested?" Joel asked.

"What, and ruin all the good publicity? No, we had a better idea. We covered up the murder and let our now-known North Korean spy do his thing," Fuzzy said.

"Only you controlled the narrative," Codi added.

"Exactly."

"You made him a double agent without his knowledge," Joel said, as the light in his head turned on.

"What can I say? we are the CIA."

With the complete picture now clear, Codi and Joel wondered what to do next on this case. There was no way they could write up what actually happened.

Fuzzy set his empty cup down. "I'll send you a document that you can use to close out your case. Let's put this thing to rest. Our agent had no family, so there is no need for closure."

Codi finished her beer and thanked the operative from the CIA for his candid information. They all called it a night, and Joel convinced Codi to let him give her a ride to her apartment.

"Please tell me you are going to get some sleep tonight," she said to him.

"I am going to get some sleep tonight," Joel repeated.

"That sounded sarcastic."

"You asked."

"Joel, the lack of sleep is not helping this case or your health. The case can wait till tomorrow. It's been waiting for sixty-plus years. Do yourself and me a favor and get some real rest tonight."

Joel looked at his partner. A subtle nod followed that gave Codi some hope.

Chapter Fifteen

FBI SPECIAL PROJECTS – WASHINGTON, DC FIELD OFFICE – 8:22 A.M.

"I did some checking up on Atlantis Kroon."

Codi rubbed her temples. "What on earth for? I thought we agreed you were going to let it go and get some sleep. There is no way we can solve this case and not cause a firestorm." It was too early in the morning for her to think clearly. She had skipped her morning swim and was still feeling the effects of the night's alcohol. She looked up at her partner who seemed just fine. "And how are you so perky this morning?"

"I actually got some sleep last night." Joel pressed on, taking a sip of his large coffee. "The address we have on her? I looked it up on Redfin. It's a twenty-five-million-dollar estate." Joel was speaking rapidly.

"So she's rich or good at the stock market, so what?"

"She runs a website that sells lilies. Do you know how many lilies you would have to sell to buy a house like that?"

"No, but I'm sure you have it all worked out. Look, Joel, we have a stack of cold cases we've got to get through. We've closed this case. I'm not interested in opening a new case based on what, exactly?"

"Remember what we used to say at the GSA?"

The General Services Administration was Codi's first job out of the military. It is where she met Joel, and they mostly chased tax evaders and government contract fraud. It was also the place where they had proven themselves with an international terrorist case.

Codi looked at Joel with one eye, waiting for the answer. He seemed to hope she knew the answer. She didn't. "What did we used to say?" she said.

"Crime doesn't pay as poorly as the GSA," Joel said, in a sing-song way. "Follow the money, Codi. It will lead you to the crime."

Joel had made a name for himself as a GSA officer by digging into financials and finding the connection to criminal activity. In truth, if you dug deep enough, just about every American cheated on their taxes in some way. Before coming to the FBI, Joel had been an expert at finding those who made a career of it.

"So this little investigation of yours is a new case? Which means I'll have to clear it with Holloway, and I already know what she'll say."

"No. For goodness sake, no. I say we don't turn in our current case quite yet. It will give us some leeway if I piggyback this search onto it."

"Give *you* some leeway. *My* case is done," Codi said. "I'm not interested in getting involved in making up a new one. You have forty-eight hours, and then I'm turning in the BLM Officer Harry Wells case and moving on."

Joel looked up at his partner, a bit hurt. But after all she had been through in the last few weeks, he couldn't blame her. He was now the one following his gut and not listening to their boss. He just hoped it didn't blow up in his face.

***

The alert was from a program Atlantis had JC design. It warned her of any outside activity on the web that involved her personally. There were three different hits on the message board, all leading back to a dead-end firewall.

She picked up the phone and dialed a number from memory, as her mind flashed with the many possibilities of who it could be. A former client, a new client, maybe a future assassin wanting into the fold. Then a concerning thought grew. The FBI had come to her house. Was there more to their questions about her dead father?

A click was followed by silence.

She pulled the Tootsie Pop from her mouth and set it in the center of its wax paper square wrapper. "JC?" she asked.

"A, is that you?" a voice responded.

"It is."

"On my way."

The hacker she employed, known only as JC, was a man of many talents. He had set up her website with the vanishing message board and 256-bit encryption. It employed two levels of firewalls and could block anyone for any reason. He had also set up the shadow program he called Overwatch that tracked searches made involving her or the *Lilies4everyoccasion.com* site. In most cases, Atlantis knew a client was coming before he finished typing her address. JC was an integral part of her business and one of the very few people she trusted, along with her two assassins.

Atlantis took no chances with her privacy or her business. Both had been carefully maintained and fine-tuned to her idea of perfection. The thought that some unknown had been looking into her personal life was upsetting. It was bad enough to have to hide from her father's public legacy. That kind of historical fame would work against everything she had built.

Ling led JC to her office. He took only a moment to set up his laptop on a side desk. It was an action he had done many times.

"Can I get you anything?" Ling asked.

"Sugar-free Rockstar, any flavor."

She left the room and JC powered up his computer. He was a skinny Eastern European with dreadlocks and a scruffy blond beard. Both ears were pierced with green jade gauges the size of quarters, and a tattoo of $E=MC^2$+CAFFEINE was flaunted on his neck. Atlantis guessed his age to be late twenties. Only his eyes gave any indication he was not just another surfer along the Southern California coast. They had laser focus. He was self-taught, starting from a young age, and had no fear with cracking or thwarting anything on the web, including banks and governments.

Atlantis watched as the man blended with his tool of choice. In cargo shorts and a faded tee, he was a dichotomy in appearances and skill in the high-level work he did.

JC typed for several moments before looking over expectantly. "Okay," he said.

"I have three hits on Overwatch," Atlantis said. "They lead back to a firewall."

JC nodded imperceptibly and dug into the code.

She felt a weight lifting from her shoulders, as she would soon have an answer.

A buzzing from one of the five burners sitting on her desk pulled her attention.

She looked down at the text. *805P*. A glance at her watch, only six minutes away. There would be no need to counter with another time.

Atlantis rounded her desk, taking a second to enjoy the view of the Pacific Ocean as the last ambient light of dusk reflected off the purple water. She opened her site to the message board and waited until the clock pushed 8:05 p.m.

As if by magic, words started populating the message board. Within a few seconds, they disappeared just as magically.

"FBI agent Whitestone came by. Knows I hired out the killing of Federal Judge, DS. Whitestone looking for *you*—V."

A flash of heat crossed her face as Atlantis reached to reply. She was not used to messages so direct and was glad she had precautions in place for such stupid clients. She paused, her finger hovering over the keyboard, staring immobile, as the last word faded leaving a blank white screen.

JC felt the sudden tension in the room and looked up from his work. "Are you alright?"

Atlantis tore her eyes from the screen and forced a pat response. "Yep."

He watched his boss for a few more seconds before returning to his code.

Atlantis contemplated the scenarios of her current situation. She was a master of strategy, and part of that excellence came with a thorough mental vetting of every possible action and reciprocal reaction. As she clicked through the options, she focused on a very specific plan of action. It was time to prepare two files for The Encyclical.

"Okay, I have something for you," JC called out.

Atlantis moved to the side desk to see what he was talking about. There was an address at the top of the page as he continued to search for information—601 4th St. NW.

"The IP address belongs to this building right here." He pointed to an outline of a building on a map of DC. "It connects to the FBI Washington Field Office.

There are at least three different divisions of the FBI that work out of that office, and I cannot track your culprit beyond that. Not without them knowing."

Atlantis slowly nodded as she remembered the two agents who had interviewed her on the phone about her father. They were from the Special Projects division. They had known about his spying, but since he was dead, there was nothing they could do about that anymore. Atlantis had felt comfortable admitting to his past. It had nothing to do with her, and it felt good to rub his success in the government's face. She was proud of the work he had done.

"Does Special Projects work out of that office?" she asked.

JC typed a few more strokes. "Yes."

"Thanks, JC, send me a bill. And put a tracker on that office. I want to know if any more inquiries are made about me. And just to be safe, let's keep an eye on Special Agents Chen, Sanders, and Strickman."

He typed in the names. "Will do."

***

The FedEx package required a signature. The Encyclical signed and then nudged the front door closed with his foot. Placing the package on his kitchen island, he reached back and hit the lights. Bright LED ceiling light cans illuminated the washed wood cabinets and gray soapstone countertops. The home was modern, with a touch of wood to add some warmth. He normally worked in his office, but today, he was drawn to the morning sunlight streaming into the kitchen. He sat on a barstool and tore the package open.

The first thing he saw was a photo of a businessman. The man had been looking right at the camera when it was taken, almost as if he was looking back at him. He perused the contents of the envelope and set them to the side. Opening the second folder, The Encyclical pulled out a small stack of papers. On top was a picture of a younger face taken at an oblique angle. There was a strong disclaimer below the picture, written by hand in red Sharpie. FBI Special Agent.

This was something new for Stuart, a federal agent. That was a mark worth going after. He would have to be very sharp from here on out.

He spent the better part of the day studying everything in the two folders, committing it all to memory. Once he felt comfortable with the information, he booked a ticket on the morning flight to New York with a layover in Philadelphia. He would disembark in Philly and disappear.

The flight was quick and painless, and Philadelphia was ambivalent to his arrival. He purchased an older Ford F-150 pickup at a used car lot and drove off into the city.

Deciding against his usual Vrbo, he made arrangements to rent a small auto shop that had gone out of business a year ago. He negotiated a six-month lease under an assumed name and paid the first two months' rent upfront. Once he was finished with the job, he would leave the leaser with nothing but a burned-out shell.

The Encyclical had a contact in Philadelphia that could get him weapons and other needed equipment, but first, he had to follow his targets and devise a proper plan. The important thing would be to keep it simple. That was his mantra, and it echoed in his head with every job.

He would take out Victor Kozlov first and then work his way up to the FBI agent. That would require something very special.

***

SA Gerald Whitestone finished typing the last sentence, updating his current case file. He was feeling the pressure to close it out, and after his meeting with Victor things were not so optimistic. He had the motive, evidence of the murders, and one vague suspect. What he needed was a little luck. He picked up his phone and called a buddy in research.

"Yellin," answered the voice on the phone.

"Hey, Yellin, this is Gerald."

The two colleagues spent a second catching up. They had worked several cases together over the last two years and complemented each other well.

"What is it I can help you with, or are you calling because you miss working with me?" Yellin joshed.

"Both. I need some financial background on a suspect I'm working. He most likely made a large payment sometime between September and October of last year, and he would have wanted to hide it. I'm sending you over what I have on him." Gerald sent the e-file as he talked.

Yellin looked over the highlights. "Okay, I'll get right on it."

The two finished up the call and Gerald closed his computer and left the office, trying to forget his problems. As he turned the key in the ignition, he flashed to the night ahead. Callie was cooking dinner for him and had refused to tell him what she was making. As a detective, he should be able to deduce what it was, but as a boyfriend, he was supposed to be surprised. He struggled for a minute until he turned right onto the street and just let it all go. He would be surprised.

"That smells amazing," Gerald said as he walked into the petite kitchen and placed his arms around Callie from behind. The action seemed to release the last bit of stress he was still holding.

She poured white wine into the pan and several large scallops sizzled as the hot butter and spices mixed with the cool liquid.

"Perfect timing. That's unusual," Callie said, without looking back.

"My job doesn't hate you; it hates anyone who would try to take me away from it."

"How do you feel about that?" Callie asked as she spun around to face him.

"I feel obligated to help those in need and am required to help myself to you."

"I can live with that," she said, finishing with a passionate kiss. "Here, make yourself useful and pour the wine."

"It smells amazing, by the way."

Before long, they were seated in the small dining room and sharing food and conversation. The food was good, but the company was better.

After a second of silence, Callie placed her fork down with purpose. "There is something that has been on my mind, and I think we need to talk."

A shot of panic coursed through Gerald's body at the words. This was almost the exact phrase the last person he had cared for said right before she unexpectedly left him. He felt frozen, unable to breathe.

"This is going to be hard for me." Callie fidgeted with her napkin before placing it on the table. "We have been seeing each other for almost a year now, and it has been wonderful."

And? Gerald's mind screamed.

"And I think we should take things to the next level."

Gerald sucked in a breath reflexively. He blinked several times before her words fully matured in his brain. "Callie Morales, are you proposing to me?"

"No." She suddenly felt that she had overreached. "Not unless you want . . . I was thinking we should move in together first."

The corners of Gerald's mouth twitched and then jumped to the sky, revealing teeth and pure happiness. "Screw that. I think we *should* get married."

Callie's face blushed with happiness. Without warning, they both moved to the floor, taking one knee, surprising one another.

"Please let me do it," Gerald said softly.

"Okay," Callie acquiesced and sat back in her chair.

"Callie . . . would you—"

Before he could finish the words, Callie interrupted, too excited to hold back. "*Yes!* I do!" She pounced on Gerald, wrapping both arms around him and smashing lips, sending both to the floor laughing and crying, lost in a feeling so deep and strong, they might never separate.

***

The office was feeling stuffy as Shannon left the conference room for her desk. She was stationed in a bullpen with several other officials from the Canadian government. After finishing up her report, she stared at her screen for what seemed like an hour. She picked up her phone and texted Joel.

"Sorry I missed you last Saturday. Hope you are feeling better. PLMK if there is anything I can do to you. XOXO"

She hit send and watched the screen, hoping for a quick reply. Eventually, her phone rang, and she went back to the job of playing liaison between the RCMP and the USA.

As the clock hit 6:00 p.m., she packed up her things and left the office. Once outside the embassy, Shannon turned left down the sidewalk. She checked her phone but had no reply from Joel. As she looked back up, she was surprised to see Codi leaning against the railing that separated the street from a small park.

"Well, this is a surprise," Shannon said.

"Thought I'd see how the other half lives," Codi said.

"You're talking about us Canadians that live above you?"

"Only geographically, yes."

The two women shared a laugh.

"Can I buy you a drink?" Codi asked.

"Only if it's the good stuff."

"Nothing but."

They walked down to a small bar on the street corner and took a table in the back. The crowd was mostly starched white shirts and contemporary dresses.

Codi ordered a couple of hard seltzers.

"That's disappointing," Shannon said after the waiter left.

"Just trying to keep things light."

"I could use that about now."

"Well, then, this isn't going to help. I'm here to talk about you and Joel without his permission."

"Okay. I've tried reaching out a few times, but he's gone dark. Is everything okay?"

Codi let the waiter deliver their order before continuing. "He saw you, Shannon."

There was a palpable flash across Shannon's eyes, but she said nothing.

"At the hotel, kissing some guy. It has sent him into a tailspin that has got him going 'round the clock without sleep, doing anything to distract himself from the pain. He's now chasing criminals that don't exist. I can't close the cases we've closed. It's making me crazy."

"Oh dear, this is all my fault."

It sure is, Codi thought.

"I should have told him. It's why I've been so hard to get ahold of. The last thing I wanted was to put Joel in danger."

Codi's eyes drilled into Shannon. *Danger?*

"I'm helping out on an undercover case with an old boss of mine. The man I was kissing is my mark."

Codi just about choked on her seltzer.

Shannon continued, "It's just a big misunderstanding. Now, it all makes sense. I told him I was going to be busy for a bit and then he just goes dark—canceled on us last Saturday and then nothing. I thought he was sick or on a crazy case like me." She took a sip of her seltzer. "So that's why he hasn't responded to my calls and texts. Oh, poor Joel."

"We gotta fix this. He's practically manic, living on caffeine and sheer will."

"I can't. At least, not right now. I'm right in the thick of things, and these guys play for keeps. Let me send him another voicemail with the details I can share. You can cover for me from the other side."

"Got it. Hit him from both directions. I'll do what I can, but you need to make this right yourself."

"Of course. I feel terrible that he's hurting."

***

The sun dipped for the day and the green-orange glow of sodium vapor lights replaced it, illuminating the gravel yard and casting harsh shadows.

Victor Kozlov left his office to take his nightly walk around his domain. Every night after everyone had gone home, he did a visual inspection of his sand and gravel yard. It was ingrained in his routine. This was his castle, his world, and he enjoyed the solitude in a domain usually filled with noise. He checked the piles of material, making mental notes about which ones needed to be refilled. Looking over the conveyor equipment, he made sure the doors on the loaders and trucks were all locked. He was a double-checker by nature. Once he completed his walkabout, Victor felt confident locking the gate and leaving the yard for the night. What he didn't know was that this routine would get him killed.

The Encyclical waited behind the large tire of a front loader. He had watched his target do this same thing the last three nights.

Victor moved between the huge mounds of gravel, each a different size. There was river rock, clean stone, base stone, marble chips, crushed stone, pea gravel, and quarry process. Eventually, he got to the sand mounds that followed—concrete sand, stone dust, utility sand, fill sand, and beach sand. He walked through the insect-looking equipment used for refilling the mounds and finally approached the trucks and loaders all parked for the night. Climbing up the ladder leading to the cab of the large front loader, he wiggled the handle before climbing back down. He was about to jump from the last rung when a voice to his right stopped him.

"That's far enough."

Victor stayed on the last rung, looking over his shoulder at the trespasser. The man was dressed all in black, including the beanie on his head.

"A little hot out to be wearing that kinda hat," Victor said, unfazed by the man's presence.

"I'll worry about my hat. You worry about getting through this night alive."

Victor saw the words as an opening, a chance to negotiate his situation. He stepped down from the rung and turned to face the man in black. "I suppose I don't have to tell you I'm very connected and whatever you do here will come back on you, tenfold."

"No, you don't," The Encyclical replied. "Now, I want you to very carefully remove the gun in your back pocket and toss it away."

Victor reached with two fingers and withdrew the black wallet gun, known as a pocket shot, from his rear pocket. The leather held a small Colt 32 auto that could be fired without removing it from the wallet. He tossed it to the ground.

"Now walk slowly over to bin number eight."

"You mean the pea gravel bunker?" Victor asked.

"That's right. Nice and slow."

Victor squared his shoulders and headed back toward bunker eight.

The Encyclical followed at a safe distance. He picked up the tiny wallet gun as he passed.

Once Victor reached bunker eight, he stopped and glared back at the man in black.

"What's this all about? I know whatever it is, I can make it right," he said.

"I know you can make it right, too, but first there must be a small penance."

"Penance for what?"

"Climb." The Encyclical used his pistol to point to where he wanted Victor to climb.

"Are you crazy?"

"Climb and live or die where you stand. It makes no difference to me." The Encyclical brandished his gun.

Victor shook his head and started to crawl over the low concrete wall that held back the pile of gravel.

"At least you picked a low pile. By tomorrow morning this thing will be filled back up," he said, gesturing to the conveyor overhead.

The Encyclical knew Victor was talking to ease his nerves. He remained quiet, watching as his target transitioned from the concrete bunker that held the gravel in place to the gravel pile, talking the whole while. The gravel was only about six feet above the border, but every step Victor took in the loose gravel caused him to slide back. He quickly stopped talking and started to breathe heavily at the exertion. It took a concentrated effort to finally reach the top of the small gravel pile.

"Okay. Are you happy?" Victor called down. He was a sweaty mess, hands on his hips, as he huffed and puffed, trying to catch his breath.

"Impressive. I was giving five-to-one odds you wouldn't make it." Without another word, The Encyclical pulled the trigger.

Victor dropped to the gravel, moaning softly. The bullet had been carefully aimed at his stomach, leaving him to die slowly, his blood spilling out across the small-sized rocks used to decorate gardens and make driveways.

The Encyclical walked casually to the conveyor belt and started the engine. It had been set in place to do exactly what Victor had said, refill the pea gravel bunker in the morning. He engaged the clutch and the u-shaped belt fed gravel up the metal arm's length, spilling the small rock out of the top and onto the pile. He heard a few screams as Victor was buried under nearly three tons of rock.

Once bunker eight looked full, he turned off the machine. There was an echo of rock falling, then silence. A small dust cloud moved up into the air and dispersed on a light breeze. The Encyclical left the yard, locking the gate behind him.

Now it was time to focus on his next target, the federal agent.

Chapter Sixteen

HOTEL ZENA – WASHINGTON, DC – 8:43 P.M.

Shannon adjusted her dress, pulling down on the front to expose more of her assets. She hated doing it, but this was one of those times it was necessary. She tapped on the hotel room door and waited. A clanking of the chain was followed by the appearance of a man she despised. She put on a forced smile as the man's eyes roved everywhere but her face. She pushed past him into the lavish suite.

Michael Amari turned from the bar and smiled as she approached. He was a man of average height and looks with thick brown hair swooped over in a modern cut. He wore a mostly unbuttoned royal blue dress shirt and a matching Hermes belt and pocket square set against black slacks and a white coat. His Hublot MP-05 LaFerrari was displayed on his left wrist. Its unique design looked more like the insides of an alien robot than a wristwatch.

They each took a second to measure the other. This was a slow dance that had taken place over three meetings now, each looking for the confidence to proceed to the business side of things. Michael pulled her toward him and embraced her with a kiss. He poured her a glass of whiskey as she joined him at the bar.

"So is tonight our night to celebrate?" he asked.

"My buyer is ready with the cash. You name the time and place, and we can make this happen." She lifted her glass to him, and he matched her action in a simple toast.

"Tony, leave us!" Michael shouted at the man who had let Shannon into the room.

He was a large lecherous pig with greased-back hair. He rumbled out of the room, and Shannon visibly relaxed.

She had insisted on not wearing a wire as the men running this operation were too careful. The problem with that was she had no immediate backup. Sure, there was a team supporting her in a van outside, but they were running blind, and the moment they showed their hand it would be all over. This made her undercover work risky. Shannon still felt she could pull it off and, in all honesty, enjoyed the danger.

Michael slid his barstool closer to her.

"That dress is quite stunning on you, but I think it would look even better on a hook in the bedroom."

"Is that so? I told you, business first, then pleasure," Shannon replied.

"You are mistaken. Business with you is pleasure."

"Perhaps. Let's see how this first exchange goes. I have no interest in being just another one of your transactions."

Michael appreciated the cat-and-mouse game, but he was getting tired of being teased. He decided to take things up a notch. He grabbed Shannon by the arm and pulled her close using his lips and tongue to force himself on her. Shannon fought in his grasp until he finally pulled back.

"Now, that was more like it. I like a fighter. You and me are gonna have a good time tonight."

Shannon stood and brushed herself off as if his grasp had left something behind. "If anybody can show you a good time, it's you." She slapped him across the face, spun, and left the room without another word, her heart pounding with each step.

As she left the hotel, she was tempted to go straight to the surveillance van and end it right then and there, but her anger made her wave them off with a simple hand gesture.

This was the third time in two weeks that she had played a very dangerous game. The man she was seeing was suspected of trafficking illegal goods into Canada through a source in DC. She had been asked to do some undercover work to gather enough evidence to arrest him. After three meetings posing as a buyer for his goods, the man was getting tired of her dodging his advances. Apparently, in his world, sex and business were good bedfellows.

Tonight, she had ended the meeting with a forceful slap to his left cheek, killing the deal. Her boss would be furious, but she was not willing to sell herself for the RCMP. It was a job, not a lifestyle. Since joining the Royal Canadian Mounted Police, Shannon had proven herself a brilliant detective. Her tenacity and drive had taken her further than most, but her occasional overreach and high-risk actions had put her in political crosshairs.

Now, she was assigned to DC, working as a liaison as her penance. Politics and paper-pushing were not the excitement she craved, and it was slowly killing her soul. The only bright side of working here was Joel. Maybe the fact they were not currently speaking was just as well. Things right now were extremely complicated.

The chance to do some undercover work had been a godsend. It had consumed her and given her that edge she loved to live on. Now, however, the operation seemed to be a complete bust. She stormed to her car and sped away, needing some time to herself. A local brewery was just the right call.

"Pendleton, rocks," she called to the bartender as she slid up to the L-shaped bar. Her burner phone buzzed, and she glanced down to read the message.

"Ok U win business only Tues at 11p Maple Leaf self-storage Calgary bring the cash"

Her gamble had surprisingly paid off. Now things were about to get interesting. Maybe this would be her ticket back to the field.

She called out to the bartender, "Make that a double."

***

The Encyclical inspected the gangplank that connected the once mighty sailing ship to the dock. *The Moshulu* was the world's oldest and largest square-rigged sailing vessel still afloat. Built in 1904, with four masts and thirty-four sails, she was a state-of-the-art cargo ship in her time. Now, she spent her days tied to a dock, converted into a unique restaurant with magnificent water views as an ode to a bygone era. She was painted blue with a fire-engine-red hull poking just above the waterline, her huge wooden masts jutting into the sky.

The gangplank looked like a small covered bridge painted with colorful maritime signal flags. The roof was canvas, and the rest was made of steel. One side was attached to wheels on the dock, which allowed it to adjust for the tides and current. The other side was attached to a short staircase built permanently into the side hull of the ship. It allowed guests to cross over without the usual steep raking angle that most gangplanks had. He inspected the connection and noticed two plates on swivels that had been bolted together near the hull.

He stooped to tie his shoe as he took out a small measuring tape and got the exact dimensions of the plates. He then stood and casually placed a small camera on the roofline attached by a magnet. It had a view of anyone approaching the gangplank from the ship's direction. With his mission accomplished, he headed to The Deck restaurant onboard for a nice lunch.

He sat on the wooden deck, looking beyond the rigging as small boats cruised past. A slight breeze lifted the humid air and made sitting in the shade almost tolerable. His lunch was a Seafood Louie salad with an ice-cold Cigar City IPA. He had two days to get his plan ready, and it was still forming in his mind.

The last three days of covert surveillance had revealed much about his target. The most important was an exploitable weakness—a girlfriend.

He had seen the two together almost every night. The Encyclical leaned on his resource through Atlantis, JC, to hack into her home computer. Then, it was relatively easy to get her schedule for the week. I mean, the girl was an actuary. She had her whole week planned and documented down to the minute. It was simple enough to pick her date this Friday night on *The Moshulu* as the kill box. Now, he just needed to clean up a few details. He had reached out to his local equipment supplier who provided the gun used to kill his first target. He gave him his requirements, measurements, and deadline. He would do a dry run tonight and be ready for Friday.

Once the moon was down and near total darkness prevailed, The Encyclical slipped the black neoprene hood over his head. He was wearing a Vector Pro full wetsuit with a black matte finish. He lowered himself over the side of the raft and into the harbor, where he inflated his BC (buoyancy compensator) just enough so that his head floated above the water without him having to swim. His gear was attached to a nearby black inflatable tube with an inner mesh. He swam away from the small craft tied to a mooring buoy. *The Moshulu* was only a hundred yards away and, other than a few lights reflecting off the dark water, it was just a silhouette, the last customer long gone. He pushed his gear in front of him, finning through the water.

As he approached, the ship seemed much larger from this perspective. He swam around the bow and stayed close to the port side hull as he moved aft. Once under the gangplank, he was completely obscured in darkness.

He began loosening the bolts holding the two steel plates together on the ship side of the gangplank. They were the main connection securing the gangplank to the ship. Without those bolts, the thing would plunge into the water.

He replaced the bolts with two powerful electromagnets rated for over two tons of shear. They resembled a U-clamp with large connecting plates. The magnets re-secured the gangplank in place as if nothing had changed. The lithium-ion batteries attached to the electromagnets were rated for twenty-eight hours. Plenty of time for what he had in mind.

Next, he shifted four weight belts, each weighing forty pounds, to another electromagnet now attached to the hull, like a limpet mine just below the waterline. Once finished and inspected, he swam back to the raft and motored away in the dark.

He would need some sleep before tomorrow's big play.

***

Codi plopped into her office chair with casual disregard. Working for the FBI had lost its zeal. The recent confines and restrictions on how she was allowed to do her job were weighing on her. The shine she had once enjoyed here was lost, and she was struggling to reacquire it. Her new boss and her policies weren't helping. She opened a document she had been wxorking on over the last couple of days. She had only managed a few words, but the meaning was clear as she reread them.

Dear Acting Supervisory Special Agent in Charge Bruster Holloway,

I would like to notify you that I am resigning from my position with the FBI effective . . .

She leaned back in her chair just in time to see her partner strolling down the hallway. She closed the document. Joel had a coffee cup in each hand and looked lost in his thoughts. Codi watched as he sat at his desk, still not even noticing his partner.

"Hey, Joel," Codi called over to him.

He turned in his chair and rolled over to Codi's space.

"Yeah?" he answered.

"Have you ever considered what you're going to do when you leave the FBI?"

"Leave the FBI? Why would I do that?"

"It's just not the same, trying to solve cases with both hands tied behind our backs."

"True. But there have—and always will be—limits placed on us as FBI agents. We will never be allowed to use the same measures as criminals. Sure, maybe right now the list of restrictions is longer than it used to be, but we are held to a higher standard. It shouldn't make a bit of difference for the victims we serve. They still need our best efforts and attention."

Codi nodded imperceptibly. "There is something we need to talk about. How 'bout you dump that swill, and we hit up Lincoln's Waffle Shop. I could go for a waffle or two."

"Swill? This is Blue Mountain out of Jamaica," Joel said, realizing he was still holding two cups. "Oh, this one's yours," he said as he handed it over.

"Okay, we take the swill with us." Codi took the cup and stood. "You're driving. I'm buying."

Codi took a sip of her coffee. "Good swill."

"I know, right?" Joel said, beaming slightly.

Lincoln's Waffle Shop was in the historic district on Tenth Street NW. The quaint little café specialized in all-day breakfast.

Codi and Joel took a seat away from the front windows and ordered their food. The waffles were golden brown and the bacon crispy.

"Codi, you're not thinking of leaving the FBI, are you?" Joel said, with a forkful waiting to be delivered.

"I don't know. Maybe I'm just trying to find my stride again."

"I think you need to get out there and shoot someone. You always seem your happiest in a gunfight."

"Are you volunteering?" she asked, with one eyebrow raised.

"What? No. I'm just sayin', you need something more than a bunch of dusty old cases piled on our desks. Honestly, we both do."

Codi nodded as she chewed. The waffle was good, as was the advice. Now the trick was making that happen.

"So what was it you wanted to tell me?" Joel asked casually.

"Shannon."

Joel's ears immediately beamed bright red. The emotion he had been trying to bury erupted right to the surface. She suddenly had his full attention. Even his mouth was too focused on her to chew.

"What you saw the other night was not what you think it was."

Joel's mouth fell open.

"She's working an undercover case. I guess it's somewhat dangerous, and she didn't want any of it to come your way."

Joel closed his mouth and tried to absorb Codi's words. He did a preemptive swallow. "You're saying she was kissing a guy as part of an undercover operation?"

"Not all stings are clean, Joel. Sometimes, you have to lie in the mud to get close to the pigs to maintain your legend."

Joel knew the word legend referred to an undercover identity. "Wait, how come you know this and I don't?" Joel demanded.

"I didn't catch my girlfriend kissing another man and then cut off all communications with her. I popped in on her and asked."

"You did?"

"Joel, you have been a bit off your rocker since this first happened. I did it for the partnership. And me."

"Undercover . . . that makes sense. Thanks, Codi." He took another bite of waffle, not even realizing what he had done, his mind a thousand miles away.

"You're welcome. Now, finish your breakfast and let's get back and close out the Officer Wells case. No more chasing after Kroon's daughter and adding to our caseload, agreed?"

"Ah, well, about that, I found something."

Codi's shoulders slumped. "Seriously?"

***

The call was unexpected. Victor Kozlov was dead.

SA Gerald Whitestone drove through the entrance gate to the sand and gravel yard. There were several police cruisers and a city morgue ambulance waiting for action. Gerald stepped out of the car and headed toward the yellow caution tape. The air was ripe with carrion, carried across the late afternoon breeze. CSI and Forensics were busy documenting everything. There were several large mounds of gravel nearly three stories high. The focus was on a pile of gravel next to a large loader that looked like it stopped suddenly mid-load. Gerald stepped to the detective in charge and flashed his badge. The man looked Scandinavian. Gerald guessed *Norway, maybe Sweden.*

"What can you tell me, Detective?"

"The victim was Victor Kozlov. Single GSW to the stomach, which we don't think killed him. It looks like someone dumped several tons of rock on him while he was still alive. He had been missing for several days, according to his employees, hence the smell. Until this front loader," he pointed at the equipment, "came up with a load of rock and half of his rotted body."

Gerald looked at the blood smear on the blade of the front loader. There were two sheets covering the two halves of Victor Kozlov lying nearby.

"That's all I have right now, some of it conjecture, but the autopsy should confirm it." The detective turned back to Gerald. "What's your concern in all this?"

"Victor was a person of interest to the FBI."

"Well, not anymore."

"Thanks, Detective," Gerald said as he turned and left the crime scene. He didn't want to be late to the restaurant tonight.

He started his car and left the yard. A buzzing from his phone had him stabbing the talk button.

"Gerald, it's Yellin. I might have something for you."

"Hang on a sec." Gerald pulled to the side of the road and opened the email on his smartphone. "Okay, go," he prompted.

"I have a payment from one of Victor's offshore accounts to a flower website."

"That *is* something," Gerald said with a dose of sarcasm.

Yellin continued, unaware of the slam, "The payment was for $300,000."

"That's a lot of flowers."

"Lilies, to be precise," Yellin added.

"This is encouraging. How on earth did you find that detail in an offshore account?"

"The teller who made the transfer mentioned it in the notes."

"Must be new. That's a break for us. Good job. Send everything to me—the name of the site and who runs it. I'll go through everything in the morning."

"Will do. Have a good weekend."

"You too." Gerald hung up and took a moment to update a few new notes in his electronic case file before pulling the car back onto the street. He was now one step closer to a very clever assassin.

The humidity and heat of the day were almost gone, especially down by the water, as Gerald walked across the gangplank and up to *The Moshulu,* a Seneca Indian word meaning "one who fears nothing." He found Callie waiting for him at a table near the port side railing. They exchanged a hug and a kiss and sat.

"How goes your case?" Callie asked.

"You know I can't talk about it, but crappy."

"Well, maybe this will cheer you up." She slid a cocktail across the table to his side.

"Yes, that should do it," he said with a smile.

Callie stirred the straw in her drink a couple of times. "So this is a first."

Gerald looked at Callie, questioning.

"First night out on the town as an engaged couple," she said.

"Yes, it is. Here's to us." He raised his glass.

They clinked and took a drink. Callie placed her glass down and looked up. "I've been thinking about this all week, and I was contemplating a fall wedding."

Gerald took a moment to fold his napkin and place it on his lap. "Fall is nice, but when you fall for someone as hard as I have, I say we take next weekend and go to Atlantic City."

He watched her reaction and decided he needed to explain.

"I mean, I'm not some spring chicken, Callie. I was sure this part of my life had passed me by. You have been . . ." He fought for the right words. "You have made me feel like I am just starting my life, my real life, and I can't wait until fall to start it."

"Okay, next weekend it is."

"You pack for three days, and I'll take care of everything else."

The night air cooled as they finished their meal one-handed, each unwilling to let the other's hand go.

***

The Encyclical wore full scuba gear over his black wetsuit while waiting under the gangplank of *The Moshulu.* He had watched from across the river as his target walked onto the ship and joined his date. He then slipped into the water and dropped below. The bay was inky black at night, and he used a wrist-mounted Navimate GPS to navigate from across the channel through the blackness.

Once under the gangplank, he surfaced, keeping just his head out of the water. He used the waiting time to attach a rope to the four weight belts still hooked to the electromagnet on the side of the hull. Strapped to his right wrist was a smartphone with a special app designed for this mission. It had a screen that displayed the image from the small spy camera he had attached to the gangplank yesterday, using monochromatic red tones, making it almost invisible to passersby. Just below the image were two buttons that required a three-second press to activate. They controlled the electromagnets holding the gangplank in place.

He slid along the ship's hull away from the gangplank, keeping in the shadows. Now, all he had to do was wait.

***

After dessert, Callie ordered a liqueur and Gerald a coffee. They sipped and chatted as the evening wore on. It was a magical night, and neither wanted it to end. Eventually, Gerald paid the bill, and it was time to leave. They left the deck and headed for the gangplank exit.

Earlier, The Encyclical had almost pressed the button twice as other couples with similar looks exited the restaurant. Finally, the right pair showed up on his screen. He immediately released all the air in his BC, making him heavy in the water. He had to use his fins to stay afloat. If he sank too far beneath the surface, the app's signal would be lost. As the couple stepped onto the gangplank, he didn't hesitate. He pressed the button to deactivate the electromagnets holding the two plates together. The Encyclical dove under the water and finned vigorously toward the gangplank. He switched on a small red mask light that pointed forward. The magnets dropped off and fell, releasing the shipside of the gangplank. It fell almost six feet before a huge splash, accompanied by a short scream, sent the couple and the steel walkway into the water.

The Encyclical took the rope he had attached to the weight belts on the hull and slipped it around the floundering man in the water. He then pressed the second button and the electromagnet on the hull released, sending 160 pounds of weight to the bottom. The rope attached to the weights pulled at the struggling man who had not yet surfaced for a breath since the downward crash. The Encyclical followed from a distance to make sure his plan succeeded, his red underwater flashlight just barely illuminating the struggling target.

The federal agent had lost a large volume of air in surprise before he was dragged into the depths of the harbor. His last bit of oxygen was used up as his brain finally processed that he was caught on something. The man eventually found the rope hooked to the back of his belt and undid his pants to escape. He pulled his shoes off with the pants and started desperately for the surface, now completely on empty. His lungs fought the urge to suck in water, forcing his body to override the reflex.

As he attempted to reach the surface, a hand suddenly grabbed his ankle and the last of his air left him. His lungs won out, and he took in a large breath of water.

The Encyclical held him for a few more moments before letting his inert form drift off with the current. He re-acquired the directions on his wrist-mounted GPS and headed for the pier on the other side of the channel. It was time to leave the City of Brotherly Love.

Chapter Seventeen

MAPLE LEAF SELF-STORAGE – CALGARY, ALBERTA – 10:39 P.M.

Maple Leaf Self-Storage was an older rundown yard with high fencing and low lighting. It had a collection of shipping containers around the perimeter and two block buildings in the center with green-painted roll-up doors every twenty feet. The flight to Calgary was unusually pleasant, as Shannon was still playing a legend, and that legend flies first class. She had covertly met with her "buyer," the detective running the sting, and they made a plan for the upcoming exchange. His primary concern was her safety, which was nice for a change.

The sign on the fence said closed, but the gate was opened by a man dressed in black as Shannon pulled up in her rental car. She circled the lot and came in behind the two black SUVs waiting to greet her. She popped the rear hatch and exited her idling car with a satchel in hand. The air was fresh and clear since an evening rain had just passed through, leaving everything with a glistening diamond finish.

Shannon closed the distance between Tony and Michael, her vehicle's headlights pinning their faces. She tossed the satchel at their feet and adjusted the mini purse on her shoulder. "There's your money," she said, standing backlit between her car's headlights. "Okay, load it up, boys. Your boss and I have some unfinished business." The extra men looked around, not sure what she meant.

Tony bent down and picked up the bag. He was wearing a black sweater that was just a bit too small for his massive torso. He opened it to find stacks of Canadian bills. He looked over at his boss with a potentially first-time-ever grin. Michael gave him a nod, and he began to count.

Michael took a small step forward. Shannon's car headlights glowed against his deep purple sharkskin suit. "Where's the buyer?"

"You are never going to meet him. That would be bad job security for me," Shannon replied.

She deliberately walked up to Michael and posed seductively. "It's all there, and I'm all here. As soon as our business is done, how 'bout some pleasure?"

Michael looked around, taking the whole site in, making sure things were copacetic. Slowly, he nodded. "Load up her car."

Two men from the second SUV holstered their pistols and popped the hatch. They started to carry cases of dry cat food toward the back of Shannon's car.

"Don't I get to see it first?" she asked.

Michael waved one of the men over. He set the case he was carrying down in front of Shannon.

She opened it and selected a box at random, ripping the top open. It was filled with salmon-flavored dry cat food.

"Okay?"

"Dig a little deeper," Michael said.

Shannon reached into the kibble and felt something hard. She pulled back and out came a Gen 5 Glock19 sealed in plastic.

"There's an extra mag in each box as well."

Shannon felt deeper into the kibble and came back with the extra mag, just as Michael had said.

"That's eighty boxes," he said. "Ten to a case, so eight cases. Just as agreed."

She walked up to Michael and put her arm around his neck and pulled him toward her, planting a kiss on his lips.

"Your men can follow us in the cars," Shannon whispered in his ear. She nodded to the back seat of Michael's SUV. He quickly got the message.

"Tony, you're driving," he said. "Have the men meet us back at the Kensington."

Michael, in a rare show of chivalry, opened the rear passenger door for Shannon. He then half-jogged around to the other side. Tony called out orders to the other two men still loading Shannon's SUV and then moved into the driver's seat.

At the top of a nearby water tower, a spotter with a high-resolution night scope watched the proceedings in the distance. He was waiting for a very specific signal. The moment Inspector Shannon Poole kissed their suspect, he radioed the signal.

Shannon reached into her mini purse and grasped the Beretta Tomcat .32 ACP pocket pistol. She skootched closer to Michael as he entered the vehicle. Tony started the engine and headed for the exit gate.

A four-man team converged from out of the dark and took down the gate guard before he could react. Three unmarked cars followed quickly behind into the yard.

Shannon placed her pistol in Michael's crotch as she whispered in his ear. "If you want to make it through tonight unscathed, do exactly as I say. Sit on your hands." Michael stiffened and reached for the revolver in his coat. Shannon shoved her Tomcat down, getting his attention. He stopped and slowly shoved his hands under his butt. She reached into his coat and removed his .357 Mongoose Nighthawk custom revolver, pointing it at Tony.

"Tony, pull over and put your hands on the steering wheel," she said as she cocked the hammer to add venom to her words.

Tony pulled to the side, rage boiling over, his muscles rippling under his sweater.

"Now, very carefully, remove your gun and toss it out the window." She followed the words by pointing the gun closer to his head. She watched as he started to comply reluctantly.

"Uh-uh, left hand."

He changed hands, rolled down the window, and tossed his 9mm out the window.

"Now, we just have to wait here for a sec."

Suddenly, from out of the shadows, three cars approached, their headlights blasting. One stopped at their SUV, and the other two continued past it into the lot. A brief gun battle played out behind them, and then silence. Two men from the car beside them quickly exited and helped Shannon contain and arrest her prisoners.

Michael tossed a threat before he was shoved into the back of a cruiser.

Soon, the whole place was a beehive of police activity.

Her mission was a success. The adrenaline drop was harsh, but throughout the operation, Shannon had felt more alive than she had in years. She breathed in the euphoria as statements were given and follow-up questions asked. It was wonderful. As the night wore on, a new thought dominated her. It was time to make good with Joel.

***

ASSA Holloway put the phone back in its cradle, processing the call. It was the SSA from the field office in Philadelphia. She had just lost one of her best agents under suspicious circumstances. The agent was working a case that involved two federal employees that had been assassinated in the same way.

The SSA had taken her agent's case file and done a cross-reference to see if the evidence connected in some way to another ongoing case. The only hit was a vague connection to the name Atlantis Kroon, and that connection was to a case ASSA Holloway's two most troublesome agents, Sanders and Strickman, were pursuing. As she considered the request, a small smile grew between the wrinkles on her face.

She popped up and padded out of her office and down the hallway toward the small conference room in her agents' bullpen. With each step, her mind formed a plan that would take away all her current troubles.

Codi and Joel had reconvened in the conference room after breakfast. They were working somewhat at cross purposes. Codi had reluctantly sent in their Harry Wells case report to appease their boss with an addendum, citing Joel's findings on Atlantis. She was not happy about their current direction, but Joel had good instincts and his somewhat manic approach lately didn't mean he wasn't on to something.

"So I heard from Shannon."

Codi stopped what she was doing and looked at her partner.

"She called last night from Calgary," Joel added.

Codi knew when to speak and when to be an ear for her partner, and right now was the time to just listen and nod.

"Turns out you were right. A big misunderstanding. I overreacted like a teenage boy. Relationships are built on trust and communication. I let all that go. My soul was so ripped apart when I saw her kissing another man that I just couldn't deal." He scratched at the back of his head. "I shut her out and buried myself in misery and busywork. It took a bold move from you to get at the truth and turn me around, something I could have done all by myself if I had just addressed the situation with Shannon like an adult and not run off to a dark place and cry." He placed both elbows on the table and leaned toward his partner. "I just wanted to say thanks. You and Shannon mean the world to me. And you . . . make me a better man." Joel wiped the emotion from his eyes.

Codi placed a hand on his arm and simply said, "You're welcome."

Joel nodded slowly, then stood and stepped to the whiteboard. "We're having dinner tonight to discuss what's next."

"That's the best news I've heard all week. Dinner is a good start. Does that mean we can drop this infatuation with Atlantis Kroon?" Codi asked.

"No, just the opposite." He began by recapping what he had found so far. He used the red dry-erase marker to make his point. Slowly at first, but the cathartic actions soon put him back to his old self as he poured through what he had uncovered.

"Atlantis Kroon, daughter of Mark Kroon, operates a website called *Lilies4everyoccasion.com.* The site is credited with taking in $4.8 million gross last year. She claims her operating costs were three million, most of that protected in an LLC. The LLC distributed a little over $1.5 million to her trust in the last year alone."

"Okay."

"I can't figure out how her operating costs were three million dollars. What was she selling, gilded lilies?" He moved as he spoke, the dry-erase marker held in his fingers like a cigar.

"We should try to order some and see what happens," Codi suggested.

"Good thinking." Joel sat at his computer and pulled up the site.

Codi leaned next to him to watch the screen.

"Ah. There you two are."

Codi and Joel looked up to see ASSA Holloway enter the room and sit across from them. They watched her expectantly as she interlocked her fingers.

"I have received a request for you two to lend a hand on a case at the Philadelphia Field Office. There was an agent following up on two suspicious murders. Apparently, your recent investigation into your suspect's daughter matched up with something their agent was working on before he died. Rather than have another agent start all over, they have requested you pick up where he left off, using your evidence as well. It will require you to work out of that office."

Codi and Joel shared a look.

The ASSA seemed a bit too happy at the prospect of them leaving. "I'm not going to lie. The two of you have tried my patience with your loose gun tactics and unwillingness to conform to my procedures. I trust you won't pick up any more bad habits while you're away."

Joel sat, dumbfounded. *Loose gun tactics? And we just closed a case using your policies.*

"Who can say?" Codi said, a bit flippantly to her boss.

"Who can say *no* to such an opportunity to prove your methods to other offices and agents?" Joel added quickly.

ASSA Holloway unclenched her fingers and laid her palms flat on the table. She took a slow breath and released it like it was her last. "I have asked travel to arrange your flight. You leave tomorrow." She stood and left the room.

Codi and Joel watched her go.

"I could kiss you right now," Codi said to Joel.

"Cheek or lips?"

"Tongue."

Joel flushed.

"You got us out of this unproductive prison. Let's pack up our notes and get out of here. I'm suddenly craving a good Philly cheese steak. After your date tonight, of course."

They gathered their evidence. Joel took a picture of the whiteboard before dismantling it, his mind drifting to the evening ahead.

***

Atlantis opened her eyes. There was a silver sliver of moonlight cutting across the foot of her bed. Without moving her head, she scanned the room. In the overstuffed chair in the right corner was a shadow. She sat up slowly as she reached for the stainless Walther she kept under her pillow. It wasn't there. The shadow raised an arm holding her gun. It swung loosely on a finger by the trigger guard loop.

Atlantis stared daggers at the figure but said nothing. The message was clear. *I can get to you.*

"My bosses are an impatient lot and require an update."

"And a text wouldn't suffice?" Atlantis said, dryly.

"They requested I send a message to get a message."

"It is not very wise to enrage the head of a murder-for-hire company."

"Are you enraged?"

Atlantis gestured to her situation. The man had broken into her home, taken her pistol while she slept, and effectively threatened her—yeah, she was enraged. "We'll see."

The silence that followed was claustrophobic.

Finally, she said, "I am starting at the top and working my way down your list."

"Why the top?"

"Professional curiosity and an opportunity I can't pass up," Atlantis replied. "The vice president will be in Los Angeles next week on a fundraising errand for the party."

Chung-Woo nodded his approval and stood. He tossed her Walther back on the bed. "Good. She needs to be silenced, and soon. I'll let them know."

"Let who know?"

"It's better if you don't know. Pardon my interruption." He slipped out the door and was gone.

Atlantis calmed her breathing. She was in a very dangerous game, but she was good at games. The North Korean government was not something she wanted on her bad side. It was time to cut things short and get her two assassins here as soon as possible. There would be no more sleep for tonight.

***

Joel approached the address and rechecked his phone's map. The place he was supposed to meet Shannon for dinner was nothing but a sidewalk on a busy street. He leaned over the railing on the sidewalk and his view was transformed. A column of trees framed a series of thirteen basins, forming a cascading waterfall that spilled down a steep hill. The water dumped into a small reflecting pond at the bottom. There were corresponding stairways that led along both sides of the water feature, allowing pedestrians to relax and explore the area.

The sign said Meridian Hill Park. It was a twelve-acre urban park in Columbia Heights with textured concrete paths, benches, and urns. The stunning flora within the grounds guarded the original longitudinal meridian marker for DC known as the White House Meridian.

As Joel's eyes followed the water flowing down, he saw Shannon waving to him from the grass landing below. He gave a casual wave back and trotted down the stairs to meet her.

There was a white blanket and a picnic basket laid out next to the water's final destination. He walked past a white marble statue of a woman relaxing in a chair known as *Serenity.*

"I thought I had the wrong address," Joel said as an introductory line.

"I was hoping to remove the distractions of other diners." *While still on neutral ground,* Shannon left unsaid.

Joel took a seat across from her on the blanket. The sun was gone from sight, but the sky held an orange glow that slowly intensified with each moment that passed. The air was still and warm, the worst heat of the day dissipating.

Shannon pulled out three small battery-powered candles and turned them on. She placed them between her and Joel.

"So what's for dinner?" he asked.

"Joel, I thought we should talk first and eat second."

He had been reaching for the basket lid but pulled his hand back like there might be a snake inside.

Shannon looked down and collected her thoughts. She spoke without looking up. "I'm sorry you saw me playing undercover intermediary between a low-life seller and buyer. It was just a role. There was nothing to it but a few kisses."

Joel looked at her with his mouth slightly agape, unsure of what to say.

"These kinds of covert jobs can require atypical actions. I don't apologize for them, however, as they led to a major arrest."

"But you apologized for me happening to see you?" Joel asked, a bit confused.

"Hang on. This is not going like I had planned." Shannon paused before restarting. "I am sorry I didn't tell you everything when I signed on to the case. I just wanted to get my old job back so badly that I kinda jumped at it before looking at all the angles."

Joel crossed his legs, trying to get comfortable on the ground.

"And the last thing I wanted was to put you in any danger," she added. "I'm a good detective, and playing liaison officer for the RCMP is killing me. What I mean to say is, I don't know what the future holds; I just know it'll be better with you in it. Please forgive me."

"I already have," Joel said, looking into her perfectly blue eyes. "But where does this leave us? Do you want to go back to work in Canada?"

Shannon nodded slightly, understanding his concerns. "My head is in the job and the job I love is in Canada, but my heart is here in DC with you. It might be a bit screwed up, but that's the truth."

"Shannon, neither one of us can predict the future. All we can do is wrestle the most out of each day we live. Let's just start there and be happy when we can and share that as often as possible."

Shannon almost exploded, as she leaped to give Joel a big hug, wrapping both arms around his neck. The candles went flying, and no one cared.

"I thought I'd lost you. I was such a mess," she said.

Joel paused the hug and leaned back. "*You* were a mess?"

***

SSA Natalie Combs shook Joel's hand vigorously. The field office in Philadelphia was much like the one in DC. It had a common area with cubicles and workspaces, and there were several small meeting rooms and a few enclosed offices. The big differences were the holding cell and the interview rooms. Special Projects didn't have those. They utilized the ones in the DC Field Office one floor below them.

"So glad you could join us. Welcome to Philly. I have read your files, and I can say without fanfare that you two have done some serious butt-kicking and name-taking. It's nice to have you here." Natalie was an older woman with a fire in her eyes and a smile on her face. She had a way of getting right to the point and never played politics with her agents. Her sandy brown hair swept around her round face, framing it into an oval. She had dull, overworked grayish skin and a collection of lines around her mouth that said *smoker*.

"Thanks," Joel said, a bit taken aback.

"Just so you know, I'm a big fan of KISS when it comes to investigations. The simplest approach yields the most accurate results."

Codi and Joel were immediately concerned. Another supervising special agent who used acronyms. This one: Keep it simple, stupid.

"And when I learned that you were working on a case that included some of the same evidence we had, it just made sense to combine assets. As I'm sure you know, we lost Special Agent Whitestone last week in a freak accident. We're still investigating that. It has been really devastating for us here. He was a great man and a great agent and won't easily be replaced."

There was an awkward moment as she processed feelings that were just below the surface.

"We're very sorry," Codi said.

"Thank you. The emotion of the event is still fresh." She took a second to remember, regained control, and pressed on. "I hope you don't mind, but I would like you to join me in an interview to start things off. It might provide some perspective." She stood as she spoke and led the way down a hallway to an interview room. Codi and Joel followed, not sure what they had gotten themselves into.

The room was compact, with a table and four chairs. There were two monitors mounted on the wall, each projecting the image of a small white room, one from a high perspective and the other from straight on. In the room was a table with a woman in her mid-thirties being interviewed. The conversation could be heard on a pair of speakers mounted next to the monitors.

"This is the woman that was with SA Whitestone at the time of his demise," she said as she sat at the table.

Codi and Joel joined her, watching the drama unfold.

"After you finished dinner what happened next?" asked the interviewer in the white room.

Callie Morales was trying to be brave, but her emotions were raw. The past week had been a blur. She wanted to help the FBI find who killed the man she loved. Or was it just a horrible accident? "I . . . we left the restaurant and headed for the parking lot."

"Did you notice anyone or anything out of place?" the interviewer asked.

"No. We stepped onto the ramp that connected the ship to the dock, and it just collapsed." She started to cry again. It had been an on-again, off-again reaction for her ever since the event. Sometimes, she would just burst into tears for no apparent reason.

The interviewer paused to let her regain some control. "Did you hear any sound or noise like a clicking or snapping before it collapsed?"

Callie stopped and tried to relive the moment, tears streaming down her cheeks as she did so. "Not that I remember."

"Okay, go on."

"The ramp fell out from under us and we both went into the water. It was so dark. I lost sight of Gerald for a second because the canvas awning was pulling me to the bottom. It was all I could do to find my way out from under it and swim to the surface. I was sure I would drown. It was the most horrible feeling."

Codi had a flashback from one of her first high-profile cases with the GSA when she had drowned and been brought back. It made her heart race just listening to the woman's experience. The memory was something she had struggled with ever since. Thankfully, Matt's heroic action had saved her life.

"I finally reached the surface. But there was no sign of Gerald. I dove back into the water many times, but it was too dark to see anything." Callie started sobbing.

SSA Combs stepped over to the speaker and turned the volume off. "I'm sorry. I thought this might have been more helpful." She remained standing, reflecting on her dead agent. Realizing her actions, she continued. "I have gone through the case SA Whitestone was working on and feel strongly that your case and his are connected somehow. There are too many coincidences and not the kind I can dismiss."

Codi understood. Coincidences were often the path that led to the truth.

"The thing is, the main suspect is in California. I hate to do this to you, but I think the best thing for the case right now is to put you in the proximity of the suspect. I have notified travel and I'm sending you west. Here is the information SA Whitestone was working on." She handed them a file folder. "The electronic files have been emailed. If there is any chance that Gerald was murdered for getting too close to whatever is going on here, you two will have to be very careful. I want those responsible caught and prosecuted to the fullest."

***

Ling opened the door for JC. He passed through the home and headed straight for the office, setting up his computer on the side desk as if the place were his. With a few clicks, the hacker was online and working. Atlantis flowed into the room a few moments later and took a seat at her desk. She watched the quirky man as his fingers flew across the keys.

"Things are happening," JC said, "and I need to fill you in personally. Those FBI agents you wanted me to track? They're here."

Atlantis seemed surprised by the information. "Here?"

"Yeah, Codi Sanders and Joel Strickman. They flew out of Philly to Orange County yesterday." He stopped typing and spun his chair to face Atlantis. "They're staying at the Ayres Hotel, probably working out of the Los Angeles Field Office's satellite department in Orange. The same place that guy Chen works out of. You know, the one that came here for the interview you told me about."

"Do you know why they are here?" Atlantis asked.

"No, nothing that detailed, but I can tell you they were in Philly for less than twenty-four hours. Whatever case they're following, it's heating up and points to here in the OC."

Philly was where Atlantis had placed a hit on the FBI agent that was getting too close to the Judge Silverman assassination. She had assured herself that with Special Agent Whitestone's and Victor Kozlov's deaths, all leads back to her were snipped. If the new agents had gone from DC to Philly and then on to California, it was possible they were on to her.

"There are only about forty million people living here," she said. "The odds they are looking for me are astronomical." She didn't sound convinced. "It would be silly, however, to stand around and do nothing while the fox eats all your chickens, especially when I employ two of the greatest fox killers on the planet." Atlantis wasn't given to hysterics or petty revenge. She didn't overreact or freeze with panic either, but right there and then, she knew she would fight to protect what was hers with the only weapon she employed—murder.

"Okay, let's take a break for a bit," she said. "We'll give them nothing more to feed on. Go ahead and take down the site. I'm going to work remotely, and I think it would be a good idea if you did as well once our operation is finished here. In the meantime, I'll get the boys in motion and send a little something over to Codi, Joel, and Chen."

"Consider it done. I'll make sure the boys have everything they need, and then . . . I always wanted to check out Patagonia." He started to pack up his laptop. "You sure you want to mess with the FBI?"

"I'm not going to mess with them, JC. I'm going to eliminate them."

Chapter Eighteen

FBI SATELLITE OFFICE – ORANGE COUNTY, CALIFORNIA – 9:13 A.M.

The FBI Field Office in Orange County, California, is a satellite department for the Los Angeles Field Office. It is run under the watchful eye of the SAC (special agent in charge) and is located at 4000 West Metropolitan Drive, Suite 200, in the city of Orange. The building is a four-story rectangle composed of white concrete and gray windows. Inside, on the second floor, is a small office that houses a select core of agents and support staff. Codi and Joel took over the back corner of the bullpen there. They requested two whiteboards and a folding table, transforming the small space into a workroom. SA Roddy Chen, the man who initially helped them interview Atlantis Kroon was assigned to get them get settled.

"My office is right there." He pointed. "If you need anything, please let me know," he said between chomps on a large wad of gum. "And please, call me Chen. That's what everyone else around here calls me."

"Thanks, Chen," Codi replied.

"Bathroom?" Joel asked.

"Down the hall. Key's on the front desk," he said with a second gesture.

Joel nodded and got back to repopulating the boards with all their information, including SA Whitestone's case as they now knew it.

"You grew up around here, didn't you?" Joel said to Codi as they were finishing setting up.

"Yeah, just south," Codi answered without looking up. "San Diego County and Orange County have a lot of similarities. Close to the beach and an easy-going vibe. The only thing that's changed is the population and traffic. That, and my favorite sandwich shop is no more."

"That's why they say you can never go home again." Joel's words were meant more for him than for his partner.

***

It took two full days to make the transfer of evidence and get everything organized. The work area was cramped and seemed to be an echo chamber for all the agents working the room. Every whisper and phone ring seemed to amplify into the back corner where Codi and Joel worked.

"I think this is worse than the fishbowl," she said.

"Everyone can see *and* hear us," he added.

Codi and Joel had done more with less, and it wasn't long before they tuned out the ever-present background noise. As far as everyone hearing them and looking up from their desks to see the information on the board—oh, well.

During the flight to Orange County, Joel and Codi dove into SA Whitestone's case. Two federal employees had been murdered with an unknown venom in an unknown way. They studied the evidence, read the reports, and looked over all the photos. There was something in the information that Joel found intriguing and familiar. He racked his brain but was unable to put it all together. The connection to their two cases came through Atlantis Kroon. Her website, *Lilies4everyoccasion.com,* had piqued Joel's curiosity, and now, with a payment of $300,000 from one of Victor Kozlov's offshore accounts just three weeks before federal judge Dabney Silverman's murder, it was a strong area of focus.

Joel had tried to investigate the website, but an unusually high-level firewall kept him from diving deep.

"What do we know?" He wrote bullet points out on the board and did a brief overview with Codi, pointing to each one as he spoke.

"Two federal employees, a senator, Bobby Carlyle, and a judge, Dabney Silverman, were both murdered using an unknown hemotoxin."

"The judge's murder ties to an ex-Russian mobster named Victor Kozlov. Apparently, he paid $300k to a site called *Lilliesforeveryoccasion.com*. That site is owned by Atlantis Kroon, daughter of a dead North Korean spy."

"We don't know a lot," Codi said. "We can prove he bought the flowers, but that's about it. A judge wouldn't give us a warrant to search her place with this weak connection."

"True . . ." Joel said, extending the word as he thought. "What do you think? Is Atlantis an assassin?" Joel wrote the word next to Atlantis with a question mark after it.

"Maybe. But something's just not quite right. Not because she's a woman. We make excellent assassins."

"I'll bear that in mind when the need arises."

"I'm thinking more like the handler for an assassin," Codi said, with growing conviction. "She's not the type to get her hands dirty. Maybe she has more than one, like a talent agent. Sits back and gets a piece of everything she sells and has real assassins carry out the hits."

They spent the next two hours rehashing the details and fine-tuning their suspicions. Joel seemed to be going over the same details for the third time when Codi interrupted his monologue. "How 'bout we try to order some flowers."

They had started the process back in DC, but it was thwarted by the sudden appearance of ASSA Holloway and her enthusiasm to kick Codi and Joel to the curb for not playing by her rules.

Joel pulled up the site, and Codi watched as he navigated through it. It was plain and concise with simple pictures and descriptions. The prices were clearly stated.

"So what are you thinking, red, orange?" he asked.

"Nothing rhymes with orange. Let's get the white."

"That's a hundred dollars," Joel said.

"It's the Bureau's money—go big . . ."

"Or go home," Joel finished as he placed the order. The screen jumped to an information page.

"That's strange," Joel said. "It's all about the recipient. There's nothing here about the buyer."

Codi looked closer and saw he was right.

"Usually, these kinds of sites require a gallon of personal information to place an order." Joel started to fill in the form. "So who should we send them to?"

Codi thought for a second. "ASSA Holloway."

Joel stopped typing. "You know this might be a murder-for-hire site, right?"

Codi said nothing.

"Come on, she's not that bad. Okay, she is that bad, but as federally deputized agents, we can't rain down a hit on her."

Several agents working nearby stopped what they were doing and looked over. Joel cleared his throat and tried to look normal. Impossible.

Codi still said nothing.

In a whisper, Joel continued, "Fine, but if they kill her, I'm not responsible."

He filled in all the information. It was fairly comprehensive. The next page was the payment page. It only had a few methods of payment, all cryptocurrency.

"Okay, now we're getting somewhere."

"And where is that?" Codi asked.

"Look, the only way to make a purchase is with cryptocurrency. That's not your average Venmo/PayPal website."

"No credit card?"

"Nope, just untraceable cryptocurrency, like Bitcoin or Stellar."

"So how did we get a hit on the $300k from Kozlov's account?" Codi asked.

Joel looked through the paperwork until he found what he was looking for. "Some underling at the bank, in their attempt to be thorough, indicated it in the Notes section of the transaction." Joel held up the photocopy of the transfer of funds from the bank to TRON. "Whoever dug this up should get a serious attaboy. TRON is one of the best blockchain-based operating systems in the world. We'd never get information as to where or to who the money went. Kozlov transferred the money from his offshore account to TRON and then used it to pay for lilies, a.k.a., a hit on the judge."

Codi didn't understand much about cryptocurrency, but the idea of being able to send and receive untraceable payments was troubling. What legitimate business would need that?

"Unfortunately, this information handwritten in the Notes section of a bank payment request is next to useless in court. The defense would discredit the employee and make this black-and-white note look like a psychedelic rock poster, and that's if we could even tie the payment to the site. Once it goes into TRON, it's a black hole."

Codi nodded. It was a thin lead, and the suspect in the transaction was dead, but those three words, *Payment to Lilies4everyoccasion.com*, had connected the two cases by the thinnest of threads.

***

The Scientist stepped aboard the F70 Princess motor yacht. She was a combination of perfection, power, and panache, with an open design and fine leather and walnut finishes throughout. The name on the back, *Cruise Control,* flashed past his view as he took the three steps that led to the side boarding entry on the aft deck. He slid the rear glass slider open and stepped inside. The first thing he noticed was the cool air. The second was the spacious feel of the galley and the salon beyond. This was an expensive yacht. He set his gear bags down and closed the slider behind him. Running his hands across his shaved head, he took in the magnificent space.

"Welcome aboard," a man said. "I went ahead and took the V-berth bedroom up front. You can have the master. It's down those stairs." He pointed to the staircase between the galley and salon along the port hull.

The Scientist looked up to see a handsome male with long dark hair and a scraggly beard a few days old. He had dark green penetrating irises that tracked like radar. He was wearing nothing but surf trunks. "I'm Stuart. The Encyclical." He reached his hand out as he spoke.

"Cameron. The Scientist. Pleasure." The Scientist had heard all about his counterpart in Atlantis's business. They had spoken a few times cryptically over the occasional phone call but had never met in person.

"Oh, before I forget, there is an aft utility room normally used for the crew. It's been set up as a workspace for us."

"Whose yacht is this?" The Scientist asked.

"I'm guessing our sponsor rented it. You know what they say about jets, boats, and women?"

The Scientist just looked at him.

"Rent, don't buy." He laughed at his chauvinistic joke.

The Scientist nodded absently as he picked up his bags and headed for the staircase. It corkscrewed down into a spacious bedroom with an ensuite and plenty of storage. He took the time to stow his gear and clothes and then headed back up to the galley for something to drink.

"So, crazy times, eh? You and me teaming up must be something special." The Encyclical spoke between sips of an aged Scotch.

The Scientist dug through the fully stocked refrigerator and came away with a Diet Coke.

"Our target package is on the table over there. I was waiting till you got here to open it. I'm thinking we should barbeque tonight for dinner and then go through everything."

On the table was an unopened FedEx package. The Scientist glanced out the expansive hull windows that surrounded the room. There were large yachts lined up in a row. Across to the other side were more of the same. This place was a millionaire's playground.

Newport Beach, California, is an ocean-side community built around Newport Bay. The large waterway is fed by the San Diego Creek and comprises six islands, all within a long peninsula that protects everything from the potentially angry sea. The bay is ringed with high-end yachts, restaurants, and homes, a place where possessions are used to show off wealth.

The Scientist realized he hadn't given his new partner an answer yet. "A barbeque—that sounds great." He took a sip of his soda and went outside to the utility room.

The space was small, only about eight by twelve feet, with a narrow worktable, a collection of tools, and some overhead lights. The Scientist set up the rest of his things, paying careful attention to his collection of caterpillars in a portable Tupperware container with small air holes in the lid and some of his more exotic poisons and toxins.

***

The Ayres Hotel was a three-story terracotta stucco L-shaped building located on the border between the cities of Orange and Anaheim. It had a small pool and a jacuzzi and was surrounded by a decent-sized parking lot. The rooms were clean and practical, with a king-sized bed and a small desk to work from. Life on the road was draining but compared to what waited for them back in the DC office, it was a nice change.

Codi listened to the soft buzzing of her cell phone's alarm as she tried to decide. Once the decision was made, she hit the button to turn it off and climbed out of bed. She fought the urge to head to the pool and start her day with several dozen laps.

Joel had gone on and on last night at dinner about the kinds of germs found in hotel pools. Apparently, the information stuck.

Instead, she did a preset bodyweight workout in the room. After a quick shower and change of clothes, she was out the door and down to the complimentary breakfast. She gave herself two more days before she would have to go somewhere else to eat. The over-processed food and soggy bacon were hard to take. She sent a short message to Matt. She was already missing him.

Joel sipped on a small glass of orange juice and pushed the dried-out eggs around the plate. He took off his glasses and checked the lenses.

Make that no more days. They would not eat here again.

After some small talk and bad carbs, they left the eating area to head into the office. As Codi was crossing the lobby, the hotel desk clerk called out to her. "Agent Sanders, I have a delivery for you."

Codi stepped over to the laminated walnut check-in area. The clerk stepped into the back room and came out with a spectacular bouquet of white lilies.

"Thanks." She carried them over to Joel. "I thought you sent these to ASSA Holloway."

"I did."

Joel took the small envelope that had Codi's name on it and opened it. The card inside read, "Sanders and Strickman, it was a pleasure making your acquaintance last week. Here are some flowers to go with your future. White lilies. They're for weddings and funerals."

"It's a message, Joel."

"Sounds like a threat to me."

"It means we're getting close."

They headed to the office, stopping at a coffee shop on the way and keeping an eye out for a tail. It was never fun to have a bullseye painted on your back. It made Joel paranoid and Codi angry. Everything they did from now on would have to be carefully calculated.

SA Chen hurried over as they entered the office.

"I see you got flowers as well."

"She sent you flowers too?" Joel asked.

"Yeah, with a note that said something about my visit to her home, followed by a fairly obvious threat."

"Let me guess, worded just right so it can be taken more than one way."

"Exactly."

Cody put the lilies down on their folding table and took a seat. She was glad for the floral scent that helped cover up the room's overwhelming redolence of testosterone and stress. Joel and Chen followed behind her.

"Chen, how 'bout you and I take a run at her house? Joel, see what else you can find out about the website and her finances. If she's a handler, she'll need to pay her assassins, and that might leave a trail we can follow. She is obviously aware of what we are up to. Let's see if we can return the favor and send a little pressure back the other way. Might cause her to slip up."

"Okay," Joel said. "On it. It's about all we have left to go on."

Codi and Chen left the office, headed toward the beach, and then south down Coast Highway toward Laguna. They passed through the quaint town of

Corona Del Mar and then found themselves out along the open coastline. Chen drove while Codi kept her window down, enjoying the familiar sea air.

Cliffs appeared ahead, signaling the incline into Laguna Beach. The ocean was blue-green, with whitecaps heading out as far as the eye could see to a slightly raised horizon.

"So what's it like working in Orange County?" Codi asked, breaking the silence.

Chen looked over at his passenger. "We get the occasional high-profile case. Mostly white-collar stuff. What about DC? Special Projects. What is that all about?"

"Cold cases, help out with case overload and anything that doesn't fit nicely into the Bureau's case designations."

"I understand you and Joel were the ones behind stopping that domestic terrorism up in Minneapolis."

"Yeah, that and a few others. We've been lucky so far," Codi said.

"Luck, huh?"

The two agents shared a look and a moment before Chen had to get his eyes back to his driving.

Codi looked out the window. A large blue and white sailboat was tacking north, its hull leaning away from the onshore wind.

Chen pulled into the circular driveway, and both agents got out of the vehicle.

"Wow, so this is how the other half lives," Codi said as they walked up to the magnificent home.

"Try the one percent," Chen replied.

They stepped up to a large steel and glass door that pivoted open after a few rings of the doorbell.

"Hi, Mrs. Ling," Chen said. "It's Special Agents Chen and Sanders, FBI, here to see Ms. Kroon."

"You no call her Kroon. She Atlantis and nothing more," the short woman spit out.

Codi tried her hand. "May we speak with Atlantis?"

"Atlantis no here. Has business out of the country. Don't expect to see her back for some time," Mrs. Ling said.

The information caught them by surprise.

"Do you know where she went?" Codi asked.

"What I look like, secretary? She no tell me nothing."

"Look, we would be happy to come back with a warrant," Chen said.

"Warrant? You bluffing. You can't get no warrant. I watch TV. I know these things." Each word carried with it more venom.

SA Chen decided to take a different tack altogether. "Mrs. Ling, this is very serious, and if you are in any way complicit, you will be arrested right along with your boss."

"I don't know that word. But I no work for her. I work for trust. You don't believe me, take a look for yourself. She not here." Mrs. Ling opened the door and gestured. "You take off shoe first," she said, pointing.

Codi and Chen removed their shoes and checked out the home. It was empty. Even some of the nicer furnishings were covered over with sheets for protection against the sunlight.

Atlantis Kroon was in the wind.

***

The Hotel Bel-Air was a sprawling complex with three pools and four bell towers. The terracotta roofs and pinkish stucco gave it a unique and traditional Spanish feel. One of the reasons it was used for presidents and royalty coming to the Los Angeles area was a specific set of buildings separated from the rest of the complex. It was an area that could be cordoned off, secured, and protected better than most. The Scientist drilled down on the website of the grounds to the presidential suite and took a virtual tour.

The vice president's trip to Hollywood was in four days, and a simple hack into the hotel's reservation system revealed an entire section of that hotel taken by just one purchaser, the US government.

The Encyclical looked at an overhead view of the Hotel Bel-Air that he pulled from the many documents in the FedEx package Atlantis had provided. He had stayed there briefly a couple of years back while doing a hit in the city, just not in a room as magnificent as this. The memory of the target splayed out in his driveway for both his wife and girlfriend to find at the same time made him smile. He'd only wished he could have stayed around to watch the fireworks.

A ship's horn blasted nearby and their boat rocked slightly against the dock as the two assassins bantered back and forth with some initial ideas. After going through the entire packet, they had a pretty good idea of what they were up against. The information was thorough and detailed. Completing the hit, that was doable. The real task was getting someone to take the fall because, without that, the US government would never stop looking for the person who killed the vice president. There would be a public outcry, and politicians would demand results.

"What we need is a Lee Harvey Oswald," The Encyclical said.

The Scientist leaned back and interlocked his fingers behind his neck. "I have a thought."

The Encyclical looked over.

"Rather than find a fall guy, how 'bout we make it look like an accident? Then there would be no crime to investigate."

"I like it. What are you proposing?"

The rear slider opened, and a young man stepped onto the boat. Both The Encyclical and The Scientist had their pistols out and aimed before the door finished opening. JC looked up and nearly wet himself. "Sorry, I guess I should have knocked. I was trying to be stealthy."

"Not the best choice around us, JC," The Encyclical said, as he lowered his gun, recognizing Atlantis's hacker.

JC held out a packet and approached the settee. "Atlantis wanted you to see this right away. We could have a problem." He set the packet down. "The FBI might be on to us. Well, three agents in particular. Atlantis wants you two to . . . well." JC wasn't comfortable saying the words. He looked around. "Nice boat, by the way. You guys aren't planning on taking her out any time soon, are you?"

The question was followed by silence.

"Right, gotta go . . . things to do." JC quickly left the boat.

The second packet was specific. Special Agent Joel Strickman, Special Agent Roddy Chen, and Special Agent Codi Sanders had become a problem and all now in Orange County. The two men spit-balled several plans of action, each one figuring out how to deal with the nosey feds. After a few impasses, they took a break to start fresh in the morning.

Killing the vice president and getting away with it would be hard enough as it was.

***

"Bad news."

"Oh, you too?" Codi said as she sat across from her partner in their temporary office.

"What's your bad news?" he asked.

"Atlantis Kroon has flown the coop."

"So has her website." Joel spun his laptop around to a blank webpage with an error message.

"She's covering her tracks. Did you find anything on her finances?"

Joel shook his head.

Codi's phone vibrated. She glanced at the caller ID and hesitated before finally picking it up.

"Special Agent Sanders. How can I help you?" she said in an overly flowery tone.

"Sanders, this is ASSA Holloway. I got a large bouquet of lilies sent to me. Apparently on the agency's dime. Was that your doing?"

"Hang on. Let me put you on speaker." Codi hit the button and laid the phone on the desktop so Joel and Chen could hear the conversation.

"What color were they?" Codi asked.

"What?"

"What color were the lilies?" Codi asked her.

"White, why? What's that have to do—"

Codi interrupted her. "Can you read the inscription that came with them?"

"Hang on, that's one of the reasons I'm calling." There was some paper rustling, and then, "'You'll want to hang on to these for your agents. They will come in handy in a few days.' What the devil is going on?"

"Thanks, boss. I gotta go," Codi said.

"Hey—"

Codi hung up and pocketed her phone. She looked over at her partners; both had shocked expressions. Her phone started to ring again, and she ignored it.

"You going to get that?" Joel said, nervously.

"I'm done playing her games. We have a very serious assassin coming for us, and we have no idea who he or she is."

"Well, I have some good news."

Codi and Chen each shot a glance Joel's way.

"I have been wracking my brain for three days, and it finally came to me. It was something I read one night a couple of years ago on an obscure website that deals in cryptosporidium and—"

"Joel! Just get to the point," Codi said, interrupting. It had been a long day, and Codi was beyond her usual patience level.

"Oh, sorry. I think I know what killed our two federal employees."

"An assassin," Chen said.

"No, the delivery."

Codi and Chen shared a look and then refocused on Joel.

He typed for a few seconds and then spun his laptop around for them to see. "*Lonomia obliqua.*"

Codi squinted at the image. It was just a fuzzy caterpillar. *What is Joel on about now?* she thought.

"Also known as the assassin caterpillar. It fits all the symptoms of our vics."

"Is that thing real?" Chen asked.

"Oh, yeah, very real."

***

The humidity, along with the floral scent mixed with unburned jet fuel, was carried on a light sea breeze. Atlantis stepped down the mobile jetway, her teeth clamped on the stick of the Tootsie Pop she was finishing up. Saipan is a commonwealth of the United States. It is the largest island in the Northern Mariana

Islands, located 135 miles north of Guam. The island had several larger towns along the coast and a few remote villages inland.

She hailed a cab and relaxed as the driver cruised through tropical scenery set against sea-foam-blue water. The home she had rented was a small A-frame style with lots of windows. It was built directly on the crushed coral sand with lush green palm trees on three sides. The back multi-pane glass slider opened up to let the outside world in. There were umbrellas and beach chairs followed by a few steps through the sand down to the water. This wouldn't be an ideal home in a tidal surge or tsunami, but it was paradise on earth, and no more late-night uninvited guests.

She had the driver haul her bags up the stairs to her bedroom and tipped him for his troubles.

The interior was warm and inviting, with leather and rattan furniture on top of bamboo floors. There were three young women lined up in the open kitchen.

"I took it upon myself to stock the kitchen and give you a selection of housemaids to choose from," said a small man with thin vellum-like skin and a shaved head.

Atlantis strolled past the three girls, inspecting them. They were each wearing a white bikini with their hair pulled back, almost carbon copies of each other. They had local island and Chinese influence in their genes with jet black hair and curvy bodies. The first two girls looked a bit intimidated as Atlantis looked them over. The third, however, made eye contact with her. The young woman had a hungry, almost animalistic, feel about her, as a slight smile grew on her face.

"I'll take this one," Atlantis said.

The little man shouted out something in a language Atlantis didn't know, and the two other girls scurried off. "Good choice. She will clean and cook and anything else you want." He gave her a brief bow and followed the other girls out the door.

Atlantis let her fingers slide across the girl's porcelain skin. "What's your name?"

"Leilani," the girl replied.

"I'm Atlantis."

The girl dipped into a brief bow.

Atlantis watched the display, satisfied that her time here on the island would not be boring.

***

It took a couple of days for Atlantis to acclimate to the time difference, but the easy lifestyle and lull of the waves would do her good. She checked her site to confirm that it had been taken down, then left a message for JC to make sure he was situated and asked him to check in on the boys.

He replied with a picture of magnificent snow-capped mountains and a caption of, *soon*. It was his job to keep tabs on the operation she had set into place and alert her to any possible threats coming her way.

Now, all she had to do was wait for her assassins to complete their operation, and then in a month or so, once the dust settled, reopen her doors for business.

This new life suited her well. Her companion was a surprisingly sophisticated cook, among other things. The laid-back lifestyle was something she could get used to. For a while, at least.

Atlantis had chosen this island for its obscurity and its close proximity to over twenty countries, giving her many back doors, should the need arise. She closed her laptop. The urge to stay informed and updated was a weakness that could give you away. She would be patient and just sit back and enjoy the sun. JC knew how to reach her.

Chapter Nineteen

NEWPORT BEACH HARBOR – CALIFORNIA – SLIP 232 – 7:22 P.M.

The next morning, The Encyclical and The Scientist met at the table in the salon.

"You look like you haven't slept yet," The Encyclical said, as his partner listlessly entered the cabin.

"Just getting used to being on a boat," The Scientist said while rubbing his hand across the stubble on his head. "Caffeine?"

"Gotcha," The Encyclical said and pointed out the coffeemaker in the galley.

The Scientist poured himself a cup. "I might not have slept last night, but I gave our little problem a lot of thought." He took a sip and let the hot liquid warm his throat. "I know how to kill the vice president and get away with it."

The Encyclical looked over at his partner with a pleased expression.

"But the first thing I like to do is plan my escape, our escape. It doesn't have to be completely locked in until we figure out all the details, but I'd like to be able to act on a moment's notice and implement a pre-designed exit strategy, especially if a few feds are sniffing around." He took another sip from his cup. "Being based on a boat gives us some unique opportunities."

"Funny, I was thinking the same thing," The Encyclical said.

The Scientist sat at the table and sipped his coffee, waiting for an energy lift. "What have you got in mind?"

"First, I think we should go on a cruise." He gestured to the helm as he spoke. "We both need to know how to skipper this boat and learn its capabilities. Let's spend the next few hours getting familiar with it and our surroundings."

The Scientist slowly nodded his head.

"Do you know how to scuba dive?"

"No. I'm not a big water guy," The Scientist replied.

"Okay. I'm planning on dropping some dive gear over the side and tying it off to the underside of the pier," The Encyclical said. "That way, I—we—can jump overboard at a moment's notice and disappear under the water."

"Nice. Maybe you can show me the basics," The Scientist said. "I'll get us a backup car and stash it nearby with the keys hidden under the rear passenger fender. That way, we can get to it and take off if needed."

"Good. That'll give us a couple different quick ways out of here. We can add one or two more as we tighten up the plan." The Encyclical stood and moved to the helm. He grabbed a map and unrolled it on the table. "There are marinas to the south and north from here and Catalina Island to the west. All possible sanctuaries for this boat. I have made arrangements for a guest slip just south of here at Dana Point Harbor." He pointed out the quaint harbor on the map. "I think we should pop down there for a night. It will give us time to get the hang of the vessel, and we can mirror our escape plans down there as well."

The Scientist looked over the map, committing the other marinas to memory. "I'll get us a second standby ride at Dana Point. Look at this." He pointed to an area marked Doheny State Beach on the map right next to the marina. "A state park with overnight camping. We could leave a car there, and if the marina ever gets too hot we just jump the fence, head up the beach, and vanish."

"I like the way you think. Good. Pick up a tent to make the campsite look real." The Encyclical rolled the map back up.

"I've also been giving our problem with the federal agents some thought."

"You should not sleep more often."

"Believe me, I'm better when I do. I think we need to take them all down in one extended operation, maybe not at the same time, but close and definitely in conjunction with the vice president."

"If we eliminate the agents and the vice president in one operation, all the focus will be on the vice president. We can just slip away and vanish," The Encyclical said.

"Exactly."

The Encyclical powered up the helm. He took the time to show his non-boat-savvy partner the ins and outs of the controls. The cockpit looked like something out of a spaceship with hi-def colored screens displaying charts, numbers, and gauges. The bottom screen controlled the two 1400 HP Mann diesel engines. The top monitors could be configured to your liking, with displays for navigation, fish finder, depth, speed, weather, cruise control, and more. He turned over the engines and let them idle.

Newport Harbor was still glassy since the typical late morning breeze had yet to arrive. Traffic was light as they passed the collection of mega yachts that saw little use from their owners. They paralleled the finger of land called the Newport Peninsula, home to the rich and famous and an epic surf spot known as The Wedge. Then *Cruise Control* motored past the extended jetty and omnipresent bait barge, keeping its wake down.

Once clear of the harbor's mouth, the ocean took on a more lively feel, but the large boat handled the current with ease.

The Encyclical pushed the throttles forward and turned south, heading for the quick trip down to the next harbor—Dana Point. He gestured for The Scientist to get behind the controls and watched as he got a feel for the boat, giving him suggestions as they went.

After ten minutes, he stood up. "Okay, all yours. Wake me when we get to the next harbor."

"What?" The Scientist said.

"You'll be fine. Trust your eyes and the gauges." Then he left for the galley to get a snack. He wanted to confirm the guest slip rental in the next harbor.

***

The University of California, Redlands, was only a forty-minute drive east on the 91 Freeway. The mostly red-brick campus was modern, with a sprawling feel amongst many trees. As they got out of the car, Joel couldn't believe the difference a few miles east made. It was like stepping into an outdoor oven. The dry heat was something he had little experience with growing up on the east coast.

The Entomology department was located in a three-story building with a curved glass entrance. It had a prestigious history, ranked as the second-best place to study bugs in the entire world.

A young man with stringy brown hair, pimply skin, and a rotund body met them on the first floor. He had deep-set eyes that disappeared the moment he turned in any direction. They introduced each other, and the conversation immediately turned to business.

"How can I help you, Detectives?"

Codi let the *faux pas* slide. She was surprised at how young the professor was, but achievement and age often had no correlation.

Joel spoke up. "We were hoping you could tell us something about the *Lonomia obliqua.*"

"Ah, the giant silkworm moth. The stuff of legends."

Codi immediately regretted following Joel out to the college. *The stuff of legends* sounded like one of his conspiracy theories gone wrong.

"What would you like to know? Her history or her habitat?" the professor asked.

"We were more interested in her toxicity."

"Got it. Well, the caterpillars store a hemotoxin in sacks at the base of each spine. Let me show you."

"You have some here?" Joel asked, with unhidden excitement.

"Oh, no such luck." He took them to a kiosk in the back of the open room. It was a carpeted space with several displays and pictures mounted on the walls. A homage to entomology.

He clicked a few keys and then input the caterpillar's name. An image popped up on the screen.

Codi leaned in to get a look at the strange-looking creature. It was an average-sized, brown-mottled worm with huge green bug eyes. Across its entire back were pale green branch-like twigs that stuck out in all directions.

"When an animal or person brushes against them, the hollow bristles you see here penetrate the skin and release the venom. It feels like maybe you brushed against a stinging nettle or received a static shock from a doorknob. Many people don't even realize they have been envenomated until symptoms appeared a few days later. You see, the venom works slowly at first. You develop some flu-like symptoms, and by the time you feel bad enough to go to the hospital, it's too late." He seemed very excited to share his wealth of information, as he clicked the screen to a picture of a woman in a hospital bed right before she died. "Authorities in Brazil are working on an antivenom but have had mixed results."

"Brazil?" Codi asked.

"Yes. It's a species that lives only in a very specific ecosystem there." He clicked the screen again to show the area of southern Brazil where the giant silkworm moth lived.

"Any idea how a person here in the United States, who never went to Brazil, became envenomated by one of these silkworms?" Joel asked.

"It's not possible. We can't even get a mating pair here, and we are one of the highest-rated departments in the world."

"What if someone smuggled them in? Is there a way they could breed them or something?" Codi prompted.

"I guess. We have many such enclosures in the lab here, and we track them through their lifecycles. Raising caterpillars to adulthood is not difficult. But getting the giant silkworm moth here? Sounds far-fetched to me. If somehow you did get them here, you would have to have a very specific enclosure built, which requires a strong knowledge base to pull it off."

The ride back to Orange County was mostly in silence as Codi and Joel took in all they had learned.

The office was nearly empty by the time they made it back in the heavy late-afternoon traffic. Joel had left a search program running on his computer, and the results were waiting for him. He took a moment to read over them.

"I got bupkis on any payments to her assassins. She has some very careful accounting methods. Plus, the Isle of Mann is notoriously secretive about its clients."

Chen walked over to the folding table. "No luck on airlines or immigration hits. Facial rec came up empty as well. Atlantis left the country either on a private jet or under an assumed identity."

"Or both," Codi added.

"Unless she slips up and uses something connected to Atlantis Kroon, she's a ghost," Chen added.

The three agents called it a night. Codi and Joel walked through the parking structure just as the security lights flicked on.

Joel's stomach grumbled. "Seafood?"

"I was thinking more like bait," Codi replied.

Joel looked at her, confused.

"We are never going to get ahead of these guys with the intelligence we have. We have no idea if the assassin that works for Atlantis is Black, white, male, or female. He or she is coming for us. I say we let them."

"Say what?" Joel squeaked.

"Let them. In the military, I was stationed in Afghanistan for a while. The squad I was in had a job tracking three Taliban terrorists who had raided a small village, killing several occupants, including two US doctors. They were on foot, heading for the Turkish border. We picked up and lost their trail so many times. You see, they were really very good and knew the terrain cold. Eventually, we were going to be called off the search and onto something the brass felt was more important. That's when we came up with an alternative plan. We decided the best solution was to get out in front of them.

"We had a helicopter drop us ten miles ahead on a small hilltop. That night, we built a big campfire, and I started singing. It was just the three of us. The other two took sniper positions on a taller hill five hundred yards away. I'll never forget that night, singing and making noise all the while waiting for a bullet to end me. With no booze, mind you."

"Terrifying," Joel said. "So what happened?"

"The Taliban had picked up two more guys on their exodus. We were expecting only three, not five, but they couldn't say no to a chance to remove a few obnoxious Americans in their path."

Joel couldn't imagine being in her situation.

"They came at us from the back of the hill, just past 1:00 a.m. I was not singing anymore by then. In fact, we were just about to give up and bed down for some shuteye. Our spotter didn't see them until they were on top of us. The first bullet removed Lance Corporal Davidson's head. Then all hell let loose as bullets from both sides flew. I dove over the campfire, pulling my trigger as fast as I could. When the dust settled, we had bagged our guys but lost a good man." Codi paused to reflect.

Joel knew better than to interrupt, so he just stayed quiet.

"I wonder if our efforts over there made any difference?" Codi asked no one.

"So your plan is to lure out this assassin so he'll take a shot at us?" Joel said the words, not believing he was actually saying them.

"That's how bait works, Joel."

***

The Scientist lowered his binoculars from the passenger side of a late model BMW 535, as the female agent entered the building, followed by her partner. He double-checked the tracker he had installed on the agent's vehicles was still sending a signal. Surveillance over the last two days had answered a few questions. The agents were just regular people, and regular people had regular routines, and routines could get you killed. He had several opportunities where he could have just walked over and blasted one or the other agent, but that was not the plan. Always stick to the plan. It would get you through unscathed.

After all, the whole point was to get things back to the way they were, not spend the next twenty years running or behind bars.

The Encyclical had talked about hitting the two agents' hotel rooms late at night with a shock-and-awe-style attack. Then make a quick trip to the nearby City of Tustin and eliminate the tall Asian agent in his home. It would be a bit messy, but it would be over and done. Nice and quick, just the way he liked it. The Scientist, however, had been convincing in his words. "There is a way to do this without the agency knowing it was a hit. I mean, accidents happen all the time, and people die unexpectantly or go missing."

***

The Encyclical stepped into the presidential suite at the Hotel Bel-Air. It was four days until the vice president was due to arrive. Room access was through a small, enclosed patio with a jacuzzi and lounge chairs. Once inside, the Spanish-style architecture gave way to a contemporary and bright room filled with comfy chairs and couches. Light from tall windows and the scent of fruits and jasmine filled the room. There was even a grand piano. The rear French doors led to a private pool area surrounded by palms and greenery. Dining and chef's kitchen to the right, sleeping to the left. He had checked in and paid under a false name all set up through JC. He could only imagine the cost per night for this room. The concierge gave his pitch and showed him around, then gracefully exited a hundred dollars richer. The Encyclical kicked off his shoes and removed the fake beard that was starting to itch. He grabbed the room service menu and looked it over. Might as well enjoy himself. He stepped into the well-appointed bathroom just off the master, where he found two identical sinks on white variegated granite.

He had given The Scientist's operation much consideration. It was a solid and clever plan. For now, he would follow along. If at any time he disagreed or things went south, he could go back to the shock-and-awe method he preferred.

He reached for the cold-water handle on the right sink and used all his strength to break it off in the closed position. He set the broken handle down next to the valve and took several pictures of the faucet. He then unscrewed the aerator on the end of the faucet and pocketed it. Now, all he had to do was enjoy his evening and get out first thing in the morning, but not before reporting the broken faucet to the concierge. He glanced at the private pool through the slider in the master. *Perhaps a swim first.*

***

TTX or tetrodotoxin is one of the deadliest toxins on planet Earth. It is a selective sodium channel blocker nonprotein toxin with no known antidote. Several animals use it as a defense system. One of particular note is the puffer fish. Toxicity starts with some general numbness and loss of body coordination. Vomiting and paralysis of the muscles follow, ultimately causing a myocardial infarction. There is currently no way back once you inject or ingest even the tiniest amount of the toxin.

The Scientist held up the small container holding the off-white powder. Using a magnifier, he coated a collection of tiny glass barbs smaller than an individual toothbrush bristle. Working in the aft crew quarters was claustrophobic, and the gentle rocking made detail work difficult, but the lighting was good and the ventilation adequate.

After coating the barbs, he let them dry. Next, he took two identical faucet aerators that matched the sample The Encyclical brought from the hotel and disassembled them to their base parts. He collected the dried barbs and encased them in a porous gel mold just small enough to fit inside the aerator. The gel would slowly dissolve as the water pushed through it, releasing the barbs to flow out of the faucet. He estimated five minutes of runtime before all the barbs were released. Anyone washing their hands or brushing their teeth with this water would inadvertently envenomate themselves with the micro shards. They were so tiny, the cuts would be virtually unfelt.

He placed one of the completed barb-loaded gels into the aerator, carefully reassembled it, and wrapped it up. By now, a work order to replace the broken faucet would have gone to maintenance, and the repair made. JC would have hacked into the maintenance log and discovered the person who had done the repair. He would then hack into his social media accounts and revamp them to show growing frustration with the current administration's policies, giving his most recent posts an all-out anti-government vibe.

Next, The Encyclical would head back to the hotel with the replacement aerators for the presidential suite just before the vice president arrived. In and out.

***

Matt sat back while the Zoom call connected. A familiar face appeared. It looked tired and even a bit desperate.

"Should I be worried?"

"No, just life on the road," Codi lied. The last thing he needed to know was that there was a deadly assassin hunting her and Joel down.

Matt knew better than to ask Codi about any ongoing cases, so he let it go and changed the subject. "How's your hotel room?"

"Seriously, Matt, that's what you want to ask me? Should I respond with, how's the weather?"

"Sorry, just worried about you, and I didn't know what to say."

"I'll be fine, as usual. Why don't you tell me you miss me or you can't wait to hold me in your arms?"

"Well, I do!" Matt stammered out.

"Well, *I do* is not very romantic, though it is good practice for our wedding day."

"Look. Let me start over."

Codi let a small grin form at the corners of her mouth. She loved getting the better of Matt and exposing his boyish, unrefined way when it came to women.

"I love you. I miss you. I can't wait to see you, and I think we should go someplace fun when you're done with this case."

"That's better. And I agree on all accounts."

"Hey, that's not very romantic."

"No, it's not, but it's the truth."

They both shared a heartfelt laugh, and the conversation flourished from there.

Codi eventually hung up, feeling renewed and happy at this unexpected moment, ending an otherwise frustrating day with an uptick.

***

The Hotel Bel-Air was busy this morning. Producers meeting with stars. Business magnets making deals, and high-priced romance on display. The Encyclical strode past the lobby with his head down, pulling a small carry-on behind him. The lobby bathroom was off to the left, and he made a beeline for it. Once in a stall, he changed his clothes into those of a maintenance worker for the hotel, including a curly wig and contacts. He grabbed a tool belt and clipboard with several reprinted work orders JC had provided. The reflection in the mirror was unknown to him. The simple prosthetics, along with everything else, gave him a remarkable likeness to Juan Juarez, the maintenance worker who had made the original faucet repair.

The vice president was due tomorrow, and the subtle ticking clock in the back of The Encyclical's mind pushed him forward. He left the carry-on behind in a locked toilet stall and moved down the hallway and out of the building. The pathway to the left was covered in tropical greens as it led past several buildings. The presidential suite was separated from other areas, and The Encyclical moved like he belonged. He eyed the key card in his hand from his stay a few days prior. JC had done his magic on it and assured him it would work. The real test was right in front of him. He didn't hesitate and swiped the card. Nothing. He swiped again, his mind filling with what-ifs. A small green LED flashed, and he pushed the door open, the what-ifs quickly melting away.

A young man in a suit sitting on the couch sprang up at the unexpected sight of The Encyclical.

"Pardon my intrusion. I am just checking up on a repair."

"Agent Kyle Breman, Secret Service. This room is off limits," said the freshly minted agent.

"That's great, but the person who will be staying here will surely want their bathroom to work."

The agent paused for a moment. "You have a work order?"

"Of course." The Encyclical showed him his paperwork. All were forged by JC and backed up on the hotel's server.

The agent clicked his radio and called in the work order to make sure it was valid. While waiting for a reply, he eyed The Encyclical with suspicion. The Encyclical knew no maintenance worker would challenge a federal agent in a stare-down, so he quickly averted his eyes to his shoes, shuffling slightly while waiting for the reply. The radio squawked, breaking the momentary silence. "That work order is confirmed. Faucet replacement yesterday and follow-up for possible leaks today."

The Encyclical's eyes lifted to the agent across from him, his brown-colored contact lenses appearing open and honest.

"Make it quick."

He turned and headed quickly to the bathroom with his new babysitter in tow. To put on a good show, The Encyclical bent under the sink and shined his light at the valves controlling the hot and cold water to the faucets. He then did a quick test of all handles to verify they were working. Quickly unscrewing the two aerators at the tip of both faucets, he replaced them with the ones he brought. He used a white rag to wipe everything he touched clean, as though he was polishing the chrome. The whole operation took about three minutes. The Secret Service agent casually watched but had no clue what transpired. A quick exit followed, and the agent went back into the bathroom and did a quick test of the faucets for himself. Both worked, but the water pressure was not very strong. *California and their water-saving tactics*, he thought. His mind went back to the daydream he was having before being interrupted, of protecting the vice president by diving in front of a shooter, not hanging out babysitting an empty room.

The Encyclical followed his mental map to the employee changing area. A maid passed by and called him by name with a cursory hello. He returned it with a quickly mumbled hi, not knowing if the person he was mimicking had an accent or not.

Inside the changing room, he found the locker with J. Juarez on it. A simple pick had the lock open, and he quickly placed the evidence he had brought on the very back of the top shelf.

A quick trip back to the bathroom stall had The Encyclical back in his street clothes and out of the hotel. The last thing on his to-do list was to kill the maintenance worker and close the loop. But first, he needed to get back. He had a date with three feds, and he did not want to miss it.

Chapter Twenty

IRVINE, CALIFORNIA – THE IRVINE SPECTRUM MALL – 9:43 A.M.

Joel and Chen drove the rental car out to the Irvine Spectrum, an outdoor shopping center with stores, restaurants, and theaters. Codi could see their car, five vehicles ahead, as she followed her partners down the 5 Freeway in Chen's personal car, a white Mazda MX-5. She had dressed in jeans and a lightweight blue hoodie, with glasses and a ball cap. Each agent was double-armed with a backup gun. She had checked their car over thoroughly first thing that morning and found a transmitter hidden underneath. This was a good sign, and she felt hopeful the assassin would make a play soon. Now it was up to them to provide a scenario that he or she couldn't refuse. Codi didn't know what to expect, but they would be ready.

It had taken about twenty minutes for Codi to convince SA Chen and Joel to go along with her plan, and even then, the enthusiasm was weak.

Protocol required they notify the SSA and have an entire support team. But that would only tip their hand. An assassin as clever and smart as this one would smell a sting and never make a move. Bait didn't work if the game fish saw the fisherman holding the line.

The plan was simple. They would take Saturday and Sunday and make themselves very available. If nothing came of it, they would regroup on Monday and devise another plan of action.

The Irvine Spectrum sits on twenty-seven acres with 150 stores and attractions. Its design is based on the unusual architecture of the Alhambra in Spain. It attracts all ages, with a large Ferris wheel on one end and a wine bar on the other. The city of Irvine, where the Spectrum is located, boasts of being the safest in America for several years running. Codi knew it would only take one run of bad luck to change that stat.

The two agents found a parking spot and headed into the center. Codi followed at a discrete distance, each agent with their head on a swivel as they moved through the masses. Bodies flowed in every direction, some seeking a specific location, others just browsing the many shops. As a Saturday mid-morning, it was crowded. Joel had a light sweat beading on his forehead as the thought of being a willing target was making him jittery and stressed.

They kept in touch simply through cell phones on a three-way conference call with simple white in-ear wired headphones to help them blend in.

"Okay, who's up for a deep-fried Twinkie?" Chen said.

"This isn't the fair, Chen," Codi answered.

"No, seriously, there is a place here that makes the best I've ever had. They deep fry 'em, dip 'em in chocolate, then sprinkle crushed almonds over the top and plop a scoop of organic vanilla bean ice cream next to it."

"I could go for that," Joel added.

"Guys, we're supposed to be—"

"Right, and what says 'I'm not paying attention; come on over and kill me,' like two guys sitting on a bench eating dessert?" Chen interrupted.

"Well, I guess you should have a say in your last meal," Codi responded.

Joel suddenly lost his appetite.

"Nice, Agent Sanders. If we get out of this, you're buying us dinner, and we're picking the place," Chen added.

"*When* we get out of this Chen, *when*. And you're on," Codi said.

***

"Okay, put this on." The Scientist handed The Encyclical a glove that looked just like a hand, including fingernails. "It will protect you from the urticating bristles."

The Encyclical put the glove on his right hand. It was a close approximation to his skin color.

Now that the vice president was handled, there was nothing more they could do on that front. It was truly a watch-and-wait game, which allowed them to focus all their resources on their federal agents.

The Scientist lifted a Tupperware container out of his bag, set it on the bumper, and opened the top.

Inside were several assassin caterpillars in a twig of leaves.

"So that's them, huh? Don't look like much."

"That's what makes them so deadly," The Scientist replied.

The Scientist had described his plan in detail, and his partner had bought in on the simplicity of its design. The tracker they had placed on the agent's car had led them to a large outdoor shopping mall in Orange County. The only downside was the woman had not come along.

Using forceps, The Scientist carefully lifted one of the caterpillars out of the container and handed it to his partner. "Take it by the feet so the bristles point out, and whatever you do, don't touch 'em." He then selected one for himself.

All they had to do was brush past the two agents they had tracked to the mall and then focus on the third. By the time the two guys started showing symptoms, they will have dealt with the female, killed the vice president, and out of the country for a little R&R. The Encyclical had to hand it to his partner; it was a clever and simple plan.

They left the parking structure, each holding his gloved hand in a reverse cup so as not to brush against any bystanders. They needed full potency for the job at hand. Once among the shoppers, they separated and eliminated possibilities. The Irvine Spectrum was laid out like a backward exclamation mark with a large walkway in the center. It intersected several courtyards and had architectural elements like water features, and, at one end, it looped around in a giant square.

All the assassins had to do was follow the path and eventually, they would pass everyone on the property. There was no need to hurry. Slow and steady would win this race.

***

Joel sat on the bench across from two circular waterfalls bordering an electric carousel. It had a menagerie of plastic animals ornately painted to attract young children and their parents for a spin. He and Chen dug into their gooey sugar rush.

"Oh my gosh, this is amazing," Joel said through a mouthful of chocolate Twinkie.

"See, I told you. Not a drop of anything healthy but orgasmic for your taste buds," Chen replied.

Codi listened to their chatter, wondering if maybe she should go get one for herself. Instead, she stepped over to the farthest water fountain and stood up on the concrete lip. It gave her a two-foot height advantage, and she could see across the entire courtyard. She pretended to balance and move to the unheard music in her headphones. She kept her hoodie on and her hands in her pockets, hoping she would blend in with the many people who came here just to be looky-loos.

To her left was a grid in the concrete that squirted large drops of water into the air at random intervals. It was filled with wet children trying to run and guess which spot would shoot up next. To her right, she could clearly hear and see her two partners sitting on a bench, lost in gastric ecstasy. It was for the best, as Joel had momentarily forgotten his fear.

From the corner of her eye, she caught a man strolling through the crowd. He was rough-shaven with a buzzed head. A loud Hawaiian shirt and blue jeans made him stand out such that she noticed and dismissed him at the same time. She continued her surveillance, letting her trained eyes go from one person to the next, not knowing the identity of who she was searching for, focusing instead on their body language and their perceived intent. A shopper doesn't track others; they blissfully stroll through a crowd focused on their destination or the people they are with.

Coming from the opposite direction was a face that caught her attention. He was handsome with flowing long brown hair. His walk had a familiar military posture and movement as he passed. He seemed to wander aimlessly in a general direction, and she almost dismissed him, but there was something not quite right. Codi tried to understand what she was looking at. The man was dressed in chinos and a light Pendleton. He had the sleeves rolled up and his hands—that was it! One of his hands was bent backward and was a little stiff. That arm was not swinging like his other arm. *Could it be an injury or something else?*

"Possible sighting," she said casually into the built-in mic on her headphone cable.

Joel suddenly swallowed his chunk of Twinkie without chewing. He almost gagged, and his face turned red. Chen's eyes darted in every direction like an owl on crack, while Joe tried to get his breath back.

"Cancel that," she followed, quickly realizing their rattled actions would give away the operation.

"What do you mean cancel?" Joel said hoarsely. "I almost swallowed my tongue."

"It's not a perfect science. I was mistaken . . . that's what cancel means. Feel free to go back to your Twinkie."

The man she was watching adjusted his course, and his arm moved forward to point his closed fist in front of him. Codi had thought he had a disability, but now she realized his current path and body language put her two partners in harm's way.

"Excuse me, ma'am, please step down for your own safety."

Codi spun around to see a security guard with his hands on his hips and a resolute expression looking at her. Rather than make a scene, she jumped off the lip and threw a few insults his way, as any other loiterer would do.

Once on the ground, however, she had lost sight of the man she was tracking. "Incoming. I say again, incoming." She ran toward her partners.

***

The Encyclical was the first to spot their targets. He gave a short gesture to his partner to get his attention. Then, using a simple hand signal, two fingers up like a peace sign, he closed the fingers together and pointed them in the direction of the agents. The Scientist nodded and used his hands in an arc to show that he would get around behind them. That would put them on a collision course with their targets from two different sides.

The Scientist moved off left, and The Encyclical slowed down, looking at a pair of cheap sunglasses in one of the center booths. Once in position, they moved in concert, closing on the men.

As he cleared the main collection of bodies in the courtyard, The Encyclical moved his hand holding the deadly organic weapon in front of him. Now it was just a matter of passing by close enough to accidentally trip and swipe his payload on the curly-haired agent with the glasses. He would count on his partner to pass by the back of the other agent and brush him on the neck. The timing was everything now, and he course-corrected, slowing his pace to match his partner's, matching him step for step as they closed in.

***

Joel and Chen had received mixed messages from Codi. The first one ended in "cancel," and now, the "imminent danger" signal. Joel started to stand, but Chen placed his hand on his knee. "Patience," he whispered.

Joel noticed that Chen had slowly moved his hand toward his pistol, using his plate of sugary goodness to cover the action. He matched the movement. His heart was racing as his eyes scanned about, trying not to move his head and give away his concern. To his left, a man approached, but he had no weapon. Joel relaxed just a bit until he noticed something in his hand.

"Caterpillar!" He jumped up, knocking Chen off the bench just as a man from behind was swiping for his neck. The man in front of him reached his hand toward Joel.

Joel raised his arm just in time as the creature was smashed and slimed across his shirtsleeve, leaving a viscous trail across the material. He reached for his gun and spun toward the assassin, but he had melted back into the crowd. He was gone. Chen and Joel stood back-to-back hyperventilating and pointing their guns. Mothers and children screamed and ran for cover. As they parted, the security guard ran at them with his pepper spray aimed like a gun. As soon as the guard saw real guns, he panicked and ran in the other direction.

The two agents slowly lowered their guns, now standing all alone in a cleared-out courtyard.

"Freeze!" Two local policemen ran toward them, guns drawn.

Joel and Chen put their hands in the air. "Don't shoot, we're FBI!"

***

The Encyclical followed the crowd out and back to their car on the fourth floor of the parking structure and got in on the driver's side. They would slip away and regroup. He waited a couple of minutes until The Scientist appeared next to the car and got in. He backed the car out and joined the many others making for the exit.

"Any luck?" The Encyclical asked.

"No. The guy got knocked off the bench just as I swiped. The whole thing went sour in a matter of seconds. I was lucky to get away." The Scientist turned slightly in his seat toward his partner. "We've shown our hand."

"I know," The Encyclical said, contemplating the variables of the situation.

They drove in silence for a bit as they distanced themselves from the momentary disaster. With the federal agents on high alert now, it was going to be a monumental task to finish the job. It might already be done if they had done things his way—*sniper rifle from a distance.* He turned left and then followed the signs to the freeway.

***

Joel and Chen were surrounded by several policemen with the now brave security guard standing behind the men in blue. Things were finally calming down as no one, miraculously, had been injured. Their phones had been confiscated and then returned once their identities had been verified on the radio. A buzzing in Joel's hand interrupted the heated discussion between the two agencies.

"Joel, you there? You guys okay?" It was Codi.

"Yeah, a couple of local cops crashed the party, but we're talking them down. We just about got sent to the morgue. You need to know there are two of them. I got a nice dose of venom on my sleeve. Don't think my shirt is gonna make it," he said, looking down at the goo on his shirt. "Unfortunately, they got away."

"I got eyes on the prize."

"What? Where are you?"

"I'm heading north on the 405. The suspects. Yes, you're right. Suspects, plural. They're both male Caucasian." She gave him a further description of the driver. The other she had not gotten a good look at. "Driving a dark blue BMW 535, license 9ENW319. Hey! Watch where you're going!" The line suddenly cut off.

"Codi? Hello? Are you there?" Nothing.

Joel hung up and tried redialing. There was no answer. He had lost her.

"Get a BOLO out on a dark blue BMW 535, license 9ENW319. We gotta go. North on the 405," Joel called to Chen, and the two agents left in a hurry, leaving the local boys to smooth things over.

***

After the foiled attack, Codi had reacquired her mark just as he blended with the crowd. She followed as close as she dared. The throngs of bodies made it easy to blend in and not be spotted but hard to keep track of a single man. Several times, he disappeared before she was able to spot him again. She sprinted for a flight of stairs as she caught a glimpse of his long hair moving up the levels of the parking structure. Codi had parked on level three. She followed the mark up to the next level along with a horde of people wanting to get away from the possible mass shooting.

She watched from the top of the stairs as he unlocked a dark blue luxury car and got inside. She took a good look at the car and turned, sprinting back to her car, like a salmon swimming against the current. Luckily, she was going downhill, making it easier to push through the up-flowing throng.

She needed to get out of the structure ahead of the car or she would most likely lose it. She popped the door locks and had the engine started before her door closed. Once out of her space, she had to ride the bumper-to-bumper line of cars out through the exit. Just outside the structure, she pulled to the curb, watching the cars flowing out like a bunch of ants escaping a flooding hill.

The dark blue car turned into a lane and passed her. To her surprise, there were two men inside, the one she had made back in the courtyard and a second man in the passenger seat. He was just a blur as they drove by. She pulled out a few cars back and followed them out of the center.

They merged onto the freeway and headed north. Codi maintained a good distance and grabbed her phone. She called Joel and put it on speaker, setting it on the dash, so she could have both hands on the wheel. As she was giving Joel her hard-won stats, an elderly woman too short to see over her large steering wheel changed lanes into Codi as if she didn't exist. Codi swerved and just managed to avoid an accident, but her phone went flying and disappeared somewhere under the passenger seat.

She tried to reach it with her fingers but found nothing but a petrified French fry. She had lost the call and couldn't pull over to retrieve it without the risk of losing the blue BMW. The men she was following were dangerous, and only the most careful actions would get her the required results.

She followed them, taking the overpass south on the 55 to Newport Beach. Codi could hear her phone buzzing under the seat but had no way of answering it. She had tried calling out to Siri several times, but the thick cushion muffled her voice too much for Siri to work. The freeway narrowed and then ended, becoming Newport Boulevard. The car continued west for the coast. As the road dropped from an incline, Codi had a good look at the Pacific Ocean in the distance. It brought back many memories. Just south of here was her childhood stomping grounds. She had a special place in her heart for Southern California, where she had grown up body surfing and boogie boarding in the waves and later long-distance ocean swimming. Her dad had died here, and her mother's ashes were sprinkled on the coast. It was the only connection she had left to them.

The car turned down Coast Highway and mixed with the high-end vehicles that paraded the area. Codi drove past a bevy of high-class restaurants that backed up to the harbor. She crossed over the Newport Harbor Bridge and followed them right onto Balboa Island, the largest island in the harbor. A couple of jogs and she found herself in a small line of cars.

The dark blue BMW was four vehicles ahead and Codi felt confident she had gotten here clean. As she looked more closely, she realized what the line-up of cars was all about. A small ferry carried vehicles and pedestrians back and forth from the peninsula across the water. There were two ferries that worked in tandem, carrying up to two vehicles per trip. They were completely flat, rising out of the water only a couple of feet. There was a small, raised control room on the starboard side and two gates to keep the cars from rolling off.

The ferries traveled only about eight hundred feet across the channel, but they cut off a six-mile drive around. The little service had been running continuously since 1919, and the whole operation showed its age with an "old-world charm."

Codi exited her car and moved to the sidewalk. There were a few pedestrians and shops along the street. She mixed in, keeping her eye on the car ahead that was waiting its turn to board. There was no way she could follow from here without being seen. With only a few cars at a time, her turn would be three back of the suspect's car. If she went on foot, she would probably be discovered, and there was no way to keep up with a car on foot on the other side.

She headed back to the white MX-5 and flipped it around, finding a parking spot. She grabbed her binoculars and tried to dig under the seat for her phone. She couldn't reach it, so she went around to the passenger side and opened the door. Reaching under the seat, her fingertips finally made purchase with the small device, and she pulled it out.

***

As they stopped in the line-up of cars waiting to cross on the ferry, The Scientist spun in his seat surveying the vehicles behind them.

"See anything?" The Encyclical asked.

"No. But I think I'll have a look. Take the car across and back around, and I'll meet you at the boat." He reached into the back seat and came away with a hat and long sleeve t-shirt with a surf logo on it. He changed out of his Hawaiian shirt and pulled the hat low on his head, adding the fake hand glove to his right hand and one very venomous caterpillar. After collecting a few more supplies and a skateboard, he exited the vehicle, staying low at first until he moved past the row of cars and up onto the sidewalk. The first thing he noticed was a white Mazda pulling out of the line-up and turning around. It pulled to the curb and parked. The Scientist walked past the vehicle from the other side of the street and then doubled back slowly. A woman exited, moved to the passenger side, and finally headed toward the railing next to the ferry. She was wearing jeans and a hoodie. He didn't recognize her initially, but the binoculars in her hand made him curious. He kept his loaded gloved hand behind him as he casually followed her back to the railing by the water for a closer look.

Codi carried her binoculars over to the railing alongside the water. She was amazed at the number of enormous yachts docked along the edge in a line of slips. She picked a spot that seemed inconspicuous and dialed Joel.

"Codi, are you okay?"

"Yeah, just dropped my phone. So here's the deal. I'm looking at the Balboa ferry crossing to the peninsula. Our guys are on it, and there is no way I can follow without them seeing me. My interest in taking on two highly trained assassins alone is really low right now. So get your butts over here and call in the cavalry."

Codi could hear Joel typing on his ever-present laptop in the background. "Balboa ferry. Got it. On our way."

She studied the car as it rolled up the ramp and onto the ferry. A small Honda SUV followed behind along with about twelve pedestrians and some bikes. The gate closed, and the ferry started its crossing, about the same time as the ferry on the other side started back toward her. She was focusing on the driver, trying to get a better look at his face.

Come on, just look this way. You know you want to. Wait a minute, where's the passenger?

A sudden rumble, followed by a body slam almost knocked her to the ground.

"I am so sorry. Been trying to learn this darn thing."

Codi spun around to an older surf dude with a skateboard. "You okay?" she asked him.

"I know, watch where I'm going." The man called out as he awkwardly stood and skated away on stiff legs.

Codi shook her head and rubbed the back of her neck, where there was a tingling sensation. She returned to her binoculars just in time to see the ferry dock and the dark blue BMW exit. There was now only one man in the car. As she tracked the vehicle along the street heading north, a sudden stab in her midsection was followed by a voice.

"Take it easy, Miss Fed. You are now in my hands." Codi looked down to see a pistol pointing at her midsection. The man slid it under his loose shirt but continued to point it at her. As her eyes moved to the face, there was recognition. It was the stupid skateboarder.

"Now, very slowly, like it's Sunday morning, I want you to toss me your phone and set down the binoculars." He had backed off just a bit, keeping a safe distance between them, eliminating any chance she might have to lunge at him.

Codi complied, tossing her phone to the man and lowering her binoculars to the ground by the strap. "Hands in your back pockets and walk." He pointed in the direction he wanted her to go with his head. He quickly pulled the sim card out of her phone while her back was turned.

"That's the second phone I've lost this month," she added casually as she started to walk.

There was a crunching sound as her phone died under the foot of her tormentor. The Scientist followed behind her, keeping a wary eye on his prize. It was important to never get too close to a captive. If you had a gun, you could always just shoot them if they tried anything, but if they got too close, the variables increased.

"I've been looking for you," she threw back over her shoulder.

"Well, glad I could help you with your quest. Now shut it, or I will end you right here and now."

Codi doubted he would make a move so close to so many witnesses, but she had no reason to expect he wouldn't kill her the second they were alone.

Chapter Twenty-One

405 FREEWAY – ORANGE COUNTY, CALIFORNIA – 11:58 A.M.

Joel and Chen had been hurrying up the 405 Freeway, not knowing where to go next. Joel was working frantically on his laptop, trying to hack Codi's phone and get her location. It took about five minutes before a red dot showed up on a local map overlay just as his phone rang. It was Codi, and they now had her position.

"Turn around. We need to head to the Newport Ferry, and we need to hurry."

Chen nodded and exited at the next off-ramp. He called the NBPD and asked for their assistance as he crossed over the freeway and back into the southbound traffic. Taking the 55 cut-off toward Newport Beach was the quickest route, and Chen pushed the rental car up over ninety.

Joel was still hyped up from his near brush with death and everything around him seemed to move in slow motion. He kept his eyes on the screen, removing his glasses to clean them as a coping mechanism to ease his nerves. This simple action let his mind wander for just a second.

"Shoot!"

"What is it? Chen asked as he glanced over, doing ninety-five down the freeway.

"I forgot to arrange for someone to feed my pets."

"Pets? How long has it been?" Chen asked.

"It's been almost a week."

"A week? Oh, no."

"They can go a week without food easy, but I need to get ahold of a friend and see if they'll help."

"What are they?"

"Sushi and Sashimi. They're Oscars."

Chen looked at him with a question on his face.

"Fish," Joel explained.

"Gotcha. New to the pet game, huh?" Chen asked.

"No, well, kinda. Had 'em for a few months now, but this is the longest I've been away."

Joel sent a quick text to a friend, hoping that the reply would be in his favor.

"How 'bout you? Any kids or pets?" Joel asked.

"Kinda both. My black lab, Cleo, is like my kid. She runs the house and my heart."

"How do you pull that off?" Joel asked, bracing for a near miss as the rental shot between two slower-moving cars.

"We don't travel like you guys at Special Projects, and I have a backyard and a really cool neighbor. She is just so on it when it comes to helping. Love that girl."

"Oh, yeah? Anything there?"

"Only if you're into octogenarians."

"Gotcha. Not . . . well, I mean they're fine and all, I'm sure. Not judging. Just not my type, per se. Forget it."

"Relax, Joel. You'll live longer."

"Coast Highway, turn left!" Joel called out.

***

After about 150 feet of walking, Codi heard the man's voice again. "Now step onto the *Cruise Control.*" She was confused for a second before noticing the name on the back of a luxury yacht to her right. Stepping up onto the aft deck, she turned back to face the assassin. He was a man of average height and looks other than an unusually long face. Slumped shoulders and an obvious blond wig on his head made him look almost insect-like. His body and actions were on full alert, and his eyes locked onto Codi with single-minded focus.

"Now, very carefully, remove your gun and toss it over the side."

Codi tried to maintain an ambivalent attitude as she did what was asked. "I hope I'm going to get that back. I really liked that gun," she said as she dropped it over the side.

"Now your badge. To me."

Codi tossed her badge toward her captor.

"Always wanted one of these," he said, without taking his eyes off Codi.

"Halloween's coming up. I'm sure you'll find a good use for it."

"Enough small talk. Keep your hands in your pockets and sit down, Indian-style." He watched as Codi obeyed.

"I'm not sure that's politically correct to say these days."

"Neither is shooting people, but I won't hesitate if you keep talking," The Scientist said as he moved onto the boat and stood on the opposite side of the deck. He kept an eagle eye on his captive, his gun hidden under his shirt in case a civilian happened by.

After about five minutes, The Encyclical boarded the boat.

"We had a little monkey on our back," The Scientist said to him.

"I see. The lady fed. Have you disarmed her?" The Encyclical asked.

"I had her toss her gun overboard."

The Encyclical wasn't convinced.

He moved over to Codi, keeping out of his partner's line of sight. He ran his fingers all over her, letting them linger on every curve. He never smiled, but the look on his face was one of pleasure. When he got to her leg, he found her backup gun and removed it. He looked at his partner with a less-than-satisfied glance.

The Scientist shrugged. "I also gave her a little kiss from my beauties."

The Encyclical paused and cocked his head. "Look at you, forcing your plan to work no matter the circumstances. Okay, nice. How long do we have?"

"We can kill her anytime. I just made sure that if everything goes bad, she won't be a problem much longer." He kept his gun aimed at Codi. "On your feet, we're going to the bow. He pointed her to the walkway along the railing. He called to his partner, "Take the inside. If she tries anything, feel free to shoot her through the glass."

Codi led them to the bow. The two assassins maintained their distance and never let their guard down. The Encyclical used the controls to lower the anchor into the water. He let the chain play out until the last link automatically stopped the electric winch.

"Okay, get inside," he said, using Codi's small backup gun in his palm as an incentive.

Codi climbed down into the anchor chain locker located on the very point of the bow. It was just big enough to fit her in a crouched position. The man who had been giving the orders stepped over and kicked the hatch closed on her. She heard the slide lock engaging as everything went dark. Her mind spun. Had she heard right? He had hit her with one of those assassin caterpillars? She tried to remember what Joel had told her. Unfortunately, she had mostly tuned him out at the time. Something about no cure and horrible symptoms, but she couldn't remember for the life of her how long she had to live. A shaft of light shined through the small hole that allowed the chain access to the locker. She scooched around until she found a halfway decent position and tried to remain calm. Getting worked up did nothing to better your situation, especially when there was a deadly venom circulating in your blood.

***

"Give me a hand," The Encyclical said as he reversed the anchor winch. He and his partner wrestled the rode chain onto the deck as it spilled from the winch looking to go back into the locker but was pulled away. Soon there was a big pile of ugly anchor chains on the bow.

"Okay, time to shove off. We don't want a dragnet following her here. We'll shoot her and dump her in the ocean once we're in open water."

They pulled out of the slip and headed for the breakwater. The ocean was choppy from the strong offshore wind, but the luxury craft cut through it with ease. The Scientist moved up to the helm watching his partner navigate the large craft. She was a thing of beauty.

***

The EEOB is accessible from West Executive Avenue just across from the White House. Originally, the Eisenhower Executive Office Building housed the secretary of the Navy, followed by the Army chief of staff. Today, it is the workplace of the vice president of the United States. The white gabled building with a gray roof and circular driveway gives a nod to colonial architecture.

Inside, modern furnishings sat amid key antiques and chandeliers. Sitting on a white linen couch with papers strewn across the glass coffee table sat the second most powerful person in American politics. Vice President Cummings was as intelligent as she was shrewd. She had taken her hometown-girl image and used her disarming style to leave many very capable candidates in the dust. A soft knock perked her interest.

"Madam Vice President, I have your three o'clock," her secretary said from the doorway of the atrium.

"Right. Send him in." The vice president tidied her paperwork before standing and shaking hands with the ambassador of South Korea.

"Mr. Ambassador, *an nyeong ha seyo.* It's good to see you again."

"And to you, Madam Vice President."

The vice president offered him a chair, and they sat and chatted for a time. Vice President Cummings kept her face neutral and unexpressive as they talked, not wanting to give anything away for free.

"The president and I are aligned in your plight, but we believe North Korea is just rattling swords, nothing more."

The ambassador cleared his throat. "I have brought you a present that might change your mind." He opened his briefcase, which had been thoroughly searched upon entry, and handed the vice president a folder.

She opened it and took a few minutes to look it over. The well-earned lines around her lips and blue-gray eyes showed concern. "Operation Redirect? What is that?"

"A North Korean kill list. They are systematically eliminating any person of power who works against them."

"All of this can be verified?"

"Of course." The ambassador shifted in his chair. "Madam Vice President, you have been a true ally for our people. You even spoke out against the DPRK's atrocities many times, and South Korea thanks you for that, but your name is on their list. This needs to be addressed. You need to be careful."

The vice president looked away for just a moment. "They wouldn't dare."

"We are talking about North Korea."

The vice president sighed. "I suppose you're right, and I appreciate your concern. I'm beginning a fundraising campaign for the party. This could be added to my speech. Perhaps someplace dynamic, like Los Angeles."

"You do me and the ROK a great honor."

***

Codi felt like a cross between a sardine and a pretzel. The boat was moving and bouncing across an uneven sea, making the small space more like a torture chamber. The three-inch chain hole that let a narrow shaft of light into the space gave her false hope. She let her fingers move across the floor, searching for anything useful, inching along with fingertips because her head couldn't bend in the confines of the space to look down. There was a small amount of sand and some trash. A PowerBar wrapper and an aluminum cap from a gin bottle. Nothing more.

She realized there was little she could do but wait for a chance to act once out of this dungeon. Her legs were losing feeling, and she would be useless at pouncing out in surprise when they finally did open the hatch. If they ever did. They might just let her succumb to dehydration—no more effort required. Her hand moved across the earbud cables around her neck. They were small flexible white rubber-coated wires with in-ear speakers at one end and a mini lightning plug on the other. She removed them from her neck and tried to think. *Come on, Codi, think like Joel.*

They had locked her in the forward anchor locker. The lock mechanism was a sliding bolt. An idea borne of desperation festered in the back of her mind and slowly made its way to the front.

The boat suddenly stopped, and the engines died, as did her plan. She braced herself to be the next victim of the deadly assassins.

Straining her ears for any clue about what was happening, she drifted back to the tingling sensation on the back of her neck when the assassin "bumped" into her. He had brushed her with one of those deadly caterpillars. She managed to just reach the back of her neck with her left hand. There was a slightly raised rash. She was already dead; she just didn't know when. The thought made her slump in despair.

Codi had finally gotten her life on track. Her career was flourishing right along with her personal life. Matt. A picture of his smiling face crystalized in her mind. She would miss him the most. That is, if there was a hereafter where you could miss someone. Codi's belief system included an all-loving God. It was self-doubt that often took over and painted a much bleaker picture. She heard muffled voices raised in anger and shook the destructive thoughts from her mind. They were unintelligible. She waited and worried as to what might be next, as deadly venom worked its way through her system.

She went back to her simple plan and focused all her energy on that. Better to be moving in a direction rather than be rudderless in fear. The problem was if she somehow got the hatch open, her legs were too numb to stand, and the helm had a perfect view of the anchor locker. She would be spotted and back in this hole, or worse, dead, before she could slither all the way out. Now was not the time.

***

The rental car pulled to the curb, and Chen killed the engine. They had tracked the location on Joel's computer to the last place Codi had called them from before her phone cut off and the signal on his computer vanished. The ferry could be clearly seen up ahead with a short line of vehicles waiting to cross.

"Somewhere over that way." Joel pointed before closing his computer. Both agents exited and moved to opposite sides of the street, walking the sidewalks looking for any sign of their colleague.

"Hey, Joel!" Chen called out, pointing with his left hand. "That's my car; she was here." He stepped over to the MX-5 and checked the doors—locked. There was nothing obvious inside.

They continued down the two sides of the street toward the ferry. Bicyclists and pedestrians moved freely about. Once up to the railing they both looked out at the blue-green bay. There was a fair amount of boat traffic and several paddle boarders plying the water. A small Laser sailboat with a yellow sail zipped in front of the returning ferry, getting a blast from its horn for coming so close. Joel pulled back, worried for his partner, and continued to look around while Chen updated the authorities on the situation and the area of focus for the BOLO.

"Hey, Chen!" Joel called, looking down at the sidewalk along the water's edge.

Chen stepped over to see what had his interest. It was a smashed cell phone.

Joel knew his partner could take care of herself, and if pushed, would push back twice as hard. She was tenacious and inventive, excellent qualities against most odds, but two deadly assassins with a kill order on her would be more than even he could imagine for her. He felt a pang course through him as reality hit home.

Joel looked up. "Upgrade the BOLO to a kidnapping."

***

Once they were out in the open ocean, away from prying eyes, The Encyclical killed the engines and let the yacht drift. The wind pushed at the sleek craft's superstructure. He pulled a Sig P320 from his belt and started for the bow.

The Scientist stood and moved his hand to the butt of his Glock 43. "I've been thinking maybe we don't have to kill her just yet," he called out.

The Encyclical stopped and turned back. His anger at their current situation bubbled to the surface, and it all focused on his partner. "I don't care what you're thinking. I don't do prisoners. We tried things your way and now we have two very edgy federal agents. They are not going to be easy to get at."

The Scientist considered his partner's words. He was right, but right was only half the picture.

"I'll tell you this," The Encyclical continued, "I'm not going to miss this chance to put one down the easy way. From here on, I'm running things. Plus, our current situation requires something more along my skill set. You can be the spotter. If you don't like it, we can separate and work from two different angles."

"Atlantis is not going to like that," The Scientist countered, trying to turn the conversation in his favor.

"She's my handler, not my mother."

Silence filled the cabin.

The Scientist stepped sideways and leaned against the booth. "Let's take things down a notch. No plan ever truly survives contact with the enemy, you know that. Just because the first pass failed doesn't mean we need to abandon the plan. We have something far more valuable on our side now than we did an hour ago. We can use her to our advantage. The fed and this." He held up a small silicon chip.

"What's that?"

"My new calling plan. I helped myself to her cell phone's SIM card. Used correctly, it works like a homing beacon, bringing her partners running to a place and time we determine. Once again, we control the narrative." He looked out the starboard window at the whitecaps moving across the water. "I caught her; that makes her mine. You can have her once I'm done, but I have to tell you she won't be long for this world, anyway." The Scientist turned back to his partner. "She got a little kiss from one of my pets, remember?"

"If that's the way you want to play it," The Encyclical conceded, his gaze locked on his partner. The Scientist returned the same look. Two killers trying to decide if now was a good time to do what they did best.

"What do you have in mind?" The Encyclical finally seemed more interested in results than a shootout that he would easily win. "If I don't like it, I can still kill her and go my own way," he said, sliding his gun back into his belt. He kept his hand on the grip, waiting until The Scientist did likewise. Slowly, they released their grips and let emotions cool off.

***

The Encyclical was convinced the best plan was to shoot their captive now and be done with it. Every movie he had ever seen screamed letting a cop live was a mistake. They always escaped in some crazy way and ended up turning the tables. A simple bullet now would end that possibility. If Atlantis hadn't put so much stock in The Scientist's skills, he would have finished him off then and there for his failure.

The Scientist followed The Encyclical up to the bow with a syringe in hand. They skirted the piled anchor chain, moving to the front hatch. The Encyclical pulled out his pistol and maintained a safe distance. One way or another, they would incapacitate the fed, maybe for good. The boat bobbed with a sudden swell and both men had to regain their balance. The wind made a tangled mess of The Encyclical's long hair, as he watched his partner unlock the hatch and raise the lid.

The woman looked up, shielding her eyes from the blinding sunlight. She seemed pathetic and small in the container, not the tough federal agent he had read about who had single-handedly taken down some serious bad actors. The Scientist raised his phone and took a picture.

"You have two choices," he called out. "I can inject you with this," he held up the syringe, "or my partner will shoot you where you sit. I personally vote for the injection because pulling your carcass out of that hole is going to suck once you're dead."

There was a moment when nothing moved but the wind. The Encyclical considered killing them both right then and there. It would never be easier. Then an arm was raised and held in the sky.

"Smart," The Scientist said as he injected her bicep and shoved her back down. "Now, smile for the camera." He took a few snapshots and then locked her back inside the anchor hold.

The Encyclical returned to the helm and started the engines.

Once *Cruise Control* was back on plane, and the tension in the boat eased.

The Scientist had a far-off look; he was processing the new information, trying to build a solid plan around it. Something that would not end up putting him in the crosshairs of his own partner. If this didn't work, he would have to act first, before The Encyclical could put him down.

He spotted the harbor mouth as it slowly grew in size.

Dana Point Harbor was a quaint I-shaped anchorage surrounded by a rock breakwater and a collection of support shops and restaurants. Once inside the breakwater, the turbulence calmed significantly. *Cruise Control* turned right, then left into the east basin where the guest slip he reserved was waiting. He spun the boat around using the aid of the bow thruster and backed her in. The Scientist jumped out and tied her up just like he had been shown. It was the first successful sign of teamwork since they had nearly separated violently. The Encyclical shut down the engines and went aft to hook up the shore power.

***

Vice President Cummings stepped into the presidential suite. It was the second stop on her tour. The party was backing her for the next election, and she had found favor in the public when her boss had not. The Secret Service agents did a quick sweep of the rooms that had been previously checked and rechecked. All was in order. She moved to the bar and poured herself a small shot of single malt. The smooth caramel-colored liquid sent a familiar burn down the back of her throat, signaling the end of a busy day of travel and campaigning. Her chief of staff did a quick review of her schedule for the following day. It would be a grind, but she was very adept at making herself the center of attention, even in this ego-driven star-studded town.

She thanked him for his recap and invited him to join her for a nightcap. The two used the unusually quiet time to relax, drink, and share war stories. As the clock moved past nine, he excused himself and left the vice president to herself. The whiskey had done its job, and she was feeling calm and even a bit happy. She laid out her toiletries in the bathroom and then relieved herself. A quick hand wash was followed by a few splashes of the warm running water on her face. She dried off and looked at herself in the mirror. At fifty-eight years old, she had carved a career as an attorney, then a senator, and now she was only one step away from the highest office in the land. Some might say it was a meteoric rise, but the years and hard work were etched on her face like a topographic map. She tried a smile. That was better. *Remember to smile.* It was one of her most redeeming qualities. She pulled herself from the mirror and sat back down on the couch. A few more details needed her attention before tomorrow's chaos and speeches.

***

They tied off *Cruise Control* to the transient berth, A12. The Scientist took an Uber up to the Newport Marina and retrieved their getaway car, parking it in the overnight camping area at Doheny State Beach.

The Encyclical lowered a complete scuba set into the water and tied it to the underside of the dock. It hung down on the rope about ten feet below the surface of the water. He pulled out a large hard case and opened it up. Inside were several of his favorite weapons, including a few more out-of-the-box choices. He set a Russian ballistic knife on the table. It had a six-inch blade and a slightly larger handle.

Next, he removed a Remington custom 300 PRC sniper rifle and mounted the Nightforce 7-35x56 ATACR scope on the rail. A thorough check and cleaning had it ready to go. He loaded the mag and placed it in the fly-fishing case he had brought with him. He set a ZiP pistol next to the ballistic knife and holstered it to his calf.

When the Scientist returned, he used a burner phone and Codi's SIM card to send a text along with the picture of Codi. The picture showed her crammed into the anchor locker. The caption read: *If you ever want to see her again come to end of Dana Point pier at 9:50. Bring all your files. You stop looking for us and we won't kill your partner. Just the two of you. Any other cops and she'll be a floater.*

A few moments later, a reply came back: *You have my word the case against you will be dropped. Just don't hurt her.*

He showed his partner the reply. "That's a whole new level of gullible," The Scientist added.

"Don't count on it. They'll shoot us where we stand for taking one of theirs."

They had waited until 9:00 p.m. to send the text, giving the agents just enough time to drive to the location if they hurried. The assassins knew there was no way the feds would drop the case, but that was irrelevant to their plan. Tonight, they would put a serious dent in the FBI's case, one they might never recover from.

"Okay, time for me to go." The Encyclical took his Sig and strapped it in a holster across his chest. He placed the ballistic knife in a slot next to it and covered both with a black windbreaker. Pulling the fly-fishing case from the table, he turned and left the salon. It would take him fifteen minutes to get into position. He walked across the parking lot to the footpath along Dana Point Harbor Drive. From there, he hung a left on Cove Road and pushed himself up the incline to the top of Dana Point cliffs, a prominent rock feature known as the Headlands rising up right next to the harbor. In the 1800s, the cliff was used to ferry animal hides and pelts from nearby Mission San Juan Capistrano via ropes to ships below.

When Cove Road made a sharp ninety-degree turn, The Encyclical jumped the guardrail and worked his way down a drainage incline carved into the side of the cliff. The ditch was built to carry runoff, but it had become so overgrown with sage and oaks, the assassin easily disappeared into the foliage. About sixty feet down, he found the small clearing he'd spotted on his Google Earth search. He opened his case and set up the sniper rifle. There was a clear view of the harbor. The many lights reflecting off the calm water were inspiring. Off to his left was the small Dana Point Pier that jutted out into the harbor.

He opened the bipod and lay down behind the rifle. The scope was exceptional in low light. He lensed the end of the pier, dialing in range and wind. It was a four-hundred-yard shot. A piece of cake for any decent sniper.

***

Darkness parted in a blurry smear, and it took a few minutes to remember her station—kidnapped and drugged inside an anchor locker. Codi blinked her eyes several more times before her vision started to clear. The boat was no longer moving, and it was night. The only good news was that she could no longer feel the pain in her pretzeled legs. They had gone fully numb. She could make out a bit of light thanks to the dock light streaming through the anchor chain hole. It illuminated the space just enough to see her hand in front of her face.

She remembered the beginning of a plan she had been forming before she'd been injected into oblivion.

Shaky fingers pulled the earbuds from around her neck. She bit the tip of the lightning plug off the wire. It took serious finger searching, but she found the aluminum cap. Smashing it between her fingers, she molded it into a wedge shape, then pressed it next to the seam beside the barrel lock. It consisted of a round piece of chromed steel that slid into a receiver and then rotated on a slot to keep it from sliding open on its own. She could see the bolts on the underside that held it in place. All her finger strength couldn't even budge them. She hammered the small aluminum wedge into place with her palm, and the gap between the door and the locker lifted just a fraction, creating a soft glow through the seam. It allowed her to feed the headphone wire out and up into the air outside. After about ten inches had been shoved out, she stopped, realizing that there was no way to get the soft wire to go over the bolt and back into the seam on the other side.

Using her front teeth, she bit the headphone cable in half, leaving a good portion of the original intact and still poking out the seam. She removed the wedge with her fingertips and repositioned it in next to the other side of the lock. Using her teeth, she stripped the rubber coating from the cut-off piece of cable, revealing two braided strands of copper wire. She twisted them together, forming a slightly thicker and stronger wire. After bending a hook on one end, she slid it through the gap and blindly tried to catch the cable poking out on the other side. It would take a lot of luck to work, but sometimes, that's all you had to go on.

The first one hundred tries resulted in failure and bloodless fingers, leaving Codi slumped in despair. She had to re-bend the copper wire into shape multiple times and was ready to quit when a chunk of braided copper pulled through on the other side. She let out a muffled scream of joy—success!

Once she had a generous amount of cable on both sides, she removed the cap-wedge. The hatch was no longer straining against the lock. It allowed the cable to move more freely from side to side. She pulled down, putting friction on the bolt, and rotated her hands in a counterclockwise direction. Nothing. Reversing the motion, she was rewarded with a small click as the barrel post knob rotated up out of the notch. She wiggled the cable back and forth, spinning it as she did, so it would slide to the open position. It was slow and painstaking work with partial millimeters achieved over minutes of effort, but the barrel pin was moving. The excitement had Codi's heart pounding. She tried not to rush as that is how mistakes are made. She spun and wiggled, spun and wiggled, working the bolt slowly out of the hasp. It took almost twenty minutes of frustrated attempts until the thin rubber headphone cable stopped working. The lock was jammed. The bolt would not move. She pulled a bit harder, and the headphone cable snapped.

She sobbed in defeat. There was no getting out. All the good she had done would end here. This would be where she'd take her love for Matt and hope for a future to the grave. The life they'd dreamed of—gone.

If only she had something to write with. She would leave him a message. Tell him how much he meant to her. Codi bowed her head and let the emotions and tears flow. It was at least good to still feel something. That would all end soon enough. She punched the hatch in frustration. It bounced. She let the pity overtake her.

Wait a minute. The hatch just bounced. Her mind was still not functioning at one hundred percent since being drugged. She realized in her muddled state she had slid the barrel lock all the way open. It wasn't stuck. It was at the end of its track.

She cracked the hatch open and peered around. The boat was docked in a slip at a marina. It was not the marina she had started in, but it was very quiet, and no one was in sight.

Codi opened the hatch all the way and pulled herself out. Her legs were worthless until blood finally started flowing through them. She dragged herself out and closed the hatch quietly. Using her arms, she pulled herself over the side and lowered her torso into the water. It was shockingly cold and like a slap in the face sobered her up from the drug hangover. She didn't hesitate as she pulled her way across the water to the other side. Along the way, she started to regain the use of her legs. At first, they just wiggled, but by the time she reached the other side, they were kicking.

***

At 9:30, The Scientist moved with his pistol and another syringe to the anchor locker. He reached down for the lock, but it was already in the open position, and the hatch popped up with ease. The locker was empty. A quick survey of the area spied a swimmer just exiting the water on the other side of the slips. He had planned to take her with him to draw the attention of the other two agents, giving his partner the perfect shot. Now he was forced to change tactics and go on the hunt. There would be no place she could hide.

He ran for the tender, untying the painter as he grabbed the outboard. It screamed to life. He spun the small boat around, heading after the woman.

The other side of East Basin was a long L-shaped peninsula that connected back at Island Way, an intersecting roadway with tall bridge access over the water. It consisted of a long, narrow parking lot and a set of perpendicular docks. The Scientist changed his mind and turned right, heading at a diagonal to the first dock. He would cut her off and work his way back along the peninsula, herding his target into the corner.

***

It started with a numb feeling in her fingertips like she'd pinched a nerve in her spine. She paused reading the documents on the coffee table in front of her and leaned back to stretch. Something was off. The vice president stood and wobbled a bit on her feet and then collapsed, vomiting up her dinner and suddenly covered in beads of sweat. She called out. Almost instantly, the two Secret Service agents assigned to her were at her side. It took a couple of questions followed by an emergency phone call before an ambulance rushed Vice President Cummings to Ronald Reagan UCLA Medical Center.

There, more questions and tests were quickly performed. The most obvious choice was food poisoning. They pumped her stomach, gave her an IV with Ringers, and rushed a blood test. Initial results were inconclusive, but a more thorough pass revealed an unknown toxin. A specialist was called in and within the next two hours, TTX was identified. By now, the vice president was incoherent and teetering on unconsciousness. The specialist demanded an immediate blood transfusion. It was imperative they replace as much infected blood with new blood as possible. Whatever tissue damage had already occurred could not be dealt with. He knew it would take a miracle to save her, but he would break every rule to do so.

***

The Scientist slammed into the dock and threw the painter around a cleat as he stepped up. He ran to the gate and jumped over it into the parking lot. There were several light poles illuminating the area in a sodium-vapor glow. Only a couple of cars remained in the lot. He could see from the dock to the street along the water. It would be easy to spot a person coming. The few buildings here were shuttered for the night. He moved forward, eyes scanning the horizon like a human terminator.

Codi climbed onto the dock and let her body recover before standing. Her soggy form left a wet humanoid shape on the concrete dock. The sky was clear and the salt air centered her mind as she tried to stand. Her legs were still trembling. Running was out of the question for now. She moved like a drunken sailor along the slip past the moored vessels, testing a few doors on some of the boats as she went. She was hoping to find a working radio and call for help, but every craft she tried was dark and locked. This was not the live-aboard area. When she got to the gate, she had to pull herself over, almost crashing to the ground. There was a gray building nearby. It provided restrooms and other supplies for the boaters during business hours. She spied a payphone booth hanging on the wall next to the bathrooms under a single spotlight. As she got closer, she grasped her folly. The phones had all been removed long ago; they were nothing but empty shells. Cell phones were the way of the world now.

The bathroom doors were locked. She turned and headed for the exit. In the distance, there was a silhouette moving in her direction at a slow jog. She recognized the shape of the assassin who had injected her. A sudden shot of adrenaline had her legs working, and she turned and ran in the other direction, not knowing it was a dead end.

Chapter Twenty-Two

DANA POINT HARBOR – ORANGE COUNTY – 9:48 P.M.

Chen pulled the car to a screeching halt next to the pier. Joel was out the door and running before the engine was off. Chen called after him in a hushed voice. "Joel! Get back here! They might be targeting us!"

Joel paused at the words, then raced back to the car.

Chen popped the trunk and handed him a vest and a shotgun. They moved out, serpentining their way to the end of the pier. A sea of ground fog enveloped the harbor, and the first few wisps moved past them. Their shoes banged across the wooden planks.

Once they got to the end of the pier, Joel looked around frantically over the side, at the pilings below, and in the water. There was a ramp near the end that dropped down to a small dock was at water level, allowing boats to tie up alongside. Joel and Chen raced down the ramp and performed another fruitless search.

"She's not here," Chen said, stating the obvious.

"I can see that," Joel snapped as he took out his phone and texted another message to the kidnappers: *We are here. Show us Codi or we are gone.*

The Encyclical watched through the scope as the two agents ran onto the pier. He had an easy shot and was getting impatient with his partner who was supposed to be motoring over in the tender with the drugged female. The fog had rolled in and fingered its way across the pier. He would not wait much longer. If the opportunity arose, he would dispatch the two men with a single round. The proverbial killing two birds with one stone was something he had on his bucket list, and with these two sitting ducks, it would be easy. All he needed was for them to line up. They had done it several times already, but his partner had not yet arrived with the girl and the tender. He needed The Scientist to collect the bodies, remove any evidence, and weigh them down under the water. It was his plan, so where was he?

Now the two agents had dropped down a ramp and were out of sight. If The Scientist screwed this up, he would personally put a bullet in his eye.

He picked up his phone, angry and frustrated, but changed his mind and put it back. Even if The Scientist didn't do his job, he would make sure his side of the equation was completed. He pressed his finger on the trigger and lined up the shot, waiting for them to come back up the ramp. He would finish these two and then tend to the others. He was done playing games.

***

Joel called out in the dark for Codi a couple of times and then checked his phone. Still no reply. He spun and ran into Chen.

"Sorry, I'm just jacked up."

"I get it. Something must have gone wrong."

"That is often the case with Codi. She tends to be taken prisoner and then ends up taking prisoners. But until I'm sure she's safe, we gotta keep looking."

"And call in back-up."

"Good idea. Let's get a bunch of bodies down here and canvas the marina. The first ping I got on Codi's phone was at Newport Beach Harbor, so the suspects must be using a boat to get around."

Chen reached out his hand. "Loan me your phone. I left mine back in the car." Joel unlocked and passed his phone to Chen. He followed behind him up the ramp, as Chen dialed his office's emergency number from memory.

***

At first, all he could see were two heads moving up and down as they walked up the ramp. The one in the front was on the phone. Soon, both agents came into clear view. The Encyclical lined up the shot and waited patiently. The fog was getting thicker as warm, moist air moved across the cool ocean. For a second, a patch moved between him and his targets. He lost sight of the two men, and then, as if God himself had set things in motion, the fog cleared for just a bit, and the agents lined up perfectly.

He slowly exhaled and squeezed the trigger, sending a 250-grain black-tipped copper-jacketed bullet at 2819fps. The bullet was designed to easily penetrate body armor and was not available for purchase in most states. In just over a second, he watched as both bodies jerked and crashed, ending up on top of each other in a motionless pile at the top of the ramp. A single retort echoed through the air before slamming the entire harbor back into silence. It was a thing of beauty. He only wished this scope had a recording feature on it. This was a shot he could watch over and over again. A rare smile crept over his face as he raised up from the scope. He picked up his rifle and placed it back in the fly rod case before scurrying back up the drainage ditch to the street.

***

Joel tried to move past Chen who was focused on dialing in reinforcements as he walked up the ramp. When Joel came up behind him, there was a sudden impact that had Chen crashing back into him with an unexpected intensity. Joel felt a searing pain and then everything went black, just as he heard the beginning of a high-powered rifle shot.

***

The phone in his pocket buzzed, but The Scientist didn't have time to answer. His target was about eighty-five yards ahead of him, standing next to a gray building.

He took off in a sprint. She spooked and disappeared behind the building, heading away from him. The Scientist figured he had about one hundred yards left of the peninsula before she was surrounded and cut off by the water. If he could get to her in time, he could easily corner her, or if she took to the water, it would be like shooting fish in a barrel as she tried to swim away.

Codi ducked behind the building and ran, putting as much distance as she could between herself and the assassin. As long as she kept the building between them, he would not have a shot at her. It would buy her a few more seconds to come up with a plan. Up ahead there were maybe five more access gates to slips lined with boats and then darkness. She was running out of real estate. Without giving it a ton of thought, she turned left and jumped over the gate onto the third to last dock on the spit.

The Scientist reacquired his target as he cleared the building. He noticed a sign for a sailing club above the door. The only light on was a porch light by the front entrance. She was running right to the end as he had hoped. She would be cornered and dealt with in mere moments. Then he could get over to the pier and clean things up. Without warning, his target cut left and leaped over the gate of one of the last slips up ahead. He lost sight of her.

A quick pursuit over the gate, and he found himself standing on a slip lined on both sides with smaller boats. There were twenty-five vessels on each side and only two post lamps leaving much of the four-hundred-foot concrete walkway in darkness. A quick glance around revealed no target. She had gone to ground.

***

Kami Snowden moved her finger around, stirring her coffee. It had gone cold, and the sweetener was reforming on the bottom. She had been on the job for just over six months, and all the excitement she had felt going through the academy had fizzled out. Night shift at Dana Point Harbor was like working at a small-town morgue. Very little action and all of it predictable, like Saturday night's drunken boater going five miles over the speed limit.

She was standing in the observation room of the slump block-and-glass two-story harbor patrol station. The second floor was all windows, providing an elevated 360-degree view. Tonight was just like every night—quiet.

Kami was a sandy blonde with green eyes and tan skin. She had maintained her college weight with a lot of exercise and had defined muscles hidden beneath the bulky uniform that was much like a blue police officer's uniform. She reached for another bite of her protein bar as a rifle shot rang out across the harbor. That was definitely a high-powered rifle shot. She ran out to the dock and listened for another, but the night was once again quiet. A swift run around the harbor might give her a clue as to what was going on. She tossed the lines on the purpose-built twenty-eight-foot enforcement boat sporting an enclosed helm and flashing lights. It was built to take on heavy seas, and using her in the harbor was like having a racehorse at a petting zoo. She started the engine and backed out of the slip. Turning north, she patrolled between the slips, looking both ways as she moved along. The fog was settling in, and visibility was dropping by the minute. She flipped on a searchlight and used it to pry into the darkness.

***

The Encyclical worked his way back down the incline toward the harbor. The fog had now won its battle, and visibility was down to mere feet. He wasn't sure if his partner had completed his task, but there was no chance he was heading over to the scene of the crime to find out. He quickly moved across the empty parking lot and onto the boat. Once there, he pulled his Sig and carefully moved onboard, taking the time to clear each room, including the anchor locker, to make sure no one was lying in wait. The Scientist and the female fed were not onboard. Something had gone wrong. He started the engines and removed all but one dock line, which he ran up to the flybridge and tied back off. Pulling a more practical rifle from his collection, a Heckler and Koch MP5 with a collapsible stock, he took the stairs two at a time to the upper helm controls. From the raised position, he could see and fire down on any interlopers with ease.

The Encyclical was now ready to leave or fight back at a moment's notice.

A harbor patrol boat cruised by unusually fast, but the captain paid *Cruise Control* no mind.

***

Codi ran along the dock, looking for a place to hide. The boats were all locked, so she opted for a different approach. On her right was a large motor sailor with a generous rear cockpit enclosed in blue canvas and clear vinyl. The clear vinyl had aged over the years, making it look more like a frosted bathroom window. Codi slipped aboard and spun the turn-button eyelets securing the bottom to the fiberglass hull. Once released, she slipped under the canvas and came up on the other side. A quick look around revealed nothing useful.

She lifted the seat hatch to the storage space under the bench and felt around inside. A small, hard item caught her attention, and she came away with a corroded rigging knife. It wasn't much against an armed assassin, but her options were severely limited. Her legs had finally returned to full function, allowing her to squat down and lie in wait.

The Scientist pulled a small flashlight from his pocket and flicked it on. He moved slowly from boat to boat, looking for any sign of his escaped prisoner. Several fishing boats with their signature flying bridges were in a row, and then came a couple of sailboats. He took the time to check each hatch to make sure it was locked. After the sailboats came an old trawler that had been left to the elements. Next was a large motor sailor with the rear section completely enclosed in a weathered canvas. The clear sections were opaque, and the once royal blue canvas a faded shell. He stepped next to the canvas, not sure how to get past it to check the door.

Codi slowly lowered her stance, poised like a coiled spring.

***

Joel's eyes fluttered open. The first thing he noticed was the pain. His chest was killing him. There was a heavy weight on top of him, and he couldn't breathe. Bile rose in his throat as he started to panic, trying to make sense of his situation. He wiggled and squirmed until he had removed the top half of the weight on his chest. He heaved in small gulps of air until his mind cleared, his chest unable to fully expand. The weight on top of him was Special Agent Chen, and he was not moving.

The whole incident happened so fast, Joel thought as he shimmied out the rest of the way from under Chen and felt around for his glasses that had flown off in the action. A quick finger check, along with the amount of blood loss confirmed his fears. Chen was dead. He then checked himself and there was plenty of blood on him as well. He was shot and bleeding out. He felt lightheaded for a second as he struggled to pull his vest off to see what was what.

His vest had taken two rounds, which were clear from the outside, but they had not penetrated all the way through. He did a double-check with his hands and even though there was a lot of blood, none of it was his. He let out a sigh of relief and shame all at once. He had heard only one gunshot before he blacked out. He checked Chen's vest. It had one bullet hole in the front and two in the back. The bullet must have fractured off one of his ribs and broken into two pieces, causing them to lose power. As they flew out the back of Chen and into Joel's vest, they never fully penetrated.

He sat next to Chen and took the time to close the man's eyes and place his hands on top of his bloody torso. He was a good agent and would be missed. He thought of the other good people who had lost their lives to these monsters, and rage slowly built within. He placed his vest over Chen's face in reverence and stood on shaky legs. His chest was throbbing, and he was unable to take a full breath. He started to walk back down the foggy pier. Someone would pay.

The sound of an approaching boat motor stopped him, and he dropped low, returning to the end of the pier, crab walking. He was hoping to see Codi and her kidnapper, but a harbor patrol boat materialized from the fog and was zooming past. He waved his hands and called out.

***

Kami had crossed most of the harbor. The fog made it difficult to see much of anything. She would never find where the gunfire had come from. It was almost impossible to determine the source from a single shot, and in this fog, it would be a waste of effort. From her recollection, it had seemed to come from the north end of the harbor, but that only narrowed it down to about a half square mile. She slowed the boat and listened as she steered. Maybe a second gunshot would give her more of a sense of the direction.

A man waving his arms on the end of the harbor pier appeared and then disappeared as the fog shifted across the water. He was wearing grey slacks and a light blue shirt. There was blood all over him. She spun the boat and pulled up to the lower dock and tied it off. Pulling her weapon, she moved up the ramp toward the top of the pier, just as the man ran down. He surprised her and she nearly fired at him.

"Hold it right there!" she screamed as adrenaline coursed through her body.

He froze with a surprised look on his face, open palms out to his side.

"I'm Special Agent Joel Strickman, FBI, and I need your help."

"Show me some identification," she countered, pointing the gun with practiced efficiency. "Nice and slow."

Joel slowly reached into his pocket and pulled out his badge. This woman was taking no chances.

"See?"

Kami slowly lowered her weapon. "I heard a gunshot. Are you okay?"

"Yeah, it's not my blood, but my partner's dead. What I need right now is for you to get on that radio and call in every police officer in the area. We need to lock this place down. There is an assassin hiding around here somewhere." Joel looked around as he spoke.

Kami gaped dumbfoundedly for a beat.

"Come on!" Joel ran past her to the boat, and she followed. He quickly filled her in on the situation with Codi, and she tossed him her cell phone while she used the radio to get help. Joel alerted the FBI, but it would be at least thirty minutes before agents would arrive.

"We're not going to be able to see much in this soup," she said as she untied the boat. "If they brought her in on a boat, they would most likely be using the transient slips on the far side of East Basin."

***

Codi held fast on the other side of the faded vinyl, ready for fight or flight. She could see the flashlight dancing about, and a silhouette following as he stepped onto the boat and moved close to the enclosure. He paused right in front of Codi, the hazy clear vinyl separating them. His flashlight poked around the site as the man held his ground.

***

Satisfied there was nothing, The Scientist was about to step off the motor sailor and go to the next boat when he noticed the canvas fasteners on the bottom were unlatched. He swung his light into the faded plastic and raised his gun.

***

Codi watched as the man moved to leave, but then he suddenly turned back. He stopped and shined his light right in her direction. As soon as he moved his pistol, she pounced. Stabbing the dull knife at her pursuer and backing the move up with a full volume leap. The opaque vinyl gave way to her violence as the stitching holding it all together had long since rotted in the sun. A large section of the clear vinyl wrapped around The Scientist, and he was flung backward. He hit his head on the railing of the next boat and fell between the dock and its hull. The index finger on his hand instinctively pulled the trigger on his Glock multiple times before it smashed on the hull of the other boat and slipped into the dark water.

Bullets blasted through the vinyl just past Codi's head as the man she had crashed into hit the other boat's hull and slipped under the water. Codi hung precariously on the other boat's railing with her toes on the dock. Using her balance, she pulled one foot forward and kicked off the other boat, launching her backward enough to collapse onto the dock. The last of the clear vinyl slipped under the water and disappeared. Codi stood and looked around for any sign of her attacker. Nothing. She waited another couple of minutes before turning back for the walkway.

The sound of a vessel approaching had her ready to bolt until she noticed the flashing blue lights. She stepped onto the main dock and walked briskly to the end. The craft spun up next to her, pinning her in its spotlight. A tall man was aiming a gun her way, but the light blinded her too much to make out anything more.

"Codi?"

"Joel?"

"I thought you were taken!"

"I was, but now . . ." She opened her arms to indicate her current situation as a free woman. "Where's Chen?"

"He didn't make it," Joel said with genuine sadness.

Codi nodded in understanding. She was getting tired of losing good people. "I had one, but he slipped under the water. Might be knocked out, maybe drowned, but I doubt it. He could have swum away, and I would never have known it in this soup." She gestured to the thick fog.

"One of the assassins?" Kami asked from the helm.

"Yeah," she said as she boarded the boat.

"The other tried to kill us with a high-powered rifle," Joel added. "He had us dead to rights, but Chen's death saved my life."

Codi stepped up and gave Joel a brief hug. "Wasn't sure I was going to see you again."

"Ditto. This is Kami, by the way. She runs the place."

Codi and Kami gave each other a nod of respect as they left the dock to continue their search.

"Head over that way. I can take you to their boat," Codi said, pointing.

***

The Scientist crawled out of the water onto the large swim step and up the molded steps to the aft cockpit of *Cruise Control.* The woman he had chased had nearly drowned him, and the swim back to the boat was fueled with fury. He dripped a trail of saltwater behind him. A voice from above stopped him in his tracks.

"What happened to your arm?"

He looked up to see his partner holding a gun on him and then glanced down at his arm. It was trickling blood. He had not even known he was injured, thanks to a burst of adrenaline.

"Minor knife wound. She got away."

"Told you we should have killed her," The Encyclical taunted.

"How'd it go on your end?" The Scientist said, trying to change the subject.

"Two down. Still waiting on the pier for you to clean them up."

"That's not going to happen now; we need to get away from here. This fog will cover our exit, but the cops are going to be swarming this place any minute."

As if on cue, the first sounds of distant sirens cut through the foggy air.

"Boat's running. You take her out. I'm going to get a few surprises in place for anyone who tries to follow us." The Encyclical tossed his MP5 down to his partner. He then climbed down and headed into the salon, leaving his dripping partner on the back deck.

The Scientist jogged up the steps and noticed the single line holding the boat to the dock. He reversed direction and untied *Cruise Control* before engaging the transmission and sending her out into the basin. He made a left turn and headed for the breakwater while rubbing the bump on the back of his head. The cut on his arm had stopped bleeding, and he was trying to focus on the path ahead.

***

The Encyclical grabbed a few supplies, and then slipped over the transom and into the water, disappearing into the inky blackness. He dove to his hidden scuba gear and used his Spetsnaz ballistic knife to cut away the rope holding it in place. He donned the BC and tank, put the regulator in his mouth, and followed that up with a mask, deciding to leave his shoes on in case he needed to run once he got out of the water.

Under the water, the sound of a second engine and the blue flashing lights skipping above the surface told him he had made the right call. They were onto

Cruise Control, and his now ex-partner would draw them away. He glanced up as the hull passed right over him, is partner unaware of his presence.

He took his time and followed the glowing dial on his compass to a predetermined exit point. Staying about ten feet under the water made him invisible, but still allowed what little light came from the harbor to help maintain his bearings. He used a modified breaststroke because of the shoes on his feet and was making decent time. He breathed slowly and easily as he pushed through the water. The post lights on the other side of the harbor were brightening as he approached the dock.

***

The police had finally spread out around the harbor. They had blocked off the main access road, Dana Point Harbor Drive, and sent a team to protect Special Agent Chen's murder site on the pier. The OC Field Office had been notified and agents were in route. Five other patrol cars cruised around the perimeter of the harbor. They were using powerful flashlights to probe the fog for anything suspicious. A live-aboard coming back from his nightly trip to Jimmy's Famous American Tavern was chased, cuffed, and interrogated. Everyone was on edge, and the lack of visibility just made things worse.

***

The harbor patrol boat passed under the Island Way Bridge and into the east basin. Kami slowed to a stop as they came alongside the guest slips.

Codi looked around. "It was right here," she said, pointing to an empty slip.

"Where did it go?" Joel asked.

"We would have seen her if she had come this way," Kami said. "That means she's heading out to open water."

"Trying to escape," Joel added.

"Not on my watch," Kami said as she reached for the throttles to head out after them.

"Wait!" Codi shouted, with her hand raised. She was looking down into the dark water. Joel stepped over to see what had grabbed her attention at such a critical time. There were bubbles coming to the surface in a discernable path. Codi made an imaginary line along the trail and estimated where they were headed. The far end of the harbor.

"I think they might have split up. Is there a dock over that way?" She pointed to an empty space in the fog where she estimated the bubbles were heading.

"That's where the charter boats dock," Kami said, before gunning the throttles and heading that way.

"Can you drop me there?"

"I don't think that's wise."

"Use the radio to get the police over here."

As if they were listening, the radio squawked to life as the police entered the harbor and started asking for details. Joel grabbed the radio and coordinated a full lockdown around the marina. He gave a brief description of the known suspects and parlayed with the officer in charge.

Kami pulled the boat next to the dock and maneuvered a quick reverse, stopping the vessel in its tracks.

"Don't let that boat get away," Codi said as she jumped to the dock.

Kami slammed the throttles forward again, and the craft pulled quickly onto a plane and exited the basin.

Codi stepped to the edge, searching the foggy water for signs of bubbles coming from the direction of her target's assumed destination. Nothing. The patrol boat disappeared in the fog, leaving behind only a diminishing engine sound.

She realized she was unarmed, and going against a trained and armed assassin was a good way to shorten your life expectancy. But with her life clock already ticking down, thanks to a certain caterpillar and its venom, Codi felt more reckless than usual. Maybe the police would arrive in time to help out, but she would not wait for that.

***

Kami cleared the five-mph buoys at thirty knots, leaving a wake that disappeared into the fog behind them. Once out on the open ocean, there was no way of telling which path the fleeing boat had taken. The visibility was maybe fifty yards, and speeding under those conditions could be very dangerous. She powered up her radar and waited for it to come to life. The nine-inch screen glowed as a blue circle with yellow details appeared. There was a large blip on a course of 340 degrees about two miles ahead. Kami course-corrected and pushed the throttles to their stops. Her chase boat could do about forty knots on a good day, and the ocean tonight was smooth as glass. She watched as the gap between her and the luxury craft in front of her slowly closed.

"What's your plan?" she called out to Joel. "I doubt they'll just pull over when we catch them, and it's not like we're big enough to push them around, especially if they're armed. The boat I saw was at least seventy feet long."

"We'll worry about that when we get there. Can we call the Coast Guard?"

"Already did, but they're coming out of Long Beach and are at least forty minutes away."

"This thing will be over in fifteen. Okay, just stay on their tail. Whatever we do, we can't lose 'em."

***

The Scientist pushed the throttles to the max as he left the harbor and made a right turn. The multi-screen display in front of him was a wealth of information, most of it foreign to him. His speed was steady at thirty-five, which made the big boat seem like it was flying, but the visibility was zero, and going that fast through the thick fog was freaky. He'd seen some boat-to-boat crashes on YouTube, and it was nasty stuff. Watching a map-looking screen on his left, he followed a parallel course to the land outline along his starboard side. He was looking for the harbor where they had been before. There were lots of places there to dump the boat and fade away into the foggy night. Atlantis would never forgive him for running off, but he had saved enough to vanish to a remote country. Besides, what had she done, if not the same thing, expecting him to stay behind and clean up her mess? Forget that.

He noticed a solid yellow color appear at the bottom of the screen. It was moving in his direction and slowly closing. He hit the autopilot and went aft to have a look, but there was nothing to see in the thick darkness. He called down to his partner to let him know they had company. After several yells, he went below and searched the boat. Nothing. The Encyclical was not onboard.

The thought of being alone on the big boat caused him to grit his teeth in angst. *How dare he.* Once this was behind him, he would take the time to hunt down and kill The Encyclical for his betrayal. This was unpardonable. He noticed the case with his ex-partner's gear sitting in the salon. He popped the lid and collected two additional pistols. After grabbing some extra mags, he headed back out to the flybridge. The blip that had been behind him on the screen was closer. He checked the distance to the harbor opening—another fifteen minutes away. He racked the MP5's slide and rested it on the chair next to him. He would make short work of his curious followers.

Chapter Twenty-Three

DANA POINT HARBOR – ORANGE COUNTY – 10:56 P.M.

The light on the dock grew brighter as he followed his bubbles upward. Pausing just a foot under the water, he did his best to make sure it was safe above. Once relatively certain, The Encyclical exited the water and grabbed onto the edge of the dock. He pulled three small devices from a waterproof pouch and set the timers for two minutes before tossing them next to the fuel pumps. He took an extra beat to make sure they were in a good position before slipping back under the water. A nice distraction would *bring all the girls to the yard* and would guarantee his safe exit.

He had parked the getaway car in the overnight lot at Doheny Beach, just a short walk from the harbor. Now all he had to do was swim to the end of this channel and hang a right. The beach was only a hundred feet away, and his car was just a short walk from there, far from where the police would soon be focusing all their attention.

***

The night was quiet and thick with moisture. Codi scanned her perimeter looking for any sign of the second assassin. Had she missed him or just guessed wrong? Neither was acceptable to her.

She heard a muffled sound across the narrow basin. There was a single dock there with three gas pumps standing in the center like tall headstones. The water around the dock rippled. Something had disturbed it. The fog was making it hard to see, but as it moved across the water, some patches were thinner. She could just make out bubbles moving in a line up the narrow basin.

As she leaned closer to get a better view, a sudden and violent explosion knocked her backward as the fuel dock across the basin disintegrated. A large piece of steel spun past Codi's head and embedded in the charter boat next to her. Her ears were ringing, and there was a pressure on her chest that felt like a car had hit her. She sat back up, grateful she hadn't been flung into the water, as she was pretty sure she had been knocked out for a second or two. The fuel dock was mostly gone, but three fuel pipes were spouting flames like World War II flame throwers. It illuminated the area in a violent yellow glow, the intense heat eradicating the fog in the immediate area.

Codi remembered the bubbles. The assassin had just triggered a diversion and was escaping up the narrow basin. She turned and staggered in the direction she had seen the bubbles traveling.

Sirens could be heard approaching the diversion as she ran past several larger ships tied up for the night. Next came a tackle store, a restaurant, and a surf shop, all dark inside. Once past the buildings, she approached four ramps extending out into the water. They were used for launching boats with trailers. Beyond that was a crane used for haul-out services. It marked the end of the basin. Codi ran past the ramps and out onto the end of one of the small finger docks pointing back into the basin.

She slowed her pace the last one hundred feet, knowing sound traveled well underwater. Once on the end, she squatted down and let all her senses take over. There was a soft rushing sound in the distance caused by the ignited fuel lines and a metallic sound from a few sailboats whose rigging clanged against their masts as they bobbed. All of this was eclipsed by several sirens closing in on the flames one hundred yards away. Otherwise, the night was quiet. She scanned the water where the fog would allow. Nothing. A shot of fear hit. Had she lost her suspect?

It started as a single bubble. Maybe just a fish, but soon more followed, all lining up as the source moved straight through the water. He was heading her way.

Codi reached into her pocket and grabbed the rigging knife. She lowered herself as she watched the bubbles go past her. Taking several deep breaths and without thinking it through, she launched herself into the water.

***

"Where do you think they're heading?" Joel called out over the roaring engine.

"Newport Harbor is the next stop north," Kami said. "He might try to lose us there and get away on foot. There are lots of places to hide. It would be virtually impossible to surround that harbor like we did in Dana Point."

"Any chance they can get a chopper up in this?" Joel asked.

"No way."

"Okay, describe the entrance for me."

Kami looked at him like he was a bit off but played along. "There are two long rock jetties that reach out into the sea. They are about three hundred feet apart. About three-quarters of the way in is a standing bait barge. After that, the channel opens up gradually to the left, and a big area of moorings divides your path in two directions."

Joel listened to the description and tried to visualize it. "Is a harbor patrol stationed there?"

"Sure. And they are much bigger than ours. Why?" Kami asked.

"I have a plan."

Joel quickly laid out his idea, and Kami listened as if her life depended on it.

"I like the way you think," Kami called back as she reached for the radio. "Halbert, do you read?"

"Newport Harbor Patrol, go for Halbert," came the reply.

"Halbert, this is Kami. I got a 10-3—"

A voice interrupted. "Kami. How's my little Dana Point water cop? I—"

Kami's face flushed, and she interrupted right back. "Halbert. Shut up and listen. There's a seventy-footer heading your way. I'm running 10-39 and working with the FBI."

There was a pause in the response.

"FBI? Slow down, missy."

"I don't have time for your games. I need you to set up a blockade at the harbor mouth, *stat.* No one gets in or out. Understand?"

There was a second pause.

"The guys we're chasing are armed and dangerous, so get yourselves ready."

"Roger that. Give me ten minutes to check things out."

"You got five, and Halbert, these guys have nothing to lose, so take every precaution." She slammed the radio's mic back down. "They have a much bigger setup in Newport than we do. Four boats, stern-to-bow, and some heavy cabling should be able to do the trick. A harbor mouth blockade is something we train for."

"Good. Now we just gotta box him in," Joel returned, "and distract him a bit."

Kami gave Joel an uneasy smile as they blasted along in the foggy ocean, radar providing their only visibility.

"What's it like working for the FBI?" she asked out of nowhere.

"Less water than you get but a lot of politics and restrictions impeding the work. Oh, and enough paperwork to start an origami school."

"Sounds like my job."

"It's the same everywhere these days. You've gotta adapt or get left behind."

Kami glanced over at the FBI man. He was tall and determined with a geeky handsomeness that had a pale cast to it. "You okay? You're looking a bit green."

"Not a big water guy," Joel said while pushing his glasses up his nose, trying to focus ahead. The enclosed helm was tight quarters for two, and Joel hung onto the door latch to keep his balance.

"Try bending your knees as we hit the swells it will take some of the jarring away. And keep your eyes focused ahead. It might help your new skin color."

Joel shot her a glance but followed her instructions. The view out the windscreen was mostly wisps of fog flying by with the searchlight ending in a total white-out up ahead. The water had a black-blue ominous feel, and Kami seemed impervious to it all.

"If you're not much of a water guy, what are you?" Kami asked, trying to take Joel's mind off his turning stomach.

"More of a computer and research kinda guy. I like to find hidden connections."

"Like puzzles?"

"Yeah, like that. I do have two pet fish."

"Oh, so you are just a bit of a water guy," Kami added with a half-smile.

"If aquariums and showers count, sure."

From out of the fog came the stern of *Cruise Control.* She was displacing a lot of water even though she was on plane.

"That's a big boat," Joel exclaimed.

"Expensive boat."

"One thing these guys seem to have plenty of is money."

"We're getting close to the harbor." Kami pointed to the glowing screen that had been displaying their target as they closed the gap. Two parallel lines grew, and *Cruise Control* was heading between them.

The Newport Harbor jetties blocked both north and south swells from entering the harbor. They were some three hundred feet apart and extended for several thousand feet. Once inside, the only thing a boat can do is go in or out. There is no other path until you completely enter the harbor. It was an ideal choke point.

"Try hailing him," Kami said. "It might keep him busy enough that he won't see our little surprise until it's too late." She passed Joel the radio.

"*Cruise Control, Cruise Control,* this is the FBI. Stop your engines and prepare to be boarded."

Joel looked over at Kami. "I've always wanted to say that.

"I say again, stop your engines and prepare to be boarded." Joel continued broadcasting over the loudspeaker. The first signs of flashing blue lights on the horizon seemed to glow through the haze as they closed in on the blockade set up in the mouth of the harbor.

Kami grabbed the mic from Joel and switched the output. "Newport Harbor Patrol, this is Dana Point Harbor Patrol. We see your lights. Be warned, suspect is coming in hot and is armed. We will pull to the side. If you have to shoot, try not to shoot us."

"Roger, we can handle it from here," came the reply.

The response had a condescending slant to it that infuriated Kami, but she pulled and slowed to the right.

***

The Scientist kept his eyes on the chase boat as he powered into the harbor entrance. They were broadcasting on a loudspeaker as if words could do him harm. As he turned back to look ahead, a lineup of flashing blue lights filled his vision. He cut the wheel hard left toward the rocks and then made a big turn to the right in an attempt to come about. At his speed, the big yacht would need all three hundred feet of width to make the turn. As she arced before the blockade of boats tied end to end with armed personnel, he opened fire from his MP5, raking the boats as he flew past. A delayed response sent bullets flying back his way that did little damage.

Once spun around, a quick glance back saw authorities desperately untying their boats to give chase. He switched out the mag and readied for round two. He would sweep back around and crash through the blockade now that it was partially dismantled. He continued the arc, keeping his eyes open for the rock jetty.

Kami and Joel had paused next to the ever-present bait barge that sat in the channel with its two pole lights illuminating its presence. It was long closed for the night and provided some protection from the return fire from the blockade.

As they watched *Cruise Control* spin back in their direction, Kami slammed the throttles to their stops.

"He's trying to escape," she cried out.

"Get us close and ram him if you have to," Joel called back as he exited the helm and dropped to a prone position on the bow. The bow was slightly lower than the hull, giving a modicum of protection. The Harbor Patrol boat rose on plane as the large yacht ahead closed the distance. Joel took careful aim as the bow wobbled and fired three times at the upper control area on the yacht. His actions were met with automatic return fire that sprayed hot lead all around him. Joel had nowhere to hide and held his breath while returning fire in hopes of keeping the shooter's accuracy down.

Sirens and lights could be heard chasing after the getaway boat. To Kami's surprise, *Cruise Control* did not head back out to open water but continued in its arc, heading back into the marina.

After strafing the small boat that had fired at him, The Scientist reloaded his rifle and continued his turn. The boat was running flat out, pushing a huge wake behind it. As he came about, several boats headed his way, but most importantly, the blockade had broken up. Through the fog, he could make out several gaps ahead. He straightened the wheel and headed for one of them.

Kami and Joel realized at the same time what had happened. The Newport Harbor Patrol had been so zealous to capture the boat that they had dismantled the blockade too soon. Their suspect was going to surge through and disappear into the clutter of the harbor.

Kami maxed out her throttles and yanked her wheel to port.

***

Codi was a strong swimmer, and she used her dive to propel her deep into the water. A shadow of a scuba diver appeared about seven feet down. The splash she made entering the water caused him to look up. He immediately realized the threat. He spun to meet her. Codi grabbed the low-pressure hose that provided breathable air from the tank to the regulator and sawed it in two with her knife.

The Encyclical recognized what his attacker was doing too late. His air supply was suddenly cut off. Bubbles surrounded him as the cut-off hose whipped uncontrollably through the water, dumping the tank's contents. He instinctively reached for the ballistic knife strapped to his calf and gave it a quick swipe at the man attacking him—no, woman. *Woman? It was the escaped fed! How was this possible?*

The glow from the post light above, cutting through the fog and ten feet of water, did little to illuminate the battle. Codi saw the blade just before it slashed her way. She sucked her midsection back as it sliced through the water and her skin. A faint dark ooze spilled and mixed with the sea. The assassin then returned the blade in a reverse arc, hoping for more damage. Codi grabbed his wrist, pulling her toward him inside the blade's arc, and blocked the return sweep all in one motion. She used her other hand to pry off his mask. Now he was out of air, and his visibility matched hers.

She swung her small blade down, aiming for the man's eye, but he ducked at the last minute, and the blade gouged his skull and broke off, leaving Codi only the handle. She let it drop and concentrated both hands on the man's knife. They spun and flung through the water as bubbles spewed, each fighting for control over the other.

Codi used her feet to push off the man's chest and her teeth to get him to release the knife with a final effort. A kick to his midsection shoved them apart and dumped a burst of air from his lungs. He would not last much longer underwater, but neither would she. The knife now in her possession, she grabbed the hilt and started back toward her prey.

The Encyclical moved backward in the water, trying to distance himself from the crazed woman who now possessed his knife. He reached for his Sig that was secured across his chest and pulled it free. His brain was screaming for him to surface, but he had one thing left to do. The killing range of a 9mm pistol underwater was six to eight feet, depending on the circumstances, before the water slowed down the bullet so much that it was ineffective.

Codi swam back at her target, keeping her new knife ready to strike. It was an odd knife with an unusually large diameter grip. It had a tab up by the tang that was familiar to her, but she couldn't recall the memory. Her oxygen was getting low, and if she didn't surface soon, she would be in trouble. The shadowy figure came into view, and she prepared to deliver a killing blow. Movement around his torso alerted her to the mistake she had just made. He had a gun and was pointing it her way. Codi tried desperately to reverse her course, but she was too slow to get away. That's when it hit her. The knife in her hand was a ballistic knife, capable of firing at an opponent.

During her time in the Marines, she had been stationed in Guam for a few months. One of the guys in the squad had pulled one of these knives from his duffle and had spent the next ten minutes bragging about it and showing how it could launch the blade out of the spring-loaded handle like a mini spear gun.

Codi could remember her response. "That's a good way to disarm yourself. Shooting the business end of your knife away."

The Encyclical fired three shots at her midsection. Then, shedding his tank and BC, he stroked for the surface to avoid involuntarily gulping in water and dying right there.

Codi saw the flash about the same time she felt the bullet's impact. It doubled her over and pounded out her last ounce of air. But not before she reached forward, pointed the ballistic knife, and pushed the lever. The Spetsnaz ballistic knife first appeared in the early seventies as part of the Russian special force's standard equipment. The handle contained a compressed spring that could be activated to shoot the knife-edge forward at 40 mph, with an effective range of sixteen feet. The blade was sharpened on both sides and thin in the middle to reduce the weight. As she pressed on the small lever at the top of the handle, the blade shot forward. It crossed the six feet of water separating them and embedded into The Encyclical's side, just as he was turning for the surface. There was a jolt from his body before hands and feet continued to kick upward.

Codi fought the pain and used her feet to propel her. Her arms felt dead. She wrapped them around her torso, squeezing against the agony. Dark blood spilled into the water, and her brain triggered her to breathe. Having drowned once before, she never wanted to do that again and was willing to black out before sucking in a breath of liquid death. She breached the surface, taking shallow gulps of air as her entire trunk convulsed with pain. To her right was the assassin. He was just above the water, moving all wrong. His mouth was moving like a fish, and his arms twitched rather than swam. His eyes shifted over to share the hatred he harbored for Codi. He started to speak, then looked as if he had changed his mind as his eyes glazed over. Codi held no sympathy for the killer and met his stare with cold, unflinching eyes. She watched as he struggled for a beat longer and then sank back into the liquid void. The knife had done its worst.

After a few moments, Codi turned for the launch ramp and kicked with just enough propulsion to move forward. She used the pain to push her onward, dipping under the water a couple of times and coming up sputtering as her feet fluttered back and forth. Finally, she reached the ramp and dragged herself halfway out of the water before collapsing. One assassin was dead. Hopefully, Joel was having an easier time of it.

***

Bullets plowed through the aluminum hull for the second time, scuttling Joel back from the bow. He took cover behind a storage locker just in front of the helm.

Kami pushed slightly ahead of the big boat, aiming for the gap to the right of the scattering blockade. *Cruise Control,* without hesitation, blasted through a smaller skiff with blinking blue lights as it tried to re-block a space in the barricade. The boat disintegrated without slowing the larger yacht one iota.

More shots were exchanged as The Scientist cleared the blockage, gaining entrance to the harbor. His rifle dry-fired, and he tossed it over the side and pulled out one of the Sigs. Now, he just needed to dump the boat and slip away into the night. A couple of police lights could be seen flashing in the distance as Newport Beach PD responded to the situation, but they would never be able to completely secure the harbor. It was just too big.

Past the entrance, the harbor doglegs left into an area of moorings, single-point anchorages that allow the tied-off boats to turn and flow with the current and tides. The slack tide had spun all the boats on mooring buoys perpendicular to the entrance, creating an unseen boat maze with little gaps in between.

With the fog still clinging to the water, visibility was spotty to non-existent. Going 35 knots in the harbor with no visibility was a risky proposition, but freedom called to The Scientist, and he had but one play left. He would not end up in custody tonight.

Kami pulled closer to *Cruise Control,* her boat slightly ahead. She pinned her spotlight on the helm of the big boat and tried calling over the loudspeaker again. Joel looked back at the disheveled blockade. Three boats had freed themselves and were giving chase, but they were almost too far behind to be seen. The suspect would get away if they didn't do something now. He hung onto the handrailing on the front of the enclosed helm and exchanged shots with the man driving the boat, his adrenaline currently countering his sea sickness. Bullets pinged back and forth, each getting close but doing little damage.

The lights of several homes came into view, and both boats had to course-correct in an instant to prevent hitting the shoreline. They had arrived at the dogleg.

***

The Scientist heaved hard to port and the seventy-footer slowly turned. The Harbor Patrol boat had taken the lead and was blasting him with a powerful spotlight that he had been unable to shoot out. Once the water opened up again, he decided to take matters into his own hands. He waited until the smaller boat closed, then spun the wheel into a collision course with the other vessel.

***

Kami tried to get Joel in close, hoping he might get a lucky shot off and end the chase. She pushed the bow over, keeping her spotlight pinned on the suspect. *Cruise Control* launched over just as she was closing the gap. There was no time to react, and the boat plowed into her bow, crushing and sheering off the front of the boat in an instant. The sudden cavity that was now the bow caused the vessel to plow into the water nose first. The speed they were traveling flipped the craft over, making it somersault across the water and partially tearing apart on impact. The Harbor Patrol boat quickly slowed and started to sink, ending its life with a sucking and hissing sound.

Kami had no time to react as her boat cartwheeled nose end first. She was tossed like a rag doll in a dryer until the enclosed helm fragmented and launched her out like a clown in a human cannon. Her body skipped across the water like a flat stone, knocking her unconscious.

***

The Scientist hit the Harbor Patrol boat at speed. There was a short, screeching sound followed by a spectacular display of physics. The smaller boat flipped across the water, breaking up along the way. A brief smile grew across The Scientist's lips as he looked back at the destruction. He flipped back around in time to see a forty-two-foot sailboat lying perpendicular to his path. There was no time to react.

The Morris M42 was built and designed in partnership with Sparkman & Stevens. Known for its luxurious accommodations and large cockpit, the yacht was striking with its indigo blue hull and white cabin and sails. The sails were stowed for the night. Inside was an airy cabin with rich teak appointments and a full galley. Only hull and mast lights alluded to its actual size in the dim light. She wore the proud moniker of *Lyoness* on her stern and a sleekness that spoke of her speed in the wind. With a displacement of over 16,000 pounds, she was a formidable seagoing pleasure craft.

The moment the bow of the speeding Princess yacht hit the carbon-epoxy Kevlar hull, its bow folded inward, each of the large vessels fighting for survival. The sound was heard throughout the harbor as both hulls catastrophically failed. The mast from the Morris was sheared off and crashed onto the Princess, smashing the helm. The Scientist was spared since he had been flung from his place into the air, impacting with the cabin before it spun sideways and the keel rotated up, taking out the entire bottom of the power yacht. The top half of the boat dove up over what was left of the sailboat and then augured into the black harbor. Steam hissed from the two diesel engines as they quickly cooled before slipping under the water. Both vessels were a total loss. Luckily, the owners of the *Lyoness,* Curt and Wendy, were not onboard. They were out visiting their grandchildren.

Joel had been lucky. As their boat flipped, he had been cast off the side of the hull and spun across the water. He came to a sudden rest just in time to see the two big yachts meet their demise. He watched several chunks whiz through the air just past him, but the body of Kami is what caught his eye. He immediately swam after her. She had landed near a white Catalina 34 moored nearby. He stroked over and managed to get his hands on her hair just before she sank and disappeared into the dark water. He pulled her to the surface and swam toward the anchor chain and hung on. She was breathing shallowly and had at least several broken bones with probably some internal bleeding. Joel needed to get her help and fast.

The Scientist leaned back. Everything hurt. For some reason, he was still above water. He had no idea how long he had been unconscious, but both boats were no longer visible. There were lots of flotsam and jetsam all around.

He realized his shirt was caught on a piece of the hull, which had kept him afloat like a life preserver. He unhooked himself and swam with much effort over to the swim step on a smaller sailboat. He crawled up and nearly passed out again, most likely needing a hospital, but his priority was to get to safety.

After he rested a moment, it was time to move. The Harbor Patrol was starting its search of the wreckage, and he needed distance between him and the authorities. The Scientist slipped off the step and stroked through the water, keeping his eyes on the warm glow coming from the homes along the shoreline. He could just make them out through the fog and knew he would be able to slip away from there.

***

Codi looked down at her stomach. There were three clearly defined blood stains growing on her shirt, besides the oozing slash just above them. She lifted her shirt and inspected the damage. With a light probing of her finger, she felt each bullet hole. To her surprise, the bullets were only an inch or so into her body. The water and the distance she had managed to put between her and the shooter had slowed the bullets' velocity significantly. She tried to pop one out like a zit, but the pain was overwhelming, and she almost passed out. Against everything she believed in, Codi might have to go to a hospital. The thought scared her, but bleeding out on a concrete ramp scared her more. She ripped off her shirt and tied it tightly around her midriff. The intense pain almost sent her to blackness again, so she laid back and waited for her head to clear before standing up. Finally, she staggered up the ramp and took a right on Embarcadero, hoping to find some help.

After about three hundred yards, she collapsed at the intersection of Dana Point Harbor Drive. She could see a barrier up ahead where the police had sealed off the road, but she would never be able to get that far.

Headlights panned across her from behind, and a few moments later an officer approached, gun drawn. Codi reached up for help, then passed out.

***

A low moan came from Kami. She was coming around. Joel rotated her torso so he was facing her as he held firm to the anchor chain. "Shh. You're gonna be okay, Kami," he soothed.

Off to his left, a sound in the water caught his attention. A seal swam past in the dark water. No, a person! Joel held perfectly still as he tracked the man, now swimming away. It was the man who had nearly killed them both.

Kami's eyes began to focus, and she realized Joel was looking at something in the water. Their target.

"I can hold on here. You go get him. There's no chance he gets away, understand?" she whispered.

"You sure?"

"Go," she said with stronger conviction than she felt. What she really wanted to do was let go of the chain and let the water take away her pain. It was all she could do to not pass out.

Joel screamed at the approaching patrol boats, "Over here!" Then, as soon as a spotlight pinned them, he carefully released Kami and made sure she had a good grip on the chain. It would be a matter of moments before the other Harbor Patrol boats were on the scene. He pushed away and silently stroked after the assassin.

Officers circled the crash site. There was debris in the water, obscured by the heavy fog. The high-powered searchlight on Kami intensified as they grew closer. It revealed a soggy but conscious woman, hanging onto an anchor chain, a weak arm raised in the air signaling her distress. An officer on the bow dove into the water to help her.

***

Joel could tell the man was injured. He was slowing down with every stroke he took. This gave Joel an idea. He used the moored boats to disguise his parallel path as he pulled ahead of his target, beelining for the nearby shore. There was a row of high-end homes along the bay with security lights on their personal docks and a few with warm glows spilling from inside.

Joel inched onto the sand and stepped into the shadows. A beat later, his suspect crawled out of the water and lay on the sand. Without his glasses, Joel could just make out the figure in the low light as he stood up and limped in his direction. Joel stepped out of the shadows and called out.

"FBI. You are under arrest."

***

The man stopped and assessed his situation. The lanky FBI agent was standing between him and freedom. Standing without a gun.

He reached behind him for his pistol but came away with nothing. It had flown off when he impacted the sailboat's cabin. The chilly swim to shore helped sharpen his damaged wits, and he looked around for some sort of weapon.

There were several private docks reaching out into the water, some with boats, others empty. Between them were small sandy beaches accessible only to the homeowners. A swim hook and life preserver were attached to the dock next to him with a swim safety sign placed there by a concerned homeowner. He grabbed the swim hook pole and used it like a bat swinging at Joel's head.

Joel grabbed a smaller lounge chair and tried to use it like a shield to parry away the attack. The Scientist swung his weapon back and forth, and Joel knocked it aside each time.

A counter swing hit a post on the dock, and the swim hook snapped off, leaving a jagged end that was now quite deadly. The Scientist changed tactics and used the aluminum pole like a lance to stab at his opponent. It cut right through the chair's fabric, forcing Joel to dodge and weave with every jab. Soon, the chair was shredded and useless.

Joel worked back around and tossed the broken chair at the assassin, using the time it offered to grab the life preserver hanging on the dock. He now had a stronger replacement shield, but there was a large hole in the middle of it.

Somewhere nearby, a dog barked and a porch light came on. It increased visibility significantly and Joel got a good look at the man trying to kill him. He had a buzzed head with a long, angry pale face and was bleeding profusely from his right leg. The pole shot out, and Joel just managed to push it aside with the preserver. The two men continued to fight with no obvious winner. Joel took a hit to the shoulder and a huge gouge poured blood. The shot of pain almost made him lower his shield, but he overcame the urge and fought on.

The Scientist saw the blood seeping from his combatant's shoulder and was emboldened. He struck repeatedly, pushing Joel back. He forced Joel over a hedge and into another yard. Each time he struck, the preserver barely deflected the hit; it was only a matter of time before he would end this.

Joel stumbled back through a low hedge almost falling on his back. The new yard had a hardscape with an eating area and a raised built-in hot tub overlooking the harbor. There were a few kids' toys strewn around as if they had been called inside right in the middle of playtime. Joel wove a path through the toys, focusing on the thrusts of the jagged pole trying to kill him.

He moved left, away from the raised hot tub he was being forced back into, and the assassin filled the space, continuing his onslaught. Joel waited for the man to get frustrated and overplay one of his jabs. He let the pole go through the hole in the preserver, twisting it to clamp the pole. He then counter-moved by pushing back at the assassin with all his might, sending the man backward.

The Scientist fell as his left foot stepped on a skateboard, and it spun out from under him.

He pulled on the pole for support, but Joel had released it, and his hands suddenly cartwheeled, finding only air for purchase. He went down in a *humph*, his head hitting the corner of the hot tub.

The aluminum pole skittered away across the concrete, echoing its distaste for the hard surface.

Joel cautiously approached the body. It was motionless. He knelt and checked for a pulse. Two arms reached up and grabbed Joel around the neck and squeezed. Joel panicked and hit him with a right uppercut, sending him back into the hot tub's concrete corner. The assassin slumped again, and Joel kept his distance, waiting to see what he would do next, but all he did was die, as blood trickled from the gash in the back of his head and a couple of fingers danced to an unheard tune.

Exhausted, Joel staggered over to the house with the light and barking dog and knocked on the back door. He needed to find his partner.

Chapter Twenty-Four

MISSION HOSPITAL – LAGUNA HILLS – CALIFORNIA – 8:09 A.M.

Joel entered the room. It smelled like disinfectant and day-old body parts. A nurse stepped past him on her way out. Once inside, he noticed Matt had taken up station in the ubiquitous chair every hospital room has. His arms were crossed over his chest, and he was sleeping with his head completely bent down.

"How long has he been here?" Joel whispered to Codi.

"Flew in as soon as he heard. Thanks for calling him."

"He must love you an awful lot to sleep in a chair like that."

"Not sure I could reciprocate," Codi responded.

"I see you're living the dream," Joel followed up, as he looked around the room. Codi was in bed with her midsection heavily bandaged. The few cuts on her face had been addressed and blueish-purple bruising seemed more prevalent that her normal skin color.

"Red Jell-O and soggy peas on tap."

"Yum. Is there room for the three of us at your table?"

Codi didn't find his humor funny, and the look on her face told him so.

"I hear you got lucky. Three bullets to the torso. The water slowed them down enough that they penetrated only muscle?"

"And a nick to my pancreas. Won't be doing any sit-ups for a while. Hey, nice glasses, by the way."

"Thanks, they're loaners. I hate sit-ups," Joel said the second part to himself as he subconsciously adjusted his temporary heavy black frame glasses.

There was a moment of silence as Matt breathed heavily, still asleep in the chair.

"Thanks," Codi offered.

She knew she should be dead or dying by now, but Joel had moved heaven and earth to get a sample of the assassin caterpillar antivenom, antifibrinolytic, air-freighted to the hospital. Brazilian scientists had been working on it recently with decent success when administered within the first few days of envenomation. It had arrived soon enough that doctors were able to stop and reverse the effects of the venom. According to the lab in Sao Paulo, she was six to eight hours away from the point of no return on its effectiveness.

"You're welcome," Joel said, knowing what she was talking about.

"So how's our case?" Codi asked.

"I have been buried in meetings with the higher-ups trying to second-guess how we ran this case. It's a real mess. You'd think taking two deadly assassins off the board would buy us some leeway."

"Apparently, not with the FBI," Codi said.

"With the death of the vice president, everyone involved is pointing at someone else. The only good news is *that* chaos seems to have most of their attention. The suspect they have is either very clever or the biggest patsy since Lee Harvey Oswald."

"That's terrible about the vice president. I liked her."

"I thought you were apolitical?"

"You gotta vote for somebody."

Joel nodded. "So how long before you get outta here?"

"Not till tomorrow afternoon, according to the doctor," a voice said behind them.

Codi and Joel turned to see Matt awake and stretching.

He added to his comment with a stern look. "For once, I'm gonna make sure she's a hundred percent before she ducks out the back door."

Joel put his hands up in surrender. "Hey, I'm with you on this. Was only asking."

"Just when I thought the three of us were going to work out," Codi protested.

There was another beat of silence as Codi slowly sat up, an effort that was extremely painful to her midsection. "Don't worry, it only hurts when I'm awake." She grimaced.

"I'm sorry you're hurting. Let me know if I can get you anything," Joel said in earnest.

Get me out of here, Codi mouthed to her partner.

"I'll handle wrapping things up with the case here. You two enjoy the Jell-O." Joel left with a hug from both Codi and Matt.

"Hey," Codi called out to him. "I owe you an answer to your question."

Joel looked perplexed as he stepped back toward his partner.

She let a small smile creep through the pain. "Handyman . . . that's the pet name I have for you. I know it sounds cheesy, but you are and always have been my go-to when things get out of control. You have a way of fixing everything and making things right."

Joel's face flushed red, and he turned and left the room. He was never good at receiving praise, but coming from his partner, it was overwhelming.

"Thought he was never going to leave," Matt said.

"Don't be rude, and don't get your hopes up. I'm out of commission for a while."

"With any luck, you have a better pet name for me," Matt said as he shifted in his chair.

"Handyman is not a bad pet name, Cuddle Cakes."

"Oh, that's rough, Knock-Out," Matt countered.

"Seriously, you asked, Noob." Codi tried to hold a straight face and almost succeeded.

"Hot Stuff."

"Goofball."

"Sticker Shock."

"Ouch."

They both started laughing, finally coming to a pause as Codi reached for her midsection. "Don't make me laugh."

"You started it. So . . . I was thinking after they discharge you, how would you like to show me your childhood haunts? We're only a couple of hours away."

"You read my mind," Codi answered. "I know a great place to stay on Coronado Island. You sure we can't go now?"

"Not a chance."

A nurse came in and adjusted Codi's covers a bit lower while asking her a few questions. Matt looked up to see a blond hunk with a chiseled face and perfect white teeth.

"Okay, don't go anywhere," the hunk said. "I'll be back in a bit to take good care of you." He dropped a patented smolder before he left the room.

Matt watched the man go. "What kind of hospital is this?"

Codi glanced at him, slightly confused by his comment.

"I think you are right," Matt said. "If you're really wanting to leave, you should."

Codi looked at him, waiting for the other shoe to drop. Nothing.

"Okay, give me a sec," she said, pulling the IV from her arm.

"Sure."

She didn't wait for him to change his mind and padded gingerly into the small bathroom.

The mirror must have been broken because the person looking back was almost unrecognizable. Codi moved her fingers through her hair and then gave up. She put on her street clothes and removed the plastic bracelet from her wrist.

Codi and Matt stepped out into the hallway and never looked back.

***

Joel looked around the room. It was a carbon copy of the room he had just come from where Codi and Matt were staying. Kami lay wrapped like a mummy with several broken bones, including a hip, femur, and clavicle. She was heavily sedated, but the prognosis was positive as all known internal bleeding had been stopped.

Joel had plucked her from the depths and saved her life. He moved over and set a bouquet of flowers he had bought at the gift shop on a small, wheeled table next to the bed.

A slight stirring from the patient caught his attention.

"Hey," she said hoarsely.

Joel smiled back. He wasn't sure what to say. He felt bad for getting her into this situation, but together, they had thwarted a major player in the underworld. So he just stood there.

"Two days ago, I was unhappy with my job," Kami started. "It had been unfulfilling for me. You come along, and it's suddenly too much. I longed for some action, real action, and then when I got it, I was overwhelmed. Guess I just . . . I don't know . . ." Her voice faded with the last word.

"You took a beating and came out the other side. You're bound to be a bit lost. It happens to the best of us," Joel said.

Kami's eyes drifted downward as she processed the information.

Joel tried to change the subject. "So when are you getting out?"

"They say at least a week. And with my hip jacked up, I'm not going anywhere fast or standing."

"I've spoken to your boss and, just so you know, you have his full respect and support. Good things are waiting for you once you get back on your feet. Focus on that."

Kami nodded her head, and a small smile lifted her face, betrayed mostly by her glistening eyes.

Joel stepped over and caressed the tips of her fingers that were poking out of her cast.

They shared a moment. "Take care of yourself," Joel said and then left her room, letting his mind go back to what was next—finding and taking down Atlantis.

***

The sun warmed her belly as she fluttered her eyes open after a brief nap. It was going to be a hot day and mid-morning sunbathing was turning into a sauna. It was just about time to head back inside. Living on an island was fun, but Atlantis missed Southern California. There was no place to get a decent milk tea and the selection of produce was dismal. She had made it a habit for Leilani to hit up the local farmers for something that resembled organic.

It had been two weeks since JC had checked in. Everything was going to plan. The vice president was dead and at least one fed had made the papers as deceased. It was time to start things back up and get to work on the next person she had been given on the list. The problem was she had lost contact with her two assassins. It was not like them to go completely dark after a job. It could be the red-hot level of their last hit. It was volcanic, but with all the evidence pointing to a guy named Juan Juarez, they should be in the clear. What wasn't clear is why they hadn't eliminated him and completely closed the loop. The second-guessing was making her antsy. Something wasn't right, and she needed answers. She reached out to JC. He could get to the bottom of this.

Leilani stepped to her side as Atlantis sat up on her lounge chair.

"I'm in the mood for a large martini," she said, glancing up at her maid.

Leilani knew her boss's needs by now and was happy to fulfill them as long as the check cleared. She turned with a plastered smile and headed back to the house. Atlantis watched as her curvy hips swayed. It was a sight she had yet to tire of.

***

The beachside cabin on Coronado Island in San Diego was small and cozy. It had a dated feel familiar to most beach rentals. Matt had paid too much money for it, but it was the height of the season, and he was lucky there was anything available. After getting Codi settled, he made a food run. She would need to spend the next couple of days flat on her back. The image inspired a bevy of perv-infused thoughts, which he eventually shook off. At least she would have good food and a proper nurse to take care of her. No more *Thunder From Down Under* masquerading as a daytime nurse.

He put the groceries away and opened the windows to let the sea breeze through. Codi was sleeping, and that was exactly what she needed. No more cases pulling her from his arms. He took a seat in the blue sofa chair in the corner of the master bedroom and let his gaze fall on his fiancé. Her chest rose and fell in a regular pattern.

Codi was a one-of-a-kind woman with a heart of steel and a façade made of granite, but somehow, she had let all that go for Matt. He was a lucky man, and he knew it. The sheet on top of her did a poor job of hiding her nakedness and Matt could see the bandages wrapped around her torso. A torso that was lean and fit supporting firm breasts and muscular limbs. The thing that had his attention was her face. It was well and truly at peace. It was a look he rarely saw, and it made him proud that his actions to get her here had done that.

The first week had been a series of predictable actions. Three meals a day and help getting to the bathroom, with lots of sleep. On the seventh day, Codi woke and called out, "I need to get some sand under my feet."

Matt set up two folding chairs by the water, and Codi slowly made her way there. The effort of lowering herself into the beach chair showed on her face, but she was determined to do it herself. They stayed and watched as vacationing families and sunbathers slowly began to populate the beach. The sense of normalcy was good, and it reminded Codi why she did what she did.

Matt was content just to hold her hand and let the world move past them.

After several hours, Matt picked up the chairs, and they headed back to the cottage.

"I've been doing some thinking."

That was never a good start to a sentence in Matt's opinion. "Oh, yeah?"

"What do you think about a hybrid?"

"You mean like a hybrid wedding or are you talking about changing how we get together twice a week?" Matt asked, trying to keep things light.

"I'm talking about a car."

Matt looked confused.

"For me. I like the Toyota RAV4 Prime and was thinking about getting the hybrid."

"Oh. Yeah, that is a really good car," Matt said, a bit too enthusiastically.

"If I'm going to stay more at your place, I will need a car," Codi added.

Matt's smile overtook his face, and he had no words for the happiness it triggered.

He placed the chairs next to the glass slider, and they headed back into the kitchen for something to drink.

"Maybe we can go car shopping tomorrow and you can take a test drive?" Matt said as he grabbed two cold Perrier's from the fridge.

"That would be great, but I was thinking about taking a test drive tonight," Codi said without taking her eyes off Matt.

Matt looked a bit disappointed. He was hoping now that Codi was feeling better they might be able to get back to some form of intimacy besides holding hands and spooning.

"I was hoping you might do the driving," Codi proposed.

Matt wasn't quite sure what she was talking about. "Why would you want me to do the driving on a car you're going to be driving?"

Codi just smiled and let him flounder, her gaze never faltering.

Matt suddenly stopped talking and looked at her as he replayed the words in his mind.

"Yes. I would love to do the driving. How 'bout now?" He pulled Codi into the bedroom and closed the door.

***

Codi stepped out of the car and tossed Matt a look and a smile. Two weeks in San Diego had done her a world of good. Matt had been the right medication for what ailed her, but now that she was feeling better, the constant thought of finding the woman who had been pulling the assassins' strings consumed her.

Matt could read Codi's thoughts, a rare occasion. It was time to get her back to what she did best. Although, in his mind what she did best was not at work.

"Have fun storming the castle," he threw out.

Codi leaned back down to meet his eyes, the most piercing green eyes that were filled with honesty and passion. She could look into them all day long.

"I always do," she threw back. "Fly safe. I'll see you back in DC soon." She banged the roofline of the rental car and walked away. Her stomach protested in pain as she took the steps into the building. It was going to be a long day.

Matt watched her walk away, his mind flashing across his memories of their last couple of weeks together. He had always found Codi to be incredibly sexy, incredibly confident, and tantalizingly independent. They were key reasons he loved her. There was no drama. She told you how things were and followed through every time. And when it came to sex, she was off the charts. How he had landed such a catch was still something he had not figured out, but he would be happy for whatever part she was willing to share with him.

Once in the office, Codi could feel the penetrating stares as she walked over to the work area Joel was occupying. Chen's death had been hard on everyone. He had been well-liked and a good agent.

She sat at the folding table, and Joel looked up, surprised. He had been concentrating so hard he had not noticed her entrance.

"Codi! You're back," he said, with a bit too much enthusiasm.

"Thanks, Captain Obvious."

"I see you're all the way back," he replied, this time, less excited.

Codi used her eyes to point toward the other agents working in the room. "I don't think they like us," she whispered.

"They blame us for Chen's death. Some feel we took too great a risk in the way we ran this case. ASSA Holloway wants us back in DC ASAP."

"I think she's going to put us on double-secret probation," Codi responded.

Joel started to ask if that was a real thing and then thought better of it. "Our recent boss, SSA Natalie Combs out of Philly, has intervened, but she could only buy us two more days."

Codi let out a long breath, exhaling through her mouth, wondering what Joel had been up against trying to work while she was off "convalescing" with Matt.

"How was San Diego?" he asked.

"Magical. How was here?" Codi asked.

"Hellish."

"Copy. Maybe we should just cut our losses and go back and face the music," she said.

"I would agree, except I have a lead on the elusive Atlantis Kroon."

Codi waited for Joel to elaborate.

"I reached out to a couple of three-letter agencies. First, the IRS has been developing a program that is capable of tracking financial transactions that you or

I could never access, specifically blockchain transactions. They have partnered up with the NSA and their OAKSTAR program."

"Isn't that the secret internet surveillance Snowden leaked about?"

"Right," Joel answered. "It's an upstream collector that can pierce Bitcoin and other such transactions. Anyway, they have passed some very solid intel our way. Our two assassins have offshore bank accounts. As does Atlantis Kroon. And I can tie payments from her to them. There was one more thing they were able to track. A shell company of hers recently paid for a beach house on an international Vrbo."

"Where?" Codi asked.

"That's just it. That part is unclear. The whole transaction seems to have been deleted right after the money cleared. There is no contact information other than the site itself."

"Sounds like a black site."

"Agreed. I did some more 'research' front-tracking from the date of the transaction and got a hit." Joel used his fingers to make a quote sign with them when he said *research*. What he meant was hacking, something Codi encouraged. The FBI not so much, not without heavy oversight.

"Facial rec at the private air terminal in Orange County nailed her. The flight plan was to Honolulu and then on to Guam. She never arrived in Guam, but the air traffic control there had her pegged on-course at 1200 kilometers out."

"So she crashed into the Pacific ocean?" Codi asked.

"I doubt it. Using the plane's fuel capacity and consumption, I narrowed its destination to one of two other locations. Micronesia or The Marianas."

He spun his laptop around to Codi. The screen showed a map of the Southwest Pacific Ocean. He zoomed in on Guam. You could see two island chains north and east of it.

"I got a buddy who is an immigration judge and gets out to Saipan, the largest of the islands, about three times a year to hear cases. He gave me a contact he trusted on the island that identified Atlantis's private jet parked at the airport. I didn't want to go through official channels in case she had someone on the inside or a digital tripwire."

"Saipan?"

Joel leaned over and zoomed in more until the upside-down *F* outline of the largest of the Mariana Islands appeared. "It's a US territory."

"Well, we can't jump a regular flight and go get her. She's been one step ahead of us this whole time. We need to find a different way."

"What are the chances ASSA Holloway will approve travel there in the first place?"

"Zero," Codi replied, and her mind began to assemble a working plan.

EPILOGUE

The jet touched down on the single runway that had originally held some of the most famous sorties in the Pacific Theater during World War II.

The long flight had been filled with Codi and Joel arguing over what they had in terms of compelling, court-worthy evidence. There were plenty of tax fraud issues, but payments to people who worked as assassins didn't guarantee a solid connection to murder-for-hire. Codi and Joel both knew she was responsible for the deaths of at least five people, but they would never prove it unless they found something more or they somehow got her to confess.

The fraud, however, was solid evidence that could lead to a conviction. For Codi, it was disappointing, much like Eliot Ness and his boys, The Untouchables with Al Capone. They wanted him for murder but only got him for tax evasion. It would have to do. Too bad the assassins were dead; they might have cut a deal in return for a confession.

The Saipan police department consisted of eleven police officers who rotated in three teams. They were not in the habit of dealing with violent criminals and had no ability to keep things quiet. It was an island, after all, and gossip and news circulated at the speed of light.

Atlantis had been ahead of them every step of the way. She had known when they arrived in Orange County and had sent them lilies as a warning. As soon as they started to investigate her, she up and disappeared. It was only by luck and a lot of hard work and determination that Codi and Joel had gotten this far.

Now that they had found her, it would take very careful machinations to keep Atlantis's incredibly wide-sweeping radar from finding out about it.

To prevent tipping their hand, Joel coordinated with the Coast Guard (USGC) based on the Northeast coast of Saipan.

Codi had reached out to a friend from her last case, Colonel Gilbert. He recently commanded a multi-agency task force with the impossible charge of bringing down a bioterror plot. He had been happy to arrange a ride for the two agents on military transport to Guam and then over to the island. SSA Natalie Combs had run interference, and their boss back in DC was mollified by thinking they were on their way back to her.

Codi and Joel were met by a late model Suburban with three heavily armed Coasties inside. Lieutenant Desoto stepped from the passenger seat of the Coast Guard vehicle and made the introductions. He was accompanied by two seamen with M4 rifles.

Codi laid out their plan and thanked the men for coming to help.

"Ma'am, we've been holed up here on this island for three months. The most exciting thing we've done is play trivia down at Crikey's on BOGO night. So thank you for having us."

"Well, when this is over, who's buying down at Crikey's?" she asked.

The men looked at each other, unsure how to answer. Finally, the youngest in the group tried his luck. "You are?"

"Hey, got the first trivia winner of the day," Codi said.

That got a round of nods and laughs from the Coasties.

Codi actually liked the idea of a few overly eager shooters on her team. Maybe one of them would put a bullet in Atlantis, and she could be done with her.

"Okay, let's go get her," Joel said.

"Hopefully, she'll put up a fight," Codi added.

The Coast Guard Suburban sped off for the other side of the island as the sun's edge dipped to the horizon, casting everything in a brilliant orange.

***

Dressed in assault black, three hooded figures moved to the house, weapons ready, one taking the back, and the other two, the front door. They didn't knock or pick the lock. It was time for a shock-and-awe approach. A message must be made. It took two attempts at the front door before the deadbolt broke through the wood jam. A simple ultrasonic pen shattered the back slider with a push of a button. There was a half-dressed young girl in the living room who looked surprised to see armed people. She let out a scream that was cut short by a burst of silenced gunfire.

Atlantis knew the sound of a silenced gunshot cold. She ran to the bedroom and grabbed her own silenced pistol. Crawling to the banister, she made a snap assessment of the action below. Three assailants in black were clearing the downstairs. She took aim. Two soft poofs from upstairs had one assailant writhing on the floor. Her shots were followed up with a fusillade of return fire up to the second-floor landing, splintering and shredding everything around her. Atlantis rolled to the back wall, just missing a bullet with her name on it. Once there, she rolled left and took another glance further down the banister. A careful aim dropped a second shooter before a returning round caught her in the shoulder and knocked her back, her gun falling to the sofa below. This gave the remaining shooter confidence, and he charged up the staircase in hot pursuit.

Atlantis knew she had seconds to decide. Thoughts of her father's training flashed through her. He had always been in favor of a strong offense as the best defense. She had no weapon or anything close she could use. That left one thing: her body. She pushed herself to her feet and ran for the staircase.

As the shooter neared the top of the stairs, an air-born figure with nothing to lose vaulted recklessly feet first. It was a move that would leave Atlantis paralyzed or dead at the bottom of the stairs, except for one thing: the body of the shooter in front of her. He managed to get a shot off, just missing his target before he was blasted backward down the stairs head over heels. The impact stopped Atlantis's forward momentum to the ground below, and she hit the staircase, just grabbing the railing to stop her downward fall. Her shoulder screamed in pain as she watched the shooter hit the tile floor below with a satisfying crack. She helped herself down the stairs and found her gun, eliminating the first man she shot who was still moaning on the floor as his blood pooled outward.

Atlantis pulled the mask off the man with the broken neck. Chung-Woo, the man behind Operation Redirect. Surely an intermediary for the North Koreans. They had come to tie up loose ends. She needed to get out of there quickly, but the loss of blood had made her light-headed. She plopped down on the end of the couch. She would just rest here for a second and let her strength return. Her eyes moved across to an unmoving Leilani. She had been fun; what a shame.

***

The quaint two-story beach home was set against a small street that fronted several exclusive beachfront properties. The warm glow of the windows was inviting, as the interagency task force drove past their destination, giving it a cursory inspection. At the end of the street, they parked and got out. Each person knew their job, and no words were necessary. Joel and two Coasties took to the beach. They would come in from behind.

Codi and the lieutenant made for the front of the house. They were expecting some sort of resistance and were well prepared. She stepped up to the front door. It rested loosely on damaged hinges, an obvious sign of a forced entry. Codi pushed it open with her toe. There was a collection of bodies lying on the floor.

Just then, Joel and his team burst into the room through a broken slider on the ocean side.

"FBI, nobody move!"

Atlantis raised her one good hand in surrender.

Joel held his gun on the woman, letting his anger for Chen's death feed him. He moved closer so he couldn't miss. A simple twitch and justice would be served. The Coasties looked at Joel a bit nervously. Was he going to kill this woman in cold blood? Codi was tempted to let him. This woman deserved to die, and she would back her partner's play. Joel tried to pull the trigger, but his hand started to shake.

Atlantis, concerned for her own safety, called out, "I'm unarmed. I surrender."

A hand gently pressed down on Joel's shaking gun hand. "Joel. It's okay, we got her." Codi pulled the pistol from his fingers and placed her hand on his shoulder, knowing full well what he was going through.

"Cuff her boys, the drinks are on me."

***

Codi and Joel walked out of the Ronald Reagan Washington National Airport terminal to a happy sight. Shannon and Matt were standing on the curb. Matt had a ridiculous sign with the words "Sticker Shock" and a heart.

It took exactly one second for the two agents to run from the exit doors into the arms of their loved ones. Joel practically teared up with emotion. All of the drama from their last couple of weeks melted away. He held Shannon like he might never let go, and she reciprocated with equal passion.

Codi and Matt paused to watch Shannon and Joel together. It was a glorious picture of happiness and joy. Much the same as they were feeling. True happiness was elusive, but it poked its head out from time to time, and it was imperative that you recognized it and embraced it for as long as you could.

"Who's up for some lunch?" Matt asked the group.

"I could eat," Codi said.

"She can always eat," Joel fired back.

"I'm starving. How does Greek sound? I know a place nearby," Codi said to the group.

"Sounds heavy," Joel replied as he pulled at his carry-on, not really paying attention to the conversation.

"Okay, what are you thinking?" Shannon threw back.

"Anything is fine with me," Joel tossed back.

"Okay, Greek." Codi tried again.

"Except that," Joel replied, now looking at his phone as he spoke.

"You said anything," Shannon countered.

"You know what I mean."

"No, we don't. Not if you don't tell us," Codi said, with consternation on her face. This was a reoccurring theme. "Joel! You're doing it again!"

Matt raised his hand to stop Codi from losing her shiz. He waited until Joel looked up. "Joel, we are all going to the Greek restaurant, and you are invited to join us."

Joel stopped and looked around at the three faces staring at him. He didn't realize the drama he was creating. "Sounds good. Let's go."

"Perfect."

The foursome laughed and headed for the parking structure.

***

ASSA Holloway stood in the hallway with her arms crossed. She watched as Joel and Codi moved in her direction, her anger building with each step they took. The two agents had gone against her will and jogged off to some Pacific island to arrest a suspect. This was exactly what she had been personally against. As they got closer, she opened her door and gestured inside. "I need a word with the both of you."

"Good, because we need to chat with you as well," Codi countered.

As she closed the door and started for her desk, ASSA Holloway exploded with venom. "I'm not sure what you two were thinking when you lied to me about returning to DC and instead ran off island hopping to—"

"Let me stop you right there," Codi interrupted. "Joel and I have only done one thing. And that's our job to the best of our ability. We are FBI special agents, and we do things the FBI way, not your FRICS way. Sorry we couldn't mold to your plans, but we have made a joint decision, and this is it."

Joel slid two envelopes across the desk, then he and Codi stood and left.

ASSA Holloway called out, "These better be your written apologies. There will be a suspension coming your way. I'm not done talking here!"

"But we are," Codi said as she let the door shut behind her.

Joel was numb as he departed the FBI Field Office. He felt as if he had been coerced into writing his resignation. But with all that had happened, Codi was right. It had to be done. He looked to his left for strength and found the gleaming eyes of his partner. They were intense brown eyes that held grit and determination like no one else he knew.

She put a hand on his shoulder and smiled weakly. It was the end of an era for both of them, and what came next was anybody's guess. But they knew together they were unstoppable.

***

Atlantis stepped from the courthouse. She was not happy. The judge had levied a three-million-dollar fine for tax evasion and penalties despite her high-priced attorney's best efforts. The more serious charges had not stuck. Her clever operating style had left little evidence behind—and most of it circumstantial. The fine was small change, but it was a battle she had lost, something Atlantis was not familiar with. The North Koreans would not let this go. Chung-Woo had failed at severing the connection between him, Atlantis, and the US vice president's demise. They would now have to deal with her directly, no middleman. That would mean either a better offer or a bullet with her name on it. She was not so easy to kill. Anger in her soul flamed up at the thought of it. She was most upset with the two federal agents who had ruined everything. She set her mind on one path forward.

Revenge.

IF YOU LIKED THIS BOOK

I would appreciate it if you would leave a review. An honest review helps me write better stories. Positive reviews help others find the book and ultimately increase book sales, which help generate more books in the series.
It only takes a moment, but it means everything. Thanks in advance,

Brent

AUTHOR'S NOTE

This is a work of fiction. Any resemblance to persons living or dead, or actual events, is either coincidental or used for fictive and storytelling purposes. Some elements of this story are inspired by true events; all aspects of the story are imaginative events inspired by conjecture. *Fatal Measure* was a true labor of love. Like life, the writing process is a journey, one meant to be savored, and to me, it's more about the pilgrimage itself than the destination. I learned a ton while writing this book, and I hope it's reflected in the story and the prose. Only you, the reader, can be the judge of the results. Drop me a line if you have feedback or just want to say hi.

Brent Ladd Loefke, 2019, Irvine CA

INTERESTING FACTS

For more facts, go to my website, brentladdbooks.com.

Quiet Bird

The Boing Model 853, also known as The Quiet Bird, was first conceived in the late 1950s and then a half-scale prototype was built in 1960. It was the first stealth technology implemented in a plane by the US. It showed very low radar cross section and launched a race to achieve full stealth flight.

MiG Defection

On September 21, 1953, Lieutenant No Kum-sok flew his Mikoyan-Gurevich MiG 15 over the 38th parallel in North Korea to a US air base in South Korea and defected. The US got a huge boost in aviation advances, as the MiG was considered a superior fighter to the F-86 Sabre. No was welcomed with open arms as a US citizen and went on to work as an aeronautical engineer. He is a hero to the US, and therefore, I used his story but changed his name, not wanting to disgrace his actions in any way, as the defector in my novel had an ulterior agenda.

Lonomia obliqua

The giant silkworm moth is a species of *saturniid* moth from the southern region of Brazil. It is famous for its larval form because of its intense defensive mechanism, urticating bristles that can inject a deadly venom. The caterpillar has been responsible for many deaths. At the time of the writing of this book, the only treatment is the use of antifibrinolytic within the first few days after envenomation.

Castor Bean and Ricin

Ricin is classified as a Type-2 ribosome-inactivating protein. It is extremely toxic if inhaled, injected, or ingested. It occurs naturally in nature, most commonly in the outer shell of the castor bean. Ricin has had its share of fame throughout recent history and in entertainment as a chemical weapon.

Murder-for-hire

Murder-for-hire, or contract killing, is a one of the oldest professions on the planet. It reached fame during the Murder Inc. days of the late thirties and forties, where hundreds of murders were carried out on behest of the National Crime Syndicate. Today, it is a growing field with opportunities across the globe.

Harley Davidson Livewire

The Livewire is Harley Davidson's electric motorcycle. It is state-of-the-art and fully bluetooth compatible. It has a range of just over 146 miles and can get you to 60 mph in three seconds. It's sleek design and ultra quiet ride is creating many fans.

The Moshulu

The Moshulu is the world's oldest and largest square-rigged sailing vessel still afloat. Built in 1904 with four masts and thirty-four sails, she was a state-of-the-art cargo ship for her time. With a length of over 350 feet and just under fifty feet in breadth, she could carry over 3,000 gross tons. These days, she is a floating museum and a first-class restaurant.

ACTUV Sea Hunter

The Sea Hunter is an autonomous unmanned surface vessel launched as part of the DARPA anti-submarine warfare program. The 132-foot-long trimaran self-piloting craft has a top speed of twenty-seven knots. She is currently in testing for the navy and operates at a fraction of the cost to comparable warships.

OAKSTAR Program

OAKSTAR is a secret internet surveillance program of the National Security Agency. It pulls data directly from top-level communications infrastructure. It allows access to very high volumes of data, which is then classified and organized using keywords and phrases. It is one of the programs Edward Snowden leaked about the NSA during his time as a subcontractor for the CIA.

ACKNOWLEDGMENTS

With deep appreciation to all those who encouraged me to write and, especially, to those who did not. I wanted to thank the following contributors for their efforts in doling out their opinions and helping to keep my punctuation honest: Jeff Klem, Natalie Call, Geena Dougherty, Carol Avellino, and Wade Lillywhite. A host of family and friends who suffered through early drafts and were kind enough to share their thoughts: my lovely wife Leesa, who is my first reader and best critic. And my editor, Cathy Hull.

A special thanks to my publisher, Morgan James Publishing, who helped make this all possible, as writing is only half the total equation. Finally, to Christopher Kirk for the cover design.

As many concepts as possible are based on actual or historical details. Special thanks to the original action hero—my dad, Dr. Paul Loefke.

Lastly, writers live and die by their reviews, so if you liked my book, *please* review it!

ABOUT THE AUTHOR

Writer and director Brent Ladd has been a part of the Hollywood scene for almost three decades. His work has garnered awards and accolades all over the globe. Brent has been involved in the creation and completion of hundreds of commercials for clients, large and small. He is an avid beach volleyball player and an adventurer at heart. He currently resides in Irvine, California, with his wife and children.

Brent found his way into novel writing when his son Brady showed little interest in reading. He wrote his first book, making Brady the main character—*The Adventures of Brady Ladd.* Enjoying that experience, Brent went on to concept and complete his first novel, *Terminal Pulse: A Codi Sanders Thriller*—the first in a series, and followed it up with *Blind Target, Cold Quarry*, and *A Time 2 Die. Fatal Measure,* the fifth book, takes our characters down another rabbit hole.

Brent is a fan of plot-driven stories with strong intelligent characters. So if you're looking for a fast-paced escape, check out the Codi Sanders series. You can also find out more about his next book and when it will be available when you visit his website, BrentLaddBooks.com.